Praise for the novels of Amanda Skenandore

The Undertaker's Assistant

"Effie's community of freedmen and Creoles in Reconstruction New Orleans is unforgettable. Skenandore's second novel is recommended for readers who enjoy medical historical fiction reminiscent of Diane McKinney-Whetstone's *Lazaretto,* and historical fiction with interpersonal drama." —*Library Journal*

"Readers who like complex characters amid a roiling historical setting will be fascinated by Effie's quest. . . . Teen readers will empathize with a young woman's search for identity and love."
—*Booklist*

Between Earth and Sky

"Intensely emotional. . . . Skenandore's deeply introspective and moving novel will appeal to readers of American history, particularly those interested in the dynamics behind the misguided efforts of white people to better the lives of Native Americans by forcing them to adopt white cultural mores."
—*Publishers Weekly*

"A masterfully written novel about the heart-wrenching clash of two American cultures . . . a fresh and astonishing debut."
—V. S. Alexander, author of *The Magdalen Girls*

"By describing its costs in human terms, the author shapes tension between whites and Native Americans into a touching story. The title of Skenandore's debut could refer to reality and dreams, or to love and betrayal; all are present in this highly original novel." —*Booklist*

"A heartbreaking story about the destructive legacy of the forced assimilation of Native American children. Historical fiction readers and book discussion groups will find much to ponder here." —*Library Journal*

Books by Amanda Skenandore

BETWEEN EARTH AND SKY

THE UNDERTAKER'S ASSISTANT

THE SECOND LIFE OF MIRIELLE WEST

THE NURSE'S SECRET

Published by Kensington Publishing Corp.

THE NURSE'S SECRET

AMANDA SKENANDORE

KENSINGTON
PUBLISHING CORP.

www.kensingtonbooks.com

KENSINGTON BOOKS are published by
Kensington Publishing Corp.
119 West 40th Street
New York, NY 10018

All Kensington titles, imprints, and distributed lines are available at special quantity discounts for bulk purchases for sales promotion, premiums, fund-raising, educational, or institutional use.

This book is a work of fiction. Names, characters, businesses, organizations, places, events, and incidents either are the product of the author's imagination or are used fictitiously. Any resemblance to actual persons, living or dead, events, or locales is entirely coincidental.

To the extent that the image or images on the cover of this book depict a person or persons, such person or persons are merely models, and are not intended to portray any character or characters featured in the book.

Special book excerpts or customized printings can also be created to fit specific needs. For details, write or phone the office of the Kensington Sales Manager: Kensington Publishing Corp., 119 West 40th Street, New York, NY 10018. Attn. Sales Department. Phone: 1-800-221-2647.

The K logo is a trademark of Kensington Publishing Corp.

ISBN: 978-1-4967-2654-4 (ebook)

ISBN: 978-1-4967-2653-7

First Kensington Trade Paperback Printing: July 2022

10 9 8 7 6 5 4 3 2

Printed in the United States of America

For my fellow Nightingales
Past, present, and future

CHAPTER 1

New York City, 1883

Travelers sluiced from the newly arrived trains onto the platforms like privy muck into the sewer, halting and sluggish. Their voices echoed through the car house, blending with the wheeze of steam and whine of metal. Daylight fought with streaks of soot and drifts of snow to penetrate the glass ceiling above. Una, however, preferred the shadows. She watched the travelers from behind one of the great ornamental trusses that supported the roof. Watched and waited.

The first to emerge were always the businessmen—bankers, speculators, oilmen, factory owners. They strode across the platform like it was their own private foyer, perturbed but undaunted by the noisome crowds. Time was money to these men, and their hurry and hubris made them easy marks should one be willing to suffer their over-perfumed clothes and superior airs. Today, Una was not.

Close on their heels came the coach class. Weary-looking women with wide-eyed children clinging to their skirts. High-falutin debutantes and their weighed-down porters. Traveling merchants with leather-bound cases of their wares. Countryfolk carting chickens and leading braying goats. Many carried little more than they could squeeze into their traveling sack. A change of underclothes. A half-eaten loaf of bread. A worn Bible with the name and address of some distant relative tucked inside. Nothing worth Una's time.

Then he appeared—the very man Una was awaiting. Well dressed, but not foppishly so. A ruddy, youthful complexion. He was a Middle West man, to be sure. Indiana, perhaps. Ohio. Illinois. Precisely where didn't matter, only that he was not a New Yorker. Judging from the way his wide eyes scanned for a signpost or placard to direct him through the throngs, he was entirely new to the city.

Una checked that her hat was securely pinned and bit her lips to bring out their color. She unfastened the latch on her travel case, holding the handles tight so it remained closed.

The man shuffled and bobbed along the platform until his eyes lit on the overhanging sign directing travelers to the Forty-second Street exits. Then his shoulders squared and step quickened. Una threaded her way through the crowd toward him. When his eyes flickered up again, this time to a large clock perched high in the central tower at the far end of the platform, Una stepped in front of him. The man barreled into her. She gave a soft cry and dropped her traveling case, its contents scattering at their feet.

"Oh, I do beg your pardon, miss," the man said.

"It was my fault, sir. I was uncertain of my way."

"You and me both. I've never been in such a large station."

She knelt to collect her scattered belongings, flashing him a timid smile when he bent down beside her. The faint scent of tobacco clung to his fine Chesterfield coat. "Largest station in the world," she said. "At least that's what I've heard."

He handed her a ribbon-trimmed bonnet and worsted wool shawl, which she carefully folded and tucked inside her bag. "You really needn't trouble yourself."

"It's the least I can do." He reached for another piece of clothing, then froze, his neck and ears reddening to match his cheeks. Una snatched the silk chemise, its smooth fabric and lace hem brushing the tips of his gloved fingers as she whisked it into her bag. In a show of embarrassment, she dropped her chin, hiding her face beneath the wide brim and drooping plumage of her hat.

"I . . . er . . ." He wobbled on his haunches, his Chesterfield brushing the dirty floor.

Una gathered up the last of her clothing and stuffed it in her bag. "Thank you," she said, latching the bag and standing.

The man stood too. "Again, my apologies, miss." He dusted off his overcoat and glanced again at the clock. "Can I see you to a carriage?"

Una dared another glance at his wide, honest face. Another timid smile. "That's very kind, but I'm departing, not arriving."

"Oh?"

"Yes, sir. Back home to Maine. I'd only come for a brief visit to comfort a sick friend."

"I see," he said, disappointment evident in his voice.

"Thank you again." Una curtsied and hurried toward the boarding trains. At the far end of the car house, she crossed the tracks and slipped into the crowded waiting room. After tucking herself into the corner, she surveyed the room. A policeman stood at the far end, besieged by an elderly man brandishing a train schedule. Una smirked and opened her bag. Wrapped inside the shawl was the Middle West man's cigarette case. Pure silver, by the look of it, and ornately etched with scrolling filigree. On the back were the man's initials: *JWC*. But those could be burnished away easily enough. If Marm Blei didn't want to melt it down.

After another glance at the copper, she slipped the cigarette case from her bag and into a pocket hidden within her ample skirt folds. It had been easy as tilly to free the case while the man worried after her scattered clothes. It practically fell out of his overcoat when he bent down to help her. Diving into the coat's inner pockets was riskier. But that lacy chemise did the trick every time. While the man bumbled with embarrassment, she'd slipped a hand inside and relieved him of a few bills from his pocketbook and two silver dollars.

Una closed her bag and strolled from the waiting room out to

Vanderbilt Avenue. The day's waning sunlight did little to warm the January air. Four separate rail companies ran lines through Grand Central Depot, each with its own baggage rooms and waiting areas. With a stash of counterfeit tickets tucked inside her coat sleeve, Una could easily pass from one room to the next and back and forth from the car house.

More than a hundred trains stopped at the depot each day, spewing dupes into the city. It was easy pickings if you were smart. Una never lingered in one place too long. Never returned to the same waiting room more than once a day. Never snatched more than she could easily hide. A good thief had her rules and kept to them.

The Middle West man, Mr. JWC, wore a watch on a silver chain and had at least ten other bills in his leather that she'd left behind. But not out of kindness. The more you filched, the more likely your mark would notice before he left the station. Una didn't always come home with the fattest haul, but she didn't get caught neither. Not often, anyway. Bail money added up, and she knew Marm Blei kept score.

Una's empty stomach grumbled. The depot basement housed a ladies' restaurant, but she seldom ate on the job. You had to be ready to sprint away on a moment's notice, and a belly full of ham and cabbage or oyster stew would slow you down. But there were good pickings in the basement—men perfumed and freshly shaven strutting from the barbershop, ladies hurrying to the toilet, railwaymen stumbling from the saloon—and Una decided to do a little more prospecting before heading home.

She slipped back into the station house through a different company's waiting room. On her way to the basement stairs, she spied a young boy dressed in shabby trousers, a patched coat, and dirty cap. Una rolled her eyes as he sidled up to a well-dressed man sporting a shiny top hat. Don't do it, you looby, she thought. The boy cast a quick glance around the room, then reached for the man's overcoat. Una lingered at the head of the stairs, even though the room was about to become a hotbed of coppers. Don't do it.

She'd been that young once. And just as stupid. Miracle she hadn't ended up under lock and key at the House of Refuge.

The boy managed to slip his grimy hand into the man's pocket. Una shook her head. Loobychin. A moment later, the boy's hand reappeared, clasping a gold watch. It was probably worth a hundred dollars, but the boy wouldn't get more than twenty for it from a fence. Less if he were working for a boss. But she had to give the kid credit for lifting it without the man's notice. Maybe he wasn't such a looby after all.

He started to slink away, and Una turned back to the stairwell. She'd gone only a few steps when a deep voice hollered, "Thief!" Every muscle in her body tightened. Her feet tingled, ready to skedaddle. She glanced over her shoulder and saw that the well-dressed man had the boy by the wrist, the shiny gold watch dangling on its chain from the boy's hand.

He'd just earned himself a spot at the House of Refuge, the boy. Scrawny as he was, he'd as likely freeze to death as finish out his stretch there. Una mounted the steps and pushed through the growing gaggle of onlookers toward the boy before her smarts could stop her. She tucked her carpetbag under her arm and threw up her hands with great show. "There ya are, Willie! Your ma's worried plumb sick over ya." She turned to the man. "This lad ain't botherin' ya, is he?"

The man's eyes narrowed. "This *lad* is a thief. He tried to steal my pocket watch."

Una clutched her breast—a bit dramatic, to be sure, but she needed to keep the man's attention. "What? Willie, is that true?"

"I . . . er . . ." The boy glanced from Una to the man's hand, still tight about his wrist, and the confusion in his face melted away. "Sorry, Aunt Mae, ya know how Ma is when she's in liquor. I ain't had nothin' to eat for three days."

Una held back a grimace. Sick was a far better card to play than drunk. But clearly the boy was green. "That ain't no excuse. Ya know ya could've come to me for a meal. Give this fine gentleman his watch this very minute and apologize."

The man's fingers slowly loosened from the boy's wrist. He'd left red, angry marks on his skin. A feral, skittish look in the boy's eye told Una he might run, leaving her on the hook for his thievery. She grabbed the back of his threadbare coat and gave him a gentle shake. "Hand it over now, ya hear?"

"Yes 'um," the boy muttered, but not before casting Una a glare. He dropped the watch into the man's waiting palm and gazed with longing as it was stuffed back in his overcoat pocket.

"And what about yer apology?" Una said.

"Sorry, mister. I won't never do nuthin' like that again."

"That's a good lad." Una kept a grip on the boy's coat and turned to the man, flashing a doleful smile. "My deepest apologies, sir. His ma's a good woman, just mournin' the loss of her husband is all. I'm sure ya understand, bein' such a fine-hearted gentleman. We won't be takin' up any more of your time." She gave the boy another shake. "But ya can best believe he'll be gettin' a good lashin' before his supper."

The man's expression didn't soften. He brushed the sleeve of his overcoat as if his mere proximity to her and the boy had sullied it. "You see that he does."

Una made a hasty curtsy and dragged the boy by the back of his coat from the waiting room. When they reached the street, the boy shrugged to free himself, but she held on, yanking him behind one of the steel support columns of the nearby elevated railway.

"What you playing at, boy?" she said. "You looking for a first-class ticket to Randall's Island?"

"What'd you care?"

She let go of his coat. "I don't. But an imp like you who don't know his head from his rear gonna get every mark in there antsy, checking their watches and leather, looking around all suspicious like. Not to mention the coppers. Makes my job and any other divers working the spot twice as hard."

"I could've gotten away."

"That man had a hold on you like a vise. You think they'll go easy on you in the Tombs 'cause you're a kid? The beak will eat

THE NURSE'S SECRET   7

you for breakfast and spit your bones out in the yard. Don't give two licks about the likes of you or me."

The boy just shrugged. Hard-headed looby, he was.

"Your parents know you're out here dipping into fancy men's pockets?"

"Ain't got no parents."

"Then you best get your scrawny ass over to the Five Points Mission. They'll feed you there. Learn you your letters too."

"And send me west with the rest of the orphans."

"Better than a life on the cross." Una's words met with another shrug. She crouched down. The boy's cheeks were chapped and mud-streaked, his nose raw and dribbling. "At least you gotta be smart. Easier pickings on the el." She nodded at the tracks above them. "Fewer coppers too. And you gotta start small—the loose change in a man's pocket or a few shines from a lady's purse. You take it all and they're gonna notice. Makes it harder to get away. A man-about-town's bound to realize his watch is missing and soon. Best wait till he's settled down someplace with his nose stuck in a newspaper or a glass of gin before going after a prize like that."

She pulled out a hankie, spit on it, and swiped it across his cheeks. "Clean yourself up some too. The best thief is one who don't look like a thief."

Once he was somewhat presentable, she reached into her pocket for a dime. "Here. Get yourself some supper. And think some on the Mission."

No sooner had she placed the dime in his hand than she felt his other hand fishing in her coat pocket. "That's good. Always easier to dip into someone's pocket when they're distracted with something else. But I ain't stupid enough to leave anything of value where the likes of you can free it."

He gave her a sheepish smile and withdrew his hand.

"You gotta be quicker too. Move in with a lighter touch. Maybe partner up with some of them boys who work the horsecars. They could teach you a thing or two."

"You got a partner?"

"No, I don't trust—"

A commotion by the depot entry snagged Una's attention. She stood and peeked around the iron beam. The man whom the boy had tried to pickpocket was outside speaking loudly with two coppers. Una frowned. He'd seemed cross but mollified when they'd left him. She turned back to the boy, yanked him close, and dove through his pockets until she found the man's watch.

"You cheeky little bastard, this is likely to wind us both in the clink."

She left the watch in the boy's pocket—better it was found on him than her—but took back her dime. "I'll go north on Fourth, you east on Forty-Second. Don't run. It'll only draw attention. And if I ever catch you in the depot again, I'll turn you in to the coppers myself."

The words had scarcely left her mouth when the boy took off running. And not across Forty-Second Street but up Fourth Avenue, the way she'd planned to go. Looby! Una tucked the handles of her bag in the crook of her arm, squared her shoulders, and stepped beyond the beam. Two women with fur hats and muffs strolled past. Una walked beside them, matching their pace. Behind her, the commotion at the depot entry intensified. A shout. A whistle. Likely the coppers had seen the boy run and unscrambled their wits enough to give chase.

Una didn't look back. She inched closer to the women, even as one shot her a cutty-eyed sneer. Una's clothes, clean and respectable as they were, paled next to these women's finery. But from a distance it was hard to tell lambswool from horsehair. Real silk trim from imitation. Certainly if you had the peanut-sized brain of a copper. Eyeing her from the back at twenty paces away, she looked the same as any young lady out for a stroll with her friends. Or so Una hoped. Rule number five: Look like you belong.

Thick-soled boots thudded on the pavers behind them. One set. Walking fast but not running. Una drew closer to the women.

"Why, what a lovely muff you have," Una said to the woman next to her, donning a pleasant smile. "Sable, is it?"

The woman looked surprised. "Why, yes. My father brought it back from the Continent."

"Russia, I imagine. I hear the finest sable comes from there. It matches your hat quite perfectly."

"Yes, they were a set."

"There's a sable-trimmed reticule at Stewart and Company that would complement the ensemble nicely." Una knew because they'd fenced such a moll-sack at Marm Blei's shop just last week. The thief said it sold for thirty dollars on Ladies' Mile. They gave him seven for it and sold it for twelve after Una had painstakingly removed A. T. Stewart's stitched-in label.

The thudding boots drew closer. Una didn't need to turn around to know it was a copper. They must have split up to look for the boy after he slipped them. Unless the well-dressed man had recognized her and pointed her out among the crowd.

The copper stalked past without a glance in her direction. Una exhaled with relief. She peeled away from the women and turned down Second Avenue. Tempting as it was to return to the depot for one more dive, she knew it was too dangerous. Stupid boy. She almost hoped the copper did catch him for all the trouble he'd caused her. And to think, she'd almost given him a dime!

She'd gone less than a block when a sniveling voice sounded behind her. "There she is! That's the rogue!"

This time, Una turned around long enough to see a bruiser of a copper barreling toward her. She ran.

CHAPTER 2

Una darted around fruit sellers and newsboys and hackneys. She leaped from the sidewalk and crossed under the el, barely making it across the street without being trampled by the approaching horsecar. Still the copper's boots sounded behind her.

She tripped over the leg of a peddler's vegetable cart and stumbled, twisting her ankle fiercely, but kept running. With her traveling bag clutched to her breast, she sidestepped and elbowed through the crowd. She'd make quicker time if she turned off the busy thoroughfare but couldn't risk trapping herself in a dead end. She needed to get her bearings. Allowing herself to slow, she pictured the checkered streets of the city like she were a pigeon flying overhead. To the west across Fortieth Street lay Reservoir Park. Its tangled walkways and overgrown shrubbery were a good place to slip the hulking tail behind her. Una headed in that direction, but doubted she could make it to the park before he overcame her. Already his clomping footfalls were gaining.

No, she couldn't outrun him. She'd have to outsmart him. She further slowed her pace, hoping he'd think her about tuckered out, and returned to the picture in her mind of the city streets. There was an alley off Madison Avenue that led to a small courtyard. Farther on was a privy pit and narrow passage out to Thirty-Eighth Street. It wouldn't leave her much time, but it would have to do.

The copper had slowed too, the fat sod. She could hear his dragging step. He probably expected her to pull up short at the nearest lamppost to catch her breath. A fair enough assumption given how even a loosely tied corset strangled a girl's lungs, and just what she hoped he would think.

The alleyway appeared in sight. Una waited for a break in the crowd, then sprinted down the sidewalk and into the alley. Clothes strung between the buildings fluttered on the lines just above her head. She dashed through the small courtyard to the privies. The cold air stank of rotting potato peels and human waste. Two overflowing trash bins sat in the corner. Una crouched behind them, drawing her coat over her head and nestling among the crumpled newsprints, withered food scraps, and soot-stained rags.

A moment later, the copper bounded into the privy yard. He whipped a hanky from his pocket to shield his nose from the stench. Una suppressed a chuckle. Coppers today had gone soft with their indoor crappers. He glanced about the small yard, opening the privy doors with his billy club just wide enough to peer inside. Then he hurried down the narrow exit at the far end.

Once the thud of his footfalls was gone, Una stood and brushed off her coat. She had a minute, maybe two, before the copper circled back. She unpinned her hat and traded it for a headscarf buried beneath the lacy chemise in her bag. A stained apron, fingerless gloves, a smear of soot across one cheek, and her transformation was nearly complete. She shrugged out of her coat and strapped her bag to her back with a worn belt she kept handy for such emergencies. If she leaned forward just so, the bag would look like a hunch beneath her coat. Before putting it back on, she turned her coat inside out. Those new to Marm Blei's crew balked when Una had covered the fine satin lining with a patchwork of ratty cottonade. She'd paid Marm Blei twenty dollars for the coat—a handsome sum—after all. But the alteration proved indispensable in times like these. She'd gone from well-heeled traveler to gnarled rag-picker with time to spare.

Rule number eleven: Sometimes the best place to hide is in plain sight.

Sure enough, not a minute later, the copper thundered back into the privy yard. Una stood hunched beside the trash cans, picking through the refuse. "You seen a woman hiding about here?" he asked her.

She looked up and met his deep-set eyes. His cheeks were flush with exertion, and his panting breath clouded in the air.

"Vhat kind of voman?" Una said, feigning a German accent.

"A thief."

Una turned back to the trash. She plucked a chunk of moldering bread from the bin, sniffed it, then tossed it to the ground. "Zat isn't much of a description. She tall or short?"

"I don't know. About average, I guess."

"Fat or sin?"

The copper huffed. "Not especially either."

"Vhat vas she vearing?"

"A blue coat and velvet hat."

Be it the cold, the smell, or a lunch that hadn't agreed with him, the copper looked about to explode with ire.

"Vone of those fancy hats vith plumes and ribbon or a simple affair?"

"I don't know," he bit out.

Una found a gin bottle buried beneath peanut shells and empty sardine cans. She held it up and gave it a little shake. A few drops of liquid sloshed inside. She offered the bottle to the copper. He scowled. Una shrugged, wiped the bottle's mouth on her coat sleeve, and drank the gin herself.

"Well, you seen anyone matching that description?"

"I'm sorry, Officer, but you just described half the vomen in this city. I'm certain I can't say."

The copper grumbled and started to stomp away.

"But zere vas a voman hiding behind zese trash cans just a moment ago."

"There was?"

"Startled me half to death."

"Why didn't you say so?"

"Pretty girl. Dark eyes. She had a little mole right here." Una pointed to the side of her nose. "You didn't say anyzing about a mole."

The copper looked as if it was all he could do to keep from reaching out and strangling her. "Which way did she go?"

Una pointed down the alley toward Thirty-Eighth Street. "Out zat vay. Turned right, I believe."

She snickered as the copper sprinted away. Gullible bastards, the lot of them. She wiped her hands on a scrap of newsprint and hobbled out the opposite end of the alley beyond the privies and their stench.

CHAPTER 3

Una kept up her hunchback disguise for several blocks until she was safely shadowed by the towering brick and wooden tenements of the city's lower wards. There, she unstrapped the traveling bag from her back but didn't bother righting her coat. A week's worth of trash, horseshit, and mud covered the streets. No point to risk dirtying the fine side of her coat when there was no one here to fool or impress.

She kept her step measured, neither dawdling nor hurried, like someone who didn't have on her person an engraved cigarette case and a host of pinched trinkets that could earn her a one-way ticket to the workhouse on Blackwell's Island. Her stomach rumbled like it had at the station. Were it not for that boy, she'd have already fenced her swag at Marm Blei's and be washing down her supper with a pint of ale at Hayman's grocer. She knew better than to involve herself with such shenanigans. The first rule of survival on these streets was to keep your head down and look out for yourself. Her mother had been a do-gooder and look where it got her—burned to a crisp like an overdone steak. Never mind where that left Una.

She nodded to Officer O'Malley at the corner of the Bowery and Grand Street. She'd told him she worked at a soap factory, and Marm Blei paid him to believe it. He tipped his hat to her and continued on his rounds. Even so, the cigarette case weighed heavy in her pocket. She'd feel better once she had a pocket full of brass instead.

A block and a half farther on, she spotted a tall man in a dark blue frock coat leaning against a lamppost. Her eyes snagged on the glint of silver at his throat before taking in his face. Barney Harris. He was pretending—not very adroitly—to be reading a magazine as if it were perfectly natural for a well-dressed reporter to be loitering in the slums. He shifted from one foot to the other, his eyes peeking above the page of the magazine every few seconds. The screeching brakes of the nearby el train startled him, and he bolted upright, bobbling his magazine and nearly falling off the curb.

Una chuckled, even as she slowed. Maybe she ought to turn down the next alley to avoid him. Marm Blei hated being kept past supper. Besides, Una didn't feel much like gabbing. But she owed him for giving her a false alibi last month at the opera house after a man accused her of stealing his signet ring.

The soprano had been magnificent that night. And if the coppers had taken her back to the station and frisked her, they'd have found more than the man's ring hidden in the folds and flounces of her skirt. But when they'd questioned her, she told the coppers she'd been in the company of Mr. Harris all night. He had, in fact, sought her out during the first intermission and shyly complimented her dress (stolen, of course, and a bit too tight). So the yarn she'd spun for the coppers wasn't entirely a lie. Thank God Barney correctly read the look on her face when she approached with the coppers and, after a moment's bubbling, corroborated her story.

Una owed him. And she hated owing anyone. It went against her rules. So despite the plunder weighing down her skirts, she continued in his direction.

"You stand out around here like soot on snow," she said, approaching him. "You take the First Avenue el in the wrong direction again?"

"Miss Kelly! A pleasure to see you. I hoped you'd be by sooner or later."

"You beat dirt all the way here from Newspaper Row to see little ol' me? I don't know whether to feel flattered or frightened."

"Flattered, I assure you. I'd have brought flowers if I thought you fancied such things."

"I fancy gold. Diamonds. Imported French silk."

"I'd try that too if I didn't think you'd take it straight to Marm Blei's back door."

She shrugged. "A girl's gotta eat."

He pursed his lips, and made a soft *hmm* sound. His gray eyes narrowed. Not in disapproval—Una had seen enough of those squinty-eyed looks to know—but in bemusement. Like she were some rare bird in a curiosity shop, songless and molting. A bird in need of saving. Could he be the man to do it? his eyes seemed to say. Could he spring the lock of her unfortunate circumstances?

He was a decent man, Barney was. Handsome in a boyish kind of way. Had enough brass in the family coffers to afford silly ornamentation like the silver tie pin he wore. (His wages at the *New York Herald* certainly wouldn't be enough.) Trouble was, he had a cage of his own—bigger, perhaps, and cast in finer metal—waiting for her if she took his bait.

So instead of batting her eyelashes and smiling shyly, she jabbed him on the shoulder, swiping his pin while she was at it. "I know ya didn't come all this way to whisper sweet nothings in my ear. What do ya want?"

He frowned and tucked the magazine under his arm. "You know anything about the murder last Saturday on Cherry Street?"

"You mean Big-nosed Joe? What of it?"

"How'd it happen?"

"Heard he was strangled. Ain't heard much else."

A woman pushing a wheelbarrow full of second-hand stockings trudged toward them. "Fifteen cents a pair," she called to anyone in earshot. A greasy rag covered her head, and a faded shawl hung around her shoulders. Una grabbed a pair and examined the darning. "Five."

"Ten," the woman said.

Una held the cotton stockings to her nose. They smelled enough of soap to wager they'd recently been washed. She fished through her pockets and handed the woman a dime. Barney, she noticed, had trained his eyes on the fishmonger and his slimy wares across the street, his cheeks flushed red.

"That eel there what got your color up or these here stockings?" she said, dangling the limp cotton in front of him before shoving them into her bag. If he blushed like that over a pair of stockings, what would he do if he caught sight of her chemise? Una half considered dropping her bag like she had at the train station to find out.

Barney cleared his throat and pulled a pencil from his pocket. He patted his other pockets—presumably in search of a notepad—then sighed and unfurled the magazine. "Undergarments aside, you mentioned Big-nosed Joe was strangled. By whom?"

Una shrugged. "Take your pick. He played so much cards half the Bend claimed he owed them money."

"The police report said he had ten dollars and a gold watch on him when they inventoried his belongings in the morgue. If someone killed him over a gambling debt, why not clean him out?"

"Maybe whoever done it didn't have time."

"But he had time to strangle him. A knife or bullet would be faster."

"And likely louder."

"That's a good point." He scribbled a few words on the magazine cover.

"What do the police say?" she asked.

"They chalk it up to an argument over cards. Hazard of the profession, so to speak."

"Probably was." Joe was as famous for his temper as he was for his beak-like nose.

"But what if it wasn't? Remember there was that prostitute found strangled on Water Street last month?"

Martha Ann. She'd been a girl at one of the fancy houses for a while, making better money in one night than Una earned in a week of hard grifting. But then, some years back, one of her regulars got jealous of another regular and carved up her face like a pumpkin. She'd been walking the streets ever since.

Una shifted her bag from one hand to the other and spoke past the thickness in her throat. "Like them coppers said, hazard of the profession."

"Both of them were strangled with a rope or belt of some sort. What if they were killed by the same person?"

"A crazed strangler running about the slums? Now, that I would have heard of."

"Not if he wasn't from around here."

"Especially if he wasn't from around here." She held up his silver pin. "Like I said, you outsiders stick out like soot on snow."

He smiled at her and took back his pin. "Point taken. Just keep your ear to the ground, will you?"

"I always do."

Barney pocketed the pin along with his pencil. He tore off the magazine's cover and tossed the rest of it to the ground.

"Hey!" Una said, snatching it up.

"Oh, sorry. I didn't think . . .there's not much worth reading inside. Nothing that . . ."

"Nothing that would interest the likes of me, huh? Probably forgot I could read at all." She brushed a limp onion skin off the top page. "And here you were talking about bringing me flowers just a moment ago."

Barney's cheeks flushed again, and he rubbed the back of his neck. "I . . . er . . ."

Una let him fumble for words, enjoying his discomfort a moment before giving him a nudge with her elbow. "I'm only joshing you. Can't let good privy paper like this go to waste."

He gave a tight laugh and glanced back at the fish stand, avoiding her gaze. Una slipped her hand in his pocket, snagged the pin, and walked away. "See you around, Barney. I'll let you know if I hear anything about your mysterious killer."

She was a few yards away before he called out to her. Una turned around.

"Be careful."

CHAPTER 4

Barney's expression—that of genuine care and concern—needled Una as she navigated the bustling streets to Marm Blei's shop. He was a good reporter, hungry, albeit a bit green. And it was high time someone gave a damn about the slums. Someone other than those stodgy reformers whose kindness always came with a catch.

Maybe she should have played the coquette and let him buy her flowers. Lord knew they cost enough this time of year to be prized alongside gold. She slipped a hand into her inside pocket and fingered his tie pin. The pointy end pricked her through her glove.

Una cursed and continued on, the cold and darkness creeping over the city.

At the corner of Orchard Street, a young ruffian dashed out in front of her to sweep the road, the bristles of his broom caked in a day's worth of dust and horse manure.

"How short are you?" she asked when they reached the opposite side of the street. The boy, with his black hair and olive skin, was familiar, but she didn't know his name.

"Five cents."

Una knew the racket. The boy's father (who likely wasn't his father at all, but a con man of the vilest sort) set an amount each day that the boy had to collect before returning home. If not, the boy would be beaten. She remembered passing by street sweepers at this very intersection with her mother nearly two decades ago. She'd been the same age as the children then, and they'd been fellow Irishmen, the children, not Italian. Una and her mother had been off on some do-good mission, and instead of giving the boy a penny, her mother had given him a roll from the basket of food they'd prepared that morning. She'd pointed in the general direction of the Points and told him about the House of Industry where he could get not only more food but an education.

"Never give them money, Una," her mother had told her. "It only perpetuates their exploitation."

Una remembered nodding, though at the time she hadn't fully understood all those big words. Now, she fished in her pocket for a coin. This late in the day, he was probably shy only a penny or two. An honest boy would have said so. But honesty didn't buy you an ear of corn or meat pie on your way home. On these streets you survived by hustling. That was the lesson her mother should have taught her. She tossed the boy a nickel and walked away.

The front door of Blei Dry Goods store was locked when Una arrived and the windows darkened. But Una never used the front door. Instead, after a glance around, she slipped into the alley that flanked the shop, picking her way past ash barrels, empty chicken crates, and a broken wagon wheel to the back door.

A bell jangled from the door when Una entered, and Marm Blei looked up from the pearl-studded brooch she'd been examining. The first time Una had seen her—this giant of a woman with long, plump fingers and shrewd, beady eyes—fear had stricken her. One misstep and this woman could flatten her like a latke. All these years later, an echo of that fear remained. Never mind that Marm Blei had taught Una almost everything she knew about thieving and saved her more than once from a trip to the Island. She doted on Una, or so the others complained. But that didn't mean she still couldn't squash Una flat.

"Come look at this, *sheifale*," she said and patted the stool next to her. *Lamb.* She'd called Una that from the very beginning.

Una set down her bag and sat beside her at the long narrow table that filled the center of the room. The store had two offices. One opened off the main shop and housed a polished oak desk and neatly kept ledgers of all official business. The other, where Una now sat, was part workshop, part receiving office for all unofficial items. Secret cubbies lay beneath the floorboards, and a hidden dumbwaiter ferried larger goods down to the basement.

Marm Blei handed her the brooch and loupe. "Tangle-foot Toby wanted sixty-five dollars for it. What do you think?"

Una turned the brooch round in her hand, feeling its weight, before examining it more closely with the loupe. The pearls were inlaid in a bed of delicately etched silver. On the backside, the seal of a well-known and high-end craftsman, *Martin & Sons*, was engraved beside the clasp.

"A fine piece. Worth at least sixty."

"Look closer."

Una brought the loupe back to her eye and studied the brooch again. At first, she didn't see anything out of the ordinary. Marm Blei wheezed softly beside her. The cold always troubled her lungs. Una raised the brooch to her nose and sniffed. No metallic smell. Pure silver, then. The weight of it confirmed that too. If it were lighter, she'd suspect the thicker parts of the silverwork were hollow. Heavier, and she'd guess silver plating concealed a cheaper metal beneath. She turned it over and studied the clasp. The soldering work was delicately done, but the clasp itself was rather flimsy. Una picked up a nearby rag, dipped it in the small pot of silver polish on Marm Blei's workbench, and rubbed it on the clasp. It remained a lusterless gray.

"The clasp isn't silver. Not pure silver, anyway. And rather cheaply fashioned."

"What else?" Marm Blei asked.

She flipped the brooch over and reexamined the pearls. They floated amid the filigree like frozen raindrops, uniform in size and color. Too uniform. Beneath the loupe's magnification, she ought to see more variation. Ought to see the tiny imperfections that marked each pearl as unique.

"Roman pearls. Fakes."

"All of them?"

"No." She gave each a scratch. A fine powder came away from the real pearls. The others—glass beads coated on the inside with an iridescent liquid made from ground fish scales and then filled with wax—gave off nothing. "About half."

Marm Blei nodded approvingly as Una handed back the brooch.

"You think it's been fenced before and someone replaced the real pearls with fakes?" she asked. "Melted down the original clasp and replaced it with this one?"

"Perchance. Smart of them, if they did. They'd have to have skill, though. An untrained hand would have damaged the silverwork removing and replacing all those pearls."

There were a few fences in town—Marm Blei included—who could manage such a feat. But it was an awful lot of trouble to go through for a handful of loose pearls and a spot of silver. Una frowned. "You don't think . . ."

"That Martin and Sons did it themselves? Seems likely as not to me. Your average customer wouldn't know the difference." She laughed and patted Una's knee. "We're not the only crooks out there, *sheifale.*"

"How much you give him, Toby?"

"Fifteen."

A fair price. Never mind that Marm Blei would turn around and sell it for fifty. She tucked the brooch into a velvet-lined box opened on the workbench. When her gaze returned to Una, the laughter was gone from her eyes. "Heard you got in a bit of a scrape today at the station."

Una shifted on the stool. Who'd ratted on her? She hadn't seen anyone else from Marm Blei's crew at the depot, but then, Marm Blei had eyes even Una didn't know about.

"It was nothin'."

"Nothing?"

"Nothin' I couldn't handle. I'm here, ain't I?"

"Yes. Late, but you are here." She studied Una a moment longer with that hard stare, then her expression softened. She patted Una's knee again. "Cook's making hasenpfeffer tonight. Never was overly fond of rabbit anyway. Show me what you've got."

Una turned out her pockets and laid the day's loot on the workbench. A gold ring. A pair of kid gloves. A few crumpled bills. The silver cigarette case. But Barney's pin she held back. She'd taken it to prove a point, not to sell it. Maybe someday she'd give it back. Maybe not.

Marm Blei counted the bills first, then turned her attention to the rest. She tossed the ring alongside a gold watch chain to be melted down later. The gloves were well-stitched with few signs of wear. Marm Blei tried to fit one over her giant hand but managed to get it only halfway on. "Oh well," she said and threw them into a basket with other bits of clothing. Next, she examined the cigarette case.

"Be worth more without these initials."

"They're not deeply engraved. Won't be but the work of a few minutes to buff them away."

Marm Blei pursed her lips, eyeing a pile of silver trinkets that, like the gold, were bound for the melting pot. After a moment, she nodded. "Suppose you're right." She placed the cigarette case alongside the brooch, then locked the box with a key she wore on a chain around her neck.

Without having to be told, Una picked up the box and took it across the room, where a faded upholstery chair sat against the wall. She moved the chair aside, pulled up the corner of the rug, and stowed the box beneath a loose floorboard.

"You'll work here in the back room tomorrow," Marm Blei said to her, handing over a few of the bills before tucking the rest in her pocket. Una didn't need to count them to know it was less than she'd hope for but more than she deserved.

"But I hate—"

Marm Blei silenced her with that steely gaze. *"Besser fri'er bevorent aider shpeter bevaint."*

Una had heard the words enough to know well what they meant: better caution at first than tears after.

CHAPTER 5

━━◆◆◆━━

Una trudged down Mulberry Street back into the heart of the slum. She climbed the steep steps of her tenement, lighting a new match on each landing to illuminate the windowless passage. Old paint peeled from the walls, and holes gaped in the plaster. The stairs were stained with years of grime ground into the wood.

Normally, Una didn't notice the dirt or the smell—that of piss and rotting food scraps—but tonight, it seemed to rise up and choke her. Why couldn't the other tenants be more careful when emptying their chamber pots and trash bins? Why didn't they scrape their boots at the door? Marm Blei enjoyed a fine set of apartments above the shop with indoor plumbing. The best fabric that came through the back door of her shop ended up upholstering her furniture and trimming her windows. The best marble work and paintings ended up on her walls. And here Una was stepping in . . . stepping in God-knows-what sticky mess on the way to her squalid room. She scraped the dark scum clinging to the sole of her boot on the lip of the stair and kept climbing.

It wasn't as if Marm Blei wasn't good to her. Everyone knew as fences went, she was the fairest one. And hadn't she taken Una under her wing all those years ago? Taught her the art of the grift? If Una were more careful with her money, she could afford a better flat. Or so Marm Blei always reminded her. *If you eat your whole beigel, sheifale, you'll have nothing in your pocket but the hole.*

Una was not yet eleven years old and had been on the streets only a few months when she'd met Marm Blei. But they were long months. Hard months. The gaunt, bedraggled reflection that peered at her from shop windows may as well have been a stranger's.

On this particular morning, she'd woken with ice crystals on her eyelashes. The baker on Worth Street who gave away his stale bread instead of feeding it to the hogs had run out by the time Una arrived at the back of his shop. The milkman who delivered up and down the Bowery kept such close watch on his cart, she couldn't sneak a single sip. So she wandered cold and hungry into the Jewish Quarter. The rags on her feet had begun to wear thin, and she hoped to find fresh scraps among the trouser makers' trash barrels. Merchants crowded the sidewalks in the heart of the quarter, selling everything from vegetables to chickens to tinware.

Una spied an unattended apple cart and scurried over. As she reached for one of the fruits, a hand grabbed her wrist. A man's hand to be sure, so long and meaty the fingers. But when Una looked up, she saw her detainer was a woman. Not the apple seller, but some well-dressed moll out for morning shopping. She stared down at Una from a towering height, her gray eyes hard, her grip on Una's wrist inescapably tight.

Before Una could mutter an excuse, the apple seller appeared. Una grimaced. This giant of a woman would rat her out for sure. Then the seller would fetch a copper, and this woman's thick hand would be replaced by a pair of iron ruffles. But instead, she said to the seller, "Half a peck, *bitte*, and an extra one for this *sheifale* here."

She handed the seller her basket and plucked three shiny dimes from the silk purse dangling from her wrist, all the while keeping tight hold of Una. When the seller handed back the basket, brimming with apples, the tall woman leaned down and handed one to Una. "See that you take more care next time."

Una accepted the apple with a smile, but the soft clink of coins from within the woman's purse was too much for her to resist. As soon as the woman released her wrist, Una snatched her purse and ran.

She hadn't gone half a block when a copper caught hold of the back of her dress. He lifted her off her feet, holding her out at arm's length the way one might a noisome alley cat. "What ya runnin' from?" he asked. Then his eyes landed on the silk purse clutched in Una's hand. "I see. I'm guessin' this don't belong to a ragamuffin like you."

Una squirmed, her heart pounding. Whatever he meant to do with her, it couldn't be good. Desperate, she threw her apple square at his nose. He hollered and dropped her. Una scrambled to her feet, but the giant woman was there before she could skeddadle. She grabbed Una's arm again. One squeeze of her meaty fingers and she could snap Una's bone in two.

But she did not. Instead, she knelt down, looking Una straight in the eye. "You're a greedy little thing, aren't you?"

Though her heart still hammered and tears threatened in her eyes, Una held her stare. After a moment, the woman chuckled. "Dauntless too. Let's see if you are clever as well." Her gaze cut to the copper, still howling behind them. "Have you heard of the House of Refuge?"

Una nodded.

"Then you know it's not a nice place."

She nodded again.

"Well then, you can give me back my purse or I'll hand you over to the policeman, who'll take you there straightaway."

Una gave a small huff and handed the woman back her purse.

"Good girl. Now, where is your family?"

At this, Una looked away.

"Ah," the woman said, a note of kindness in her voice. "Then you shall come with me, *sheifale.* You want to be a thief? Obey me, and I will teach you to be a thief. A good thief. A smart thief. Then you can have all the apples you want." She stood and withdrew several more coins from her purse, pressing them into the copper's hand as she walked past him. "No need to worry about this one, Officer." She glanced over her shoulder at Una and kept walking.

Una hesitated a moment, then followed, snatching her apple from the ground and giving the copper a wide berth.

Fourteen years, and she hadn't looked back.

Now, Una opened the door to her ramshackle flat. The main room was dark, and the coal stove unlit. Her roommates—three other women who also dove pockets for Marm Blei—weren't in, but one had left the window cracked. Cold air fluttered the flannel curtain. Una stomped across the room and slammed down the sash. She didn't bother with the stove, frigid as the flat was, nor the kerosene lamp that sat on the table. Instead, she lit a candle and went into the windowless closet that served as their bedroom.

Maybe Marm Blei was right. Best to lie low in the shop tomorrow. She'd outwitted that copper, sure. And she doubted any of the dupes at the train depot could describe her beyond the plainest terms. Female. Twenty-five, or thereabouts in age. Brown hair. Fair skin. She dressed in muted colors that made her eyes look more brown than green. Always wore a hat with a wide brim, even though current fashion favored a shorter one, to obscure her face. Besides, if that copper didn't have wax in his ears and feathers for brains, they were looking for a woman with a mole on her nose. Misdirection. One of the earliest tricks Marm Blei had taught her.

But that looby of a boy, he'd gotten a good look at her. If they caught him, he'd squeal for sure. Play it up like stealing the watch had been her idea. They might even cart him down to headquarters and show him Chief Inspector Byrnes's rogues' gallery. Would he be able to spot hers among all the photos on the wall? It was an old photo and likely a bit blurry as she feigned a sneeze right before the bulb flashed. But there weren't many women on the wall. Only a few dozen among the thousand or so pictures of thieves and criminals rumored to be posted. Some men boasted of their place on the wall. Una wasn't that stupid. Secretly, though, it was a point of pride.

Never mind the boy. She wasn't going to sit around this cold, empty flat all night like some penitent Quaker. Marm Blei hadn't explicitly forbidden Una from going out tonight. She didn't have to. Una knew the rules. And one of Una's own rules—seven—was to follow Marm Blei's rules. But Una was tired of living under the woman's thumb. She shrugged out of her coat and flung her carpetbag to the corner. The pages of Barney's magazine were curled and rumpled when she pulled it from her pocket. Wouldn't matter none in the privy, though. She tossed it alongside her bag. After counting out half of her money, she carefully peeled back a flap of plastered newsprint covering a hole at the base of the wall. To the right of the opening, concealed within the wall, lay a small tin box. She pulled it out and opened the lid. Inside were a few dozen coins and bills, and an ivory cameo necklace.

The necklace had belonged to her mother. One of these days, she'd take it to Marm Blei and sell it. One of these days when cameos were back in fashion or the price of ivory was higher. She added Barney's tie pin to the stash along with half—no—a quarter of the day's earnings and returned the box to its hidey-hole.

Her first stop was the grocer two blocks down for a mincemeat pie and cup of spiced wine. There, she ran into her roommate Deidre. With long red hair and a small, pointy nose, Deidre was as beautiful as she was witless—which made her a good pal on the streets. Deidre provided the distraction while her partner raided pockets. She and Una had worked together some when they were young and both new to Marm Blei's crew. As soon as she had any say, however, Una insisted on working alone. Too much trouble to worry about herself and someone else. Especially when that someone else had all the smarts of a pigeon.

But Deidre did make for good company. From the grocer, the two of them moved on to a cock-and-hen club across the street. Honest men who labored at the docks and the dump sat beside safecrackers and sharpers, talking about the upcoming alderman elections or who would best whom at tonight's bare-knuckle boxing match. All were happy to buy Una a drink, but, more often than not, they expected something in return. An ear for their sorrows. A stolen kiss. A tussle in one of the rooms above the bar. If a fellow were particularly handsome and she were in the right mood, Una might accept the offer. Tonight she bought her own whiskey and let the professionals, with their rouged cheeks and low-cut bodices, handle the men.

In the alley behind the bar, a game of pins was underway. Una bet on a few matches. She smoked a cigarette and huddled alongside the other spectators, lobbing curses that would make the devil himself blush when one of the players missed a pin. Deidre pulled her away to a dance hall on Church Street, but not before Una had emptied her skin of all but a dollar.

At the dance hall, Una nursed a drink at a table by the wall while Deidre whirled and swayed in the arms of one beau after the next. For her part, Una refused the men who tottered over to the table, palms sweaty and eyes hopeful, asking for a dance. She'd never been overly fond of the sport. What did dancing have to offer besides the effusion of bad breath and risk of smashed toes? Instead, she stewed about Marm Blei and the way she continued to treat Una like that same apple-stealing looby she'd been all those years before. Una was the best pocket-diver and conwoman in Marm Blei's crew. Maybe it was time Una started on her own.

Deidre sat down beside her, her cheeks flushed and eyes smiling. "Ain't you gonna dance?"

"No," Una said, taking a long pull of whiskey.

"Bet if that reporter fellow were here, you'd be on your feet and shakin' your hips in a jiffy."

"We've got a business relationship. That's all."

"You tellin' me if he made you an honest offer you'd turn him down? Humbug."

The thought of such an offer soured the taste of Una's whiskey. Barney wasn't a bad catch. As dogged as he was bumbling when it came to securing a scoop, and she liked that about him. But what would she do if she were his wife? Cook and clean and chase after their little brats all day? She could barely boil a potato. Or say he had enough money to hire other women for that—his silver tie pin suggested he might—what then? Una had no intention of sitting in some stuffy parlor all day like one of those listless animals they kept caged at Central Park.

"What can I say? An honest life ain't for me."

Deidre snickered. "You'd rather end up like one of them?" She nodded toward a woman at the far side of the room. The theater crowd had just arrived, and right behind them the prostitutes.

Una didn't begrudge these women. Never mind what Father O'Donoghue said on Sundays; everyone had to eat. But theirs was a profession even more dangerous than hers. She'd seen the bruises. Watched more than one wither away or go mad from disease. Not to mention what happened to Martha Ann or the likes of Helen Jewett, who'd wound up with an ax in her skull.

"I'm doing just fine where I am, thank you," Una said, though she wished she'd put more money in her tin and less into the hands of the alleyway gamblers. One good haul would make up for it, though.

Deidre shook her head and returned to the dance floor. Una finished her drink with one swill but decided against buying another. The alcohol had settled warmly inside her, giving her limbs a light, tingly feeling. Another drink and that tingling sensation would turn to numbness, the warmth to a fiery spark. The wrong look or gesture and that spark would ignite. She'd woken enough mornings with bruised knuckles or a blackened eye to be wary of one too many drinks. The Kelly blood ran hot, her father had said. But more often than not, he'd ended up a blubbering mess. Morose and sentimental until he liquored himself into a stupor. More than once, Una had put her hand on his chest, fearing he were dead, only to feel the sluggish expansion of his lungs and the lazy thrum of his heart. Maybe meanness skipped a generation.

Una was just about to leave when one of the theatergoers approached her table. They were young men, the lot of them, smug and self-important. After the curtain fell on *Marriage by Moon-light* or whatever silly play they'd seen, they'd lied to their wives and mothers about going to the Union Club for a nightcap, then rallied their cronies for a night of slumming. For them, Una and every other working-class sop in the place were simply the next round of entertainment.

"Someone as lovely as you ought to be dancing," the man said to her.

It was as much a command as it was a compliment, and Una bristled. "Someone lovely as me ain't got no interest in dancing with—" She'd been about to say *a weak-chinned fop like yourself* when the twinkle of his ruby-studded cuff links caught her eye. "With . . . with just any gentleman, but one as estimable as yourself, why, I could hardly refuse."

He held out his gloved hand, and Una readily accepted. She smiled her prettiest smile. Spoke only the proper, well-mannered English her mother had taught her when the man asked her questions. Thankfully, that wasn't often. He wasn't interested in conversation, after all. Una could tell that straightaway when his hand drifted from the small of her back to below her bustle. She repositioned his hand, but not without a coquettish glance that suggested it could return there in time. And not without carefully unfastening his cuff link.

It was two more dances before she could find occasion to liberate him of the other, during which time she fed him lies about a certain whorehouse on Church Street where they might take a drink before heading to her room. But when another couple bumped into them, and Una secured the second cuff link, she excused herself to the sidelines to retie her boot, only to escape out the back door into the alley when the man wasn't looking.

She took the long way home, wandering amid the nest of factories and warehouses along the Hudson River. The man at the dance hall had been easy prey. And she couldn't deny the satisfaction of getting over on someone who'd foolishly thought himself the predator. But pinching a man's cuff links didn't count as lying low. Not in Marm Blei's book. Hot as they were, she'd have to hold on to the goods for at least a few days to avoid Marm Blei's suspicions.

Unless she used another fence. Una smiled despite the sudden lash of icy wind off the water. Traveling Mike Sheeny made rounds through the Sixth Ward this time of year. Marm Blei need never know.

CHAPTER 6

Una spent the next day in the back room of Marm Blei's dry goods shop, buffing away the maker's marks on a cache of metalware. It was tedious work, and as the hours wore on, Una itched to be out on the streets.

Every so often, the doorbell would jingle, and a new buyer or seller would appear. Una watched from the corner as Marm Blei hustled and haggled. Most of the small, less expensive goods she acquired were sold alongside her stock of legitimately purchased items in the store. But large, unique, or expensive loot was either melted down or hidden away with a particular back-door buyer in mind.

Una admired Marm Blei's shrewdness even as she begrudged her controlling hand. True, the money and goods Una forked over to her day after day paid for the cadre of aldermen and judges and coppers who—most of the time—looked the other way and let Una and the rest of Marm Blei's underlings be. If Una had been arrested yesterday, she'd be out on bail already, and, likely as not, the charges would be dropped. If not, Marm Blei had lawyers on retainer.

But Una *hadn't* been arrested. She'd gotten out of the scrape using her wits. Sure, a thief like Deidre needed Marm Blei's protection. Her pickpocketing skill was rudimentary at best, and her ambition extended about as far as Una could spit.

Una wanted more. Precisely what more, she wasn't sure. But she certainly wouldn't find it here, buffing and polishing, a mere hand puppet. When the curtain fell and the hat went out, she, Marm Blei, reaped all the coins.

Well, Una would be doing some reaping of her own later tonight. The cuff links she'd pinched last night were worth over a hundred dollars. Traveling Mike wouldn't give her more than thirty for them, maybe forty-five if she promised to send more of her business his way. All that money was going straight into the tin. She wouldn't drink or gamble away a cent of it. A nice dinner at Delmonico's wouldn't hurt, though. *Filet de boeuf* and *asperges hollandaise. Glace napolitaine* for dessert. A fine cordial afterward. Never mind they wouldn't seat her unless she spruced up her duds and found a man to accompany her. But that could be arranged. Una could almost taste the sweetness on her tongue.

By late afternoon, Una had buffed the goblets clean of any markings their former owner could identify.

"You've a good eye for detail, *sheifale*," Marm Blei said, inspecting her work.

"Can I go then?"

"Always in a rush."

"I . . . er . . . wanted to make it to the pig market before sundown. Damaged eggs go for a song there."

Marm Blei shook her head and waved her off. A strange, needling sensation pricked the back of Una's neck as she grabbed her coat. Guilt? They were only a lousy pair of cuff links, and it wasn't as if Marm Blei was hurting for business. She mumbled *"gut Shabbes"* over her shoulder and hurried out before her nerve failed her. Yesterday when she'd seen the boy about to be hauled over to the police, she'd forgotten rule number one: Look out for yourself. She wouldn't be forgetting that rule again.

Outside, puffy gray clouds choked the sky, and a light snow was falling. Just in case Marm Blei or one of her eyes were watching, Una hurried home by way of Hester Street, waving off the miserable street urchins offering to brush away the snow-turned-mud from her path. Peddlers crowded the sidewalks, calling out their wares. Tin cups for two cents. Hats for a quarter. Tattered coats—*good as new!*—for a dollar. The smell of freshly churned horseradish and warm bread mingled with the stench drifting up through the sewer grates. The gong of an ambulance sounded above the din, and the horse and wagon dashed past, splattering Una with mud.

"By jiminy," she muttered, brushing off her coat and shaking out her skirts. When she'd first seen these hospital wagons some dozen years before, what a marvel they'd seemed. Now, they were just another nuisance.

Una arrived home to find her roommates arguing over whose turn it was to lug the ash bin down to the trash. "I did it last week," she said before they could wrangle her into their argument. She hung her coat on a peg on the wall and hurried to the bedroom. It took three tries to light a candle. Once the sputtering flame had gathered into a steady burn, she eased shut the door. Una had known her roommates for years, Deidre since they were twelve years old. They drank together. Brawled together. Went on heists together. They were the closest thing to friends Una had. But that didn't mean she trusted them. They all kept a stash of money hidden somewhere—in the wall, beneath a loose floorboard, behind a secret panel in their trunk. Una even slept with her boots on, a holdover from when she first left home and slept on the streets.

She hadn't left by choice. Not really. Soon after her mother's death, she and her father were evicted from their home. He'd given up all pretense of looking for steady work and spent his days and his money drinking. All their nice things—from the crystal vase and silver tea service Great-grandma Callaghan had brought from Ireland to the lace tidies her mother had sewn to the porcelain doll Una had gotten for Christmas just the year before—were sold. They moved to a boarding house and then a tenement in Five

Points. By then she'd gotten used to rifling through his pockets for loose change to buy bread, milk, or potatoes.

Whereas before, Una had attended school, taken piano lessons, and practiced cross-stitching, now she spent her days wandering the streets, scrounging for coal or picking through trash barrels. Her father was often gone to some saloon or other by the time she returned home. One day, she opened the door to their dingy flat to find the last of their meager possessions gone—taken by the rent collector to cover a month's worth of debt—and another family moved in. All she had left of her old life was her mother's necklace, tucked beneath the collar of her dress. She searched for her father long into the night, finding him in a back alley drinking hole, far too in his cups to comprehend what had happened. The other men in the bar laughed as she pleaded and tried to rouse him to his feet. In the end, she gave up, filching the last coins from his pocket and stomping off into the night.

The Points in the daytime was a crass, boisterous place. In the dark hours after sunset, it was sinister and menacing. She found a secluded corner in the rear yard of a nearby tenement but didn't sleep. Each time her eyelids would droop closed, a creak or clatter or scream would startle her awake. The next night passed much the same. She caught snatches of sleep during the daytime only to be roused by a copper's boot or billy club.

Experience was an unforgiving teacher, but Una learned quickly. After her boots were stolen when she took them off to sleep, she never let her eyes close again without anything of value hidden away or securely strapped to her body. She spent a few days with a band of river pirates, then fell in with a gang of other street children who taught her how to fight and forage and cuss up a storm. Then with Marm Blei, who taught her how to steal.

Una had run into her father again a few years later. Instead of a saloon, he was stumbling out of an opium den. She hesitated before approaching him, worried he wouldn't recognize her. She was clean and respectably dressed again—Marm Blei insisted everyone in her crew look presentable—and at least a head taller. At first, his glazed eyes stared right through her. Then, for a moment, they seemed to clear. "Una, *a stór*!"

My treasure. He hadn't called her that since she was a small girl. Before her mother's death. Before the war. When they'd all been whole and healthy and happy. But just as quickly, the glassy, faraway look returned to his eyes. She slipped several dollars into his pocket and watched him shuffle away.

Una shrugged off the memory. Rule number fourteen: Don't waste time on the past. She listened at the bedroom door to ensure her roommates were still fighting about the ash bin, then retrieved her tin from the wall. The ruby-and-silver cuff links glimmered in the candlelight. A handsome pair, to be sure. Solid and well made. She'd not take less than forty for them. She slipped them into one of the hidden pockets of her skirt along with Barney's pin. Maybe she'd sell it after all, depending on Traveling Mike's offer. She grabbed her brass knuckles too—just in case he tried to nab the cuff links without paying up.

Una had only just secreted the tin box back inside the wall when the door opened, and Deidre traipsed in.

"I drew the damned short stick." She flung herself down on the nest of straw and rags that was her bed. None of them had proper mattresses or bed frames to raise them off the floor. But someday Una would. The cuff links stowed in her pocket were proof that she was moving up in the world.

"Best get it over with before the snow gets worse," she said.

"I'll give you a nickel if you do it."

"Not a chance."

"Fine. You got any paper I can use in the privy? Might as well make the most of my trip."

She grabbed Barney's magazine, tore out the first few pages, and handed them to Deidre. "Here."

"What's it say?"

"What do you care? You're just gonna wipe your ass with it."

"That don't mean I don't like to know what's going on in the world. Besides, I like it when you read. Gonna learn myself someday."

"Yeah, right after you find yourself a rich husband and move into a house on Millionaire's Row."

Deidre wadded up one of the sheets of paper and threw it at her. "You swallow a hornet's nest on your way home today?"

"No." Una stood and straightened her skirt, careful not to rattle the cuff links in her pocket. As an afterthought, she wedged the magazine into another pocket—a page or two might come in handy if she found herself splashed with mud again—and then extended a hand to Deidre, hauling her up from the floor. "Sorry."

"Don't know why you get so sour when Marm Blei has you work in the shop. Wish she'd ask me."

"It's a punishment, not a reward. Besides, you ain't careful enough. Remember last time when you forgot to remove the name stitched inside that fancy fur coat? Marm Blei had a hell of a time explaining that one to the coppers."

Deidre pouted. "That weren't but one time."

"And the crystal cup you mixed up and put with the glass ones? How about that time you—"

"Okay. Uncle!"

A backward glance to be sure the flap of plaster that covered her secret trove lay smooth against the wall, and Una followed Deidre from the room.

"Where you off to?" Deidre asked when Una grabbed her coat.

"Nowhere that's any of your business." Her words came out sharper than Una intended, and she added, "Just for some eggs." Rule number twenty-seven: Once you pick a lie, stick to it.

"I'll come along," Deidre said.

"No!" Una all but shouted. She took a calming breath and continued, "I ain't gonna wait while you shlep the ash bin down to the yard and back. I'll bring you some back."

"And a pickle. Or maybe one of those sausages from Grutzmacher's."

"I'm not going that way," Una said over calls for sausages from her other roommates too.

"I bet she's off to see that reporter she's sweet on," Deidre said to them and then smirked at Una. "We can all clear out for a while if ya wanna bring him back here."

Una shook her head while the women laughed, not bothering to correct them. Better they think she was on her way to shake the sheets with Barney than guess at the truth. She flung her scarf around her neck and left them to their snickering.

Outside, snow continued to fall but slower than before. A fat flake here and there. Like the clouds had turned themselves inside out and were shaking out the final dregs. Una walked quickly but measured. She met passersby in the eye and smiled. Twilight had crept over the city, offering Una a few minutes of shadowy cover until the streetlamps flickered on.

The neighborhood had transformed since she'd been a girl. Brick tenements had replaced many of the old wooden ones with fire escapes crawling up their sides. The new rubber factory spewed smoke into the air. The trash didn't pile up quite as high along the streets. She heard Italian spoken now. Greek and Chinese. The thick Irish brogue like that of her father had vanished from many voices like a wrinkle ironed out of a shirt.

But some things never changed. Street children still huddled over steam grates. Beggars rattled their tins. Gangs prowled the alleys. The Democrat ticket won. A boxing match, a free lunch, or a burning building were still the surest things to draw a crowd. And there was no such thing as an honest thief.

At the corner of Centre and Pearl Streets, Una stopped. Pallid light dribbled from the saloon's frosted windows across the street. She glanced casually in the direction that she'd come from to be sure no one from Marm Blei's crew had followed her. A few paces off, a man cranked out a tune on his barrel organ. Una stepped closer, listening to his song as she scanned the street again. Night's deepening shadows made it impossible to see the faces of anyone more than half a block away, but Una couldn't wait around forever. She tossed a coin to the small monkey roped to the organ grinder's side and crossed the street to the saloon.

Inside, the air was warm and heavy with the scent of stale beer. A quick sweep of the dimly lit room, and she spotted Traveling Mike at a table in the far corner. A snifter of brandy sat before him. His wooden peddler's case rested on the floor beside his chair. Unlike Marm Blei, who seldom did business outside of her store, Traveling Mike was a nomad who conducted his fencing business in rear tenement yards and alleyways and abandoned cellars throughout the city. Operating entirely out of his dingy peddler's case, he couldn't move large items like fur coats or marble vases, but if a thief had something hot—a diamond ring, a gold watch, a pair of ruby cuff links—and needed it gone quick, Traveling Mike was your man. Word on the street was that he cleared thousands of dollars a year.

Una was one of only two women in the joint, the other being an old, leather-skinned barmaid, and every eye followed Una as she crossed the room toward Traveling Mike. The din of voices and clanking glasses diminished to a murmur. An ambulance bell clamored from the streets outside. The soggy hem of Una's skirt swished over the sawdust-strewn floor.

Instead of sitting down at his table, she took a chair one table over beside a middle-aged man with an overly waxed mustache. She smiled at the man and said, "Buy me a drink?"

He blinked once, then stood so quickly he nearly toppled his chair and scurried to the bar. Una waited until he was out of earshot before whispering, "I've got some swag that'll interest you."

She didn't look at Traveling Mike as she spoke but knew he'd heard her by his soft chuckle.

"That so?"

"I certainly ain't here for the weak beer and lousy company."

Another chuckle. "I thought you was one of Marm Blei's girls. You know she don't take kindly to turncoats." He had the slow, lulling accent of a Southerner but there was an edge of danger beneath his words.

"That's my concern, not yours." The mustached man was returning with her drink. She dared a glance in Traveling Mike's direction. "Well, you interested?"

He downed his brandy in one gulp and stood. "Wait ten minutes, then meet me in the alley half a block down Pearl Street." He picked up his peddler's case and started for the door just as the mustached man sat down again. He pushed half a pint of pale beer across the table to her. Cheap bastard. He could have at least splurged on a full pint. The beer tasted like rat piss—or what Una imagined rat piss to taste like—but she needed whatever jolt of courage she could get. Traveling Mike was right: Marm Blei didn't take kindly to turncoats.

She managed to pass the next ten minutes without having to say much—the mustached man was happy to do the lion's share of talking. She permitted his eyes to wander from her face down to the swell of her breasts and flair of her skirt around her thighs. But when his hand sought the same liberties, she slapped it away and stood. Half a pint of rancid beer only bought you so much. Time was up anyway.

Outside, the sluggish fall of snow continued. Una studied the passersby before starting toward the alley Traveling Mike had indicated. As she walked, she listened for the squeaky hinges of the saloon's door to be sure no one followed her. The cold had deepened along with the dark, and her breath rose like steam from her lips. Ice crystals collected on the brim of her hat. She peered into the shadowed nooks and doorways, assuring herself she was alone. Then, just as she reached the mouth of the alley, a hand reached out and grabbed her.

CHAPTER 7

Una yanked free and spun around, stepping back as she did so and sinking into a defensive crouch. One hand slid into her pocket and latched around her brass knuckles. The other shot up to absorb a strike. Her vision narrowed, and her attacker's shape took form.

"Jiminy, Deidre! What the hell are you doing here?" Una lowered her arm. She'd been so intent looking out for one of Marm Blei's hired roughs she'd missed Deidre behind her all this time.

"You ain't out getting sausages or eggs."

"Grutzmacher's was sold out by the time I got there."

"You could tell that from three blocks away?"

Una's hand tightened around the brass knuckles in her pocket. She'd never use them on Deidre but damned if she didn't want to at the moment. "How come you're following me? I told you not to come."

"I ain't following you." Deidre looked down, gnawing on her bottom lip. "Least I didn't start off following you. But when I saw you heading off in the opposite direction of old Grutzmacher's shop, I got curious."

She stepped closer and jabbed a finger at Deidre's chest. "You thought I was off to see Mr. Harris? Thought you'd cutty-eye us like a peeper."

Deidre shoved her away. "I know you ain't out to meet that

reporter. You ain't interested in anyone or anything you can't use or sell."

"That ain't—" Una stopped. It was true. Never mind that it stung to hear it said aloud. "That ain't the point. You got no business following me."

"And you ain't got no business sipping beer in the same bar as Traveling Mike."

Una kept her voice steady, even as her heart floundered. "Oh, he was there? I didn't notice. I'd come to meet a—"

"Didn't notice my ass. He's the reason you went out tonight. Not for eggs or to see that reporter. Marm Blei would be none too pleased if she knew."

The growing cold prickled over Una's limbs. What would Marm Blei do to Una when Deidre ratted her out? No transaction had occurred between Una and Traveling Mike yet. Could she deny it? Even if Marm Blei believed her, she'd be suspicious of Una from here on out. No, the best way was to embroil Deidre in the deceit with her. That would ensure Deidre's silence.

She grabbed Deidre's arm and pulled her close. "Listen, I got a pair of cuff links I'm fencing. Rubies and real silver."

Deidre's eyes widened. "How much you think you can get for them?"

"At least twenty. I'll throw you twenty-five percent if you stay quiet. Wait here and I'll—"

"Fifty, and I'm coming with you."

Una considered a moment. Traveling Mike might be put off by the appearance of someone else. No doubt it would harden his bargain. And if Deidre tagged along, she'd be privy to the negotiations and know the real amount Traveling Mike paid. There'd be no way around tipping Deidre her quota.

She let out a huff of breath that rose like a ghost into the air. The longer she dallied the greater the chance Traveling Mike would grow impatient and leave. Hell, he may have left already. And she couldn't risk Deidre blowing the gab. "All right. Fifty percent. But don't say a word. This is my negotiation."

They followed the alley to a small rear yard, the fallen snow muffling their footfalls. The shadowy outline of broken-down crates and rotting barrels cluttered the yard. Brick and wood buildings rose around them on all sides, blocking out the light from the street. Tattered curtains and thin squares of flannel shrouded the windows—few as they were—that faced the yard. The pale glow peeking through tears and around the seams suggested firelight within but offered no illumination. Behind them, the noise of the street was a distant murmur—voices and footfalls indistinguishable from the crunch of wagon wheels over the icy pavers. The same far-off sounds echoed from the opposite end of the alley, where only a sliver of the street was visible.

"Damn it," Una muttered, fishing through her pocket for a matchbook. She'd bickered so long with Deidre that Traveling Mike had given up and left.

Deidre managed to strike a match first. The kindling flame momentarily illuminated the yard. A blanket of snow covered the flotsam, glittering and white. It made a strange, dissonant contrast to the dark smudges of soot and slop that stained the walls. A flash of movement ground level caught her eye, and her gaze drifted downward just as Deidre screamed. She dropped the match, and the yard went dark before Una could fully process what she'd seen. A man? Crouched beside another man sprawled on the snowy pavers? A belt or length of rope wrapped around the sprawling man's neck?

Una instinctively backed away. Her feet tangled with a pile of rubble, and she fell against the wall. The brick was hard and cold against her back. Despite the blackness and Deidre's continued shriek, she had the sickening sense that the crouched man had risen and taken a step toward them. If there had been a man at all. Una still wasn't sure what she'd seen.

She fumbled through her pockets. Tie pin . . . cuff links . . . knuckles . . . the damned magazine. Where were her matches? She'd had the flimsy box within her grasp only moments ago. Deidre stopped screaming and fumbled with her own matches.

She scraped one, two against the striker, but they didn't ignite. Finally, Una found hers and managed to light one.

Only one man remained in the yard—Traveling Mike. He lay faceup on the ground, eyes open and red. Blood-tinged spit dribbled from his lips. Dead. Una need not listen for breath or feel for a pulse. She'd seen this dull-eyed stillness enough to be certain. His peddler's case lay closed at his side. The snow around him was dirty and troubled from a struggle. The skin on his neck was raw and red, but the belt—if that's what she'd seen—was gone.

Una swept her gaze around the yard again to be sure the other man wasn't hiding behind a barrel or trash bin. There had been another man, hadn't there? She'd caught only a glimpse before Deidre dropped her match.

"Where'd he go?" Deidre said.

Una felt a wash of relief—she *had* seen another man—followed quickly by a prickling dread. "We have to get out of here." She pushed off against the wall and grabbed Deidre's arm. Her fear-muddled brain began to clear. Boot prints trailed down the narrow passage at the far end of the yard. Behind them, a jumble of prints—hers, Deidre's, Traveling Mike's, and perhaps even the killer's—all leading into the yard. None heading out. She tugged Deidre in that direction.

"Shouldn't we . . . ?" Deidre gestured weakly at Traveling Mike.

Did she mean to close his eyes? Rearrange his twisted limbs in a more peaceful repose? Pry open his peddler's case and divide the spoils? This last idea wasn't a bad one, but they hadn't the time. "Are you mad? Half the damned city must have heard you scream. Coppers will be here any minute."

"Maybe we should stay and tell 'em what we seen."

Una lit another match. Even in the warm, peachy glow of light, Deidre's face looked drained of color. She'd seen bad things, Deidre, growing up in the slums. But not like this, Una realized. Not murder. She gave her friend's cheek a light slap. "We're gonna pad like a bull to the street, then play it cool. Just two ladies out for an evening stroll. We ain't heard nothin'. Ain't seen nothin'. Got it?"

Deidre rubbed her cheek and nodded. As the match burned down to a nub, Una cast a final glance at Traveling Mike. Then she ran. Deidre's footfalls sounded close behind her. She'd almost made it to the street when a wiry, baby-faced copper rounded the corner into the alley.

Una skidded to a stop in the slick snow. Deidre ran into her from behind, and they both nearly toppled.

"Who goes there?" the copper shouted, fumbling to unclip the lantern from his belt.

Shoving her way past Deidre, Una scrambled back toward the yard. She could escape out the alley at the far end like the killer had. Hopefully Deidre would follow, but for now, it was every woman for herself. She dashed through the darkened yard, tripping over crates and half-broken boxes and something soft and malleable that may have been an arm. A glint of light at the far end of the narrow alley promised an exit, but Una's feet slowed as she thought again of Traveling Mike's case. He must have hundreds of dollars' worth of stolen goods. Enough to get her out of the slum and free of Marm Blei for good.

She glanced over her shoulder to gauge the copper's distance. His lantern was but a pinprick of light at the far mouth of the alley. Perhaps Deidre was putting him off with some story or another before she herself would run. Una had enough time to go back for the case. But before her feet could turn around, she crashed into a stone wall in the middle of the alley.

Una staggered back and rattled her head. Not a stone wall, but another copper. In the dim light, she could just make out his tall bruiser of a frame. He clasped the collar of her coat before she had the sense to slip around him and flee. She tried to shrug off her coat, but he reached out with his other hand and locked his meaty fingers around her arm.

"Going somewhere, missy?"

Una stomped on his toes with the heel of her boot. His lined faced didn't even flinch.

"I didn't think so," he said.

CHAPTER 8

———⊰•⊱———

At the station house, Una was dragged before the sergeant. He sat behind a railed enclosure in the main hall. Gas lamps sat on either end of his broad desk, casting him and his open blotter in a jaundiced glow. His mustache was unevenly trimmed, one side bushier and the other trailing beyond the corner of his thin lips as if he'd been in his cups while shaving.

He dipped his pen in the inkwell and gazed up at her with a bored expression. "Name."

Una's hands were fastened behind her back with rusty handcuffs. The copper she'd so unceremoniously met with in the alley still held tight to her arm, his fat fingers sure to leave a bruise.

"I haven't done anything wrong, Sergeant," Una said, speaking with the same slow, Southern sway Traveling Mike had. "Your officer simply accosted me on my way home for no apparent reason."

The copper released her arm and dug inside a leather satchel strapped to his belt. He pulled out a fistful of objects and tossed them onto the sergeant's desk. Una's brass knuckles. Her matchbook. The rumpled magazine. Barney's silver pin. The ruby cuff links, however, made no appearance.

Back in the alley, he'd pushed her against the rough brick wall, pinning her hands above her head as he frisked her. The bricks were damp from the snow and smelled of soured vegetables.

He'd pulled his leather glove off with his teeth and searched her barehanded, groping his way over her breasts and between her legs before fishing through her pockets. "Can't be too thorough with you tramps," he'd said into her ear, his breath a sweaty cloud against her skin. And thorough he had been, finding all of the secret pockets sewed into the folds and flounces of her skirt. He'd taken everything, including the cuff links, before wandering his hand back to her breasts for a final squeeze.

By then, the stale beer in her stomach had risen up her throat and into her mouth, tinged with acid. Instead of forcing it back down, she vomited on the copper's brass-buttoned arm. He shrank away, cussing. Lucky for him, she'd drunk only a half pint of that rancid beer, not a full one.

Looking back, that had been her opportunity to run. But thoughts of Traveling Mike and his killer, of the copper's sticky breath and rough hands, still muddled her mind. Before her muscles could quicken, the copper pushed her back against the wall—that too would leave a bruise where her cheek struck the brick—and wrenched her hands into cuffs.

Now, the sergeant poked at her belongings with the end of his pen, clearly still disinterested. "Name," he said again.

"Dorothea Davidson," Una replied. She may not have had the sense to run from the alley when she'd had her chance, but she spent the handcuffed walk to the station coming up with her ruse. First and foremost was thinking up an alias she hadn't used before. "And like I said—"

"What's the charges?" the sergeant said, looking beyond her at the officer.

"Disturbing the peace, vagrancy, and theft."

Una looked back and scowled at the copper. These were the type of charges two-bit officers leveled against prostitutes when they wanted to make trouble for the women. Never mind that they helped themselves to these women off duty just as much as other men. Never mind that some, like this goddamn copper, helped himself to any woman, on duty or off.

She turned back to the sergeant, struggling to hold back the flurry of profanities ready on her tongue. A Southern gentlewoman who'd come to the city with the innocent intent of visiting a sick friend wouldn't cuss, after all. "Why, that's preposterous! I've not stolen anything. And unless you Yankees find it a crime for a lady to be out on her own after dark, I've not broken any other laws either."

The copper behind her snorted. "And that silver pin? What use does a *lady* like yourself have for that?"

"It belonged to my late husband, thank you very much. I keep it with me always. As a memento."

"How come you got so many secret pockets about your person, then?"

"The crime in this city is legend. Pickpockets, street urchins, confidence men. I had my servant girl sew in these extra pockets as a precaution." Una turned to face the copper who'd dragged her here from the alley. "Safe from all but the most *prying* hands."

He glowered down at her. Una smirked in return. If he didn't cough up the cuff links, the case against her was thin as Thursday soup.

The sergeant held Una's magazine by its spine and shook it. When nothing fell from between its pages—no stolen bank certificates or counterfeit bills—he frowned and dropped it back onto the desk. "Remove this woman's handcuffs, Simms, and give her back her things."

"But there was a commotion back in the alley off Pearl Street, and I caught this woman fleeing."

The sergeant's dull expression held.

"She smashed my toes and vomited on me too!"

Instead of indignation, the sergeant responded with a tired chuckle. "Smashed, did she?" He looked Una over from head to foot and chuckled again. Then he returned his pen to its rest and closed his blotter.

The roundsman, Simms, grumbled, but did as he was told, wrenching her arms up to unlock the cuffs. As soon as she was freed, Una wasted no time scooping up her things and stuffing them back into her pockets. The cuff links were a loss, but one she was happily willing to eat, considering how close to arrest, perhaps even for murder, she'd come that night. Good thing the copper hadn't investigated any farther into the alley before hauling her to the station. The retched-up beer might have had something to do with that. She smirked again and started for the door.

Before she managed more than a few steps, a bell rang from the far side of the room. A small, bespectacled man rushed to the telegraph receiver beside the bell. Una quickened her pace.

"Sergeant!" the man called, waving a thin strip of paper that the receiver had spit out. "There's been a murder. Two-seventy-six Pearl Street tenement. Rear yard."

"Wait a minute," she heard that lug of a copper Simms say behind her. "We was just there."

Una kept her eyes on the door. She was already halfway there. Once outside, she would run. The commotion of voices and stamping feet rose. Only a few more steps.

A meaty hand grabbed the back of her coat and spun her around. "Not so fast, missy."

Una scarcely had time to case her cell for weak bars or rusted-out hinges before footfalls sounded down the cellar steps. She knew better than to hope it was the guardsman come to set her free, but when she saw Deidre being led to a cell catercornered to her own, Una's stomach tightened. Deidre's cheeks hadn't regained any of their color. Her red hair was a tousled mess, and she'd lost her hat. The jailer locked her inside with a grating twist of his key, then stomped away.

"Deidre," Una whispered, pressing her face between the bars of her cell door. "Deidre!"

Deidre appeared at the door of her cell. "Una? I thought you got away."

"Thought the same of you. You didn't blow the gab, did you?"

"'Course not," she said, but something in her expression gave Una pause.

"Good."

The air in the cellar was musty and cold. It smelled of rusting iron, damp earth, and the sharp, sweat-like stench of despair. Deidre drew her coat tightly around her and kicked at the cracked stone floor. "Some mess you got us into."

"I told you not to come."

"Marm Blei is gonna be so mad she'll be pissing blood. You never should've—"

"Shh," Una hissed. No telling how many of the cells were occupied and who was listening. "Just keep your yapper shut, and we'll be fine."

The stairs creaked again. Two coppers, neither of whom Una recognized, descended from the main hall above. One stopped before Una's cell. The other at Deidre's.

"Miss Davidson?" the man in front of Una said.

She answered in the same Southern lilt she'd used with the sergeant. "Yes?"

"I'd like to ask you a few questions."

Una's gaze flickered to Deidre's cell. Damn her for following Una. Everything tonight had gone awry. They need only keep their heads, Una reminded herself, and tomorrow they'd be back on the streets diving pockets. Deidre's eyes met her own, her dark pupils crowding out the green of her eyes. Not a reassuring sign. This was exactly why Una worked alone.

The copper unlocked Una's door and stepped inside, blocking her view of Deidre's cell. His cheeks were clean shaven despite the late hour, his mustache, unlike the sergeant's, impeccably trimmed. Instead of a roundsman's uniform, he wore a suit with a shiny detective's badge pinned to his lapel. He set the lantern he carried on an upturned crate by the door. Fingers of light crept up the dank walls. "You know that other woman?"

"No, sir," Una said, seating herself on the splintery bench at the far end of her cell. She smoothed her skirt and crossed her ankles in a ladylike fashion.

"One of our officers said he saw you two together in the alley off Pearl Street."

"My dear detective, just because two women are walking astride one another in the same direction does not mean they're acquainted."

"I see. Why did you run from him?"

"It was dark, and I did not realize he was an officer of the law."

"And how did you come to be in the alley in the first place?"

"I was lost."

"Lost?"

"I'm a stranger to this city, you see. Only here to visit a sick friend."

"And the charges?"

Una gave a simpering laugh. "Do I look like a thief and vagrant to you?"

"I learned long ago, miss, not to be deceived by appearances." He took a few steps closer. "For all I know, you could be a cold-blooded killer."

Una tried to laugh again but managed only a thin croak. "Killer? Why, whatever do you mean?"

He moved the lantern to the floor and dragged the crate over to the bench, sitting down in front of her. "Listen, I know it wasn't your idea. It was your friend's idea, right?" He nodded in the direction of Deidre's cell. "She had something illicit to sell and brought you along in case things went sour. Maybe offered you a share in the profits. But Mr. Sheeny wasn't interested. They argued, and before you knew what was happening, she was pinning him down and telling you to strangle him."

Una drew back. Despite his tidy appearance, the detective's breath stank of rot. He didn't really think she and Deidre had something to do with the murder, did he?

"Or was it the other way around? You had the goods and

brought your friend along. Safety in numbers. A woman can't be too safe. Not on these streets. Am I right? Or maybe you're the type who works as a team. Maybe murder was your plan all along so you could get your hands on Mr. Sheeny's case. I hear they found over five hundred dollars in fenced goods inside."

Una held his steely gaze, knowing if she looked away he'd read that as guilt. But she didn't speak. Rule number twenty-three: When a lie isn't working, don't complicate things with the truth.

The detective leaned back. "That's all right. No need to say anything. I'm sure your friend is jabbering enough for the both of you." He stood and slowly pushed the crate across the cell with his foot. It scraped atop the floor—a loud, rasping noise that blocked out whatever snatches of sound Una hoped to hear from across the jail in Deidre's cell. Despite the chilled air, sweat gathered along the seams of her corset. Clever bastard, this detective.

The accent disappeared from her voice. "You can't possibly believe either one of us had anything to do with Traveling Mi—er—anyone's killing."

"Here's the deal, Miss Davidson, or whomever you are: You admit that your friend there committed the murder, and I'll take down your statement and let you go free."

Una crossed her arms and looked pointedly away. He must think her an idiot. There was no evidence connecting her and Deidre to Traveling Mike.

He shrugged and picked up his lantern. "Suit yourself. But you'd better hope your friend is as quiet as you are. Otherwise you'll spend a lifetime on the Island wishing you'd piped up."

The mention of Blackwell's Island made Una's skin tighten around her bones. She'd spent ten long days there once thanks to a trumped-up charge and bad-humored judge. (She had, in fact, been prospecting for wallets, but the witless copper couldn't pin her with the crime, so instead hauled her in for disorderly conduct, claiming that no respectable woman would be found on the streets at so late an hour without an escort. The police justice had agreed.) She'd been sentenced and shipped off to the Island before Marm Blei could intervene. Ten days at the workhouse with its vermin-infested cells and Una had vowed never to return.

But Deidre wouldn't turn on her. They'd been friends for years. Made it through dicier scrapes than these. If they both kept quiet, these coppers wouldn't be able to pin them with anything. Certainly not murder.

Why, then, couldn't she suppress the shiver prickling its way down her back? She recalled Deidre's pale skin and her fear-filled eyes. Una's trembling worsened.

"I'll just go see how my partner's questioning is going. He's a real hardnose, that one. Probably got himself a sworn statement already." The detective reached for the door.

Una leaped to her feet. "Wait!"

CHAPTER 9

———— ⊷•⊶ ————

Look out for yourself above all others. It was rule number one for a reason, and even if it meant Deidre ended up on Blackwell's Island serving a life sentence for murder, Una was ready to use it. Never mind that her mouth was suddenly parched and her stomach roiling as if she'd swallowed a bucket of ash. She paced as she waited for the detective to return with pen and paper to take down her statement.

Marm Blei could get Deidre out of this. She had half the city's prosecutors and judges in her pocket. Not to mention the police. It was just a matter of throwing enough brass the right way. Una plunged her hands into her pockets to keep from worrying her skin off. If need be, they could stage a prison break. Marm Blei knew all the right people for that too. Not even the Tombs was impenetrable. She fingered her matchbook and Barney's pin and the cool brass knuckles. They hadn't bothered to frisk her again before throwing her in the cell. She had a quick jab and mean uppercut, but this didn't seem like the kind of situation she could fight her way out of. No, she'd tell the detective whatever he wanted to hear, then go straight to Marm Blei.

When the detective returned, he wore a strange smile. As he reached into his pocket for something, Una realized he hadn't brought a pen or paper.

"Do you want my statement or not?" she said, trying for more confidence than she felt.

Again that strange smile. He withdrew his hand from his pocket and held out something shiny for her to see. The ruby cuff links. "Tell me about these."

"I've never seen those before in my life."

"No? Officer Simms said he found them in your pocket when he frisked you in the alley."

It was all Una could do not to snicker. How convenient that the cuff links suddenly reappeared in Officer Simms's pocket now that a murder investigation was afoot. Clearly he found a lousy commendation more enticing than the cash he could have gotten by selling them. Stupid lug didn't know how much rubies were worth.

The detective continued, still holding out the cuff links. "The same alley, may I remind you, where Mr. Sheeny, a known fence, was murdered only moments before you were apprehended."

The clink of keys and whine of metal sounded outside her cell. The detective stepped aside so she could see out through the bars of her door. Deidre's cell was open, and she was being released.

"But I . . . you haven't heard . . ."

"We won't be needing a statement from you, Miss Davidson. Your friend already told us everything we need to know. Unless, of course, you'd like to corroborate her accounting of the murder."

Una brushed past him and clutched the bars of her cell door. Her heart seemed to have taken wings and was beating frantically at the back of her throat. "Deidre!"

Her friend winced and gave an apologetic shrug as she passed. "It ain't personal, Una. You'd've done the same thing."

"I most certainly would not have!" Una called after her. Deidre mounted the cellar steps and didn't turn around.

When the door to the main hall slammed shut, Una turned back to the detective. "Whatever she told you was a lie."

"And the yarn you were gonna spin is the truth?" He laughed.

"You crooks are all the same. You'd stab a knife into your own mother if it meant saving your skin."

His sour breath reached clear across the cell. Give her a knife, and she'd show him what she could do. Rearranging that smug smile into a permanent frown would be just the start. Men like him believed themselves above their animal instincts. Men who'd never been cold or hungry or left to scramble out of the gutter on their own. Give him a few nights alone in the Tenderloin or Hell's Kitchen or Mulberry Bend without his warm wool coat and shiny pistol, and he'd meet another side of himself. The side who'd steal another man's boots right off his feet. Who'd snatch a crust of bread from a child. Who'd rat out his own friend.

Besides, he'd gotten it wrong. It was Una's mother who'd betrayed her.

He tucked the cuff links back in his pocket. "Here's what I think happened . . ."

Thanks to Deidre's loose tongue, the version of events he'd concocted had snatches of the truth. But when it came to Traveling Mike's murder, it was as outlandish as snow in July. Una countered with her version of events. Yes, she'd sought out Mr. Sheeny in the hopes of selling him the cuff links—cuff links she'd found, mind you, not stolen. No, she hadn't bullied Deidre into coming along. In fact, it was Deidre who'd suggested the fence in the first place. No, the bargaining hadn't ended in an argument. And no, she most certainly had not killed Mr. Sheeny over it. Here, Una told the truth. She described the darkness of the yard. The flare of light from the match. The shadowy figure she'd seen crouching beside Traveling Mike's body.

"What did he look like, this shadowy figure?" the detective asked in a sniggering tone.

"I don't know. It was too dark to see. That's the whole point." She closed her eyes and thought back to the moment Deidre's match had flared. "He wore a suit and cap. Black, maybe navy blue . . . and buttons. I remember the light glinting off them."

"Was he a Negro? An Oriental? A white man?"

"A white man . . . I think."

"Tall, short, fat, thin?"

Una opened her eyes. "I don't remember."

"I see. So we should be on the lookout for a white man of non-descript build wearing a dark-colored suit and cap. Do I have that right?"

"Yes."

"So approximately half the men of this city." He snorted. He'd seated himself on the bench in her cell, legs outstretched as if he were lounging before a fire, as if she'd been sharing banal pleasantries and not the description of a killer.

Una continued to pace. She reached inside her pocket again and slipped her fingers through the holes of her brass knuckles. She'd ruled out fighting as a way free of this mess, but it was nice to imagine, just for a moment, clocking the detective upside the head.

"I'm telling you the truth."

"Forgive me, Miss Davidson—or whatever your real name is—if I'm a bit skeptical of your version of the truth."

"You think it's more likely that I—a mere woman—killed Mr. Sheeny all on my own?" Una hated being thought of as weak and helpless on account of her sex. If she had a mind to do it, killing a man—even one as tall and able as Traveling Mike—was not outside her means. But she also wasn't above playing into the detective's prejudices if it meant saving her own skin.

"It takes surprisingly little pressure to strangle a man. Under the right circumstances, that is."

Una remembered the belt she'd seen around Traveling Mike's neck before the murderer fled, then she recalled what Barney had said about Big-nosed Joe and Martha Ann. They had been strangled in the same way.

"It's the same man," she said aloud to herself.

"Same man as what?"

Una glanced at the detective. "There've been two other killings lately. Both in poor parts of the city. Both strangled. I think the man who killed Traveling Mi—er—Mr. Sheeny, murdered them too."

The detective laughed so hard he nearly slid off the bench. Una gripped her brass knuckles tighter. He didn't care about the truth or solving the murder. Not when he had so tidy a suspect already in custody. One crook was as good as another to him.

"You're not lis—"

He held up his hand and stood. "Save your cockeyed stories for the judge. Though I'll warn you, he doesn't take any kindlier to your ilk than I do."

CHAPTER 10

Una passed a sleepless night in her cell. Every time she closed her eyes, she had visions of the steamboat that would ferry her away to an abysmal life on Blackwell's Island. She remembered the icy perspiration that slickened the workhouse walls when she'd landed there at sixteen thanks to that phony disorderly conduct charge. She remembered the bathwater, thick and lively with other prisoners' filth, that she'd been forced to bathe in. Remembered the flea-infested straw that covered the ground of her overcrowded cell. The hours spent weaving rag carpet with bone-chilled hands. The windowless "dark cell" she'd been confined in for sassing the watchman.

Two women had died during her short sentence there—one from dysentery, the other from the dank cold. Rounders, those who wound up in the workhouse every few months, told her things were just as bad in summer when the sun baked the building, and cockroaches overran the place. The penitentiary on the far end of the Island, where more hardened criminals like those convicted of murder were sent, was rumored to be worse still.

But Marm Blei would intervene before she ever got there, Una reminded herself, rolling from one side to the other atop the hard, narrow bench. Even if that traitorous Deidre didn't tell her of Una's lot, Marm Blei would know by morning. She'd arrive

THE NURSE'S SECRET   63

first thing with her gaggle of expensive, uptown lawyers in tow. They'd make easy work of the charges against her. After all, she hadn't actually committed any crime.

But dawn came, a pale trickle of light through the iron bars of her high-up window, and Marm Blei didn't arrive. It was still the Sabbath, Una reminded herself. The jail keeper waddled by to collect her sour-smelling chamber bucket and later with a ladle of water for breakfast. Una paced her cell, pausing every time she heard the door to the main hall above open. She watched the light outside her windows shift and brighten, the delicate crystals of ice that had gathered on the glass overnight melt away.

At last, long after sundown, Marm Blei did arrive. Alone. Perhaps her lawyers were on their way. Or upstairs already negotiating with the sergeant. Una rushed to her cell door.

"*Sheifale*," Marm Blei said, with a slow wag of her head. "*Klug, klug, un fort a nar.*"

"Did Deidre tell—"

Marm Blei held up her hand. "I heard about everything."

"They're charging me with murder."

"I know."

"But you'll get me out, right? On bail, at least, until the charges are dropped. You know I'm good for it."

"I can, *sheifale*. But I won't."

Una rattled her head. Had she heard right?

"Deidre told me you were meeting Traveling Mike to fence some goods. A pair of ruby cuff links, I think she said."

"That's not—"

"*Shveig!*" she said in her cut-through-stone voice. Una fell silent. After a moment, Marm Blei wagged her head again and continued more softly. "Of all the girls, Una, you were my favorite. Such promise, you had. But no patience, I see. And no loyalty."

"It was nothing. I just wanted to see what Traveling Mike would offer. I wasn't going to—"

"One rotten apple spoils the rest." She started for the stairs. "Good-bye, Una."

"You're going to leave me here to stand trial for murder over a lousy pair of cuff links?" Una called after her.

Marm Blei did not turn around but said over her shoulder, "You're a smart girl, Una. Too smart sometimes for your own good. You'll figure something out."

Una's stomach dropped. She rattled her cell door so fiercely the rusty hinges cried out in protest. For years she'd given Marm Blei everything she had. Every silk purse and gold watch and silver bracelet she lifted. And in return, she got peanuts. Meanwhile Marm Blei dined on fine china plates (stolen of course, but still), enjoying the protection of her thugs and fancy lawyers. That protection was supposed to extend to Una as well. That was the deal.

The jail keeper hollered from the top of the stairs for Una to quit her racket or else. Or else what? Una was already facing murder charges. But she released the bars and stepped back from her door. Rule number four: Don't draw attention to yourself. Besides, she needed to think. To figure a way out of this goddamn mess. Easier to do that here than in the back of the Black Maria on her way to the Tombs.

But corralling her thoughts proved impossible. Marm Blei's words had struck her like a horse hoof to the gut. Una still hadn't recovered her breath. This was why she didn't trust people. Why she worked alone. Why she'd gone to see Traveling Mike in the first place. Marm Blei felt threatened by her. By her potential. Well, Una would show her. When she got out of here, she'd double down on her efforts, perfect her con, move beyond the town-toddlers to bigger, richer prey. Make Marm Blei green with envy over all the goods she was turning.

Una brought her hands to her face and gave her cheeks a sharp pat. Riches and revenge would have to wait. First she had to free herself. She walked in slow circles around the cell. What were her assets? Brass knuckles, a matchbook, enough magazine pages for a hundred trips to the privy, and Barney's damned pin. Nothing of much use. What she really needed was money. Enough to bribe the guards or pay for a half-decent skinner. But even if she had that kind of brass—which she didn't, not even in her secret tin—how would she get her hands on it from behind cell bars? No, she'd have to find a chance to flee and figure the rest out in hiding.

Night passed into morning, and she still didn't have a solid plan. Officer Simms lumbered down the stairs and collected her for transport. As he locked a pair of cold, metal handcuffs around her wrists, an idea sparked in Una's mind. Barney's pin was too fragile to pick the lock of her cell door or the Black Maria's fat iron padlock. But it might work on the handcuffs. And Officer Simms, lug that he was, had done her the great favor of cuffing her hands in the front instead of behind her back where she wouldn't be able to see what she was doing.

Now all Una needed was a sliver of time—thirty seconds would be enough—when she wasn't guarded or locked behind a door.

But Officers Simms didn't let go or even loosen his grip about her arm as he dragged her from the cell, up the stairs, and outside to the awaiting transport. Now she'd have twin bruises, one on each arm, thanks to his mean sausage fingers. She'd hoped a melee in the hall or some disturbance out on the street would provide her the opportunity to run. But none of the drunks or tramps or madmen she'd been counting on appeared. The street vendors crowded along the sidewalk weren't bickering. The horses weren't biting or whinnying. Not even the newsboys, who were always up to mischief, drew Simms's gaze.

"Looking forward to seeing you at the trial," he said, hoisting her into the back of the Black Maria like she were a sack of rotten onions. "Always makes my day to watch you crooks squirm beneath them bright lights."

Una landed in the wagon on her hands and knees. If she didn't escape now, there was little chance of doing so at the Tombs, where twice as many coppers milled about. So much for waiting for a distraction. She'd have to cause one herself. She hauled herself up onto one of the splintery bench seats and reached into her pocket. Just as Officer Simms was closing the door, she dropped her brass knuckles onto the floor and wedged them with the toe of her boot into the jamb. The heavy door shuddered, unable to close fully. Officer Simms tried again. This time the entire wagon rattled with the force of his effort. But the knuckles remained, now partially embedded in the wood of the jamb.

He cussed and swung the door open, glaring at Una. When he looked down to see what the trouble was, she kicked him in the face. Officer Simms staggered back, blood spurting from his nose. Una leaped from the back of the wagon and ran. She didn't look back. Nor did she slow to get her bearings.

Churchgoers crowded the sidewalks in their Sunday best. Carts and buggies lumbered down the streets. The snow had begun to melt, leaving the ground muddy and slick. Una darted, slipped, and skidded around the obstacles. Her handcuffed wrists made it all the more difficult to pick up speed.

Several minutes on and her side ached sharply. Her wheezing breath tasted of blood. Shouts and whistles sounded behind her.

She turned down one street and up another. For a moment, the clamor of her pursuers faded, only to redouble a few moments later. Soon they'd be coming for her from all directions.

She needed a place to hide and quick. But her air-starved brain lagged behind her feet, noticing an open window or overgrown bush only after she raced past them. Alleyways overhung with laundry branched off from the streets, but she didn't dare go down them. Not without a better idea of where she was. Otherwise she risked trapping herself at a dead end.

Her leg muscle cramped, forcing Una to slow. The distance she'd managed to put between her and the coppers would narrow to nothing if she couldn't work the cramp out soon. She stopped long enough to give her leg a quick rub and gulp down a breath. The air smelled sour here, like a rotting egg. The Gas House District!

Una hobbled onward, but this time with purpose. A scrim of gray smog belched from the nearby gasworks, blotting out the sky. The fumes clung to everything here—the dilapidated tenements, the streetlamps and telegraph poles, the storefronts and their dingy awnings. It wasn't a place one lingered by choice, and Una hoped that would play to her favor.

She hurried up a broad avenue, then down an intersecting street toward the river. Even without the aid of street signs, she knew where she was. At Avenue A she hesitated. Across the street lay Tompkins Square. With its many trees and bushes, it would be the perfect place to hide. But instead of crossing the street and escaping into the park's wilderness, Una turned left and then made a quick left again. If Una thought Tompkins Square the perfect place to hide, the coppers would think so too, and in a matter of minutes, the park would be crawling with them.

Instead, she slipped through a break in the rusted fence along Eleventh Street and into the old Catholic cemetery. New burials had been banned in Manhattan for decades, and the cemetery had become a run-down, desolate place. Cracked tombstones listed in the ground. Others had fallen over completely. Bits of trash and dead leaves crunched beneath Una's feet. She crossed herself, then hurried along. Between the smog from the gasworks and shadows cast by the surrounding tenements and saloons, it felt like dusk had fallen though it couldn't be much past noon.

When Una was a child, her father had filled her head with stories and warnings about the dead. Beware the spirit of the last corpse buried in a cemetery, for it watches over the dead, waiting its turn to ascend to heaven. If you stumbled over a grave and fell, you'd be dead within a year. To whistle in a cemetery was to invite the devil. She knew these were just old-world superstitions, but the skin on her arms prickled nonetheless, and she trod with extra care to avoid falling.

She'd take angry spirits over coppers any day. At the far corner of the cemetery, Una found a tombstone large enough to conceal her from view should anyone from the street peer inside. She hunched down behind it and retrieved Barney's pin.

CHAPTER 11

⊰⊱

It was just past dawn the next day when Una arrived at her cousin's rowhouse near Murray Hill. It had taken her over an hour to unlock her handcuffs with Barney's silver pin. But she'd remained in the cemetery long after, listening for the telltale clunk of coppers' boots. Not until night had fallen and the clamor of the streets died down did she venture out. By then, she'd said the rosary five times to ward off ghosts and worked out a semblance of a plan.

Even though the coppers didn't know where she lived, Una couldn't go back to her tenement. It was too close to Marm Blei's shop and she didn't trust the woman not to snitch to the police. And it wasn't only Marm Blei. All Una's former acquaintances in that part of town—the grocer, the street sweepers, the matchbook peddlers, the rag pickers, the other pocket divers she shared her flat with, and Deidre most especially—could no longer be trusted. The stash of money and trinkets she'd hidden in the wall of her room were irretrievable.

That left her without a cent in her pocket or friend to call on. Never mind the discomfort in her chest—indigestion, she was sure—when she considered the loss of her mother's cameo necklace. It wouldn't help her now, even if she had it. But her mother had left her something else too. A cousin. And though Una had never believed any of that *blood is thicker than water* horseshit, that didn't mean she was above using such sentiments to her advantage. Rule number sixteen: Don't write anyone off until they're dead.

Una waited in the shadows across the street until her cousin's husband, a foreman in a wallpaper factory, left for work before approaching the house. He'd never liked her, Ralph—or was it Richard? Stealing his pen the last time she'd visited probably hadn't helped. It was a garish pen, a fat gilded thing covered in filigree that he waved about as he spoke as if he were the damned king and not some second-rate foreman making ten times as much money as the women he bossed about. Besides, he suggested Una was illiterate. Vulgar and witless were his precise words, if Una's memory served. Not spoken directly to her, of course. That was the way of these lace-curtain Irish. They snickered and sniveled about you behind closed doors. The low Irish still had the courage to insult you to your face. So she'd filched the gold monstrosity from Ralph/Richard's pocket, written *Thank you kindly for the pen* in large, tidy letters on a sheet of stationery embossed with his initials from the desk, and left without saying good-bye.

That had been six years ago. Time enough, she hoped, to soften the resentment. Una rapped on the polished oak door and waited. When no one answered, she knocked again. It made her edgy to stand with her back to the street. Last night, she'd found a tattered shawl hanging over the rail of a fire escape as she slunk and crept across the city. It was still wet from the day's washing, but she slung it over her shoulders anyway. Not much of a disguise, but better than nothing. Now, in the maddeningly bright morning light, the shawl, with its fraying hem and soot-stained wool, made Una feel all the more conspicuous in this hoity-toity neighborhood. She tugged it off and knocked a third time.

At last, the pad of feet sounded from within. The door opened just wide enough to reveal a sliver of her cousin's face. Her hair was still tied up in rags and sleep crusted at the corners of her eyes. She blinked several times, then frowned. "Una?"

"No, Claire, his holiness the pope. Of course it's me. Let me in." Una didn't wait for her cousin to reply but pushed against the door until it opened enough for her to slip inside. The gathering daylight filtered in through gossamer-covered windows flanking the door, casting the foyer in a pale glow.

Claire shuffled back, her nose wrinkling and frown deepening. "Blessed Mother Mary, you look awful. Smell awful too."

A night's stay in jail would do that to a girl. Never mind all the running she'd done. Or her sojourn in that derelict cemetery. But she wasn't about to say any of that to Claire. As young girls, they'd been great friends. Like sisters, it was said. Now they were all but strangers.

Claire's mother had never approved of her sister's choice in husband, a culchie fresh off the boat with few prospects. After the war, with all his loafing and drinking, she approved of Una's father even less. The families had already grown apart, both in richness and affection, by the time Una's mother died. Her aunt had offered to take Una in, to care for her and continue her education, but Una's father refused. They'd walked away, Claire's family, noses upturned and heads wagging, and Una hadn't seen any of them until she'd looked Claire up six years ago and come around, not with the intent to steal anything, but simply to size up her cousin and former friend.

Claire's cool reception hadn't surprised Una. Nor had her husband's haughtiness. But her thinly veiled pity had raised Una's dander. Now that pity was the only currency Una had. She smoothed her dirty and wrinkled skirt, then met Claire's wary gaze.

"I got in a bit of a scrape and need a place to stay."

"Stay? How long?"

Una shrugged. She hadn't thought beyond getting here. "A week. Maybe two. A month at the most."

"Are you mad? If Randolph knew I'd let you in for any longer than a second, he'd throw a conniption. That was his favorite pen, you know."

"You didn't let me in, *cousin*. I had to barge in. Not very familial of you."

"I thought a tramp was banging on my door so scarcely did I recognize you."

Una smiled around clenched teeth. A tramp indeed! She glanced in the mirror that hung over a marble-topped table against the far wall. Her hair stuck out like a feather duster around her lopsided hat. A splattering of mud dotted her collar. Her lips were chapped and nose red from the cold. "Well, now that you see I'm not a tramp, merely your long-lost cousin fallen on hard times, can I stay?"

Claire crossed her arms over her housecoat. It was a deep burgundy velvet with fur trim. Rabbit, no doubt. *Randolph* couldn't afford ermine or mink on a foreman's salary. Still, it looked softer than anything Una had ever worn.

"What happened?" Claire asked. "Your husband kick you out?"

"I'm not married."

"Running from a jealous lover, then?"

A sigh slipped out before Una could help it. What kind of rubbish was Claire reading? She sat down on a lacquered bench along the wall and began unlacing her boots. Her blistered feet ached like the dickens. "No."

"I didn't say you could stay," Claire said in a squeaky voice, her arms still locked in front of her. "You in trouble with the law?"

"Of course not."

"Well, you will be if Randolph finds you here." She dropped her arms and began to pace the small foyer. "Is it money you need? Is that it? I knew something like this would happen someday. Ma always said you were from bad stock."

"We're from the same stock," Una said, pulling off one boot and then the other, and dropping them loudly onto the floor.

"On your paternal side, I mean. Speaking of your father, why can't you go running to him for help?"

"He's dead," Una lied. Half lied, really. She hadn't seen him in almost as many years as Claire. He'd graduated from the bottle to the pipe and may well be dead. Una certainly couldn't go wandering about Chinatown, peeking her nose into every opium joint along Mott Street to find out. Not now that she was a wanted woman.

Claire mustered a fleeting expression of sympathy and continued to pace. "Well, you can't stay here. Randolph's up for a promotion at the factory and can't tolerate any disruptions right now. And what would the neighbors say if they saw you? They didn't see you, did they?" She peeked around the gossamer curtains as if to be sure. "He's running for assistant alderman and—"

"No one saw me. I swear. Nor will they. I mean to lie low." Una's stockings were damp and sticky where the blisters had bled through. Her mouth was dry and her stomach rumbled. She wouldn't be surprised if it had gnawed a hole in itself by now. She stood up and took Claire's hands, forcing her to still. "Please, for old times' sake. I haven't anywhere else to go."

When she didn't reply, Una blinked several times in rapid succession, as if she were trying to hold back tears, and continued in a thin, hitching voice. "I've always envied you, you know. Your pretty hair. Your big house. A mother who loved and looked out for you. Ever since the fire I . . ." Una sniffled and looked away, praying Claire would take the bait.

"Oh, very well," she said at last, yanking her hands free and sighing dramatically. "You can stay a few days. That's all. And you'll have to sleep in the cellar. Randolph mustn't know you're here."

CHAPTER 12

⟶•⟨⟩•⟵

Una felt like a rat, nesting in her cousin's cellar amid the sacks of potatoes and onions, creeping around the upper levels of the house only when Randolph was away. But it was far better than prison.

Claire made no secret of her disdain for the situation. When Una emerged from the cellar, she followed her around like an overattentive shop clerk. Not solicitous, but suspicious. She doled out cooking scraps and the cold, leftover bits of meals with the same pious repugnance Una had met with at the Five Points Mission as a girl. No amount of hot soup was worth that kind of treatment, and she'd left the Mission after one night. She'd leave here too, just as soon as she could figure out her next move.

Three days after her arrival, Una lay awake on her makeshift bed of rags and old flour sacks. The quiet above told her it was not yet dawn. Usually Randolph's blundering footfalls woke Una as he dressed and readied for work. But today it had been the thunder of coal tumbling down the chute. Coal dust bloomed in the air as it struck the cellar floor. She could smell it more than see it and felt it settle on her skin.

Unable to fall back asleep after such a clamor, Una lit a candle and tugged on her coat for added warmth against the dank—and now dusty—air. As she rolled from one side to the other, trying to get comfortable, the items in her pockets crunched beneath her weight. She pulled them out and set them on the floor beside her. Barney's silver pin was bent and nicked from her long and tedious battle with the lock of her handcuffs. Even if she dared bring it to a fence—which she most certainly didn't—it wouldn't be worth more than a dollar.

She'd need far more than that to get out of New York. At least ten dollars for a train ticket and traveling necessities. Even that wouldn't get her safely beyond the police's reach. Her insides ached at the thought of leaving the city. The streets were dirty and crowded. The summers were hot and muggy. Winters were bleak and cold. Passersby were just as likely to step on you if you fell as to offer a helping hand. The smell of the place could make your stomach turn. And Una loved it. Every narrow alley and crumbling tenement. She'd been born in New York. Come of age in New York. Had always believed she would die in New York. But if she didn't get out, the only part of the city she'd ever see again would be Blackwell's Island.

She picked up the magazine and unfurled the pages. The lettering on the top page had worn away to an indistinguishable smear of ink, but inside the pages were better preserved. Her eye snagged on an article titled "A New Profession for Women." She snickered and thought of the women slaving away in the corset and button factories. Those who sewed shirts by candlelight in their homes for pennies a week. The maids and other domestics laboring night and day in the mansions on Millionaire's Row. If that was the type of profession the author was talking about, Una would stick to thieving, thank you very much.

But curiosity got the better of her, and she read on.

For many years Bellevue Hospital, the chief free public institution of the kind in New York, has been famous for the high medical and surgical skill, its faculty embracing many leading members of the profession in the city. For many years to come it is likely to be popularly associated with an-

other high development of the curative arts—the results of
founding in 1873 the Bellevue Training School for Nurses,
and a new profession for women in America.

Nursing? The idea called to mind grim-faced women who scolded and neglected the invalids in their care, stealing their drafts and tonics until the nurse herself was pleasantly drunk and utterly useless. Una had encountered plenty of such women in her younger days visiting the bleak hospital wards when her father's war wound was acting up or he'd imbibed too much whiskey. But that was not the type of women the article was describing. Intrigued, Una read to the end.

Apparently some well-to-do women in New York had gotten it in their heads that the hospitals needed reforming, and what better place to start than with the careless and disorderly nurses. They decided to start a training school and contacted some famous nurse in England about how to do it. Under her guidance, and with a large endowment from the wife of a railroad mogul, the Bellevue Hospital Training School for Nurses was born. Trainees underwent a two-year program during which time they received free room and board and a modest monthly stipend. When they graduated, they found ready work in hospitals and private homes across the country.

Una sat up and grabbed a piece of licorice root from a sack on a nearby shelf. Claire had expressly forbidden her from rummaging through the food stores, but chewing helped Una think. Perhaps she wouldn't have to leave New York after all. Good old rule number eleven: The best place to hide is in plain sight.

By that evening, Una had completely reworked her plan. Instead of fleeing to Boston or Philadelphia or however far she could manage to travel, she would stay in New York disguised as a trainee at Bellevue's nursing school. The police would never think to look for her there. The case against her would eventually grow cold and be forgotten. As long as she steered clear of Marm

Blei and her underlings, Una could return to her old life. Except now she'd have an even better con than before. No more waiting around crowded train platforms for a mark. People would actually invite her into their homes, thinking she could care for their ailing loved ones, when all the while, she'd be plotting the perfect heist. Of course she'd need to be smart about it, or word would get around about the thieving nurse. But patience, care, and misdirection were among her better skills.

Only one problem stood in her way: gaining admission to the school. According to the article, the qualifications were exceedingly strict. Ideal applicants were twenty-one to thirty-five years in age, single, literate, and religious. Una handily met these requirements. True, she hadn't been to mass in more months than she could count, but when her mother had been alive, they'd never missed a Sunday. Add in all the holy days and St. Patrick's feast day, and it was enough to make up for her recent truancy. She was also of a strong constitution, industrious, and without physical defects. Obedience had never been her strong suit, but she could manage that as well. The other qualifications, however, would take more cunning to fake. She'd need to forge transcripts showing she had received a good education as well as letters of reference to prove she was of "conscientious and sympathetic" character.

She'd spend the better part of the day pacing the cellar and chewing through most of Claire's licorice root before she devised a way to secure such documents. Were she not hiding from the police and blackballed from Marm Blei's crew, getting forgeries would be easy. Marm Blei knew three or four men skilled in that trade. But those connections were lost to Una now. She'd have to rely on her own connections: Claire, who could probably be pressed to write a fake reference if it meant getting Una out of her cellar, and one other person whom Una remembered only after grabbing the silver tie pin to clean beneath her nails. Barney.

Getting across town to Newspaper Row proved no easy feat. It took two days of pestering before Claire agreed to lend Una a dress and twenty cents for the el. But even in a fresh, respectable gown, her hair washed and modestly styled, Una felt conspicuous. After nearly a week of cellar dwelling, her senses were raw and excitable. She flinched at the bright sunlight and spooked at the street car's clanging bell. A dozen times she squelched the urge to look behind her or hasten her step. You're just another lady out for a stroll, Una reminded herself. The more she believed it, the more others would too.

But however much Una might blend in among the ladies promenading about town, she was still wanted for murder. One misstep or unlucky encounter, and she'd be back in handcuffs. The sooner she could return to the safety of Claire's cellar, the better. She'd mapped out in her mind the quickest route to Barney's office and left Claire's house at noon when the coppers would be busy scrounging for a midday meal. If things went well with Barney, she'd be traveling back to Claire's, forged papers in hand, at the start of the evening rush. A crowd always made it easier to blend in. There was, of course, the issue of Randolph, but Claire assured her that today, like every Tuesday, he'd stop by a bar on Forty-Ninth Street on his way home to attend the ward Democrats meeting. That gave Una a few-hour cushion to get back to the cellar before he arrived.

She made it to the el station without incident, paid the fare, and climbed the iron steps to the platform. When the train arrived, she found a seat beside a man reading the newspaper. He paid her no mind as she sat down, making no effort to contain his sprawling knees and elbows. The perfect mark, Una thought. It would be so easy to slip her hand into his coat pocket and pilfer whatever treasures were inside. Her body's response to the delicious idea was second nature: pulse quickening, muscles tightening, senses sharpening. She'd missed this sensation more than the liquor and cigarettes and gambling of her old life. But she kept her hands clasped in her lap. Too risky.

Instead, she wandered her gaze about the car, out the filmy window, then back to the man. A headline at the bottom of his newspaper caught her eye. The thrill she'd felt only moments before vanished. Her hands went cold, and her feet rooted to the tremulous floor. Conwoman Arrested in Connection to Sixth Ward Murder Slips Police, it read.

Una leaned as close as she dared toward the man to read the article. Before she got halfway through, the man flipped to the next page. She'd seen enough, though, to make her skin feel two sizes too small. Violent and cunning, the article had said of her. It listed four of her past aliases, including the one attached to her picture in the rogues' gallery at headquarters. Had Officer Simms perused the wall of photographs and made the connection? That foul-breathed detective? Or had one of Marm Blei's associates tipped them off? Either way, the open streets of New York suddenly felt a lot more dangerous.

The el rattled along at an interminably slow pace. Every time it stopped and new riders boarded, Una's stomach clenched in anticipation of some copper lumbering aboard and recognizing her or some nosy onlooker making the connection between her and the woman in the newspaper. This latter notion was ridiculous, of course. Even if the second half of the article had given a novel-worthy account of her appearance, anyone who read it would be expecting a dirty, bedraggled woman with mean eyes and a shifty countenance.

Una breathed in slow and steady to calm herself. When her stop arrived, she walked with her head high from the car. She'd made a living playing off people's expectations. Their preconceptions and narrow-minded assumptions. The stakes were higher now, but the game was the same.

Still, her heart didn't fully settle into its regular rhythm until she was safely ensconced in a simple, straight-back chair beside Barney's desk. He didn't have his own office but was one of more than a dozen reporters working in the cramped second-story newsroom. Overhead gas lamps lit the room. The air smelled of paper, cigarette smoke, and burned coffee. A telegraph receiver chirped from one corner over the murmur of voices and clack of typewriter keys. No one had paid much mind to her arrival except Barney, who'd dropped the ham sandwich he'd been eating into his lap when he saw her.

"Una . . . I . . . what are you doing here?" he asked after having ushered her to his desk. "You look . . . different."

By different, she guessed he meant respectable. A fair enough observation as the last time he'd seen her she'd been disguised as a rag picker. His desk sat in the corner of the crowded room. A draft from the large, double-paned window behind him ruffled the stack of papers beside his typewriter. He still had a smear of mustard and a few crumbs on his trousers. Una leaned forward and brushed the crumbs onto the floor. The tips of his ears reddened.

"I need your help," she whispered, even though the desks nearest Barney's were empty, his colleagues likely gone to lunch.

"With what?"

Una hesitated and cast another glance about the room. She trusted Barney, but the less he or anyone knew, the better. Rule number six: Only give away what you absolutely must. "I need a few documents manufactured."

He frowned. "What kind of documents?"

"Nothing illegal. Not strickly speaking, anyway. Just a school report and letter of reference."

"For whom?"

"Me."

His expression remained wary. "What sort of undertaking are you about that you need a letter of reference from a bottom-rung reporter like me?"

"Oh, Barney, don't sell yourself short. Besides, it wouldn't be from you."

"I don't understand."

"The recommendation would be from Father Connally of St. Mary's Parish in Augusta, Maine, and an exemplary record from St. Agnes's Girls' School there."

"I didn't know you're from Maine."

"I'm not."

"I'm afraid I'm still not understanding. What's this all about?"

Una sighed. One of the other reporters crossed the room to a nearby cupboard and rifled through the shelves. She waited for him to return to his desk, new typewriter ribbon in hand, before she spoke. "Have you heard of the new training program for nurses at Bellevue Hospital?"

Barney nodded.

"I'm applying."

"You want to become a nurse?" He furrowed his brow as if the idea was hardly fathomable.

Una straightened. "What's wrong with nursing?"

"Nothing. It's just . . . the women at the training school are, well, of a particular mold that . . ."

"That what?"

"Er . . . well . . . frankly, that you don't conform to."

"I can conform to whatever mold I need to."

"Una, what's the meaning behind all this? You can't expect me to believe you've had a sudden change of heart and mean to go from a slum dweller and a grifter to a nurse." He laughed. "Really, have you seen those women? They shuffle about the wards with their dour expressions and neatly pressed uniforms, muttering nothing but 'Yes, Doctor' and 'Right away, Doctor.' It's the last place I'd think you'd want to go."

"That's exactly why I'm applying. I need someplace"—she dropped her voice again to a whisper—"to lie low for a while. Someplace no one will look for me."

"Listen, if you're in trouble, I know a lawyer who could help. A friend from university."

Una shook her head. "No skinners."

"Maybe I could help, then. You can come to stay with me and—"

Una took his hands. They were stained with ink and smudged with mustard. "You don't want a girl like me in your life, Barney. Trust me."

He looked down at their clasped hands and swallowed.

"The papers? Please."

At last, Barney nodded.

Una squeezed his hands before letting go. "Who knows? There might even be a story in it for you someday."

CHAPTER 13

———⟫◦⟪———

Bellevue Hospital loomed as inviting as a prison beside the East River, its bulky gray outline blending with the gloomy winter sky. Just beyond its shadow across Twenty-Sixth Street, stood a far handsomer building with a multitude of windows and white stone trim. No. 426—headquarters of the nursing school. Una climbed the short flight of steps to the entry, tugging down her shirtsleeves before knocking. The dress, another borrowed from Claire, fit so snugly through the waist that her lungs could only partially expand. The hem rose dangerously close to her ankles, and the sleeves barely reached her wrists. But it was the nicest dress Claire would permit her to wear and far more suitable than Una's own dress.

The door opened, and a woman not much older than Una peered out. She wore a simply cut dress of blue wool and matching cap. Her honey-brown hair was trained into a tight, low-lying bun. She might have been beautiful were it not for the coldness of her eyes and the sharp, unsmiling line of her mouth.

"Miss Kelly, I presume," she said in a flat, almost bored-sounding voice.

As with all the other pieces of the story Una had invented, she thought it best to stick to the truth when she could. Including using her real name. Besides, one could hardly spit in New York

City without striking a Kelly, the name was so common. (But beware, a Kelly was likely to spit back.) And she'd never given any variation even close to it to the police.

"Yes, I'm here to interview for the nurse training program."

The woman looked Una up and down the way Marm Blei inspected a piece of jewelry she thought might be fake, then stepped aside for Una to enter. "Two more minutes, and you would have been late." She sounded almost disappointed that Una had *not* been late, as if then she wouldn't have had to go to the trouble of opening the door. "Punctuality is an essential trait for a nurse trainee."

I'll show you a punctual kick in the ass, Una thought, but said instead, "Thank you. I'll remember that."

She followed the woman through the foyer and down a wide hallway. A plush Oriental rug covered the polished floorboards, and watercolor prints of country landscapes hung on the walls.

"I am Miss Hatfield, one of the head nurses at the school," the woman said, leading Una into a large room lined with bookshelves. "We'll conduct the interview here in the library. Superintendent Perkins and Mrs. Hobson from the Board of Managers will join us presently."

She gestured to a set of four wingback chairs arranged around a small table where a tea service had been laid out. Una sat in the chair closest to the door. You never knew when you might need to make a quick exit. Leaning back, she sunk into its plush cushions. Her fingers trailed over the soft velvet, and she smiled, imagining herself lounging here in the warm quiet, day after day, while the police searched for her in the slums. It was a more perfect hideyhole than she'd hoped.

Miss Hatfield sat opposite her, perching on the edge of the chair like a nun at mass, back straight and arms tucked to her sides. She had the expression of a nun too, severe and disapproving. Una immediately straightened. She crossed her ankles and folded her hands in her lap the way her mother had taught her as a girl. Clearly, the interview had already begun, and she wasn't earning good marks.

"It's a lovely library," Una said, after a prickly stretch of silence. Freshly cut flowers—a luxury in winter—decorated a nearby table, perfuming the air. Large windows framed in billowing curtains lighted the room. Marble busts stared from atop the bookshelves.

"A woman like yourself, who's had only a quotidian education, can be assured of spending a great deal of time here. *If* she's accepted, that is."

Quotidian education! Una had been quite proud of the school record she and Barney cooked up. "I assure you, the classes at St. Agnes's were most rigorous."

Miss Hatfield pursed her lips, and looked out the window. "Yes, I'm sure you thought so."

Una hid her clenched teeth behind a smile. Had she met such an insufferable woman back in the slums, she would have cleaned out her pockets then strode away, splashing her skirts with mud. But they were not in the slums, and Una needed this position desperately. So she smiled on and said in her sweetest voice, "Where did you do your studies?"

"The Keenbridge Academy followed by two years at Vassar."

Una had never heard of either of these schools, but Miss Hatfield spoke as if God himself had been a pupil there. Thankfully Una didn't have to feign more than a moment's veneration before two other women entered the library. One was dressed in cascades of silk velvet, the kind imported from Venice Marm Blei could sell for twelve dollars a yard. She had a plump face, lined but still pretty, and the careless grace of a blue blood. The other woman had a quieter demeanor, perhaps owing to her age. (Una guessed her at least fifty.) Her dress, like that of Miss Hatfield, was simple in cut and impeccably pressed. Her gray eyes flickered with the shrewdness of a safecracker casing a bank, but there was a warmth in them too that caught Una off guard.

The women joined Una and Miss Hatfield around the tea table, introducing themselves as they sat. The silk-wrapped woman was Mrs. Hobson, a founding member of the school's Board of Managers. The circumspect woman was Miss Perkins, the school's superintendent. It was she, Una knew from the article, who would ultimately rule on Una's suitability.

Mrs. Hobson poured the tea, then asked Una a few basic questions about her upbringing—where she'd been born and raised, what her family life and education had been like, what sort of hobbies she practiced. Una had spent days rehearsing her story, and it rolled easily from her tongue. In keeping with rule number twelve, Una had kept the lie simple, cleaving as much to her real life as possible. The fewer the falsehoods, the easier they'd be to remember. She had indeed attended Catholic day school—though here in New York, not in Maine. And for only five years, not twelve. There had been a Father Connally too, but he was long dead and would sooner have become an Orangeman than write Una a letter of reference.

When her own life strayed from the idyllic and genteel, Una borrowed from her mother's. Granddad Callaghan had been a glass merchant. A far more estimable profession than her father's sometimes occupation of day worker and all the time occupation of drunk. She did mention his service in the war, though, which garnered an approving nod from Mrs. Hobson and Superintendent Perkins. Miss Hatfield only yawned.

Una could tell from their open posture and intent expressions that they bought her story. Even Miss Hatfield, though she clearly wasn't impressed. Now was the time to press home her advantage. "My mother, a woman of tireless charity, was killed in a house fire when I was nine. By the time the firemen arrived, there was nothing they could do." She paused and turned toward the window, blinking several times before continuing. "I knew after that I wanted to help people. To allay the suffering of those in need. When I read about your training school, I knew nursing was the perfect means to accomplish that and . . ." She turned back to the women, her eyes suitably misty. "And honor my mother's memory."

Mrs. Hobson dabbed a tear with her napkin. Miss Hatfield

shifted in her chair, for once skittish of Una's gaze. That would teach her for being so haughty. Miss Perkins's expression, however, was harder to read. She set down her teacup, waving off Mrs. Hobson's offer to pour her more.

"Miss Kelly, while I applaud your noble intentions, you must understand that nursing is a demanding profession. It requires more than goodwill. A nurse must be industrious, disciplined, intelligent. No matter the circumstances, she must perform her duties with calmness, exactitude, and efficiency. Quick observation and a stout constitution are essential. Do you believe you possess such qualities?"

"Most assuredly."

Miss Perkins pursed her lips as if she wasn't sure. She sat back in her chair and continued to study Una. "We've had nearly a thousand applicants this year. Only a handful will be selected. Of those, a third are likely to be dismissed during their first month as probationers."

Una felt the trickle of sweat between her shoulder blades. Her teacup clanked loudly against its saucer when she set it down. She'd not realized so many women had applied.

"Many applicants we can dismiss out of hand," Miss Perkins continued, "by virtue of incapacity, physical weakness, or belonging to the ignorant, uneducated classes."

"Bad breeding," Miss Hatfield added, looking squarely at Una.

"Then there's the question of character," Miss Perkins said.

Una's mouth was dry, but she didn't trust herself not to spill her tea or break the dainty cup if she took it in hand again.

"There is, perhaps, no calling in life which demands a more constant exercise of Christian virtue than nursing the sick," Mrs. Hobson said. "You said you're religious, Miss Kelly?"

Una nodded.

"Catholic, I infer from your school record and references," Miss Hatfield said with the same thinly veiled disdain she'd had upon greeting Una at the door.

"Yes."

Miss Hatfield glanced at the other women as if to be sure they'd heard Una's damning response.

"I thought . . . The advertisement I read said Christians of all sects were welcome to apply."

"Indeed they are," Mrs. Hobson said with an uneasy smile. "Though we haven't had any Catholic trainees before."

Una silently cursed herself for being so foolish. Odious as the thought was, she should have added Protestant to her list of lies.

"Of course, the doors of Bellevue are open to anyone, no matter how mean or poor," Miss Hatfield said. "So many of our patients share your faith. But I do wonder how you'll get on with the staff and other trainees."

Beneath her too-short sleeves, the hairs on Una's arms bristled. Her pulse thudded loudly in her ears. Nevertheless she managed a smile. "I've been fortunate in my life to have friends and acquaintances of many creeds and should hope to here as well. After all, did Jesus not befriend the Gentile as well as the Jew?"

Mrs. Hobson patted Una's knee. "Well said, my dear. We certainly shan't hold your faith against you."

But a glance at Miss Hatfield, whose smug expression had soured, and Una wasn't so sure. She turned to the superintendent. Surely it was Miss Perkins who had the final say in her acceptance. The woman sat forward again in her chair, arms uncrossed and hands loosely clasped. All good signs. But her body angled slightly away from Una, and she hadn't once smiled. Her eyes were bank vaults even the best thief couldn't crack.

Una's pulse hadn't quieted. If anything, with each passing second, it thudded louder until she could scarcely hear her own breath. What would she do if they rejected her application? Already Claire was itching to turn her out. Her chances of making it out of New York now ran even with that of winding up on Blackwell's Island. Only a sucker would bother with odds like that.

"I understand you have many more applicants than you can accept," Una said, struggling to keep her voice light and even. "And some of them, many perhaps, have more illustrious qualifications than I do. But I assure you, none of them want to join your school as earnestly."

Several moments passed, and none of the women spoke. The thudding in Una's ears slowed to a murmur. What more could she do besides throw herself to the ground and beg? Una had never begged. Not a day in her life. Not even when she'd first left home and hadn't a single cent or scrap of food. But she would have begged now if she thought it would help.

"I like your spirit, Miss Kelly," Superintendent Perkins said at last. "Every nurse needs a bit of pluck. But understand this: the Bellevue training program is an exacting undertaking. The hours of study and practice are long. Insubordination or disobedience will result in immediate expulsion. Do you understand?"

"Yes," Una said without hesitation. She held her breath as Miss Perkins glanced at the other women. Mrs. Hobson nodded. Miss Hatfield sighed and shrugged.

The hint of a smile crossed Miss Perkins's lips. "Welcome to the Bellevue Hospital Training School for Nurses."

CHAPTER 14

⟫━◦━⟪

Four days later, Una was back at the large gray-stone building on Twenty-Sixth Street, this time as a bona fide nurse trainee. A probationer, really, but Una wasn't one to quibble over titles. Besides, she'd pass her probation easily enough.

Her few possessions fit easily inside the valise she carried. Claire had given it to her on the condition that she never came by begging favors again. Una had agreed, though she couldn't resist stuffing the last of Claire's licorice root into the valise and swiping another pen—this one sterling silver—from Randolph's desk on her way out.

To Una's relief, a tall, middle-aged woman answered the door when she'd knocked, not the snooty Miss Hatfield. The minute the front door closed behind them, the knotted muscles in Una's back began to relax for the first time since the night of Traveling Mike's murder.

"We try to keep things as homelike as possible here," the woman, who'd introduced herself as Mrs. Buchanan, the resident housekeeper, was saying. "After all the grim work you ladies see at the hospital, you need a place of refuge to fortify the spirit."

The great building was not like any home Una had ever lived in, certainly not since her mother died. The thick velvet draperies, the warm wood paneling, and the plush rugs blunted the noise and bustle just outside the door. Both the foyer and the adjoining parlor were well-appointed without the insufferable frills she'd spied through the windows of the so-called fine homes about town. Even Claire's house, though smaller, was crammed with doilies and lace-trimmed cushions and shiny knickknacks.

Una hadn't been impressed, not at Claire's nor when strolling down Millionaire's Row. Of course, the gilded mantel clocks and marble urns caught her eye. She looked not with longing but valuation. How much might that golden statue fetch her? Those decorative feathers? That crystal vase?

Here at the training school, or "nurses' home," as Mrs. Buchanan had called it, the decor was more modest. Not austere like the Mission or House of Industry, but not putting on airs either. Still, if Una cleaned it out, she'd clear a pretty sum. But she wasn't here for a quick grab. Deidre or some other thieves Una knew would be sorely tempted by the watercolor paintings on the walls or brass knobs on the lamps or the porcelain tea service in the cupboard. Not to mention all they might find if they raided the nurses' bedrooms above. But not her. Una was playing the long game. Besides, it violated rule number ten: Don't steal from your housemates unless they steal from you first.

Mrs. Buchanan showed Una around the first floor. Most of the other probationers had arrived earlier in the day and were upstairs in their rooms unpacking, Mrs. Buchanan explained of the near-empty rooms. The rest of the trainees were at the hospital. They did pass by a few second-year trainees who were enjoying a day off. Those who looked up from their reading or knitting smiled, but no one seemed to take too keen an interest in Una. That was fine by her. She wasn't here to make friends. The fewer people who noticed her, the better.

In addition to the parlor, there was a large dining room where the nurses took their meals. Beyond that was the kitchen—Cook Prynne's domain, though Una could help herself to a biscuit and a glass of milk between meals—and rear yard with nothing more than a spigot and a few clotheslines.

"Where are the privies?" Una asked, imagining she'd have to trudge into some adjacent yard to find the festering and overflowing privies that served not only the entire school of nurses but the neighboring residents as well.

Mrs. Buchanan smiled and led Una back inside. She opened the door to a small room off the back hall and stepped aside so Una could peek in. An ornately carved wooden box with a hinged lid sat against the far wall. Two pipes connected it to another box high above. A brass chain with a wooden handle dangled beside it. Next to this contraption was a waist-high cupboard crowned with porcelain. Twin spigots hung over a wide, inlaid bowl.

"What is it?" Una asked.

Mrs. Buchanan chuckled. "A water closet, my dear."

Una inched inside but hesitated before lifting the lid atop the shorter box. She'd read about these indoor privies but never actually seen one. Beneath the lid was another porcelain bowl with a dark hole leading away to the ground. Una dropped the lid and hurried out of the room, burying her nose in her sleeve.

"What about the sewer gases?" she asked once the door was closed and she could safely uncover her nose. "Don't they make you sick?"

Mrs. Buchanan waved her hand. "That's poppycock. On cold winter days like these, this closet is a godsend."

Una managed a weak smile and nod but was relieved when the tour took them away from the small room and its poisonous gases.

Their next stop was the demonstration room, a square space twice as large as Una's old flat, stocked with bandages, bedpans, and stoppered bottles of various shapes and sizes. Then came the library. Una had been so intent on not bungling her interview that she hadn't paid much attention to her surroundings when she'd sat here four days before. Between the tables and armchairs, several dozen women could be comfortably seated here, though only a few occupied the room now. The books, though neatly displayed on the shelves by size and topic, were not for ornamentation, as Una suspected many private libraries were. Their spines were cracked and covers worn. And they weren't all medical textbooks either. Una noticed the names of several authors whose stories and poems Una's mother had read to her as a girl. She reached out and brushed her fingers over their spines.

"You're welcome to any book on the shelf," Mrs. Buchanan told her. "Just be sure to return it to its proper place when you're through."

Una pulled back her hand. What was the point of some fanciful story if it didn't put food in your stomach or shoes on your feet? "Might you show me to my room?"

"Yes, yes, of course. I'm sure you're eager to settle in and meet your roommate. I'll go fetch some fresh linen, then show you up."

Una wandered from the bookshelf to the far side of the room where a heap of coals glowed behind the grate of a polished stone hearth. Roommate, Mrs. Buchanan had said. Singular, not plural. Una had imagined all the trainees sharing the same room. The idea of one roommate instead of dozens sounded positively luxurious. Maybe the months she spent here while the fuss around Traveling Mike's murder blew over wouldn't be so bad after all.

On the wall to the right of the hearth hung a framed letter. It seemed odd to go to all the trouble of framing a simple letter and mounting it on the wall like a piece of art. Unless perhaps it was from President Arthur himself. She drew closer to see who it was from. But only the first page of the letter was displayed, with the rest perhaps tucked behind. It was addressed simply to "sir" and began, "I wish your association God-speed with all my heart and soul in their task of reform . . ." and went on to discuss the duties and instruction of nurses. "Nurses are not 'medical men,'" it read. "On the contrary nurses are there, and solely there, to carry out the orders of the medical and surgical staff, including, of course, the whole practice of cleanliness, fresh air, diet, etc." It described the nurse as an intelligent, cultivated, and moral woman. Ignorant, stupid women, the letter's author said, were always headstrong.

Una snickered. Though she'd been accused of being headstrong a time or two herself, she found it was those women who fancied themselves well-bred and moral to be the pigheaded ones.

The soft patter of footsteps sounded behind her, and Una turned around. The woman who approached her could have stepped right out of the silly pastoral paintings that decorated the walls. Though made from quality wool, her dress had the simple, straight cut of a country bumpkin. Unlike city women, whose skin—no matter the hue—looked matte and sallow, she had a dewy complexion with undertones of pink and copper brought out by the sun. Her warm, smiling expression hid nothing. Were they meeting like this in a park or train station, she was exactly the type of woman Una would fleece.

"Can you believe it's truly a letter from *her*?"

"Her?"

"Miss Florence Nightingale. The founding committee wrote to her for advice when they were establishing the school. This is her return correspondence. Did you know that her school in London has trained over five thousand nurses who are in service now all over the world?"

This woman might be from the country, but she spoke fast as a New Yorker and with a sugar-sweet enthusiasm that made Una's teeth ache. Una took a step back—for the woman was close enough to pick *her* pockets—and stumbled into the ash bucket beside the hearth. Luckily, neither she nor the bucket toppled over.

"I'm Miss Lewis, by the way, but you can call me Drusilla. I'm sure we'll be great friends. I feel so fortunate to be here I may well burst."

Pinned between the hearth and the wall, Una winced, fearing that Drusilla may well burst for all the nervous excitement she seemed to have pent up.

"I've always wanted to be a nurse," Drusilla continued. "Haven't you? Ever since I read Miss Nightingale's *Notes on Nursing* when I was ten. Can you believe—"

Mrs. Buchanan came to Una's rescue with an armful of bedding. "Pardon the interruption, Miss Lewis. I wanted to show Miss Kelly up to your room before Cook Prynne needs my help with supper."

"Our room?" Una asked, shimmying around Drusilla.

"Yes, you're roommates."

"Roommates!" Drusilla squealed. She looped one arm through Una's and collected the bedding from Mrs. Buchanan. "I'll show her up."

Mrs. Buchanan smiled appreciatively and toddled off, leaving Una to Drusilla's clutches. She rattled on about this Nightingale woman up two flights of stairs and down a long hall. Though lamps burned at frequent intervals along the walls, Una found herself reaching for her matchbook out of habit. Unlike the narrow passageways of her tenement, where people had to squeeze and shimmy around one another, here at least three women could walk abreast, giving Una no excuse to slip her arm free from Drusilla's.

Their room was twice the size of the cramped, closet-sized room she'd shared with Deidre and the other women back in the slums. Two beds with plump mattresses and polished wood frames fit snugly inside. Each had a matching nightstand at its head and a wooden trunk at its foot. Against the far wall between the beds stood a wardrobe taller than Una and twice as wide.

She hovered in the doorway while Drusilla got to work making Una's bed. This was where she'd be staying? There had to be a catch. She scanned the wall for nicks and cracks, but the plaster was smooth and unblemished. She took a deep sniff and then another. It smelled funny. Soap, maybe. But something floral too.

"I hope you're not disappointed," Drusilla said, glancing at Una with concern. "I heard a few of the other trainees whispering about how dreadfully simple the appointments are. But I find them more than satisfactory. Don't you? This is a school, after all, not some holiday villa in Newport." She spread a quilt over the bed, gave the pillow a fluff, and turned to Una, who still tarried in the doorway. "Well?"

Una took a step inside and peeked behind the door. Two hooks hung on the wall, one already occupied by Drusilla's coat. Otherwise the slender space behind the sweep of the door was empty. What had she been expecting? This wasn't some narrow alley where a thug might be waiting to spring. Or had she thought Drusilla was part of some con duo, here to lure Una into the room where her partner waited to knock Una on the head and rob her? The idea was so preposterous Una had to swallow a laugh. She knew conwomen who worked such a grift. Drusilla couldn't be more unlike them if she tried. True, she might yap Una's ear off, but there wasn't a guileful bone in her body.

Nevertheless, Una checked her pockets before hanging her coat on the wall. She set her valise beside the trunk and poked at the bed. The mattress sprung back beneath her finger. Whatever was inside, it wasn't straw or rags. She poked it once more, then leaped onto the bed, landing on her back with her arms and legs spread. The wooden frame groaned but held. The mattress hugged her body without sagging.

Drusilla gave a nervous chuckle and sat down opposite Una on her own bed, the picture of ladylike poise. Una remembered what Mrs. Hatfield had said during the interview about bad breeding and wiggled into a more decorous repose with her legs together and hands folded across her stomach. Hopefully, Drusilla wouldn't go squealing to their superiors.

To her surprise, Drusilla kicked off her slippers and lay down too. "Let's take a nap before supper, shall we?" she said with childlike delight as if she and Una were conspirators in the same game.

Una closed her eyes. After all the scheming it had taken to get here, she was, in fact, desperately tired.

But not a minute passed before Drusilla spoke again. "Aren't you going to take off your boots, silly goose?"

Reluctantly, Una unlaced her boots and pried them off her feet. She waited until Drusilla had closed her eyes, then hid them beneath her pillow. Guileless or not, Una wasn't about to chance waking up to find her only pair of boots stolen.

CHAPTER 15

The next day, Una hurried across Twenty-Sixth Street, shoving her arms into her coat sleeves and pinning on her ridiculous white cap as she ran. Drusilla scampered at her side. Una had told her she needn't wait, but Drusilla insisted and lingered by Una's side as she threw on her uniform like a stray dog after you've made the mistake of giving it a bone.

Una had woken on time that morning. With Drusilla's loud footfalls and incessant chatter, it was impossible not to. But she'd fallen back to sleep as soon as Drusilla went down to breakfast. Early mornings had never been her cup of tea. Those poor souls bustling to work with the dawn had lean pockets anyway. Better to wait for the fat pickings that strolled out later in the day.

When Drusilla came to fetch her coat, Una had woken again. Now, they trailed behind their fellow trainees in peril of being late their very first day. To make matters worse, Drusilla stopped and stepped aside every few paces to accommodate even the slowest of wagons. By the time they reached the far sidewalk, Una had grown so exacerbated by their halting pace and Drusilla's endless streams of "excuse me," "pardon me," "after you, please" that she grabbed her roommate's hand and yanked her through the crowd.

Bellevue was a hulking gray fortress that took up two whole

blocks along the East River. It rose five stories at its center and branched out like an ill-shaped letter T with the top end fronting Twenty-Eighth Street. A high brick wall surrounded it on all sides, save the back where it was bounded by the river dock and the Twenty-Sixth Street side, where a temporary wooden fence had been erected during construction of a new gatehouse.

"What a lovely building," Drusilla said, stopping on the snow-covered lawn just beyond the partially built gatehouse.

More like a blockhouse, Una thought, remembering a similar gray-stone building on Blackwell's Island. She shuddered and tugged Drusilla onward. They took the curving, iron-railed steps that led to the double-wide entrance two at a time, arriving in the main hall just as Superintendent Perkins called the corralled trainees to order.

"Welcome to Bellevue Hospital, ladies," she began. "Today you embark on a momentous journey. One that will require discipline, obedience, and the utmost fortitude. Not everyone will weather the journey. Those who do, however, will be rewarded with a livelihood of great usefulness and divine purpose."

Una worked a finger beneath the scratchy collar of her uniform. *Divine purpose?* One would think they were about to enter a nunnery. She glanced from Superintendent Perkins to the other trainees. Some, like Drusilla, listened enraptured. Others looked afraid, as if the lot of them were about to be thrown in the middle of a cockfight. Still others wore thinly veiled smirks of conceit. These were the women who, like Miss Hatfield, had illustrious pedigrees and egos to match.

Una already had a useful livelihood. Perhaps not useful to others, but certainly useful to herself. As for divine purpose, staying alive and out of prison was purpose enough. Besides, her mother had subscribed to such absurd notions as usefulness to others and divine calling, and look where it got her. Let these other women embark on a journey. Una's only goal was to keep her head down and not get expelled so she could stay out of the coppers' clutches. If she learned a few skills to use on the streets, a new ruse to get not only into people's pockets but into their homes, so much the better.

When Superintendent Perkins finished her address, she introduced the head nurses standing at her side. Three of them oversaw the medical wards; the other three, the surgical wards. Miss Hatfield was among the latter.

"These esteemed women will be in charge of your day-to-day training and oversee your work on the wards. They began like you, probationers in the program, and have risen to this position through hard work and rigorous study. Listen faithfully to what they say and obey their every direction. In a year's time, the best among you might also earn the title of head nurse."

Una glanced at Drusilla, who stood nodding eagerly beside her, and couldn't help but roll her eyes.

Superintendent Perkins took her leave, as did five of the head nurses, whose supervision was needed on the wards. That left Una and the other trainees in Miss Hatfield's "capable" care.

She waited until Superintendent Perkins ascended the stairs to her office before addressing them. "Look around you," she began in the same smug voice Una remembered from her interview. The trainees' heads turned this way and that. Una didn't know if they were meant to be looking at one another or the hall in which they stood. None of it, not the other women dressed alike in their blue and white seersucker uniforms, nor the room with its whitewashed walls and marble-tiled floor seemed of note. Three portraits hung on the wall to her right—all stodgy-looking men, physicians according to their gold-plated placards. On the wall to the left was a roster of the current medical and surgical staff. Una hoped she wouldn't have to memorize these men's names and their positions. *Hey you*, generally worked in the slums. A nickname if you cared to be polite. But if the self-important expressions of the men in the portraits were any indication, *Hey, you* or *Lazy-eyed Joe* wouldn't do.

Thankfully, when Miss Hatfield continued, she didn't mention the list of physicians. "You are not nurses. You're not even nurse

trainees. You're probationers. Barely above the coarse and ignorant women who scrub the floors. And at least ten of you," she said,
"maybe as many as fifteen, won't be here in a month's time." She
strode back and forth in front of them, the click of her boot heels
on the marble, echoing as she spoke. "Passing your probation is
not an easy feat. Nervousness, forgetfulness, disorderliness"—her
eyes stopped on Una—"tardiness will not be tolerated or excused.
Do you understand?"

The women nodded.

"If there's anyone who would like to leave, you may do so now
without judgment. Anyone who perhaps feels outmatched by the
women beside her or unequal to the challenge ahead." Miss Hatfield's mean blue eyes again came to rest on Una.

Una returned her cold stare. Miss Hatfield was nothing com-
pared to the gangsters and swindlers and coppers she'd dealt
with in the slums. But that didn't stop Una's hands from turning
clammy or her heart from thudding against her breastbone. So
much for keeping her head down and going unnoticed.

"No one?" Miss Hatfield said after a ponderous silence. "Very
well. Let's begin."

Miss Hatfield's words proved prophetic not two hours later, before they'd even finished their tour of the hospital. On the twenty-
fifth ward, they passed the bedside of a man newly arrived after
an accident in the ironworks factory. Three doctors and a nurse
crowded around him. When the nurse scurried away at the doctor's command for morphine, Una and the other probationers were
able to see the man's injuries. His right leg stuck out at an unnatural angle beneath the knee. Bruised and swollen, his face re-
sembled an eggplant. But it was his arm that was most gruesome:
gnarled and bloody with only a splintered stump of bone where
his hand and forearm ought to be.

Several of the women around Una gasped. One retched into a
nearby bucket. Another swooned, smacking her head on the floor
as she collapsed. Drusilla clutched Una's arm and looked away,

her rosy cheeks draining of color. Once Una was sure Drusilla wasn't going to swoon as well, she peeled her clammy fingers from her arm and stepped closer to the bedside, curious what the physicians were doing to save this man's life. A tourniquet had been wrapped around the man's mangled arm to stanch the bleeding while two of the doctors discussed whether it was wise to operate immediately or wait for the man's vital signs to stabilize. The other doctor probed the man's head as if checking for cracks in his skull, unhindered by his screams.

The blood-soaked sheets did not trouble Una. Nor the mauled flesh. She'd seen worse in the slums. But his screams reverberated beneath her skin, settling uncomfortably inside her, and she found it a great relief when the nurse returned with morphine.

When the doctor—a young man dressed in a well-tailored suit with still, serious eyes—went to plunge the syringe into the patient's arm, the patient, in his pain-induced delirium, knocked the syringe out of the doctor's hand. It landed on the floor with a clatter, rolling to a stop at Una's feet.

"Miss Kelly," she heard someone say behind her.

She turned around and saw Miss Hatfield scowling at her. "Step back. You mustn't get in the doctors' way."

Una hadn't been within three paces of the doctors and would have liked to hear their verdict on when to operate, but she obliged Miss Hatfield and fell in with the other trainees. The woman who had passed out was awake now and sitting up, her face the color of withered cabbage and a goose egg growing on her temple.

Miss Hatfield dispatched one of the helpers who cleaned the wards to see the woman back to the nurses' home, then ushered the rest of them on to the next ward. Undoubtedly, the woman would be packed and gone by the time they returned for supper.

"No dawdling, now," Miss Hatfield said, eyeing first a sallow-cheeked woman who tottered at the rear, and then Una as if hoping to catch her straggling too. "We're already behind schedule."

"I don't think she likes you," Drusilla whispered to Una as they walked. "Though I can't imagine why."

Una only snorted. Her Irish name was one reason. Her unremarkable school record was another. But Una suspected there was something more, something Miss Hatfield had disliked about her from the first moment they met. Whatever it was, Una had to figure it out, and quick, otherwise Miss Hatfield would be on her like mud for the rest of her time here. And if Miss Hatfield had her way, that wouldn't be very long.

CHAPTER 16

For her first rotation, Una was assigned to ward six, a surgical ward overseen by Miss Hatfield. Her first day was a harried blur of fetching supplies, mopping up vomit, and lugging soiled dressings down to the waste barrels in the rear yard. At the end of her twelve-hour shift, she trudged back to the nurses' home alongside Dru. (She was too tired to even say her full name or bother to ask whether Dru minded the nickname.) Dru chattered on about her day with the energy of a child who'd eaten too many sweets. Una nodded every so often but didn't listen.

Her feet and back ached worse than when she used her ragpicker ruse and spent the entire day diving pockets along Market Street, hunched over and hobbling. Or that time she'd lifted the pocketbook of a U.S. marshal and had to crisscross the city twice over to elude the coppers. The short walk from the hospital seemed like a mile, and when at last they arrived, Una was famished. She attacked her supper like a street urchin, soaking up the soup Cook Prynne served with a roll and shoving it in her mouth. Several bites later, she looked to find all the women staring at her.

"We were just about to say grace, Miss Kelly," one of them said. "Would you care to join us? Or don't papists bother to give thanks to the good Lord before they eat?"

Begrudgingly, Una set her roll on her bread plate. "Of course

we do. We just don't make such a big show of it." She clasped her
hands and bowed her head. When the snooty woman finished the
prayer, Una made a slow, deliberate sign of the cross. "Is it okay
with God if we eat now?"

When no one replied, she reached for her bread, then, thinking
better of it, picked up her spoon instead. She'd raised their dander
enough for one night. Dru took up her spoon as well. Soon they
were all sipping their soup in silence.

The next day passed little better. Una refused to risk being poi-
soned by the sewer gases leaking from that strange contraption
in the water closet, so she slipped out after breakfast to use the
privy three buildings down. Both stalls were in use when she got
there, and though she could easily relieve herself in the corner
of the yard, it wouldn't do for anyone to see a Bellevue nurse
trainee hiking up her starched skirts and pissing on the ground.
But the wait made her late for morning lecture. Not late in the
normal sense of the word. In the slums you could arrive just about
any time, and no one paid you mind. Even at Sunday Mass, so
long as you sneaked in before Father O'Donoghue started reading
from the Gospel, you were considered on time enough to meet the
week's holy obligation. But Miss Hatfield hadn't the magnanimity
of Father O'Donoghue. She stopped speaking mid-sentence when
Una cracked open the door to the demonstration room and slipped
inside.

"Good of you to join us, Miss Kelly," she said once Una had
shimmied past a few of the women to an empty spot at the back of
the room. "We were just discussing the importance of cleanliness
on the ward. Perhaps you can enlighten the other trainees on the
composition of dust."

Dust? Was this a joke of some sort? But there wasn't the slightest glimmer of mischief in Miss Hatfield's eyes. "Dust is made up
of . . . er . . . dust."

A few of the trainees laughed, though Una doubted they could
have given any better answer to such an absurd question.

"Incorrect." Miss Hatfield dragged her finger over the top of the supply cupboard beside her and then held it up. "Dust is comprised of both organic impurities and the germs of disease, hence the importance of its careful and thorough removal. How, then, should we clean it?"

After a moment's silence, Una realized the question was again directed at her. "With a feather duster?"

"Incorrect once again. If I were as ignorant as you on the principles of cleanliness, I would make a greater effort to arrive on time for lecture."

Una couldn't very well tell her there'd been a line at the privy, not without facing more ridicule for avoiding the water closet, so she kept her mouth shut.

"Is there anyone who can enlighten Miss Kelly on the proper instrument for dust removal?" Miss Hatfield said, unfixing her glowering eyes from Una and casting them about the room. "Anyone?"

Una snorted, then covered the noise with a cough. See, she wasn't the only *ignorant* one among them when it came to dusting.

Then Dru timidly raised her hand.

"Yes, Miss Lewis?"

"A damp cloth or sponge?"

"Precisely. Why?"

"To avoid raising the dust."

"That's correct. A soft-hair broom may be used if care is taken. The woodwork and windows must be dusted once a week in this manner, the floors at least twice weekly. Always with carbolized water."

Miss Hatfield droned on about the various chores necessary to maintaining a clean ward. Then she informed the trainees she would demonstrate how to dress a bed.

Una fought back another snort. Surely none of the trainees were so daft as not to know how to make a bed. But when she glanced around, everyone was watching Miss Hatfield intently.

Loobies, the lot of them. Perhaps instead of insisting applicants be well-bred and refined, they should require common sense and basic domestic skills.

Later, when they arrived on the wards, Una and the other trainees were tasked with implementing the skills Nurse Hatfield had bored them with that morning. Una begrudgingly got to work dusting windowsills, rinsing bedpans, and changing out the linen. It wasn't half so hard as Nurse Hatfield had made it seem. She could have spent all morning in line for the privy, missed the lecture completely, and saved herself the browbeating without being any the worse for it. So what if she'd already forgotten how to make carbolized water. Juice from the spigot worked just as well. And never mind which sheet came first. She'd slept for years on a single sheet and pile of straw and was as healthy as a May hedge in bloom.

By midafternoon when Nurse Hatfield made her rounds through the ward to inspect Una's work, the bedpans were cleaned and stowed away on their appointed shelves, the tabletops and windows were dust free, and every empty bed was neatly made. She stood by as Nurse Hatfield ran her fingers high and low, hunting for dust, and smiled to herself when they came up clean. But apparently clean wasn't sufficient for the head nurse. She brought the tips of her fingers to her nose and inhaled.

"What ratio of carbolic acid to water did you use?"

"About that, I—" Una was saved from answering when the second-year trainee hurried over to them. A new patient just brought down from the operating theater had begun to hemorrhage. Nurse Hatfield quickly examined the patient with Una and the second-year peering over her shoulder. Blood had soaked through the surgical dressing that stretched halfway across the man's belly and oozed down onto the bed. Una watched as she peeled back the bandage to reveal a jagged line of stitches sopped in blood.

"Fetch me a basin of carbolized water, Miss Kelly," Nurse Hatfield said, her voice steady and cool. "One part carbolic acid to forty parts water, as I'm sure you remember from this morning's lecture."

Una hastened to the storeroom. Behind her, she could hear Nurse Hatfield interrogating the second-year about the man's condition before dispatching her to fetch the surgeon. Una found a jar of crystallized carbolic acid. She measured out half an ounce and dissolved it in twenty ounces of water. A faint but sharp odor unlike anything she'd smelled wafted from the basin of liquid. So that was what Nurse Hatfield was sniffing for, Una realized.

She returned to the patient's bedside with the basin, grabbing a sponge and stack of soft rags along the way. First, Nurse Hatfield used the water to clean her hands. Then she wetted a few of the rags and wiped the man's incision. Fresh blood leaked around his stitches but not so much as to suggest the type of grave internal hemorrhage the second-year had been afeared of.

"A simple case of delayed clotting, as I suspected," Nurse Hatfield said, more to herself it seemed than to Una. Already the bleeding had slowed to a trickle.

"So he'll live?"

"That remains to be seen." She turned to Una. "Get rid of that sponge you brought over. It's entirely ill-suited for cleaning and dressing a wound."

"Right, why didn't I think of that?" Una said before she could check the sarcasm in her voice.

"A sponge, Miss Kelly, is liable to convey poisonous matter from one wound or sore to another. Tow or cotton-wool soaked in water are far better as they can be destroyed after use."

"I was only trying to help."

"Until you understand the principles of cleanliness and its role in disease transmission, you can be of little help."

Una grabbed the sponge and stalked back to the storeroom. Sponges, tow, rags, cotton-wool—how was she supposed to know the difference between such things? Nothing she did would ever satisfy Nurse Hatfield. Never mind that she'd also brought rags—which Nurse Hatfield had been perfectly content to use—and of her own accord, no less. On the streets you used what you had. A shirtsleeve in place of a hankie. A corncob in place of privy paper.

When Una returned from the storeroom, she found the second-year trainee trying to remove the soiled draw sheet from beneath the patient. Only there was no draw sheet. In consequence, blood had soaked through the under sheet to the mattress. Both would have to be washed and disinfected, and the patient moved to another bed. Nurse Hatfield strode to the other empty beds Una had dressed and yanked off the blankets. Not one was made to her liking.

She commanded Una to dress them again in the proper fashion: under sheet, rubber sheet, draw sheet, upper sheet, blanket. She stood by with arms crossed as Una worked, pointing out every wrinkle and ill-tucked corner. When at last she was satisfied, she bid Una take the bloodied sheets and straw mattress down to the laundry.

"When you're done with that," she said, "report to the third floor."

"What for?" Una asked, gathering up the soiled linen.

"To explain yourself to Superintendent Perkins."

CHAPTER 17

The boiler house, laundry, and kitchen occupied the lawn behind the main hospital building. Despite the high brick wall that blocked First Avenue and the other nearby streets from view, Una could hear the clatter of horse hooves and rattle of wagons. Vendors called out over one another, peddling matches and buttons and roasted chestnuts to passersby. A mule brayed. An organ grinder cranked his machine. The muffled sounds were so close and familiar yet seemed to belong to another world. Her world.

In one arm, Una carried the linen basket, heaped to the brim. In the other, the straw-filled mattress, doubled over and tucked against her side. She waddled more than walked, stopping every few steps to rebalance her load. What in damnation was she doing here? This wasn't how she'd imagined things would work out. Waking up at the hateful hour of dawn. Dusting and cleaning like a maid. Squirming beneath Nurse Hatfield's barbed gaze until everything was just so. Not even Una's comfy bed and Cook Prynne's warm meals were worth all this trouble. Hell, even life on the Island would be easier than this.

But as soon as Una shouldered open the laundry's door and stepped inside, she knew that wasn't true. Half a dozen women hunched over washboards and wringers, sweat matting their hair.

Others churned vats of boiling water and linen, their cheeks reddened from the sweltering steam. They were bone-thin, these women, with vacant eyes and flea-bitten skin. Workhouse women, carted over from the Tombs or ferried in from Blackwell's Island. They carried out their assigned tasks—washing, churning, wringing—like women half-dead.

Una handed over the soiled bedding and hurried out. Her throat was tight and armpits sweaty, and not just from the hot, lye-smelling air that followed her out. If the coppers found her, she'd have nothing but a lifetime of suffering and drudgery to look forward to. Just like these laundry women. Her uniform might be scratchy, her roommate a chattery bore, Nurse Hatfield an insufferable prig, but Una mustn't forget what awaited her if she failed here.

When she reached the third floor, Una smoothed her apron and straightened her cap before knocking on Superintendent Perkins's door. Upon entering, Una was relieved to find Nurse Hatfield was not there, though she suspected the head nurse had filled Miss Perkins's ear with enough poison to expel Una thrice over. She'd have to do her very best cajoling if she hoped to stay.

It was a larger office than Una had expected with a polished oak desk, several bookshelves, and a separate sitting area with cushioned chairs and a lacquered tea table. The usual bric-a-brac hung on the walls: needlework, pictures, old-fashioned wood prints, a plainly carved cross. The wards were dressed much the same, with the addition of various placards put up by religious societies quoting Isaiah, Jeremiah, and the book of Psalms. Several large windows looked out over the back lawn and cityscape beyond, but only one was unshuttered.

Miss Perkins gestured to a straight-back chair opposite her desk, and Una sat. She folded her hands in her lap, as much to still their trembling as to appear ladylike, and met Miss Perkins's gaze with an innocent expression.

"Nurse Hatfield tells me you've had some difficulties today," the superintendent said. As during the interview, her voice, her posture, her face offered few clues to what she was thinking. She'd make a good conwoman.

"I had trouble seeing Nurse Hatfield's demonstration this morning from the back of the room and got a few things mixed up. I'm quite confident now that I know the proper order of things. It shan't happen again."

"Perhaps your unfortunate position in the demonstration room had something to do with your tardiness."

"I was only a minute or two late. My roommate couldn't find her cap, and we—"

"But Miss Lewis wasn't late."

"We found her cap in the very nick of time, and she hurried off to lecture, but I still had my—"

"Miss Kelly, I did not bring you into my office to hear your excuses." Her eyebrows had pulled together to form a furrow that deepened as she spoke. "Either you are suitable for this program or you are not. Your behavior today leads me to believe the latter."

Una leaned forward in her chair. She'd taken the wrong approach but still wasn't sure what the right approach was. Flattery? Obsequiousness? She felt the same sweatiness and throat tightening as she had at the laundry. "Please, Miss Perkins, give me another chance." Her voice quavered without artifice. "I am suited to this program. I promise."

Superintendent Perkins leaned back in her chair and steepled her hands. Seconds ticked by, but she seemed in no rush to speak. Una sat as still as she could, hoping the woman would read her desperation as earnestness.

How foolish Una had been to think that she could dally her way through the program unnoticed. More foolish still to underestimate Miss Hatfield and the grudge she held against Una. Neither mistake would Una make again. If she weren't expelled first.

At last, Superintendent Perkins spoke. "Nursing is not a divertissement for bored young women. It is a profession. A calling.

Inefficiency and insubordination will not be tolerated. If I see you in this office again—for any reason—before your month's probation is up, you'll be dismissed. Do you understand?"

"Yes, thank you. Yes." Una stood before Miss Perkins could change her mind. "You shan't regret this, I promise."

CHAPTER 18

The next morning, Una forced herself out of bed the moment she heard Dru stirring. She used the water closet instead of the privies down the block, pinching her nose and holding her breath the entire time. It turned out that the strange cord dangling from the box above the toilet brought a gush of water that flushed her urine from the pot. She pulled the cord three more times out of sheer curiosity and would have stood looking longer had she not become dizzy for want of air.

Miss Hatfield stared cutty-eyed when Una arrived for lecture—on time and attentive. Clearly she was disappointed Superintendent Perkins hadn't given Una the boot and was itching to catch her next slipup. But Una wouldn't give her the slightest excuse to haul her up to the third floor again.

That proved easier said than done, though. Whatever principle the trainees learned in morning lecture—the importance of ventilation and sources of bad air in the sick room, temperature, deodorizers, the difference between absorbent and antiseptic disinfectants—Nurse Hatfield expected Una to have mastered by afternoon rounds. If Una had opened the windows to encourage the circulation of fresh air, Nurse Hatfield would stalk up and down the ward, making sure each patient's bedclothes were sufficient to keep them warm and screens were in place to block them from the slightest draft. If Una had the windows closed and stove lit to expel impure air through the flue, she would interrogate Una as to whether the cooler air being drawn in from the hall was itself fresh and properly ventilated. If Una set out bowls of charcoal to absorb deleterious substances in the surrounding atmosphere, Nurse Hatfield questioned why she hadn't used porous clay instead, though she'd said herself in lecture that the two were interchangeable.

It didn't help that the moment Nurse Hatfield arrived, every patient, resting quietly only moments before, was suddenly in need of a bedpan or glass of water or warm fomentation. While the second-year trainee handled anything requiring medical knowledge or skill, these common drudgeries fell to Una, who frequently found herself juggling water pitchers and linen and metal basins sloshing with vomit or piss back and forth across the ward as Nurse Hatfield quizzed her about the different types of antiseptic. But though she sometimes confused Condy's fluid and chloralum, or let the ward's temperature stray a degree or two from the prescribed range of 65 to 68 degrees and was chastened for her negligence, she was not summoned back to the superintendent's office.

Two weeks in, Una felt like she'd finally gained her footing in this strange place of ordered bedlam. It wasn't so different, after all, reading a patient like she'd read a mark. A greenish cast to a patient's cheeks, and she was quick to fetch a basin lest he vomit. Dry lips and tongue smacking meant he'd soon be in want of water. A tight expression and skittish eyes told her the patient needed a bedpan but was too embarrassed to ask.

She'd even begun to anticipate Nurse Hatfield's arrival. As on the streets, those ruled by habit made easy dupes. In addition to rounding with the physicians in the late morning after the trainees' lecture, Nurse Hatfield visited each ward again in the afternoon. She always began on the second floor at two o'clock, after taking tea with Superintendent Perkins and the other head nurses, inspecting wards seven and eight before descending the stairs at the east end of the north wing. From there she continued in ascending order beginning with ward one. Taking into account that she spent an average of twenty minutes scrutinizing each ward, Una could expect her at four o'clock and seldom a minute before. So the wall clock's single, low gong at three thirty served as Una's warning. She tidied the long table in the center of the ward, smoothed the patients' blankets, tucked in loose sheets, and emptied any malodorous basins. By the time she heard Nurse Hatfield's clipped footfalls approaching, she was ready to greet her with a serene, if fake, smile.

Una was so intent on keeping the ward clean and Nurse Hatfield mollified that she hardly noticed anyone else at the hospital. Doctors came regularly to check on the patients, visitors sat at the bedside, kitchen staff delivered meals, workhouse women scrubbed floors and washed windows. But unless Una was tripping over a worker's mop or fetching a distraught wife a hankie, she was too busy to pay any of them much mind. The physicians issued their orders to the second-year, seemingly oblivious to Una, even as they pushed aside the screens she'd carefully arranged to protect patients from drafts and tossed their dirty equipment on her newly made beds.

One morning, arriving at the ward after morning lecture, Una noticed one of the patients sweating and shaking. He'd had some surgery or other and been brought to the ward two days before. When she asked if he was cold or feeling ill, he replied in gibberish. She might have taken him for a foreigner and shrugged it off, but they'd had a perfectly articulate conversation in English just the day before. Besides, she'd spent enough time with her father to recognize the signs. As the second-year was busy redressing another patient's wound, Una slipped the man a cup of brandy and went about her work.

Not long after, a group of several physicians arrived accompanied by Nurse Hatfield for morning rounds. They moved their way from one bed to the next like a rent collector and his thugs move through a tenement, heedless of anyone's purpose but their own.

When they got to the addled patient, they carried on as usual, an older man with a trim, graying beard lecturing and questioning the younger men. The patient, Una happily noticed, was no longer sweating or trembling. When one of the physicians asked him how he was feeling, he answered back in plain English. But then the older physician leaned down, nose to nose with the man, and sniffed.

"Who's given this man spirits?" he shouted.

The second-year who'd been following behind the group, picking up discarded bandages and tucking the patients back in, scurried over. "No one, sir."

"I smell brandy on his breath plain as day. How can we undertake the second half of his operation when he's been allowed to imbibe scarcely an hour beforehand?" A flush had crept into his cheeks. He turned back to the patient. "Who gave you drink this morning?"

The patient rattled his head. "I don't right remember, Doc. Could've been an angel."

"An angel." The physician snorted. "Was she wearing blue and white?"

"I think so."

"And a puffy cap?"

"Sounds about right."

The physician turned back to the second-year. Her posture seemed to shrivel, and she took a step back. Una, watching from across the room, grabbed a basket of laundry and tiptoed toward the door.

"I didn't give him anything," the second-year said. "I swear. It must have been the probationer."

All eyes flickered to Una. Three more steps, and she would have made it to the door.

"You," the physician said to her. "Come here."

Una set down the basket and wiped her hands on her apron to buy herself a moment's time. Her heart inched into her throat as she tried to figure another way out of the situation. The physician's cheeks grew redder. Nurse Hatfield could barely contain her smile as if she were already envisioning hauling Una up to the superintendent's office.

"Hurry up, girl. I haven't got all day."

His brusque, self-important tone settled it for Una. She walked over with her shoulders back and head high.

"Did you give this patient brandy this morning?"

"I did."

The physician blinked.

"He's got a bad touch of the horrors, this one."

"The horrors?"

"I think she means delirium tremens, sir," one of the younger physicians said.

Una nodded. "If he'd gone much longer, he'd have had a fit."

The older physician scowled at her. "And what makes you at all qualified to make such a diagnosis."

Experience, you old bloat, Una wanted to say. Instead she told him about the man's sweating, trembling, and nonsensical speech.

"That could be the manifestation of several ailments, not just delirium tremens."

"Yes, but with the yellowing about his eyes, I thought there was a good chance he'd been in his cups—er—imbibing strong spirits for a great while. If he'd been admitted suddenly for surgery and not had time to dry out, well, then the horrors—delirium tremens, I mean—seemed a plausible cause."

The physician stepped closer, the others giving him a wide berth. "You are a nurse. No, not even a nurse, a probationer. You are not and never will be a doctor. It is wholly beyond the scope of your duties, not to mention your intellectual capacity, to diagnose and treat patients. Your job is, or was"—his eyes cut to Nurse Hatfield and back—"to carry out my orders. Quietly. Efficiently. Without question or conjecture."

Una itched to haul back and punch him. And why not, if she were already about to be expelled? Her fingers were closing into a fist when one of the other men said, "I gave her the order, sir."

Both Una and the older physician turned to look at the man. It was the same young doctor who'd had enough sense to know that the horrors was the same damned condition as the fancy named "delirium tremens." Una had seen him a time or two before on the ward, usually in the company of other physicians. Despite his neatly trimmed mustache, he had a youthful face with a faint dappling of freckles across his nose. His hair, a bit too long, was the color of cherrywood and curled upward at the ends despite a generous slick of pomade. Were it not for his eyes, which had the stillness of one who'd seen and endured the thorny courses of life, Una would have thought him far too young to be a doctor. As it was, she questioned whether he was having a go at her or simply was a fool.

"I . . . er . . . noticed the patient's symptoms this morning on my way up to the theater and instructed this nurse to medicate him with brandy until we could confer on the best course of treatment."

The older physician glowered at him. "Why didn't you speak up sooner, boy?"

Color bloomed across the younger physician's face, from the tip of his nose to his ears. Before he could respond, the other man continued, addressing the group at large. "What are the appropriate treatment options for delirium tremens?"

"Hydrate of chloral or opium," another of the young doctors said with a hint of smugness.

"Very good, Dr. Allen. Both are suitable options that would not preclude surgery today as the administration of such a significant quantity of brandy has done." He turned to the freckle-nosed doctor. "A mistake, I think, your grandfather would not have made."

"Yes, sir," the chastened doctor muttered, though he too looked like he wished to sock the old man.

Hydrate of chloral was ordered for the patient and the physicians continued their rounds. Nurse Hatfield followed them, but not without a sharp glance in Una's direction. You won't wriggle free next time, her eyes seemed to say. The second-year elbowed

Una in the ribs. "No matter what the doctors tell you, leave the dosing of medicine to me, probationer."

Una nodded. Her heart still beat high in her throat alongside her voice box. Her limbs tingled like they did when she narrowly escaped the coppers. It took her a moment to order her thoughts and remember what the dickens she'd been doing before this whole mess began. Even once her hands were occupied again dusting the patients' nightstands, her mind raced and gaze wandered to the young doctor. Just what was he about, anyway? What advantage was there in speaking up for her? Surely he meant to lord this over her somehow.

Una realized she'd been dusting the same table for several minutes, rubbing with such vigor patches of the varnish were gone. She rattled her head and moved on, but not without another glance in the doctor's direction.

A few minutes later, she overheard the stodgy old physician adjourn for lunch. Nurse Hatfield and the doctors dispersed. Una's taut muscles relaxed at their departure. Now maybe she could finally focus on her tasks. But the young doctor remained, lingering at one of the patient's bedside. Una waited for the second-year trainee to disappear into the storeroom, then stalked over to him.

"What's your angle?" she whispered.

He looked up from the patient. "Excuse me?"

"You and I both know you didn't tell me to give that man brandy."

"Would you rather I have let you take the blame and be expelled?"

"Yes. No." Una huffed. "But I don't mean to live under your thumb because of it."

The doctor laughed—a pleasant, guileless sound that disarmed her.

"You're not like the other nurse trainees. What's your name?"

She hesitated a moment, then narrowed her eyes to make it plain she didn't trust him. "Miss Kelly."

"Well, Miss Kelly, your astute observation may well have saved that man's life. If he'd started to seize during surgery, who knows what could have happened. A slip of the hand, a nick with the scalpel, and he could have bled out right there in the operating theater. Not to mention the risk of aspirating. You don't need a cup of brandy to do it. A convulsing man's own bile and saliva is enough."

Una glanced down the row of beds to where the man lay resting. She'd never saved anyone's life before. A strange lightness pushed at the walls of her chest. She frowned. Do-gooding was more trouble than it was worth, she reminded herself, and went against all her rules.

"I should have recognized it myself," the doctor continued. "My father tried to give up intoxicating spirits on more than one occasion."

When she turned back to him, his eyes had drifted from her to stare at some spot on the floor. "I thought physicians were supposed to come from good families. Cream of the crop and all that." The man's cheeks reddened, and Una regretted the impertinence of her remark. "Not that I believe any of that hogwash. Good men drink same as bad. And most have their reasons."

He looked up at her again with an obliging smile. His ivories were almost white and straight enough to be fake. What a price they'd fetch!

"You take far more liberty with your words than any of the other trainees I've met also," he said.

Her stomach tightened. She *had* been far too familiar with him, using words like *hogwash*. She ought to be more guarded. Stick to her demure, well-bred woman ruse. But it wasn't just his laugh that disarmed her. He seemed different from the other physicians, though not in any obvious way. The expensive brown wool suit he wore was just as stodgy. His posture just as self-assured. And yet, it was as if he too didn't quite fit in. "You mean I'm not mute."

"That you certainly are not. Dr. Pingry about had a convulsive fit himself when you walked up and plainly admitted you'd administered the brandy. The look on his face alone was worth standing up for you."

The second-year's footfalls sounded at the far end of the ward as she emerged from the storeroom carrying an armful of supplies. Una took a step back and busied herself dusting the nearest bedside table. She didn't need to add immodestly fraternizing with an intern to her list of the day's misdeeds. "I can stand up for myself, thank you very much."

That irksome chuckle again. "I have no doubt, Miss Kelly."

CHAPTER 19

The next morning, instead of crowding into the demonstration room or hurrying straight to the wards, Una and the other trainees were shepherded into the library. The furniture had been pushed to the far side of the room and in its place sat several rows of chairs facing a blackboard that had been wheeled in for the lesson. Though Una would have preferred a seat at the back where she might be able to catch a few more minutes of sleep, Dru tugged her to the front row.

Beside the blackboard was a table where dozens of bones had been laid out on a velvet cloth. Una's skin prickled, not on account of the bones themselves, but their reminder of her long hours in the cemetery near the Gas House District. She touched her forehead, beginning the sign of the cross, but stopped and pretended to be straightening her cap instead. The other trainees would think her superstitious and simple if they saw her crossing herself on account of a few old bones.

"Do you think those were dug up and stolen from a grave?" one of the women seated behind her whispered.

"People still do that?" asked another. "How much do you think they get paid?"

Una swiveled around in her chair. "There's no money in grave robbing anymore."

The women eyed her like she were three-day-old bread. "How do you know?" one of them asked.

"I . . ." She couldn't very well tell them that she knew a man who'd once made a living digging up bodies and selling them to medical colleges. The good ol' days, he'd called it, back before the passage of the infamous Bone Bill, when a man could get thirty dollars for a fresh corpse.

Dru saved her the trouble of coming up with a demurer explanation. "In 1854 the Act to Promote Medical Science and Protect Burial Grounds was passed in the New York State Legislature," she said over her shoulder as pleasantly as if they were speaking about tea cakes. "All vagrants dying, unclaimed and without friends, are given to the institutions in which medicine and surgery are taught for dissection."

The women turned their three-day-old-bread look on Dru, who only smiled and turned back to the blackboard. Una faced forward as well, but not before giving the women her own, superior smirk. With any luck, the rest of the day's foibles would be as easily surmounted. Too bad she couldn't keep Dru and her encyclopedia-like brain on hand in the hospital. Then again, she'd likely suffer a dreadful earache from all Dru's chatting. Never mind that they were supposed to be silent as corpses themselves on the wards.

Luck favored Una again when another of the head nurses, not Miss Hatfield, came forward to address the class. "Good morning, ladies. Today will be the first of many lectures presented by the hospital's esteemed body of physicians. These lessons will cover a great breadth of topics, beginning today with human anatomy, presented by Dr. Pingry of the Second Surgical Division."

Una winced as the pompous old doctor she'd met yesterday strode forward. So much for her luck holding. The women clapped. Reluctantly, Una did the same. He was too old and self-absorbed to remember her, she assured herself. Besides, dressed in their caps and uniforms, one trainee looked so much like another, who could tell them apart? But when he surveyed the room, his eyes halted a moment on Una, and his lips compressed as if he'd tasted something sour.

Then, without preamble, he began his lecture, describing the human body as an intricate machine, the skeleton being the underlying apparatus upon which all else functioned. He alluded to a complex interior of vessels, marrow, and a latticework-like tissue called cancellous. But he brushed that quickly aside, saying it was beyond the scope of the lecture and their intellectual capabilities. As nurses, they need only know which bones fit where.

Beside her, Dru's shoulders slackened. Clearly she would have delighted in such minutiae. Una also found it interesting to imagine the bones inside her not merely as stone scaffolding but as a complex, living part of her. Simple descriptions of long bones, short bones, flat bones, irregular bones, and how many there were of each were patently boring. It didn't help that Dr. Pingry spoke in a flat, droning voice punctuated every so often by the squeak of his chalk on the blackboard.

Una's gaze drifted to the window. The heavy velvet drapes were drawn aside, but a wispy veil of white gossamer obscured the goings-on outside. Una couldn't remember the last time she'd spent so many days straight indoors. Even when the winter air was bracing and the streets a sloppy mess of mud and snow, she'd enjoyed meandering through the city. The world felt bigger then. Freer. She got up when she pleased, bought a roll and cup of coffee if she were hungry, and went to whatever spot she fancied for the day. Sure, she had her reasons—it was slim pickings at the train depot on a Saturday while Central Park brimmed with fat-pocketed promenaders—and her rules, but no one stood over her shoulder telling her which mark to pick or inspecting her technique. Marm Blei didn't care as long as she brought back the goods and didn't get herself into trouble.

Damn those lousy cuff links. Damn Deidre and Traveling Mike and the goddamn police. Were it not for them, she'd be out there now basking in the chilly air and bustle of the city instead of sitting here on this uncomfortable wooden chair listening to this odious old man blather on about . . . about . . . Jiminy! She had no idea what he was talking about anymore.

Una retrained her focus on Dr. Pingry, hoping she hadn't missed too much of the lecture. He'd moved to stand beside the table and was holding up a short, squat bone with a hole in the center and winglike protuberances on either side.

"There are thirty-three vertebrae, exclusive of those which form the skull. Each is classified according to the position they occupy in the spinal column, seven being found in the cervical region, twelve in the dorsal, five in the lumbar, five in the sacral, and four coccygeal. Can anyone tell me to which region this vertebra belongs?" Dr. Pingry glanced about the room and continued, clearly not expecting anyone to answer. "The cervical region. Note the relatively small size and that it is broader from side to side than front to back."

He held up examples of the types of vertebrae, describing their bumps and notches with strange terms like *pedicle*, *lamina*, and *spinous process* that Una hoped she wouldn't need to remember. Then he drew a long, flattened S on the blackboard and described the proper curvature of the spine.

"Who can describe for me an ailment associated with the improper formation of the vertebral column?"

Dru raised her hand. "Scoliosis, when the spinal column curves sideways."

"Correct. Depending on its severity, it can cause pain, numbness, and even damage to the heart and lungs. Anyone else?"

A few more women offered up answers. Then Dr. Pingry's gaze landed on Una. "What about you? Can you name a disease related to the spinal column? You seemed most eager to supply your thoughts yesterday."

Una ignored his smug stare and thought back to her life on the streets. The slums drew all sorts of ill-shaped folks—those with clubbed feet and shrunken limbs and twisted backs—but Una didn't know the fancy medical names of any of their ailments.

"No?" he said with appreciable glee. "I thought not." He gave his silk waistcoat a sanctimonious tug and addressed the class. "Moving on to the bones of the cranium. There are eight—"

"Hunchback," Una blurted out.

Dr. Pingry turned back to her. "I beg your pardon?"

"A disease of the spine. Hunchback."

"I can only presume you mean kyphosis, which itself is a *condition* associated with several ailments, not a disease in and of itself. Now as I was saying, there are eight bones that compose the cranium . . ."

Una found herself itching to punch him again. He was a slight man with only a few inches of height on her. She'd brawled with men half his age and come out none too worse the wear. But as gratifying as the thought may be, Una couldn't risk so much as a scowl in his direction. He didn't have the power to dismiss her from the school. Only Superintendent Perkins did. But he could go sniveling to her about any perceived slight or flash of disobedience.

So Una folded her hands in her lap and trained her face muscles into a mask of quietude. She need only listen, or appear to be listening, and Dr. Pingry would have no charge to lay against her.

But when Dr. Pingry finally quit his spouting and asked the head nurse to pass out slates and chalk for the examination, Una's quietude vanished. Examination? If she failed, he'd have a legitimate gripe to take to Miss Perkins.

Una felt like a schoolgirl again, taking the slate and chalk in hand. Felt the same nettlesome whir in her stomach as she had before an arithmetic test or geography recitation. That she'd been a good pupil in those days, earning top marks for both her schoolwork and behavior, wouldn't help her one lick now. And though one failed examination might not be enough to get the other probationers expelled, Una had no doubt it would be enough for her.

"When I hold up a bone," Dr. Pingry told them, "write down its name, type, and location in the body. Afterward, you may have five minutes to review your answers before bringing me your slate for evaluation. Are there any questions?"

Yes, Una wanted to say. Why the hell didn't anyone mention an examination at the beginning of the lecture? Then she might actually have listened. She had to admire the doctor for this omission. It was the sort of wily trick a con man would use. But that didn't diminish her hatred for him either, nor calm her whirring insides.

Thank God Dru was seated beside her. As Dr. Pingry held up the first bone, Una feigned to write the answer while her gaze slid to Dru's slate. *Clavicle, long bone, located in the shoulder area.* Before Una could copy all that onto her slate, Dr. Pingry moved on to the next bone, and she was obliged to look up. It wouldn't do to be caught cheating.

He progressed all too quickly through a dozen bones. Some, like the vertebrae he'd made such a fuss about, Una recognized on her own. Most she had to copy from Dru. Years of thieving had trained her eyes to be quick, and what she didn't get on first glance, Una figured she could copy at the end during the time Dr. Pingry had allowed for review. But after the doctor set down the final bone, Dru took only a moment's gander at her slate before standing and presenting it for evaluation.

Una swallowed a curse and looked down at her slate. Only half the answers were complete. One or two she could guess at. The occipital bone looked like a flat bone . . . or maybe irregular . . . no, flat, and surely it was part of the skull. But most she could scarcely recall and had no idea about their positioning in the body. She shifted in her chair so she could peek at the slate of the woman seated to her other side. But she had fewer answers written down than Una. The responses she did have were nearly illegible. Una would have to cheat off of someone else's slate. But whose? Thanks to Dru, she was seated in the front with almost no options. A sidelong glance was one thing. Turning clear around to gawk at the slates of women behind her was another thing entirely.

What she needed was a commotion. Something to distract Dr. Pingry, the head nurse, and other goody-goodies who might squeal if they caught her cheating. But unlike the busy train station where someone or something was always kicking up a fuss, the nurses' home was decidedly lacking in commotions.

"One more minute," Dr. Pingry said.

The whir in Una's stomach became a riot. The blank lines and half-written answers on her slate went in and out of focus. She needn't tally her responses to know there was too little white amid so much black. And too little time. No hope waiting for a commotion. She'd have to cause one herself.

A line had begun to form, crowding the small space between the front row of seats and display table, as women waited to have their answers evaluated by the doctor. Una smiled. A crowd was the perfect cover. Now for the commotion. Another trainee approached from the back, slate in hand, and Una saw her chance. Just as the woman neared the table, Una stuck out her foot. The woman tripped, floundered forward, and collided with the table. The woman remained upright, but the table toppled, landing with a thwack on the wooden floor. Bones rolled and scattered.

Una leaped up and reached out to steady the woman. "Are you all right?"

"Yes, I . . ." The woman looked around at the mess, her cheeks turning the color of pickled beets. "I tripped over something and . . . oh, I'm so clumsy."

"Just a fold in the rug, I'm sure," Una said, giving the woman's arm a squeeze before glancing at the slate she held limp in her hand. "Here, I'll help you pick everything up."

Dr. Pingry grumbled and scowled as they righted the table. "Mind that nothing has broken."

The woman nodded, the color in her cheeks deepening. She set her slate down on the table as they began to gather up the bones. Una took her time retrieving ribs and vertebrae and other bones whose name she still hadn't learned, laying each carefully down on the table while surreptitiously glancing at the woman's slate. By the time all the bones were found, Una had memorized everything she needed to complete her answers. The woman thanked her profusely and got back in line. Una followed, filling in the blanks on her slate just in time to present it to Dr. Pingry.

Up close he smelled of cigar smoke and camphor. A breakfast crumb was tangled in his graying beard. He'd given the other trainees' slates only a cursory appraisal, check-marking the answers they got correct and striking through those that were wrong, all the while wearing a disinterested expression as if the women hardly warranted his time. Even when one of the women failed and pleaded with him in tears to retake the examination, he simply shooed her away, unmoved.

But Una's slate he scrutinized with interest, marking her incorrect responses with such thick, heavy lines she thought his chalk might break.

"But it *was* a vertebra," she said, pointing to one of the three answers he'd obliterated.

"Yes, but you failed to specify which type."

Una was sure he hadn't marked the other women's responses incorrect for the same omission, but she fought the urge to argue. She'd still gotten enough right to pass. And there were other ways to get even. When he handed back her slate, she slipped her other hand inside his suit coat and took his pocket watch as well.

That evening, Una lay on her bed dangling Dr. Pingry's watch above her. Dru was still downstairs in the library reading this or that medical text and wouldn't be up until they turned off the gas at ten. It wasn't a particularly fine watch, more utilitarian than ornate, with no front lid and the initials *CJP* carved into the back. It might fetch her ten dollars, twelve at the most. Not that she'd dare venture into the city to hawk it. But having it here was a danger too. What if Mrs. Buchanan went rifling through her things and found it? It violated rule number nineteen: Never steal something you can't sell, and also the new rule she'd set for herself about not pilfering anything while she was in hiding.

Una sighed and dragged herself out of bed. It had been almost second nature, dipping into the doctor's pocket. And served him

right for grading her unfairly. But she had to be more careful.
More to the point, she had to be smart. She'd come within a hair-
breadth again of being expelled, and she couldn't rely on Dru always being on hand with the correct answers.

She opened up the lid of her trunk and made a small tear in the
cotton lining along one of the sides. She slipped the pocket watch
through the tear. It slithered down between the lining and wood,
striking the bottom of the trunk with a clang. Not a perfect hidey-
hole, but at least out of sight. She closed the trunk and plodded
downstairs even though she'd much rather dress for bed.

A dozen women sat scattered about the library. Some flipped
through magazines. Others played chess or cards. Two chatted
quietly by the dwindling fire. She spotted Dru at one of the tables,
a thick textbook splayed open before her. Una thought again of her
soft bed or how nice it would be to stick her feet out beside the fire.
But she willed herself across the room to Dru. The textbook was
open to a diagram of the sternum and rib cage. Hadn't she gotten
enough of bones for one day? Una wanted to ask. Instead she said,
"Can I join you?"

Dru looked up with delight. "Of course."

CHAPTER 20

⟹◦⟸

Two days later, Una arrived at ward six to find the second-year seated on a stool with her head cradled in her hands. A bucket was wedged between her knees. She glanced up at Una with bloodshot eyes, then grimaced and threw up into the bucket. Una fetched a damp cloth, returning just as the second-year threw up again.

"Are you all right?" Una asked. "Perhaps you should lie down a moment."

The second-year shook her head.

"Shall I go find Nurse Hatfield?"

"No!"

Una took a step back at the sharp reply. She'd never heard the second-year speak above a whisper.

"I'm fine," she said more quietly. "It will pass, I just need a moment."

Her face was pale and beaded with sweat. Her legs trembled around the bucket. Whatever ailed her, it likely wouldn't pass in a moment or anytime soon, but Una let her be and went about her work.

Though they were assigned the same ward, she and the second-year hadn't interacted much. Una wasn't even sure of her name. Miss Caddy? Miss Catson? Miss Carlisle? Whatever her name, she'd made it clear that Una was a lowly probationer, whose standing on the ward was barely above that of the workhouse helper women and the unwelcome rats. Una's job was to dust, make beds, roll bandages, attend to the personal cleanliness of the patients, and otherwise stay out of the way. Only when and *if* she passed her probation would Una be worth notice.

But that hadn't stopped Una from noticing her, and—come to think of it—the second-year had been acting strange the last few days. Resting often. Picking at her lunch. Popping in and out of the water closet.

Half an hour passed, and the second-year had managed to stand and attend to a few patients, only to rush back to her bucket. When she finished dry heaving, she waved Una over. "Mr. Kepler in bed four is having surgery in an hour. I'm supposed to accompany him." She winced and clutched her stomach as if she might retch again. "If I'm not well enough to attend, I need you to go in my stead."

"Are you mad? I haven't the slightest idea what to do in the operating theater."

"Another nurse will be there to assist the physicians. You need only wheel the patient upstairs and be on hand to fetch supplies."

"But I—"

"It's only a lithotomy procedure. It shouldn't take any longer than an hour."

"Nurse Hatfield would never countenance such a cracked plan."

"She won't know. You'll be back long before afternoon rounds."

Una crossed her arms and eyed the second-year head to toe. "Why don't you want Miss Hatfield to know you're sick? You ain't contagious, are you?"

"Of course not. It's just a passing—" She grimaced. "A passing trifle."

Suddenly it hit Una. "You're apron up!"

"Whatever are you talking about?"

She leaned closer and whispered, "In the family way."

"I most certainly am not." But a sudden flush of color from throat to forehead belied her words.

Consorting with men during a trainee's tenure at the school was strictly forbidden. A flirtatious smile was enough to get you expelled. A baby would do the trick quicker than you could let out your laces.

"They'll find out sooner or later," Una said, but not unkindly. She'd known dozens of women who'd found themselves in the same predicament and not always by choice. "Unless you mean to go to an abortionist."

The second-year shushed Una with her hand. "Four months, and I'll have my certificate. No one's going to find out unless you tell them. And God help me if you do, I'll—"

"I won't tell anyone. It's not their business no how."

The second-year looked relieved. "And you'll go with Mr. Kepler for his surgery?"

"You promise to give Nurse Hatfield a good report about me for the rest of my probation?"

She nodded.

"All right, I'll go, so long as it's like you say, and I won't have to do anything more than fetch supplies."

But the more the second-year described what Una was to do, the more unsettled her own stomach became. First, she must bathe the patient and dress him in a loose-fitting gown that could easily be removed once they reached the operating theater. Then a stretcher must be prepared, and the patient carried upstairs. When Mr. Kepler was situated on the operating table, Una must ensure that all of the following were on hand: towels, wash-hand basins, soap, hot and cold water, carbolic acid, carbolized oil, small bowls to receive the discharges, sponges, flannel and muslin bandages of various sizes, cotton wool, tow, lint, charpie, linen compresses, pins, needles, and thread.

"And make sure the sponges are free from sand or pieces of shell," the second-year reminded her as she readied Mr. Kepler on the stretcher. "During the procedure, the assisting nurse will hand you the bloodied sponges to clean. Wash them in cold water and squeeze them as dry as possible." She fussed with the bow at Una's neck and straightened her cap. "For heaven's sake, try to look competent and don't tell anyone you're a probationer."

If she was well enough to do so much bossing, maybe she was well enough to take the patient to surgery herself. Una was about to say so when the second-year hurried to the bucket and heaved up the last of her breakfast.

Two orderlies arrived, fitting long wooden poles through the side loops of the canvas stretcher Una had laid out beneath Mr. Kepler. They raised him unceremoniously from the bed and carried him from the ward. Una glanced back at the second-year. This was an awful plan. True, if Una didn't botch things, she'd have leverage. And with both Nurse Hatfield and Dr. Pingry eager for her expulsion, Una desperately needed an ally.

But if she made a mess of things, Una would get the boot right alongside the second-year. Not to mention this man's life was on the line. Picking people's pockets was one thing. Her marks were all fat chuffs anyway who could afford to be charitable. But Una didn't need the weight of Mr. Kepler's death hanging over her. Not when she already felt partially responsible for what happened to Traveling Mike. The skin on her arms prickled at the thought of him lying dead in that alley. Even though she hadn't any part in his murder, he wouldn't have been there if it wasn't for her.

Una rattled her head. The second-year was flapping her hands for Una to hurry along. Her expression—that of untempered desperation—didn't bolster Una's confidence. She took a deep breath, then scuttled off, following the orderlies through the interconnected wards, past the main hall, and into a tiny room.

"Get the door," one of the orderlies said to her.

Una looked around but didn't see any door. The orderly sighed and nodded to a latticework of metal folded like an accordion. When Una tugged, the metalwork unfolded into a floor-to-ceiling gate that closed them inside.

But what were they doing in such a small room? There'd

scarcely be space for the surgeon, never mind his equipment. And if Una remembered correctly from her tour of Bellevue that first day, operations took place on the fifth floor, not the first.

A moment later, Una had her answer. A creaking sounded above them, and the entire room lurched upward. Una gasped and braced herself against the wall. The orderlies chuckled.

"Ain't you ever been in an elevator before?" one of them asked.

Una straightened but kept a hand pressed flat against the wall just in case. "Of course I have," she lied. "I was caught off guard, is all."

The creak and whir of the machinery made her heart race while the strange sensation of moving upward roiled her already uneasy stomach. She had heard about ascending rooms in fancy hotels and stores, thinking you'd have to be mad to trust a few ropes and pulleys with the weight of an entire room. Had she known just what sort of death box she was stepping into, she'd have gladly taken the stairs.

When the elevator finally stopped, Una made sure there was solid ground on the other side of the gate before tugging it open. She stepped out on shaky legs. She'd ridden in an elevator. An elevator! She'd be a legend in the Points if they knew.

But Una had little time to relish in her triumph. The orderlies bustled with the stretcher down a short hallway and into a large oblong room. Sunlight streamed in through a bank of double-tall windows at the far end. Tiered seating curved halfway around the room, rising at a precarious pitch above the operating stage where a lone table sat.

Una's mouth went dry as a church wafer. Already men were crowding into the seats, pressed together shoulder to shoulder, and spilling onto the steps. The second-year had warned her that a few medical students might be in attendance to observe, but Una hadn't expected a floor-to-ceiling audience.

The orderlies hoisted Mr. Kepler onto the table, withdrawing the poles from the stretcher and then departing. Mr. Kepler too seemed overcome by the enormous room and gaggle of onlookers, glancing at Una with fearful, pleading eyes. She went over and took his hand. It was cold and sticky with sweat. Or was that her own sweat?

She realized she ought to act the part of a nurse and say something comforting, but she didn't trust her voice not to warble. Instead she gave his fingers a sound squeeze and bared her teeth in what she hoped was more smile than grimace.

"Who are you?" a female voice said behind her.

Una turned and saw a plump, heart-faced nurse staring at her. "I'm . . . er . . . Nurse Kelly . . . filling in for Nurse . . ." Damn it, Una had again forgotten the second-year's name.

"Nurse Cuddy?"

"Yes!"

"You've worked in the operating theater before?"

Una nodded, fearing how hollow *yes* would sound.

The nurse stared at her a moment, her eyes—already too small for her face—narrowing until they all but disappeared. "All right, then. Get to it."

Una nodded again and glanced about for the storeroom. Several doors opened off the theater stage. She picked one and walked confidently toward it. Nurse was a ruse like any other, after all. It only worked if you wore it well. The door she'd picked led to a dark broom closet. She closed it quietly and tried another. This one opened to a large storeroom stocked with various-sized basins, sponges, towels, and bandages of every sort. She filled her arms with all the supplies she could remember from Nurse Cuddy's long list and a few others just in case.

Back in the operating room, she laid everything out on a long table. At some point between mixing up a bowl of carbolized water and readying the washing basins for the sponges, Una's hands stopped trembling. In addition to setting out several bleeding-bowls, she filled a wooden tray with sawdust and placed it under the operating table. A floor slick with blood could cause the surgeon to slip, Nurse Cuddy had warned her.

She struggled to ignore the murmur of voices from the seats

above as she worked. The low hiss of the kettle set to boil on the small iron stove. But eventually, even her thudding pulse quieted.

When the assisting nurse finished readying her own table of shiny metal supplies, she came over and appraised Una's, sending her back to the storeroom for a few more sponges and another square of flannel. Then she sent her to fetch more water for the kettle, chastening her that the air must be kept moist and pure.

Just as Una returned with the water, the team of surgeons arrived, led by Dr. Pingry. Una froze, the kettle whining beside her. She'd been too preoccupied remembering how many towels and buckets and bandages were needed that she hadn't considered who might be performing the surgery. She shuffled back until her rear hit the wall, hoping to somehow blend in with the plaster. Surely he'd recognize her again and recall that she was a mere probationer with no business in the operating room.

But she may well have been an ornament on the wall for all the attention he gave her. He grabbed a blood-stained smock from a nearby peg and threw it on over his suit, walking right past the bowl of carbolized water she'd prepared to disinfect his hands. He stopped center stage beside the operating table and addressed the crowd of medical students.

"You are here today to witness a lithotomy for an unpassable bladder calculi. I will begin the procedure by . . ."

Unlike when he'd lectured to Una and the other nurse trainees, his voice now was resonant and lively. He spoke at length about the patient and his condition, gesturing to Mr. Kepler but never actually looking at him, as if he were no different from the table of bones he'd displayed for the trainees.

The two other doctors who had entered with him didn't bother with smocks but took off their suit jackets and rolled up their sleeves. Una winced, recognizing one as the young doctor who'd saved her from being expelled over the unfortunate brandy incident. Dare she hope he wouldn't notice her either?

Both men washed their hands in the bowl of carbolized water before joining Dr. Pingry beside the operating table. After he'd finished his bombastic description of the forthcoming procedure, Dr. Pingry introduced the two younger men as his senior and junior interns, Dr. Allen and Dr. Westervelt. Una noticed a wave of murmurs through the audience at the name Westervelt. The doctor whom Una recognized colored about the ears. She'd seen that name before, Westervelt, but couldn't remember where.

She refilled the kettle, then slunk along the wall back to her supply table, stepping as softly as possible to avoid notice.

Dr. Pingry turned from the audience to Mr. Kepler and scowled. "Why isn't the patient in the correct position, nurse?" He said this to the assisting nurse, who in turn glared at Una. She gave an apologetic smile.

Despite her evening study sessions with Dru, Una had no idea what a lithotomy actually was. While the assisting nurse wrangled Mr. Kepler's feet into stirrup-like contraptions that raised and spread his legs, Dr. Pingry turned back to the audience. "This is why women will never be surgeons. They'd just as soon enter the bladder from the mouth as the perineum." The medical students chuckled, and the nurse flashed Una another squinty-eyed glare.

"There," Dr. Pingry said, turning back to the operating table while still speaking loudly enough for the audience to hear. "Now that we are at last ready, my junior assistant will prepare and administer the ether while Dr. Allen assists with the procedure."

Not Dr. Westervelt, but "the junior assistant." Even Una registered the slight. She wondered if he felt the same way Una had under Marm Blei's heavy thumb, stifled and unappreciated. But his expression was impassive as he approached the supply table. He grabbed a towel and wad of cotton without looking at her and returned to the operating table. Una was both relieved and perturbed that he didn't notice her.

She watched him make a cone with the towel and a sheet of folded newsprint, then stuff the cotton inside. The assisting nurse handed him a bottle of ether. He placed the cone over Mr. Kepler's nose and mouth, instructing him to breathe in deeply as he dropped ether onto the cotton through the top of the cone. Soon

Mr. Kepler's hands unclenched, and his entire body relaxed like one asleep.

"He's ready," Dr. Westervelt said, and the procedure began.

Aside from cleaning a few bloodied sponges, Una had little to do. She stood on her tiptoes so she could watch as Dr. Pingry made a small incision beneath Mr. Kepler's scrotum. She didn't wince at the blood and was amazed when Dr. Pingry, after much pontificating, removed a jagged yellow stone the size of a peach pit. He held it up for the audience to see, and several in the audience grimaced and squirmed.

When Dr. Pingry pulled several wax ligatures from the buttonhole of his lapel and began to stitch up the incision, Una's attention drifted back to Dr. Westervelt. He'd stood intently at the head of the operating table throughout the procedure, occasionally administering another few drops of ether. She seldom found well-bred men handsome. Their skin was too pallid and their knuckles too smooth. They walked straight-backed and square-shouldered with unearned swagger. But for a man of this class, Dr. Westervelt wasn't entirely unpleasant to look upon. Beneath his polished exterior, Una sensed a certain grit.

He glanced up from the table and met her gaze. Una hastily looked away as a flush of heat crept up her neck. With the surgery concluded, Dr. Pingry dismissed the antsy crowd. He tossed his smock, further bloodied, onto Una's table and rinsed his hands in a bowl of water.

"See that any discharges from the wound are cleaned away at once," he said without looking at her. "And keep a strict accounting of the urine he passes." Then he exited the operating room, Dr. Allen and Dr. Westervelt in tow. Una breathed easier than she had since stepping onto the elevator. She'd done it! Una Kelly, thief in hiding, had made it through an entire surgery disguised as a nurse. If she could manage this, surely nothing could stand in the way of her passing probation.

CHAPTER 21

Una's elation at having survived the operating theater lingered through the following day and the next. She didn't grumble dragging herself from bed in the predawn darkness. She didn't roll her eyes waiting for mealtime prayer to end so they could finally eat. She didn't yawn conspicuously listening to Dru prattle on about her day. The genius of her plan—to hide at the school until things on the streets cooled down—was irrefutable. Never mind that only a few days before she'd been so fed up with Nurse Hatfield and Dr. Pingry she was ready to handcuff herself and walk straight to the nearest police station.

Three days on, however, Una's cheer, if not her resolve, had begun to wear thin. Morning sickness still plagued Nurse Cuddy, and not just in the mornings but throughout the day, leaving Una to scurry about the ward preparing fomentations, applying leeches, and dressing wounds in addition to her usual duties. What she'd thought she'd gained by covering for Miss Cuddy in the operating room—namely an alliance in which she held all the trump cards—proved to be a more complicated and less beneficial relationship. Una was now complicit in Miss Cuddy's secret. A fact Miss Cuddy could and would use against her. "But Miss Kelly knew all along," was all she need say, and Una would find herself back in Miss Perkins's office and, shortly thereafter, on the streets. Yet another reminder why Una should keep to herself. After all, she had secrets enough to bear.

A new patient arrived on the ward just after midday. "Was mindin' me own business when a horse and buggy came outta nowhere and run over me leg," the man told Una as she settled him into a bed. But judging from the strong smell of whiskey on his breath and the shabby state of his clothes, he'd likely passed out in the gutter after a night of drinking and been mistaken for a pile of trash. Lucky for him it was his leg and not his head in the wheel's path. As it was, his lower leg—or tibia and fibula, as Una now knew thanks to Dru's tutelage—was shattered and tomorrow would have to be amputated.

She cut off the man's trousers and helped him out of his muddy shirt and coat. He smelled not only of liquor but of horseshit and sweat. His head and his nether regions teemed with lice. One look at him, and Nurse Cuddy was suddenly and conveniently too ill to help bathe him. Instead, she sat by, cataloging the man's meager belongings as Una fetched soap and water and scrubbed the man clean.

It reminded Una of her younger years, after her mother's death, when her father would pass out drunk in his own vomit, leaving her with a bleak choice: clean up the mess or inhale the sour smell all night long. She'd hated her father in those moments. Hated the war and all the soldiers who came back whole, while her father left the better part of himself behind. Hated her mother for dying and leaving her in his blundering care.

Una had been nine when her mother died in a tenement fire. The blaze began from an unwatched oven in the basement bakery. The building, some thirty years old and constructed entirely of wood, was quickly consumed in flame. Earlier that year, the city had passed a law requiring all tenements to have fire escapes—a law many landlords soundly ignored. So there had been no escape for her mother and the needy family she'd gone to visit until the firemen arrived with their ladders.

They'd argued about it, Una's parents, just the night before.

Why did she insist on goin' out into the meanest parts of the city, her father had said, helpin' those that ought right help themselves, stretching their own food and money thin?

"'Tis the goodly thing to do," her mother replied. Then—so quietly Una, listening through her bedroom wall, could hardly hear—she said, "'Tis my money anyway. You haven't worked in weeks."

A bottle smashed against the wall then, sending Una scrambling back into bed. The front door slammed. A few moments later, she heard the swish of the broom, the tinkle of glass, and the muffled sound of her mother's tears.

Una jogged her head. She hadn't thought of such things in years. Her nerves crackled like live embers beneath her skin. No point in wasting time on things done and gone, she reminded herself. But she couldn't shake the feeling that maybe she'd been unfair in her anger.

When she'd finished the man's bath, Miss Cuddy handed Una a cotton sack with the man's belongings. "Nothing but tattered clothes and instruments of the devil. Take it all outside to the waste dump."

Instruments of the devil? That was sharp censure coming from a woman apron up and not married. But Una didn't say so. Nor did she complain that her feet were tired, back sore, and nerves raw. Never mind that she'd already made two trips to the dump that morning. She took the sack and headed for the stairs. Whatever these *instruments* were, Una wanted to know.

Instead of heading to the overflowing waste barrels in the back yard, Una exited onto the front lawn overlooking the East River. She'd swam in the river as a girl, diving for bananas and other exotic fruits that spilled over the brimming decks of the ships arriving from the Caribbean. After she'd left her father and was on her own, she joined a gang of river pirates who were impressed with her dauntless swimming. In the cover of night and fog, they'd row with muffled oars along the wharves, casing the sailing vessels moored along the river. When they found one to their liking, the men would climb aboard and grab whatever loot they could carry one-handed down the rope ladder back to the rowboat. Una's job was to dive for whatever they dropped. It was dangerous work, as you had to be on the lookout for both coppers patrolling the river and the ship's crew. One boy, little older than herself, was thrown overboard by an irate coxswain and drowned before they could reach him.

Una leaned against a tree and rummaged through the sack. It hadn't been the boy's death, nor the constant threat of arrest, nor the icy chill of the water that had driven Una to other means of grifting after only a few nights with the gang. She'd left when she realized, according to the men's harebrained calculations, a wee thing and lass to boot wasn't entitled to but a paltry share of the spoils.

Her fingers brushed the cool smoothness of a bottle. Whiskey, judging from the patient's breath. She rattled the bottle inside the sack. No more than a swig or two remained. She also found a small pouch of tobacco. Instruments of the devil indeed. Una smirked and glanced about for someplace hidden to enjoy them.

A broad entrance beneath the north wing of the hospital caught her eye. She peeked inside. Eight hardtop wagons were parked one beside the other in a large open bay, each painted black with the word AMBULANCE emblazoned in gold along the side. One of the wagons—No. 3 according to the designation painted on its front panel—already had a horse harnessed to the chassis.

In the far corner of the bay sat a man in a black uniform. His legs were propped up on a low stool and his cap was pulled over his eyes. Una started to turn away when the fire-gong mounted on the back wall suddenly sounded. The sleeping man startled awake and scrambled to his feet, hurrying to a small table where a telegraph receiver sat. The fire-gong sounded twelve times, then a short string of clicks chirped from the receiver.

Una heard footfalls clomp behind her. She flattened against the wall just inside the entrance and watched from the shadows as a doctor hurried down the front steps of the hospital. He carried a large black surgical bag. The man who'd taken down the telegraph message was already seated on the driver's bench, reins in hand, by the time the physician reached the ambulance and clambered into the back with his bag.

The driver made a clicking sound with his teeth, shook the reins, and the ambulance sped out of the bay. Una's skirt fluttered in its wake. The wagon dashed across the yard in front of the hospital and out the unfinished gatehouse, sounding its bell as it turned down Twenty-Sixth Street. Passersby scrambled out of the way.

She watched until the ambulance disappeared from view, then tiptoed deeper inside. The bay sat quiet and seemingly empty now. A large clock ticked high above on the wall, reminding her that Miss Cuddy would soon be griping at Una's long absence. Let her gripe, Una decided, heading past the line of wagons. She deserved a moment of peace after bustling about all morning attending to both of their duties.

A stable adjoined the far end of the bay. Hay crunched beneath her boots, and horses whickered as she passed. The air smelled of dust and horse sweat and manure, but it was a pleasant change from the commingled scents of dying flesh and disinfectant on the wards.

Una found an empty stall and slipped inside, skirting the piles of dung. After a furtive glance over the walls at the neighboring stalls, she reached into the sack and pulled out the man's liquor bottle. A flea had hopped from the man's filthy clothes onto her shirtsleeve. She flicked it away and used her sleeve to wipe the mouth of the bottle. The whiskey burned her throat as she swallowed.

Little over a month had passed since she'd drunk that stale, weak beer at the bar, counting down the minutes before meeting Traveling Mike, but it seemed like half a lifetime ago. She drained the last few drops of whiskey, letting them settle on her tongue before swallowing.

She'd been too preoccupied escaping and evading the coppers to notice any of the ill effects of drying out. If there'd been any at all. Una had never been a boozer. Not like some of the cons she knew. Not after seeing what it had done to her father. But the whiskey, rotten as it was, tasted divine. Like her old life. She upturned the bottle one more time, shaking it in vain above her open mouth. Then she rummaged through the sack for the man's tobacco, rolling the last of his leaves into a squat cigarette before realizing she didn't have any matches. She upended the sack onto the ground and squatted over its spilled contents. He must have a matchbook stowed somewhere.

"Can I help ya?"

Una started, falling back onto her rear, just missing a pile of horseshit. A man with orangish-blond hair stood in the doorway of the stall. His black trousers matched those of the driver she'd seen earlier, but instead of a brass-buttoned jacket, he wore only a flannel undershirt and suspenders.

"I . . . er . . ." Una stuffed the scattered clothes and empty liquor bottle back into the sack. Where was the damned cigarette? She looked around the mess of hay but couldn't find it. "I was just taking these things to the waste barrels and got a little lost."

The man extended his hand and helped her up. "I'll say. You one of them new probationers?"

Una nodded. She heard the faintest trace of a brogue in his vowels, like one who'd left Ireland very young or took great pains to hide his accent. "I best be on my way," she said, brushing her hands on her apron. "If you'd be so kind as to direct me toward the dump."

He didn't move, his broad frame blocking the doorway of the stall, his pale blue eyes fixed on her like tar on a sail. Una fought back a shudder.

"Forgive me for staring, but ya look mighty familiar," he said.

Una's heart plummeted into her stomach. Did he know her from the slums? Had he somehow seen her photograph in the rogues' gallery? He was a large man, with arms and shoulders muscled like a boxer's. His hands were workman's hands, strong and callused. But Una rarely forgot a face. One good look at a man, and she could recall the cut of his chin or crook of his nose years later. This man, she didn't know. It unsettled her all the more that he seemed to know her.

She shimmied around him and started toward the ambulance bay.

"Wait, ya dropped something." The man trotted after her, holding up the cigarette.

Una grabbed it and stuffed it inside the sack. "What instruments of the devil these patients bring in with them." Her voice sounded more thin than pious, but the man nodded.

"I hear ya. Satan's circus, this city is."

Una nodded, too emphatically, and started again for the exit. The man kept pace beside her. "What's your name, if ya don't mind me asking?"

"Miss Kelly," she said without looking at him. She didn't want to give him any more chances to connect her face with whatever memory it was attached to.

"Kelly, eh?" He seemed to ponder the name a moment, and she wished she'd had the sense to lie. They were halfway through the ambulance bay when he stopped and slapped his thigh. "That's it. That's where I seen ya."

Una stopped too. Her heart now beat somewhere near her toes. It was nearly two hundred yards from the ambulance bay to the half-built hospital gate. She could run, but she'd never make it to the street before he caught her. Instead, she slowly turned to face him.

"St. Stephen's," he said, grinning.

"I'm sorry?"

"Kelly. You're Irish, right? I saw you at mass last Sunday at St. Stephen's. Second to last pew if my memory serves me."

Una exhaled. She had indeed been at St. Stephen's last Sunday, the first time she attended mass in years. The other women at the nurses' home who hadn't been called to the wards had scattered to their Episcopal and Congregational and Reform Dutch churches. It would have seemed suspicious had Una not done the same. The incense had stung her eyes. The weak wine and stale wafer roiled her stomach. Or maybe it was the specter of her mother chanting *Credo in unum Deum* and *Agnus Dei* beside her.

"I'm Conor McCready," the man said, holding out his hand until Una shook it. His skin was warm and not as rough as it had seemed. "Glad to see they're letting our kind into the school now."

Una managed only a thin smile. Miss Hatfield certainly wasn't glad, and Una suspected she wasn't the only one. "You . . . er . . . work here?"

"Ambulance driver," he said with a proud smile. "Let me show you around."

Una hesitated. She really ought to get back to the ward to help Miss Cuddy. But part of her was curious too. How many times had an ambulance's gong sounded in the slums, or the shiny black wagon raced past her on the street, and Una wondered what was going on inside?

She glanced at the clock ticking high on the wall. Two hours before Nurse Hatfield made her rounds. "All right, just a quick peek, then."

Mr. McCready—Conor, he insisted—walked her around the nearest ambulance, describing how it was made from the best and lightest-weight materials. The cabin sat high above the wheels so the patient was less apt to be jostled about on uneven roads. Gas lanterns and reflectors helped with night travel. He let her climb onto the cushioned driver's bench and depress the foot pedal that sounded the warning gong. It echoed through the bay and stables, making the horses stomp and whinny.

She climbed down, and Conor brought her around to the back of the wagon. The cabin had a moveable floor, he told her, that could be drawn out to receive patients. He climbed inside and offered her a hand. Una waved him off.

"I better not," she said, affecting a shy smile. "Superintendent Perkins wouldn't approve."

His pale cheeks colored slightly. "Oh, of course."

Superintendent Perkins would not have approved of her climbing onto the driver's seat and sounding the gong either. She wouldn't approve of her being here at all, Una suspected. But a twinge of unease in her stomach—probably from the sour whiskey—made her glad to have a ready excuse not to climb in beside him.

She watched from the ground as he pointed to a bench for the surgeon and another for the patient, if he were well enough to sit. The cabin also stored a stretcher and a wooden box stocked with splint material, oakum, handcuffs, a stomach pump, a straitjacket, and a quart of brandy. Other supplies, he told her, like bandages and a tourniquet were kept in the surgeon's bag. From the carefully arranged cabinet to the mud-free wheels to the polished side panels, it was clear Conor took great pride in the wagon and was meticulous in its upkeep.

He climbed down and latched the back gate, boasting no one knew the city's layout better than him and the other drivers. "There isn't a street or alley or turnabout we don't know. And we're quick too. Why, I can cover a mile in five minutes flat. Less if it ain't the business district."

Una apparently did not look duly impressed, for he quickly added, "The coaches and broughams I bet you're used to traveling in don't break a ten-minute mile, if that."

Unless she counted the police wagon, Una hadn't ridden in a carriage for years. Certainly nothing as fancy as a coach. But she wasn't about to correct him. "Is that so? I confess, I never paid much mind to how fast I was traveling. But thank goodness you do, seeing as you drive with such noble purpose."

His cheeks colored again.

"I better be getting back to the ward. Thank you for the tour."

"My pleasure, Miss Kelly. I'll see you Sunday at St. Stephen's, then. Maybe we might share a pew."

Una staved off a grimace and nodded. She'd hoped to double back to the nurses' home after everyone was gone to church and steal another hour of sleep. So much for playing hooky. Besides, it seemed wise to stay on friendly terms with Conor. Una had enough enemies.

CHAPTER 22

⟫⟶◦⟵⟪

Una plopped down beside Dru at the table in the library. "What's on the docket for tonight?"

"Dr. Janssen is giving a lecture on the vascular system tomorrow, so I figured we ought to do a little primer."

Una sat back and loosened the laces of her boots. She hadn't any idea what the vascular system was but knew Dru would soon enlighten her. If having to slow down and explain things— sometimes two or three times—bothered Dru, she made no show of it. She always left room for Una at her table and had two cups of warmed milk and honey for them to sip while they studied. Una would have preferred brandy or at least strong coffee. But not since early childhood had anyone bothered to make Una a cup of anything, so she wasn't about to complain.

The other probationers didn't take to Dru any kindlier than they did to Una. Sure, Dru yapped as much as a Tammany politician on election day. And used a roll instead of her knife to steer peas onto her fork like all countryfolk did. (Better than her fingers, which Una would just assume use if she weren't trying to be ladylike.) And was cheerier than anyone in their right mind ought to be. But Una suspected the real reason was jealousy. Pure and simple. She could see it in the other women's pinched faces every time Dru answered a question correctly or got full marks on an examination.

Petty fools the lot of them—which suited Una fine. She had Dru and her big brain all to herself.

But tonight, Dru didn't seem quite herself. She wore a heavy, closed-lipped smile instead of her usual bright one. Her gaze wandered restlessly about the room. Mr. Gray's book of anatomy— usually already opened to the exact page they needed, with several others marked for reference—sat pushed back and closed. Instead of opening it, Dru circled a spoon through her milk, round and round and round, long past the point of dissolving the honey. The steady tinkle of the spoon against the cup harried Una's nerves and drew stares from across the room. When at last Dru set aside the spoon, she didn't even drink but pushed the cup and saucer away.

Una grabbed the book and thumbed through the pages to the table of contents. The Vascular System, a general anatomical introduction, page seventy-five. The introduction began with several drawings of tubelike structures, some straight and banded, others branching out and twisting like tree roots. Dru glanced at the drawings, then quickly away.

"Okay, what's wrong?" Una said.

"Hmm?"

"You're not acting at all like yourself."

Dru straightened and dredged up another halfhearted smile. "It's nothing. I'm sorry. Where were we?"

"We haven't even begun."

Dru reached for the book, but Una got to it first, leaning forward and planting her elbows atop the pages. "It's not nothing."

"Careful, you'll wrinkle the pages."

Una grabbed the corner of the top page and started to tear it from the spine. Dru stayed her hand. "Okay, okay . . . it's just, well, the vascular system."

"You got something against the vascular system?"

"Not the whole system. Just . . . well . . . blood."

Una started to laugh but then, registering the pained expression on Dru's face, faked a cough instead. "Blood?"

"Shh!" Dru looked over at the trainees seated at the other end of the library, then leaned closer. "The sight of it makes me sick. Once I actually fainted."

"But you grew up on a farm. There must have been blood everywhere. Pig blood and chicken blood and goat blood and—"

Dru shushed her again, but the first sign of a real smile played on her lips. "It's not animal blood that gives me trouble. Only human."

"That's why you turned all pasty-faced our first day at the hospital. What have you done since? You must be sick all the time on the ward."

"I haven't seen much blood. I mean, not really. Not up close. Have you?"

Una thought back to the operating theater: the dirty sponges, the surgeon's slick hands, the slow stream of blood trickling off the table into the trough of sawdust below. And then there were all the bloodied dressings she'd changed while Miss Cuddy was off retching into a bucket. Most probationers, Una realized, had spent the last three weeks doing little more than dusting. "Er . . . not much. A spot on the sheets now and then."

"Even that doesn't bother me. Once it's out of the body, that is. It's just seeing it flow out of the body that—" She stopped and gagged. "Oh, Una. What am I going to do? If I get sick or swoon on duty, I'll be expelled for sure."

Not necessarily, Una thought wryly. But then, Miss Cuddy's infirmness was only temporary. "You didn't think about this when you applied to be a nurse?"

"Of course I did. But I wanted to be a nurse so badly. I thought . . . I *hoped* once I got here my affliction might be cured."

This time, Una did laugh. "You thought by seeing *more* blood you'd suddenly get better?"

"Well . . . yes. Like the more times you eat brussels sprouts, the less awful they taste."

Una had never heard of brussels sprouts, let alone eaten them. If she didn't like the taste of something, she spat it out and didn't touch the food again. But maybe Dru had a point. Like during her stint at Blackwell's Island. One night sleeping on that flea-ridden straw and she itched so badly she'd have peeled off her skin with a razor if one were at hand. But by the end of her stretch, she hardly noticed the bites.

"Maybe I should just hand my resignation in to Miss Perkins now and spare myself the embarrassment," Dru said and began to cry.

Una searched through her pockets and handed Dru her hankie. "Don't be ridiculous."

But it was clear from Dru's crying, which progressed now into full-fledged sobbing, that she was serious. What would Una do if Dru *did* leave? Whose tests would she cheat from? Who would help her understand all this medical jabber? What kind of noisome woman would take Dru's place as her roommate?

Una couldn't let that happen. She swiveled in her chair to face Dru, reaching out a tentative hand. What was she supposed to do with this blubbering mess? How was she supposed to comfort her? Thieves didn't cry. Not unless it was a part of their act. Didn't matter if they were men, women, or children. Una gave Dru's shoulder a few quick pats the way she'd seen coachmen do with an unsettled horse.

Dru took that as an invitation to hug Una and sob all over her collar. Una tensed. The women across the room gawked and whispered. Una returned their unkind stares until they looked away. She recalled how her mother had rubbed her back in slow, steady circles when Una was sick and did the same for Dru. At first, her crying intensified—loud and shuddering—and Una feared she'd done something wrong. But after a minute or so, Dru calmed, and her tears slowed.

She drew back and wiped her cheeks. "I don't know what I'll do if I can't be a nurse. It's all I've ever wanted since the first time I—"

"I know, I know. Since the first time you read that Miss Eveningbird's—"

"Nightingale."

"Nightingale's book. Don't you think there were things she wasn't good at when she first started nursing over there in . . ."

"Crimea."

"Crimea. Exactly. Why, I bet she couldn't tell an under sheet from an upper sheet. And you know Miss Hatfield would find issue with the way she tucked in her corners."

Dru chuckled. She dabbed her eyes once more, then handed Una back her hankie. "Thank you. I'm so lucky to have a friend like you."

Una's shoulders, which had only just begun to loosen from her ears, tightened again. "I . . . It's nothing."

"I still don't know what I'm going to do, though."

"How many times have you been sickened like this?"

"Twice."

"Only twice?"

"After fainting that time when I was thirteen, I've been careful to look away at the first sight of blood."

"Thirteen! You mean to tell me it's been a decade since all this happened?"

Dru nodded sheepishly.

"Hell—er—goodness, you might be cured already."

"Do you think so? It doesn't seem like the sort of thing that just goes away."

"Only one way to find out."

Una grabbed Dru's hand and dragged her to the kitchen. The room was empty, but she could hear Cook Prynne puttering around in the cellar below. No time for ceremony, then. She seated Dru on a low stool—less distance to fall if she swooned—and rummaged through the drawers and cupboards.

"What are you doing?" Dru asked behind her, a note of unease in her voice.

"You'll see." She found a knife, tested its sharpness, then sliced the pad of her pinky finger. The cut stung, but only a little. She hadn't gone very deep. More importantly, a steady stream of blood trickled down her finger. She turned from the cupboard with her hand outstretched.

"Una, you've cut your—" Dru rose, wobbled, and quickly sat back down. Her face had gone the color of ash. She started to turn her head.

"No, don't turn away. Look."

Dru winced, but trained her eyes on Una's finger. She lasted six seconds—Una counted under her breath—before whipping her face away and clutching her stomach.

"It's hopeless," Dru said between uneven breaths.

"Nonsense." Una washed away the blood at the sink. The cold water stung her finger anew. Six seconds. Certainly not a feat to brag about, but it was a start.

She'd spied a bottle of cooking sherry at the back of one of the cupboards when looking for the knife and poured Dru a small glass. After a few sips, Dru looked well enough to stand. They snuck into the demonstration room, and Una grabbed a scrap of tow from one of the shelves. She handed it to Dru. "You do it."

"But I can't."

"The cut is hardly bleeding anymore. Besides, you said you wanted to be a nurse, right?"

Reluctantly, Dru took the tow in one hand and Una's pinky finger in the other. Her skin was clammy, and her hand trembled. She bound Una's finger with all the grace of a drunken ox.

Una laughed, examining her handiwork. Here was a woman who could recite every bone in the body, who knew the difference in exact degrees between a cool and temperate bath, who could mix a bowl of antiseptic faster than anyone at the school, and she couldn't dress a simple cut.

"Hopeless, like I said."

Una held out her hand. The loose dressing sagged. "On the contrary, it's a thing of beauty."

Dru's expression tottered. Una winced, fearing another crying fit. Instead, Dru laughed. Una joined in, laughing until her ribs ached.

"No more talk of resigning, you hear?" Una said when their laughter petered out. "We'll get you used to the sight of blood one way or another."

"Not before you run out of fingers."

Una feared she was right.

CHAPTER 23

Each night for the next three days, Una and Dru stole into the kitchen and performed the same test. Six seconds stretched into eight and ten and then fifteen. Dru protested each time that it was madness for Una to cut herself on her behalf and thanked her profusely afterward, saying she'd never had a better friend.

Una wished she'd knock it off with this friend business. It gave her dyspepsia. This wasn't friendship. It was business. If Una was to stay in the training program, Dru had to stay too.

But fifteen seconds staring at a measly finger wound wasn't the same as seeing a man whose leg had been gnawed off by a machine or assisting as the surgeon operated. Eventually Una *would* run out of fingers, and she wasn't about to go cutting anyplace else. No, they needed a more radical plan to cure Dru once and for all.

Una thought about this the next day on the ward as she helped Nurse Cuddy—whose morning sickness had finally begun to ease—prepare a patient for an enema. Perhaps she and Dru could sneak into the operating theater during a procedure. But two extra nurses—whether squeezed in among the gawking medical students or standing off to the side of the stage—were sure to draw notice. They might ride out with Conor in the ambulance. But there was no guarantee whatever emergency they were called to would involve blood. They could sneak into a bar in the Bowery or Hell's Kitchen. A fistfight was sure to break out once everyone got good and liquored. But Una couldn't risk being seen in either of those places, and she suspected Dru would sooner quit the training program than step into a saloon.

"Hold him still," Nurse Cuddy said, pulling Una from her thoughts. They had rolled the patient onto his side with his knees drawn up. Una cradled the man while Miss Cuddy delivered the enema: milk and eggs thickened with arrowroot to supplement what little nourishment the man could take by mouth.

Dr. Pingry and his interns arrived soon after for rounds. While they quizzed Nurse Cuddy about this patient's elevated heart rate or that patient's pus-filled wound, Una snuck off to do her own chores—dusting and bed making and bandage rolling. But her gaze drifted back to the men, Dr. Westervelt in particular. She was sure he'd recognized her last week in the operating theater. Why hadn't he said anything to Dr. Pingry or Nurse Hatfield? She didn't trust a man who had dirt on someone and didn't use it to his advantage. Then again, what advantage was there to getting her expelled? Perhaps he hadn't mentioned the incident to her or her superiors because in his hoity-toity world she, a probationer, was insignificant.

Una plunged her dust rag into the bowl of disinfectant with more force than intended. Carbolized water sloshed over the sides, spilling onto her apron. She heard a low chuckle and turned to see Dr. Westervelt gawking at her, covering his laughter with a fist.

No one else seemed to have noticed. They stood around a nearby bed peering at a sickly patient who'd only yesterday been up and lively. "An early case of pyemia," Dr. Pingry was saying. "Wouldn't you agree, Dr. Westervelt? . . . Dr. Westervelt?"

He cleared his throat, returning his gaze to the patient. "Yes . . . er . . . most assuredly."

"And what treatment regimen would you recommend?" Dr. Pingry's voice was sharp.

"Er . . . debride the wound and irrigate it with a disinfectant of five percent carbolic acid."

"Not cupping or bleeding?"

Una moved closer with her rag, absentmindedly dusting a nearby table as she listened to their conversation. If they bled this man, that could be the ticket to curing Dru of her squeamishness. Una would only need to sneak her over to watch. But glancing sideways at the men, she saw Dr. Westervelt draw in a tight breath like a man steeling his courage.

"No," he said. "I would recommend neither of those things."

Dr. Pingry seemed to puff up like a toadstool. Clearly he wasn't used to being told no. "You and your modern notions. Your grandfather cured many a man of pyemia, and he did so without listening to the council of charlatans like that damned Lister. Your father, on the other hand . . ." He let his voice trail off, then turned to Miss Cuddy. "Half an hour of dry cupping will do wonders for this man. See to it straightaway."

Dr. Westervelt's neck had reddened at the mention of his father. Had the conversation happened in an alley over a game of pins, it would have ended in fisticuffs, Una ventured. But then, neither man seemed the back-alley type.

Dr. Pingry patted his waistcoat and grumbled. "Still can't find my damned watch."

"It's eleven thirty, sir," Dr. Westervelt said, pointing to the wall clock hanging nearby.

"I'm perfectly capable of reading the time. Let's break for lunch. And I suppose you'll be wanting to take part in all that transfusion nonsense this afternoon."

"Yes, sir. If possible, sir."

Dr. Pingry turned his narrowed eyes upon the senior intern Dr. Allen, who hadn't the courage to speak but only nod.

"Very well. But mark my words, the infirm require less blood, not more."

Una, who'd continued to listen to their conversation as she

dusted, perked up at the mention of blood again. Nonsense or not, whatever this transfusion was, she and Dru must attend.

Dr. Pingry strode from the ward, Dr. Allen following at his heels. Dr. Westervelt remained behind. He took another gander at the man's wound before reapplying the dressing. "Some beef tea too," he said to Miss Cuddy. "If he'll take it. And a charcoal poultice for the wound. After you've finished the cupping, of course."

Miss Cuddy nodded and hurried to the storeroom. Dr. Westervelt turned to go.

"Doctor," Una called, remembering her quiet-as-a-mouse nurse voice only after several nearby patients startled awake. She reassured them with an apologetic smile and hurried after the doctor.

He stopped beside the door, his somber expression brightening. "Miss Kelly, what can I do for you?"

Drat, he remembered her name. Better if she were just one, indistinct face among the sea of nurses scurrying about. But speaking boldly to Dr. Pingry, sneaking into the operating theater, and spilling carbolized water all over herself didn't exactly help her blend in.

"You and Dr. Pingry were speaking about a transfusion. What is that?"

"We take the blood of one man and give it to another."

"All of it?"

He laughed, his too-perfect teeth flashing. "No, only a little."

"How?"

"Cannulas are inserted into both men's veins and connected by a long tube. The blood of the donor flows into the veins of the other man."

Una grimaced. Maybe Dr. Pingry was right. This transfusion procedure sounded like something out of *Frankenstein*. "Are they dead?"

Another laugh. "No, I assure you, both parties are very much alive."

However monstrous the procedure sounded, it was the perfect opportunity to fix Dru. "And it's happening this afternoon?"

THE NURSE'S SECRET   159

"Why? Do you plan on sneaking in to watch like you did in the operating theater?"

The hint of a smile betrayed his mocking tone, and though she couldn't quite tell if he fancied her or simply thought her strange, now was the time to seize whatever advantage she had. She looked down at her feet a moment, then flickered her gaze shyly upward. "Actually, I was hoping you would take me. And my . . . er . . . classmate, Drusilla. Nurse Hatfield would never permit it otherwise. My classmate and I, we're both quite interested in matters of the vascular system."

Dr. Westervelt eyed her with suspicion. "Is that so?"

She continued her coquettish game, shuffling a foot over the floorboards and looking away, only to boldly meet his eye again. "It would be most edifying to watch the procedure alongside so esteemed a physician as yourself."

"'Esteemed'?" His expression darkened. "I think perhaps you mean my grandfather."

Una floundered. She might as well have stepped knee-deep in manure. "I . . ."

He started to walk away.

"I care as much about your lineage, Dr. Westervelt, as I do a flea on a horse's rear." She winced at the ill-chosen expression but continued with the truth. "I . . . I very much wanted to see that procedure, and you're the least odious physician I know."

He stopped but didn't turn around. Una cursed under her breath. She should never have let her mouth run like that. Calling a doctor odious, even if he were only a junior intern, was not the sort of nurse-like behavior Miss Perkins would condone. He shook his head slowly, and Una cursed again, her stomach plummeting. But then, instead of turning around and berating her or stomping upstairs to the superintendent's office, he chuckled again.

"Very well. I'll speak to Nurse Hatfield about the procedure," he said over his shoulder. "But you must do me a favor in return."

Una hesitated. Rule number fifteen: Never indenture yourself to anyone. But Dru needed this and she needed Dru. "If you get my colleague and me in to see this transfusion, I'll do you any favor—within the bounds of decency—that you ask."

"We have a deal, Miss Kelly," he said and strode away, leaving Una to wonder just what this favor might be.

Dr. Westervelt was true to his word, and two hours later Una and Dru stood beside him in a small room on the second floor. The drapery had been drawn open, and sunshine lit the room. A bed sat near the window, and in it lay a pale, sickly-looking man. Another man, undressed down to his shirtsleeves and trousers, sat a few feet away from the bed. Supplies glinted on a nearby table alongside two porcelain pitchers of water and an empty metal basin polished to a high sheen. Half a dozen doctors and two nurses fretted about the room, smoothing the bedsheets, checking the sickly man's pulse, inspecting the instruments like actors readying props for a show.

"What if I swoon in front of all of these people?" Dru whispered to her.

Earlier, when she'd told Dru about the procedure and her plan to get them inside, Dru had come up with dozens of excuses why she couldn't possibly come. The windowsills needed another dusting. The chamber pots a fresh scrubbing. The ventilation close monitoring. Never mind that her ward gleamed from floor to ceiling, and there wasn't a draft to be found. Una had to all but drag her away.

Now she reached out and squeezed Dru's cold, shaky hand. "You won't pass out. Besides, they're all too bothered to notice anyhow."

"But what if—"

"Just lean back against the wall real calm like, and I'll brace you up."

Dru nodded but didn't look all that convinced.

"You sure your friend wants to be here?" Dr. Westervelt asked her a few minutes later when Dru began to pant. "If she gets any

paler, they'll mistake her for the patient and wind up transfus-
ing her."

"She's fine. Overexcited is all. What's taking so long anyhow?"

Just then the door opened, and another man entered, carrying a
big black box with three wooden legs. He pried the legs apart and
stood them on the ground.

"We had to wait for the photographic department to arrive."
Dr. Westervelt nodded to the newly arrived man.

Una's skin prickled with a sudden chill. The only other time
she'd been around a photograph machine was at police headquarters. No wonder the doctors and nurses were in such a dither. At
least she, Dru, and Dr. Westervelt stood against the back wall
safely behind the camera's big glass eye.

The photographer, a lanky man with deep-set eyes and a
hooked nose, strode around the room, observing the interplay of
light and shadow, adjusting things this way and that. Meanwhile,
two doctors led the seated man to a scale and jotted down his
weight.

"That's the donor," Dr. Westervelt said to her. "They'll weigh
him again after the procedure to determine how much blood was
taken."

"How can they assure the blood will flow from him to the patient and not the other way around?"

"Gravity. There are several stopcocks fitted along the transfusion apparatus and a rubber bulb to help control the flow as well."

"And the donor. He won't be harmed in the process?"

"Some have swooned or developed an infection at the site of
blood withdrawal, but a powerful and heavy young man like this
should be just fine."

"But if it's dangerous, why not use animal's blood or that of a
dead man?"

"They've tried animal-to-human transfusions in the past
without success," Dru said before Dr. Westervelt could respond.
"Lamb's blood, dog's blood, bull's blood. All were lethal to the

recipient. The blood of a deceased man cannot be used because of issues with coagulation. Once the heart stops beating, the blood immediately begins to clot. I've read of experiments with phosphate solutions to defibrinate . . ."

Una hadn't the slightest idea what she meant by *coagulation* or *defibrinate* but was glad to hear Dru prattle on more like herself. Dr. Westervelt seemed duly impressed. The two of them chatted quietly until the photographer announced he was ready, and the procedure began.

The donor rolled up his shirtsleeve, exposing his inner arm. A doctor grabbed a scalpel from the supply table and made several superficial cuts in the bend of the donor's elbow until a vein was exposed. A basin had been placed on the floor beneath the donor's outstretched arm. Blood dribbled from the cuts, pooling at the man's elbow and dripping into the metal basin. *Plink. Plink. Plink.*

Dru sucked in an audible breath and whipped her head to the side, her gaze falling to the floor.

Una took a step closer so that their shoulders were touching and grabbed Dru's hand. "Don't look away."

Dru mewled softly, keeping her face to the floor.

"Come on. You have to look. He's about to puncture the vein." When Dru still didn't look, Una added, "I think it's the femoral vein, right? Or maybe the pedal vein."

"Don't be a goose, the pedal vein is in the foot. They're using the brachial vein." She peeked over as if to be sure.

"And what's that thing the doctor is using? Looks like a lapel pin to me. Or maybe he got into his wife's needlework."

Dru gave an exacerbated huff and turned her full gaze on the man. "It's a cannula. Sharp at one end like a needle but hollow so the blood can flow through."

They both watched as the doctor inserted the cannula into the vein. Blood spurted from the opposite end of the cannula once the tip was inside. Dru swayed but did not look away. The doctor fastened a tube to the end of the cannula, the pale rubber darkening as it filled with blood. A stopcock halted the flow halfway down the tube.

The sickly man's vein was similarly cannulated. Both sets of tubing were joined at either end of a rubber bulb and the stop-cocks opened. Blood flowed between the men, aided by the occasional squeeze of the bulb. Una held fast to Dru's hand. Her face remained pallid, and sweat dappled her forehead. But she hadn't fainted.

"Miraculous, isn't it?" Dr. Westervelt whispered to Una.

She nodded, though until that moment, she'd been too focused on Dru to appreciate what they were watching. Here was a dying man, pale and shriveled, who might yet live on account of another man's blood. How many other men and women might be saved? Her thoughts strayed unbidden to her mother, or rather the charred body that had been her mother. Might there someday be a cure for fire-eaten flesh? Might Una herself administer such a cure? She pushed the ridiculous thought aside. She was here only in hiding. Hers was the life of a thief. Always had been. Always would be.

The doctors hovered around the men while nurses cleaned the blood splatter and covered the exposed veins with gauze. Once the scene looked presentable, the photographer hid himself and the back end of his machine beneath a black drape. "Look at the patients, not me," he said from beneath the drape. The doctors and nurses retrained their attention on the procedure. The photographer fiddled with the secret workings of his camera, then threw off the drape. "The scene needs more gravitas." He pointed to Una, Dru, and Dr. Westervelt. "You three, go stand in the back behind the others."

Una's insides tightened.

"Oh no," Dr. Westervelt said. "We're not part of the procedure. Only here to observe."

"Then observe from over there." He gestured impatiently to the narrow band of empty space between the others and the far wall.

Dr. Westervelt glanced at the doctor who'd opened the men's

arms and now stood squeezing the bulb between them. He nodded. Dr. Westervelt crossed the room and wedged himself in behind the others.

"Well?" the photographer said to Una and Dru, who hadn't
moved. "Hurry up. This man doesn't have an infinite supply of
blood."

"No, we can't," Una said. "We—"

"It's all right," Dru whispered. "I shan't faint." And she tugged
Una to their place at the rear of the tableau.

"Remember, eyes on the men," the photographer said and disappeared again beneath his drape.

Una's pulse bounded in her veins. Pressed against the wall between Dr. Westervelt and Dru, she felt like a mouse whose tail
was pinned beneath the paw of an alley cat. She loathed to be
caught in another photograph but had nowhere to run.

"Hold still!" the photographer hollered.

Una dropped her chin and inched closer to Dr. Westervelt—
closer than was strictly proper—so that his shadow obscured part
of her face. Damned Dru and this entire cockeyed plan. The camera's shutter snapped open. A moment later, it closed, capturing
Una's likeness and the rest of the miraculous scene forever.

CHAPTER 24

That Sunday after mass, Una took the Third Avenue el uptown to repay the favor she'd promised Dr. Westervelt. Whereas once she'd relished being out in the city crowds, now her skin crawled like she had a bad case of lice. There were fewer people who might recognize her on the Third Avenue el than the Sixth, a more direct route to Central Park, but she didn't take a full gulp of air until she reached the Seventy-Sixth Street station and was no longer trapped inside the rumbling car.

Her disguise—that of a well-to-do and respectable lady—would fool the coppers, she reminded herself, and all of her old chums, as long as they didn't look too close or too hard. Mrs. Buchanan had done wonders with her coat, scrubbing out the stains and mending the tears. If she found the patched inner lining and warren of pockets suspicious, she made no mention of it. With the addition of Dru's fur hat, stole, and muff, Una looked positively highfalutin. Still, she felt far safer dressed in her nurse's uniform behind the thick stone walls of Bellevue.

She entered the park through Miners' Gate and wound her way down a muddy lane toward Bethesda Fountain. The leafless boughs of elm trees crisscrossed overhead. Yesterday's snow had been shoveled into dirt-speckled berms on either side of the lane. Couples passed, arm in arm. Women pushed bundled infants in strollers. Packs of young boys raced by with sleds. Despite the gray clouds stretched overhead and slight chill in the air, everyone seemed to relish being outdoors away from the mayhem of the city streets.

Una preferred the mayhem. Easier to slip away into. But she didn't want Dr. Westervelt's favor hanging over her head any longer than necessary. Best settle the score and be done with it. Even if that meant meeting him here in the great wide open of Central Park.

The day after the transfusion, he'd waited until the other doctors had moved on with rounds and Miss Cuddy was busy in the medicine closet before approaching her. When he said to meet him at the Bethesda Fountain that Sunday afternoon, Una had been struck mute with surprise. In the past, when she'd been obliged to someone, it usually meant hiding hot goods for him or handing over half of her take. Some men asked for more intimate favors, which she satisfied with a swift knee to their groin.

"Trainees are forbidden from visiting places of amusement," she'd said, recovering her voice.

"You found yourself into the operating theater. I believe that's off-limits for probationers."

"That was not my idea. Miss Cuddy wasn't well and—"

"And you found your way into the transfusion room, with my help, I might add."

Una frowned and glanced at the medicine closet to be sure Miss Cuddy was still measuring out patients' noontime medication. "After I find you at the fountain, then what? Trainees are also forbidden from socializing with gentlemen, doctors or not, as you well know."

He flashed her a disarming smile. "Then we best not tell anyone."

"Easy for you to say. I'm the one who'll be expelled if we're caught."

"The park's always crowded on a Sunday. No one will notice us, I promise. I just want to spend the afternoon with you."

A suspicious response, but not one that warranted a knee to the groin. Not yet. "Fine. Sunday at the fountain."

Now, as the angel-topped fountain came into view, Una wished she'd insisted on a different favor. Not only did she have to keep a lookout for coppers, but hospital staff as well. She'd beg off after half an hour and stay clear of favors from here on out.

She spied Dr. Westervelt before he saw her. He wore a woodsy-green Chesterfield coat, brown gloves, and bowler. A sharp crease ran down the front of his trousers as if he'd had them pressed only moments before. At least he hadn't costumed himself with a cane and top hat like many of the other well-heeled fops strutting around the park. Instead, he carried a leather satchel slung over one shoulder.

She watched him circle the fountain with a slow, easy stride. He carried himself differently here than at the hospital. When rounding with Dr. Pingry, he wore his confidence like a shield. Here he seemed free of that burden. He still had the straight-backed assuredness of someone who'd known both adoration and discipline as a boy, but his movements were freer, as if he were no longer on the defensive.

Una tried to remember the last time she felt that way, not under the weight of some guise, but free. It had been weeks now, since before the death of Traveling Mike. But maybe not even then.

Dr. Westervelt caught sight of her and smiled, his countenance relaxing even further as he strode toward her. He hadn't been certain she would come, Una realized. She felt suddenly self-conscious of her appearance. Maybe the fur hat and muff were too much. She didn't want him to think she'd dressed up on account of him.

"Miss Kelly, it's a pleasure to see you. And a fine day, don't you think?"

Una tugged on her stole and glanced around, not at the snow-covered lawns but at the faces of those around them, assuring herself she didn't recognize anyone.

"A bit cold," she said, though Dru's furs kept her plenty warm.

"I've got just the ticket for that." He gestured to the frozen lake beyond the fountain. "A little ice-skating ought to get the blood flowing. What do you say?"

Una hesitated. Dozens of skaters glided across the icy surface, most in loose groups of two or three. But the lake was large with fingerlike inlets pressed into the wooded shoreline. No one here at the fountain or on the surrounding paths would be able to get a good look at them. The other skaters would likely be too preoccupied with their own merriment to pay them any mind. He couldn't have picked a better spot to pass the time unobserved.

But Una hadn't skated since she was a girl, and then only once or twice.

"It's quite safe, I assure you," Dr. Westervelt said, pointing to a red flag that fluttered atop Belvedere Castle. "They only fly that when the ice is thick enough to skate upon."

"I haven't any skates."

"I brought my mother's for you to use." He opened his satchel and pulled them out for Una to see. "They're a bit old but still in good repair. I sharpened the blades myself this morning."

Unable to contrive another excuse, Una nodded, and they picked their way from the fountain to the lake's edge. A group of children sprinted past, their blades kicking up puffs of snow. Then an elderly gentleman, whistling a pleasant tune. If they could do it without falling flat on their backsides, so could Una. She strapped the skates to her boots and took a deep breath before stepping onto the ice.

Her ankles wobbled and arms wheeled as she tried to balance on the thin blades. It hadn't seemed this precarious when she was five, but then, all the memories before her mother's death were a bit hazy. She waited until she stopped tottering, then ventured out another step.

Behind her, Una heard Dr. Westervelt buckling his skates, then felt the stir of air as he glided past her graceful as a goddamn swan. She shifted her weight to one shaky foot and pushed off with the other, hoping to overtake him with similar aplomb. Instead, she lurched forward, head jutted out and shoulder slumped like a buzzard. Her balance faltered again. She tried to compensate by throwing her weight backward only to overcorrect and find her skates slipping out from beneath her.

Dr. Westervelt spun around and caught her flailing arms just before she toppled.

"I'm sorry, I should have asked whether you knew your way around the ice."

"I need a moment to right myself is all."

"I thought, well, I shouldn't have presumed . . ." He was still holding on to her, though her wobbly legs had steadied, his gloved hands encircling her forearms. Dru's muff dangled from her wrist between them.

She looked down, giving her cheeks a moment to cool, then raised her chin and met his gaze. Something in his eyes struck her. An earnestness. A vulnerability. Whatever it was, it unnerved Una, and she pulled away. "Thank you, Doctor, I think I've got my balance now."

But when she tried to push off from the ice again, the tips of their skates crossed, and she nearly fell again but for Dr. Westervelt's quick reflexes and stable hand.

"Please, call me Edwin," he said, once Una was no longer in immediate peril of falling, and proceeded to instruct her on the basics of skating. He spoke not like a physician lecturing her on the principles of digestion or application of dressings, but as if they were old friends, and soon she was skating with a semblance of ease.

"Don't they ice-skate in winter where you're from?" he asked as they made their way to the center of the lake. He skated within easy reach of her, closer than would be proper were they strolling on solid land but seemingly permissible here on the ice.

"What makes you think I'm not from the city?"

"*This* city? New York? You're nothing like the women here."

"Is that so? And what is it that makes the women of New York so very different from others?"

He paused a moment, his expression thoughtful. "They care overmuch for correctness, I suppose. They hardly ever laugh. Or venture an opinion."

"And do you not think it's the men of the city who have made them so?"

"I'm certain of it. We're little better ourselves, so caught up in good form."

"Are you equally certain that *all* women of the city are this way? What about the washerwomen and the factory workers? Or the fruit sellers and shirt stitchers?"

"You mean working women? I hardly know."

"I, Dr. Westervelt—"

"Edwin."

"Edwin. I am a working woman. Or will be once I pass my training."

"That's different. Nursing is a respectable profession drawn from a respectable class of women. You can hardly compare yourself to domestics and rag pickers."

Una stopped, her skates making a grinding noise on the ice. "Can't I? Are we so very dissimilar in our wants and needs?"

Edwin glanced over his shoulder, then circled back. He looked perplexed, his head cocked and lips pressed into a thin line. He'd spoken with derision about women not speaking their minds but seemed at a loss when one actually did. Una stood with her arms akimbo. Her legs still wobbled, but only slightly. She waited for him to say of the poor what she'd heard a hundred times from the reporters and pastors and do-good society women who flocked to the slums. Recalcitrant. Immoral. Unclean.

Instead, his expression turned chastened, like that of a little boy who's been caught throwing stones at passing carriages or pulling his sister's pigtails. "You're quite right. I forget myself sometimes and find myself parroting the sentiments of my grandfather." He took off his bowler hat and ran his fingers through his carefully groomed hair, leaving the reddish-brown locks, which seemed more inclined to crimp or curl rather than lie flat, in a tousle. He was handsomer this way, Una thought and felt a pang of disappointment when he tugged his hat back on. "There's an eagle's nest at the far end of the next inlet. An impressive sight if you haven't seen one. But I . . . er . . . understand if you want to go."

She glanced behind her at the distant shoreline. She'd satisfied her promise. The longer she stayed, the greater the risk someone would recognize her. But it was refreshing being here on the ice with him. She'd missed being outdoors, the briskness of the winter air, the layered sounds and smells. Besides, Edwin's company wasn't entirely intolerable. She'd never met a man who forthrightly admitted when he was wrong.

"I suppose I have a little time to see this eagle's nest."

He smiled that dazzling smile of his—his teeth were real, she'd decided—and they started toward the inlet. As before, he matched Una's pace, neither rushing nor cosseting her.

"Maine," she said after a silence.

"Main what?"

"That's where I'm from. Augusta, Maine."

He laughed. "And you never learned to skate?" He peppered her with more questions about herself—what line of work her father did, whether or not she had siblings, what made her want to come to Bellevue. After having repeated the story five or six times now, the lie came easy. And though she quickly tried to steer the conversation to safer territory, he persisted with his questions. What did she think of New York? The park? Had she heard of Coney Island and would she like to go when it opened in the spring?

"You could join the Pinkerton agency for all the questions you ask."

"I'll remember that in case things at the hospital don't work out."

She asked him then about his upbringing and found herself listening with interest instead of wondering about the time or worrying over other skaters. His family had lived in New York for generations—the very type of blue bloods her father had left

Ireland hoping to escape. To his credit, though, Edwin didn't boast about his lineage and seemed almost skittish of the discussion. He spoke of becoming a physician like it was an obligation, not a choice, and confessed his grandfather had once been a surgeon at Bellevue.

Una suddenly realized why she'd recognized the name Westervelt when first she heard it. "That's your grandfather's portrait in the main hall?"

Edwin nodded, looking more sheepish than proud even though his grandfather must have been some big bug to earn such a place on the wall.

"And your father, was he a doctor too?"

His skates rasped loudly over the ice, and for the first time, Una struggled to keep up. "No. He dropped out of medical school in favor of a business venture." His voice was gruff when he said this, and Una didn't press him for more details, but after a minute, Edwin continued. Because of this business venture—Edwin snickered as he said the words—his father had been gone traveling for much of Edwin's youth. He drank and gambled and even kept a mistress in New Orleans. The war years were the only time he made any money, and only then as a profiteer and cotton smuggler.

At this, a flush of anger crackled beneath Una's skin. Her father had returned from the war maimed inside and out. His father with pockets fattened with gold. *Yellow-bellied rascal* she wanted to call him. But the shame and bitterness in Edwin's voice stayed her tongue. She remembered walking beside her father to Union Square one Decoration Day, his blue uniform smelling of must and beginning to fade. His limp seemed to pain him less that day, and he walked a little straighter. His breath was free from the stench of whiskey. It was one of the few happy memories she had of him. Edwin seemed to have none.

"Where is he now, your father?" she asked him.

"Dead. Drank himself into a stupor and choked on his own vomit in some New Orleans slum."

"I'm sorry," Una said, surprised at how sincerely she meant it. They had more in common than she'd realized, and some pesky part of her wished she could be as honest with him as he'd been with her.

"It's me who should be sorry. What kind of a cad poisons a lovely afternoon with such melancholy?"

"Not such a cad that the fresh air can't make up for it."

"I don't know why . . ." He pulled off his hat and tried in vain to smooth down the locks he'd ruffled before. "I haven't spoken about such things in years. But I figured you'd hear about it eventually." He gave up with his hair and replaced his hat, glancing at her askew. "I really can be quite charming."

"Is that so? And modest too, I see."

They both chuckled, then skated in easy silence until they reached the end of the inlet. Edwin scanned the shoreline. "There." He pointed to an indistinct cluster of trees, their branches overlapping.

Una squinted and shook her head. "I don't see it."

He skated to her side, stopping so close the cloud of his breath warmed her cheek, and pointed again. Una's entire body hummed like the rails beneath an approaching train, and her eyes struggled to focus. She smelled cloves and winter mint when he exhaled and couldn't help but wonder what his mouth tasted like.

Then she saw it, the mass of interwoven sticks, nestled at the union of three thick limbs. It was far bigger than she'd expected, perhaps five feet wide and several feet deep. A dusting of snow crowned the rim. What kind of bird was responsible for such a wonder? The only eagles in New York she'd ever known were those on the backside of a coin. Her eyes were suddenly misty and her throat thick. "I've never seen anything like this in the city . . . er . . . any city before."

"Bald eagles were far more common in New York's early days. Hunting and egg collecting have made them scarce."

Una vaguely remembered a man who'd come to Marm Blei's back door trying to sell a cache of eagle feathers. She'd paid him a nickel apiece. A dime for the white tail feathers. The thought now made Una sick. She swiped at her eyes before turning back to Edwin. "So the eagles who built this nest are gone?"

"Just for the season. They tend to stay near open water in the winter. But they'll be back in April to lay their eggs. The park workers keep an eye on them to make sure they're not disturbed."

"The same pair come back every year?"

"Yes, eagles mate for life."

Una became conscious again of how close they were standing. She glanced around. The nearest skaters were dozens of yards away, laughing, gliding, spinning, oblivious to anyone else on the ice. Just as she had foolishly been. Una had rules, after all. And being here with him like this, letting him distract her, was breaking far too many.

She tried to slide her skates backward to put some distance between them, but the end of one of the blades caught on the ice. She grabbed the lapels of Edwin's coat to keep from falling back.

"Sorry, I—"

Edwin seized the moment to lean down and kiss her. Una froze, but it took only a moment for her surprise to thaw. She held fast to his coat and kissed him back. He tasted even better than he smelled.

CHAPTER 25

⟶⊷◆⊶⟵

Una couldn't focus. When Nurse Cuddy had asked for cod-liver oil, she brought her linseed meal instead. When Una readied a bath for a patient, she forgot to add hot water, and the man yelped, stepping into the cold tub. When she came to collect the leeches off a patient, she couldn't get them to relax their hold, realizing only once they'd gorged themselves and dropped off on their own that she'd sprinkled them with sugar, not salt. Eventually Miss Cuddy relegated her to dusting, a task she'd already completed for the day, though not with great care, and one where she could affect little harm.

Today Superintendent Perkins was meeting with each of the probationers to inform them whether they'd been approved to continue on in the training program. Una's appointment, one of the last of the day, wasn't until three that afternoon. She'd tried to work out whether it was a good sign or a bad one to be scheduled at the end. Was Miss Perkins meeting first with those she intended to expel or saving them for last? When Una learned Dru had a much earlier appointment, she guessed the latter. Of course, the order might be fixed in some other way or entirely at random, but Una's insides had knotted nonetheless.

Only a month and a half had passed since her arrest. Not nearly long enough for the coppers to have forgotten her. If Superintendent Perkins booted her from the school, Una would be right back where she'd started, but with no place to go and no money to get gone.

Though she hadn't gotten into any official trouble in weeks, Nurse Hatfield always found something dissatisfying in her work. A hint of a draft. A speck of dust in the corner of a windowsill. A bedsheet that hadn't been pulled taut enough. Dr. Pingry hadn't warmed to her either. Her only hope on his account was that he found her too insignificant to muster a complaint.

The only reprieve to these thoughts and the growing certainty of her expulsion came when Edwin and the doctors made their morning rounds on the ward. Then Una was harried by a different type of thought: that of their kiss at the park two days earlier. Their lips had met for only a moment, but she'd felt the jolt of it clear down to her toes. Nothing like the stale, perfunctory kisses she'd known before. She couldn't remember whether she or Edwin had pulled away first, only the aching desire to feel his lips again. Propriety had gotten the better of them, though (or in Una's case, good sense), and they'd skated back to the fountain in shy silence.

She had no question now that kissing him had been a mistake. If by some miracle she did pass her probation, what then? She couldn't very well carry on a secret affair with him. Not when she was supposed to be lying low and the mere act of talking to him could get her expelled.

The trouble was, Una had enjoyed their afternoon on the lake. More than she had any afternoon in as long as she could remember. The fresh air. The snow-capped eagle's nest. The easy conversation. The kiss. For a brief snatch of time, she'd forgotten she was on the run from the police. Forgotten she'd been disavowed by Marm Blei and her crew. Forgotten she was a poor, Irish slumdweller. But Una couldn't afford to forget.

If such thoughts plagued Edwin, he didn't show it. He hardly even looked at her during his rounds. True, Una had made a point of not looking at him either. And when their gazes did meet, his eyes seemed to smile, even as his lips did not. They were quite handsome eyes, she realized, the deep brown color of tobacco. Dangerous, distracting eyes. Today, as always, Una quickly looked away. She was almost relieved when he and the other surgeons moved on to the next ward, leaving her to worry again about her meeting with Superintendent Perkins.

When three o'clock finally arrived, Una made her way to the third floor. On the stairs, she passed another of the probationers. Una didn't know her name but remembered sitting beside her during Dr. Pingry's anatomy lecture. Una had tried to cheat off her slate, only to find it as blank as her own. Now, as the woman hurried down the stairs, Una saw she was crying. Undoubtedly, she'd been sacked. Una stopped but couldn't unknot her tongue quickly enough to offer a comforting word.

By the time she arrived at the third floor, her heart beat as loudly as the bells of St. Stephen's. Did the same fate await her? She crossed the hall to Miss Perkins's door with slow, deliberate steps. A full minute she waited there before summoning the courage to knock.

"Come in," Miss Perkins called.

Una entered, closing the door behind her as softly as one might lower the lid of a coffin. If she told Miss Perkins her entire family in Maine had died last week from influenza would she take pity on Una and let her stay? Maybe she should say they'd been killed by rabid wolves. Or were snowed in on account of a blizzard and forced to eat one another in hopes of surviving. Surely that was a pitiful enough fate to warrant a second chance.

She sat down in the straight-backed chair facing Miss Perkins's desk and pulled out her handkerchief. It would be a more convincing performance if she cried.

But before she could begin her tearful story of cannibalism and wolves (the more tragic, the better), Miss Perkins reached across her desk and handed Una a sheet of paper.

"Congratulations, Miss Kelly, you've passed your probation. This is a contract detailing the terms of your schooling. Should you leave before your two years of training are complete—"

"I passed?"

The hint of a smile cracked Miss Perkins's staid expression. "Why, yes. Did you think otherwise?"

Una half nodded, half shook her head.

"You didn't have the smoothest of starts, that is true. But you've earned satisfactory marks on your examinations, and Nurse Cuddy tells me you're proficient in your duties on the ward. Moreover, the patients speak quite highly of you."

"They do?"

"As you have undoubtedly discerned during your probation, the clientele here at Bellevue is of a . . . modest sort. Some inevitably feel looked down upon by the nurses for their want of cleanliness or gentility. But none of the patients I spoke to about you made such complaints. Indeed, many said they felt soothed by your presence."

Una caught herself before muttering, *They did?*

"The program only grows more rigorous from here. And you'll be expected to maintain the utmost decorum and obedience. It's a mark of distinction to be counted among the Bellevue graduates and wear the school pin. Former students have found success all over the country. But you must commit to completing two years' training and pass the final examination before such distinction is conferred."

She handed Una her inkwell and pen. The contract was written in simple terms, outlining the program's duration, the near-endless list of behavior expectations, the inclusion of room and board, and a monthly stipend of ten dollars. Embossed at the top of the page was the school's seal—a crane surrounded by poppies and capsules. It was the same image, set against a backdrop of blue, she'd seen emblazoned on graduates' pins encircled with the words BELLEVUE TRAINING SCHOOL FOR NURSES.

Una brushed a finger over the seal. It was a point of pride for the graduates to wear the pin and something other trainees— especially Dru—talked about incessantly. She imagined for a mo-

ment the way it would look affixed to her uniform. Shiny, yet
modest. A glimmer of hope for those whom she encountered. A
pronouncement that here was a woman who could help and heal.
A goodly woman. A wise woman. A woman to be trusted.

Miss Perkins shifted in her chair, bringing Una back to her
senses. She marked her name at the bottom of the page, scarcely
waiting for the ink to dry before handing it back. Two years was
more than sufficient time to wait out the coppers—that was her
objective, after all. In the meantime, she was assured of warm
food, a roof that didn't leak, and a fancy indoor privy. Hell, she
might stay the full two years and receive her diploma. That little
blue pin wasn't a token of hope, but her entry card into homes
across the eastern seaboard. No more diving pockets in crowded
train depots. Una would move into the ranks of high-class profes-
sional. After all, who would suspect the obliging and sympathiz-
ing nurse when a silver spoon or pearl necklace went missing?
Not when she'd come from the country's foremost training school.

Superintendent Perkins stood and ushered Una to the door.
A small reception had been laid out in the medical board room
on the first floor for the newly designated trainees, she told her,
which Una was welcome to attend.

Una stopped in the doorway. "Thank you for having faith in
me, Miss Perkins."

She smiled again. "Just see that you continue to make good on
that faith."

Downstairs, the long oak table in the board room had been
pushed against a wall and covered with a swath of lace-trimmed
muslin. A porcelain tea service sat at the center, surrounded by
trays of cookies and tea cake. The newly initiated trainees clus-
tered about the room in small groups, speaking in quiet but animated tones. All six head nurses were in attendance, including
Miss Hatfield, who shot Una a flinty, pursed-lipped glance when
she entered. A few of the physicians mingled among the women.
Thankfully, neither Dr. Pingry nor Dr. Westervelt had chosen to

attend. Women from the governing board were there too, looking out of place in their frilly silk day gowns and plumed hats. Even Mr. O'Rourke, the hospital warden, had made an appearance.

Dru hurried over to Una and took her hand. "Can you believe it? We did it! Of course, I never had any doubts on your account, but I was quite certain I would be asked to leave on account of my . . . well, you know, my former frailty. But thanks to you . . ." She tugged Una to the table and poured her a cup of tea, chatting all the while. They filled their plates with sweets and joined a group of women standing beside one of the long windows overlooking the front lawn. The sun had slipped free from the patchwork of clouds covering the sky, and its light played atop the East River's choppy waves.

Among the women was Mrs. Hobson, whom Una remembered from her admission interview. She wore a shiny, pearl-studded brooch affixed to her collar. Una couldn't help but guess at the price it would fetch on the streets. Twenty-five dollars? Thirty if the latch was pure silver.

"You ladies must be overjoyed at passing your probation," Mrs. Hobson said.

The other trainees replied with demure nods and polite *Yes, thank yous*. But Una, still eyeing the brooch, blurted out, "Happy as a safecracker in a bank."

Everyone stopped sipping their tea and eyed her with confusion.

"Just . . . er . . . something an old acquaintance used to say. What I mean is yes, quite overjoyed, thank you." And it was true. The day's worry had subsided. She felt lighter than she had in weeks as if the pall of Traveling Mike's murder might finally be lifting. She drank her tea and nibbled on a square of shortbread. What would Marm Blei say if she could see Una now, a bona fide nurse trainee hobnobbing among doctors and society women? And that slippery detective who thought her nothing more than street trash. She'd loved to see his aghast expression upon learning she'd been right under his nose the entire time. Not that she had any mind to tell him. Maybe someday, when she was rich and well-settled, she'd send them both an unmarked letter just so they'd know how much they'd underestimated her.

Mrs. Hobson padded away to congratulate the rest of the room while Dru and the others chattered about which wards they hoped to be assigned for the coming weeks. Those on the first floor had to be kept immaculately clean to keep away the rats, but the upper floors would grow stuffy and sweltering come summer. No one wanted to be assigned the basement, where the alcoholics dried out in dank, prison-like rooms.

Una didn't care where she landed next so long as it was not another of the surgical wards Nurse Hatfield oversaw. She excused herself from the women and went to freshen her tea. As she stirred in a lump of sugar, a frazzled-looking orderly near the door caught her eye. He scanned the room, then hurried over to Warden O'Rourke and whispered something in his ear. The warden's expression darkened. He set down his teacup, smoothed his hands down the front of his suit, and followed the orderly out.

Una watched them go, then rejoined the circle of women beside the window. The conversation had turned to speculation about the operating theater.

"Won't it be awful with all those medical students staring down at you?" one of the women said.

"Their attention is so fixed on the surgery you could hike up your skirts and dance the cancan, and they wouldn't notice," Una said.

"You've been in the operating theater?" one of them asked.

"No . . . I've just . . . er . . . heard about what it's like."

Another of the women leaned close. "And have you really seen a cancan?"

"Of course not," Una said, trying her best to sound scandalized. "But I did see a drawing on a handbill once."

"Is it true they really lift their skirts all the way above the knee?" Dru asked, leaning in too.

"Above the knee what, Miss Lewis?"

All of them startled at the sound of Nurse Hatfield's voice. Dru's cheeks went ashen. "Umm . . ."

"Above-the-knee amputation," Una said. "We were just discussing the best type of dressing to apply in such cases."

Nurse Hatfield narrowed her eyes. "And your conclusion?"

"Well, er, the best type of dressing in these cases is—"

"One-and-a-half-inch plaster to keep the skin flaps together," Dru said. "Followed by lint and a square of oiled silk."

Nurse Hatfield gave a soft harrumph and walked away. The other women did likewise, casting Una sharp glances as if she were uncouth for having brought up the cancan at all.

She and Dru fell into laughter as soon as they were out of earshot.

"You're not like anyone I've ever met, Una. How do you think so quickly on your feet?"

"Me? How does someone who until only a few days ago couldn't stand the sight of blood know what dressing to use on an amputated limb?"

Dru shrugged. "Books, of course." She went to get another cookie, leaving Una with her thoughts. Dru wasn't a friend—that was against her rules—but it was nice to have someone she could laugh with.

She sipped the last of her tea and glanced out the window. The sun had disappeared behind the cloud cover, turning the once-sparkling river flat and gray. Movement in the foreground caught her attention. The movement took shape, and Una's hand went limp, the teacup and saucer slipping from her grasp. Both shattered as they struck the floor. Her gaze flickered to the splinters of porcelain about her feet, then back to the window. Warden O'Rourke stood on the lawn near the entrance to the Insane Pavilion. With him were two men in blue wool uniforms. Coppers.

CHAPTER 26

The Insane Pavilion was a new, single-story brick building that ran the length of the south side of the lawn to the river. Una had never been inside, not even on her initial tour, as it was one of the few locations of the hospital not staffed by the training school. She'd learned through hushed conversations with Miss Cuddy that Superintendent Perkins refused to supply nurses for the pavilion because of insufficient physician oversight. Instead, the attendants were semi-inebriates recruited from the lodging houses, their skill commensurate with their abhorrently meager wages.

A single resident physician oversaw the ever-growing number of patients. He, along with a city-appointed Examiner in Lunacy, reviewed each case and made out the necessary certificates to commit and transfer the patients to the asylum on Blackwell's Island.

On several occasions as she'd crossed the darkened hospital grounds after her shift, Una had heard cries from within the pavilion or seen shadowed figures behind the barred windows. Some of the nurses refused to pass by the building at night unless accompanied by the watchman. Una had met enough so-called lunatics to know it was a convenient label for many who simply didn't fit in. Even so, she crossed herself and whispered an "Ave Maria" when walking past the building on particularly black nights.

Now, however, she had to get inside, no matter what sort of pitiful horrors lay within the walls. Mrs. Hobson and the other matrons from the governing board had flocked to Una when they heard the crash of her teacup, fussing over her pallid complexion and unsettled gaze. Overexcited, they pronounced her and shooed her out of the boardroom to rest for the remainder of the afternoon.

But Una had not returned to the nurses' home for rest. Instead, she'd hidden in the stairwell alongside the warden's office until she heard him return from the yard. Then she slipped outside, hovering in the shadow of the arched entryway until she was certain the coppers were gone.

What business had they been about? Surely they weren't here looking for her. Her heart quickened again, thudding against her chest like a bird trapped in a chimney. Police came to Bellevue for all sorts of reasons, she reminded herself. They brought drunks and tramps in all the time. Invalid prisoners received care on the wards under police supervision. But that didn't explain the orderly's urgency or Warden O'Rourke's grave expression. Una had to find out the reason.

The sun hung low in the sky, still muted by clouds, casting long pale shadows across the yard. Not as safe as darkness, but if the coppers suspected she were here, she couldn't wait for nightfall. She crept down the steps and along the edge of the hospital, her seersucker skirt rasping against the stone wall. It wouldn't do for anyone from the governing board to see her sneaking about the lawn when she ought to be resting at the home. When she neared the entrance to the Insane Pavilion, she stopped, straightened, and then crossed the lawn to the door with a purposeful, unhurried stride. Rule number five: Look like you belong.

A sharp odor struck Una's nose as soon as she entered the pavilion. Not that of disinfectant, which she'd become accustomed to smelling throughout the hospital, but something more akin to the rear yard of a saloon where the stench of every possible bodily excretion mingled in the air. She covered her nose with a handkerchief and proceeded down the wide corridor that bisected the building, looking for the orderly she'd seen earlier. Roughly hewn doors lined either side of the corridor. A glance through the peephole revealed crowded cells lit only by the waning daylight. Patients huddled on straw beds, their breath clouding in the cold air. Others paced the small confines of the cell or stared despondently out the barred window.

Una's skin prickled. She knew what awaited these patients on Blackwell's Island, rich and poor alike: the Octagon. A place notorious for its filth and disease where they'd be doused with freezing water or strapped to flea-ridden beds or tied up in straitjackets with scant hope of leaving.

Little better awaited Una if the coppers found her, she reminded herself, and continued on, doing her best to ignore the moans and erratic shrieks echoing from the cells. She found the orderly on his hands and knees in the last cell, mopping up a pool of vomit. He eyed her nurse's uniform with a mix of suspicion and surprise. The patients in the cell were staring as well, some with a languid curiosity, others with a keenness so sharp it could cut through bone.

"You lost, miss?" the orderly asked.

"I wanted to ask you a few questions."

"Your patients complaining about their supper? Well, you're barking up the wrong tree." He tossed his soiled rag into a bucket of sudsless water. "I had nothin' to do with them missing ham hocks. If you ask me, the cook done stole 'em outta the soup pot himself."

"No, nothing like that."

"I ain't responsible for no missing laudanum neither."

"Actually, I was wondering about the police officers who were here earlier."

The orderly stood and carried his bucket from the cell, leaving behind a long streak of vomit to dry and crust on the floor. He had the unlined face of a youth but moved with the shuffling gait of an old man. "You saw 'em, eh?" He walked past her without saying anything more, locking the door and dumping out the bucket in the nearby water closet.

Una followed behind him. "Warden O'Rourke seemed rather unnerved by their visit. Do you know what it was about?"

"What's it to you?"

"Superintendent Perkins asked me to look into the matter." It was better to avoid naming someone else in a lie, but Una needed some leverage. "In case there was some danger to the nurses she needed to be made aware of."

The orderly snorted. "Whatever the danger, it's come and gone now."

"What do you mean?"

"We had a suicide last night. Over on the female ward." He nodded to a cluster of cells farther down the corridor beyond a sliding door of steel bars. "The doc at the morgue thought nothing of it, but you know how them coppers are. Always sniffing around when they think there's a chance a little brass might come their way."

"Brass, as in money?" Una asked, trying to sound naive.

He nodded. "A bit suspicious, it was. How it happened, I mean. Not the sort of thing the warden wants to read about in the papers."

Una's knotted insides untangled with his words. The coppers' visit had nothing to do with her. How the dickens had she ever thought it had? No one but Barney knew she was here. And Bellevue wasn't exactly the first place you'd come looking for an escaped murderer. Certainly not among the staff. Present company excluded.

A laugh bubbled up inside her. She cleared her throat to hide the sound. "That's good to hear, thank you. I'll be sure to relay this to the superintendent."

"'Good'?"

"Well, no, not good, but at least nothing to worry the other nurses over." Una turned around and started for the door, eager for a breath of fresh air.

"Ain't you wonderin' what was suspicious about it?"

"About what?" she said over her shoulder.

"The suicide."

Begrudgingly, she turned back to face him. "Please, en-lighten me."

"Don't know."

"You don't know?"

"Like I said, it happened on the female ward." He shuffled to the door that separated the wards and banged his empty bucket on the bars. "Madge!"

A woman peeked her head out from a nook at the far end of the corridor. "What, you chucklehead?"

"Them training school nurses are in a dither wantin' to know about that gal who hung herself."

Una winced at their shrill shouting. No wonder the patients here were mad. She would be too with such noise.

The woman, a short, stocky creature with unkempt hair and a missing front tooth, waddled to the door. She stared at Una a moment before saying, "Well, what do you wanna know?"

"Actually, I don't—"

"She was askin' why them coppers were here. I told her they came with their palms up and peepers closed."

"Ain't nothing to see anyway," the woman said. "She hanged herself plain and simple."

"With what?" Una asked. She knew enough about the care of insane patients to know that ropes and laces and other such things were to be kept out of the cells.

The woman shrugged. "A length a cloth. A belt." She held her thumb and index finger an inch and a half apart. "Something about yea wide if the bruising on her throat's any indication."

The image of Traveling Mike splayed out on the snowy ground flashed in Una's mind. "Did you say a belt?"

"Maybe. Whatever she used to do it was gone this morning when we found her."

"Gone? But how is that possible?"

"One of her cellmates likely took it and hid it somewhere."

"Did you ask them about it?"

"Can't. One's so mad she thinks she's a bird and only answers in chirps and squawks. The other's a mute."

"But surely you would have found it when you searched them." Una's voice was thin, her words clipped. "You did search them, didn't you? The cell too?"

The woman nodded. "Me and them coppers. Nothin'."

"Then how can you be sure it was a suicide at all?"

"What, you think one of her cellmates killed her? Strangled her dead without the night attendant hearin'?"

Or someone broke inside and killed her, Una thought but didn't say. The dank, odorous air grew heavy. Paranoia was getting the better of her. There was no cause to believe the woman was murdered like Traveling Mike. Knowing that didn't make it any easier to breathe, though. She tugged at her collar, then plucked the cap from her head and fanned her face. When she looked back at the woman, she found her staring intently.

"Hey, don't I know you from somewhere?"

Una shoved her cap back on her head. Her fingers trembled as she pinned it in place. The overhead gas lamps burned too dimly for Una to fully make out the woman's features, but at first glance, she hadn't seemed familiar. "I've been working at Bellevue for several weeks. I'm sure we've passed on the grounds."

The woman shook her head. "Before that. From somewhere else."

"I'm afraid that's impossible." Una's voice remained thin. "I've only just relocated from Maine."

As the woman continued to stare, it was all Una could do not to fidget or back away. She blinked slow and steady, keeping her eyes fixed on the greasy scarf the woman wore over her wiry hair. "Thank you for your assistance. I'm sure it's like you say, nothing suspicious to report. Miss Perkins will be most pleased." She turned and, though her feet itched to beat wood, walked calmly from the pavilion.

CHAPTER 27

—»◦«—

"Detail for me, Miss Kelly, your observations about this patient."

Una blinked and rattled her head, her surroundings sharpening back into focus. The ward around her was quiet, lit with morning sunlight. The nutty aroma of oatmeal gruel, fresh from the kitchen, wafted through the air. A fire crackled in the stove. Even so, Una shivered. She set down the cloth she'd been using to wash the patient's face and hands and turned to the head nurse. "I'm sorry, what?"

"Imagine I'm the physician about my morning rounds, and this is my first time seeing this patient, what would you report?"

"Her pulse rate is normal. No fever or chills. Her breathing—"

"From the beginning, please. Remember, there are many important things the physician must know, which only the observant nurse can tell him."

Una nodded. "This is Mrs. Riker, she's thirty-nine years of age, married with—"

"Stand up, Miss Kelly. You mustn't address a physician while seated."

Una swallowed a sigh and stood. She much preferred Head Nurse Smith to Miss Hatfield but already was weary of her exacting standards. "This is Mrs. Riker, she's . . ."

For the next several minutes, Una described everything she could remember about the patient—her condition and weight and drinking habits, her previous bouts of ill-health and the health of her family members. She described her skin: color, perspiration, location and duration of eruptions, redness, and swelling. She described the quality and rate of her pulse, the frequency and regularity of her respirations.

"And her alimentary canal?" Miss Smith said when Una had finished. "You forgot to mention anything about the state of her hunger and thirst, her bowel habits and evacuations, whether she has passed any gallstones or worms."

"There was nothing of note, so I figured—"

"It is not for you to decide what is or is not of note. You must relay everything to the physician and leave him to decide."

Una looked down and nodded. Half the time, it seemed like the doctor was hardly listening to her. Other times, he rushed her through her report with an exacerbated wave of his hand. But she knew better than to argue the point with Nurse Smith.

She hoped that the interrogation was over, but just as Nurse Smith turned away, the patient gave a weak cough, which brought on a whole new round of questions about the character, frequency, and duration of this "worrying symptom." Una stumbled through her answers. Her thoughts had been so far away this morning that she couldn't recall whether the woman had coughed like that before or not.

After a further lecture on the importance of correct observation, Una was sent to air out the blankets on the balcony. The new ward Una had been assigned, ward twelve, was a female medical unit on the second floor. A bank of five tall windows lined one side of the room, opening onto a narrow wrought-iron balcony.

Una raised the sash of one of the windows and clambered out with an armful of blankets. The brisk morning air stung her cheeks. Tendrils of fog rose off the river and crept across the lawn. Five days had passed since the coppers' visit to Bellevue on account of the suspicious suicide in the Insane Pavilion. She'd kept careful watch for their return, but so far they had not. She'd kept an eye on the papers too. Whatever Warden O'Rourke had paid the coppers hadn't been enough to keep the story from leaking to the press. The *New York World* had run a shamelessly titillating piece two days ago—"Mysterious Suicide in Bellevue's Lunatic Ward"—but mentioned nothing of the police investigation. Instead it suggested the woman had hanged herself with a leather belt, which her cellmate, the bird woman, had mistaken for a worm and afterward eaten.

Rumors flitting about the hospital were less absurd. The laundry women speculated that the dead woman had used a blanket to hang herself. Natural that her cellmates would have untied it from the window bars and used it to keep warm, seeing how drafty that ward was, they said. Others speculated that the night attendant had found the woman dead and removed whatever it was she'd used to kill herself, hoping that the death might be ruled natural. The attendant had, after all, been fired the very next day on account of negligence.

Una flapped the blankets to remove any dirt or lice and laid them over the iron railing. Already the gossip about the hospital was dying down. So why couldn't Una focus? The coppers hadn't come on account of her and likely wouldn't be back to do more snooping into the case. A simple suicide. Even the *New York World* thought so, and they'd be the first to run with more nefarious rumors. Una was safe. Her plan to hide away here was working perfectly. No one suspected she was anything but a charitable-hearted girl from Maine.

Except maybe the day attendant in the Insane Pavilion. Una had thought about her as much as the coppers these last few days. She smoothed the last of the blankets out over the railing but lingered outside in the cold, misty air. People mistook strangers for acquaintances all the time. That was why confidence schemes worked. Some thieves made their entire living by it. If you could find out someone's name and a bit about them—where they grew up, where they studied, where they had family—you could greet them like long-lost friends. Rather than admit they didn't know you, the poor sucker would smile and buy you a drink. Before the night was over, they'd convince themselves that yes, they did, in fact, know you and happily lend you ten, fifteen, twenty dollars to buy your poor, sick child medicine. A sum you promised to pay back the very next day, but of course, never did.

Was Una being taken by such a scheme? What did the day attendant have to gain from saying Una looked familiar? Maybe it was all just a mistake. Una couldn't keep worrying on it, otherwise she'd worry herself right out of her position at the training school. The woman hadn't recognized her, and that was that. Besides, in the end, it would be the attendant's word against Una's. Who would believe such a coarse, unkempt woman over her?

She climbed back through the window and crossed to the stove to warm her hands. No more letting her mind wander. Between keeping the ward clean and remembering what each patient had eaten, how much they voided, and how frequently they coughed, she had more than enough to think about. She was about to return to her work when her gaze snagged on the flickering flame behind the stove grate. The night of Traveling Mike's murder came back to her. The flash of light as Deidre lit a match. She couldn't shake the similarity between his strangling and the woman's suicide. A belt, the attendant had said. That was precisely what she'd seen around Traveling Mike's neck. Or thought she'd seen. Everything had happened so quickly. Could there be a connection between the deaths?

Una gave a weak laugh and turned away from the stove, smoothing her apron and eyeing the long row of patients awaiting her care. Of all the cockeyed ideas she'd had, this was the most absurd. What did she suppose happened? That the frowzy attendant murdered Traveling Mike and then the woman in the Insane Pavilion the very same way? It would explain why the attendant recognized Una. But she wasn't even on duty when the woman died. Besides, the person Una had seen crouching over Traveling Mike's body in that alley had been a man.

Right?

She pressed her fingers into her eyes and laughed again. The worry of the past few days was making her doubt her memory. She shrugged off the idea and got back to work, ignoring the chill that lingered beneath her skin.

CHAPTER 28

As Una was leaving the hospital that evening with the other trainees, she spied Edwin leaning against the doorjamb of the doctors' dining room. Their eyes met for the flash of a moment, and he inclined his head toward the stairwell at the far end of the hall. It was a slight movement, one someone less trained in observation would have missed. She might not be practiced at assessing the character and frequency of a patient's cough, but Una could certainly read a man's behavior. How else could she pick the perfect dupe?

Not that Una thought of Edwin as a dupe. If anyone was a dupe in this situation, it was her. To meet him like this—here at the hospital where anyone could stumble upon them—was beyond foolish. But instead of pretending not to have noticed, she gave a quick nod.

"I forgot to tell the night nurse something important," she said to the other trainees. "I'd better go back."

"We'll wait for you," Dru said cheerily, even as the others rolled their eyes and grumbled. Una couldn't blame them, not with a warm supper waiting at the nurses' home.

"No, it could take a while, what if she's busy and all. I'll be fine walking back on my own."

Dru looked unconvinced as if crossing the street and walking half a block alone were as perilous as a midnight stroll down Bottle Alley. Una squeezed Dru's hand. Her concern, though entirely unfounded, was touching. "I'll have the night watchman escort me."

With Dru appeased, the women hurried out while Una turned around and started up the main staircase. She climbed to the second story, followed the hallway to the narrower flight of stairs at the far end, and crept back to the first floor. She sat on the bottom step and waited. The old brick bones of the hospital creaked around her like a giant troll shifting on its haunches. Otherwise it was quiet.

Her mind strayed to the Insane Pavilion—the dead woman, the attendant, and Traveling Mike. Could they truly be connected? She unpinned her cap and loosened the bun at the nape of her neck. Her thoughts were so mired she didn't hear Edwin's approaching footfalls and startled when he opened the stairwell door.

"Forgive me, Miss Kelly. I didn't mean to frighten you."

It wasn't him Una was afraid of, even though everything about him whispered danger for her plans. "You didn't. I was just lost in thought."

He started to say something in reply when footsteps sounded on the stairs above. He grabbed her hand and led her from the stairwell. As soon as they were out in the open, he let go, and Una found herself missing the warmth of his touch. He passed through two adjoining wards, down a short flight of stairs, and out a heavy door covered with sheet iron into the night. Una followed a safe distance behind. Once she made it outside, she realized they'd exited onto the grounds between the north wing and Twenty-Eighth Street. To her right lay the ambulance stables. To her left, a low-slung brick building Una didn't recognize. Its windows were dark and only a faint swirl of smoke puffed from the chimney.

Edwin stood in the open doorway of the building, waiting for her. She looked about to be sure no one else was lingering around the grounds, then joined him. He closed the door behind them and struck a match. The vast room swallowed its feeble light.

"Where are we?"

Edwin grabbed an oil lamp from a peg on the wall and lit the wick. The light flared then settled into a soft glow, illuminating the room. Shelves filled with bottles lined the walls. A stone mortar the size of a soup pot sat on a nearby counter, its wooden pestle—itself the size of a chair rung—resting to one side. Copper vats borne aloft on iron stands were scattered around the room alongside metal boilers and enormous glass beakers. The air smelled sharp and faintly metallic.

"This is the drug department's manufacturing laboratory," he said. "Pharmaceutical preparations for the entire city are made here."

"And they keep it unlocked?"

Edwin patted his jacket pocket. "Skeleton key. All the doctors have one."

Una wandered farther into the room. Ropes and pulleys dangled from the ceiling. At the far end, an open hatchway led down to the cellar where dozens of brandy barrels were stacked. A drunk would have a heyday in here. Or a thief, for that matter. Or a pair of furtive lovers. She turned around and looked at Edwin. "Did you bring me here to assail my virtue with a kiss again?"

She said it in a light, teasing voice, but Edwin's cheeks colored. "No, I . . ." He thrust his hands into his trouser pockets and rocked back on his heels like a boy caught stealing sugar from the tea tray. "I'm sorry if my forwardness at the lake offended you."

"So you brought me here to apologize?"

"No. I mean, yes. I mean, no. Not really. Not entirely. I just . . . wanted to see you again."

Una smiled at his sudden shyness. Another man she might suspect of artifice, but not Edwin. "You see me every day on the ward."

"Yes, but then we're both just playing our prescribed roles."

Una ignored the aptness of his words, keeping her voice blithe. "And what role are you playing? That of the obsequious intern?"

Edwin's expression hardened, and she regretted her flippant

remark. He slipped his hands from his pockets and tugged down on his suit jacket in the same manner she'd seen the fusty Dr. Pingry do. "Studious, I should think, is a more suitable descriptor. Discerning and duteous. I have my grandfather's reputation to live up to, after all."

"And your father's to live down."

He frowned and glanced at the lamp he'd placed on a nearby table as if he meant to grab it and leave.

"I don't mean that as a criticism," she said. "We're all trying to live down something."

Edwin didn't reply, but he didn't storm out either. Were Una trying to fleece him, she'd drop the subject. Say something flattering like how well-liked he was among the nursing staff or how clever he sounded during rounds. (When he wasn't trying to impress Dr. Pingry.) But Una's aim wasn't to distract or bemuse him so she could pinch his pocketbook. She felt the same desire he did—to taste again the freeness they'd known at the lake when they hadn't been trainee and doctor, but simply two people enjoying each other's company. She crossed the room, lifted herself onto the counter beside him, and sat. It wasn't the most decorous of perches, but her feet ached after the long day's work.

"Perhaps being a bit like your father wouldn't be such a bad thing anyway."

Edwin crossed his arms and leaned against the counter opposite her. Jars of medicine rattled on the shelf behind him. Clearly this wasn't the assignation he'd had in mind. "You never met my father."

"No, but I've known lots of men. And women. *Alleh meiles in ainem, iz nito bei kainem.*"

Edwin gave her a confounded look, and she added, "Just something an old acquaintance said. It means, 'no one possesses all the virtues.'"

"I'll say."

"Your father must have had some qualities you admired."

He stood brooding for a moment, then ran a hand down his

face and sighed. "I guess he . . . he didn't pretend to be someone he wasn't. I suppose there's virtue in that."

His words landed like a billy club to the gut. Una had spent half her life pretending to be someone or other she wasn't. But she managed a weak nod.

"What you saw was what you got. Society's good opinion be damned." He winced. "Er—pardon my language."

"I'm sure my delicate ears will recover."

A fleeting smile cracked his hard expression. "Sometimes I wish . . ."

"Wish what?"

"Wish I had the courage to be my own man."

"You don't want to be a doctor?"

"I do. Very much. But a different sort of physician than my grandfather or Dr. Pingry would have me be. There's a symposium next month in Philadelphia about Dr. Lister's principles of aseptic surgery. I—" He stopped and shook his head. "I'm sorry, you don't want to hear about this."

"On the contrary, I do."

He told her more about Lister and his methods. About the symposium and Dr. Pingry's objections to his attending. His entire countenance enlivened as he spoke, and Una found herself listening intently.

"You simply must attend, then," she said when he'd finished. "Dr. Pingry's good opinion be damned."

Edwin laughed. "You shouldn't miss me were I to go?"

"Miss you!" Una feigned a gasp. "That's rather presumptuous of you, Doctor. I think I should hardly notice you gone."

He grabbed his chest dramatically. "Ah, Miss Kelly, you've struck me with a mortal wound."

At this, Una found herself laughing too. How easy it was to shed the day's worries when she was with him. To forget Nurse Hatfield and Traveling Mike and the police—even if just for a moment. How easy, and how dangerous.

He stopped laughing and took a step closer. His hands fidgeted at his sides until he buried them in his trouser pockets again. His gaze was once more skittish. Did he mean to kiss her? She knew better than to permit another such advance. What happened at the lake had been a mistake. A blissful, foolish mistake. One she couldn't afford to make again. Why, then, did her lips tingle with anticipation?

To both her disappointment and relief, Edwin came no closer. "All jesting aside, Miss Kelly, I'd hoped you might agree to see me again. To let me court you. Privately, of course. I should not want to jeopardize your position at the school."

Una blinked. A kiss she was prepared for. But this? She slipped off the counter and inched away from him. "Why would you want to do that?"

"Because you're the most captivating woman I've ever met. Witty, kind, high-spirited. You challenge what I say instead of simpering in agreement."

She continued to slink away until she found herself pinned between the counter and a vat of sharp-smelling liquid. "I'm not those things."

Edwin chuckled. "See, you're challenging me even now."

"I can't," she said without conviction.

"Is it me you disprove of or the necessity of deception?"

"It's not you," she blurted out before good sense got the better of her. "You're . . . rather captivating yourself. But I . . ."

He took another step toward her, his air of confidence renewed. "Then please, give me an earnest chance. That is, if you could abide keeping such a secret."

Una's hands felt suddenly sweaty and her mouth dry, as if she'd been caught red-handed in the middle of a heist. Part of her wanted to distract him with a swift kick to the shin and run. But the larger part of her wanted to shrink the distance between them. Wanted to taste his winter-mint breath. Wanted to be the woman he thought she was.

Two more steps, and he was close enough to kiss her. Una's body hummed like an electric bulb. Instead of kissing her, though, he took her hand. "Please, say yes, Miss Kelly."

"Una."

"Una." He said it like it were the kind of sweet wine one savored on the tongue before swallowing. "Is that a yes?"

She couldn't afford more distractions. The coppers' recent visit had reminded her of that. And everything about Edwin—from his dashing smile and too-perfect teeth, to his warm candor, to his heart-quickening touch—was distracting. Una pulled her hand away and shimmied past him toward the door. "I can't, Doctor, I'm sorry. I have enough secrets in my life."

CHAPTER 29

Una knew the idea that the Insane Pavilion attendant was involved in Traveling Mike's murder was farfetched. Crazy, even. The two deaths weren't connected.

But, absurd as it was, Una couldn't put the notion to rest until she got a closer gander at the attendant.

The next morning, while the other trainees squeezed into the demonstration room to learn about dressings, bandages, and splints, Una slipped out the back door and made her way to the hospital. She'd made Dru promise to teach her everything she missed that evening during their study hour.

"What if one of the head nurses realizes you're missing and asks where you are?" Dru had asked.

"Tell them I was too sick to get out of bed."

"I couldn't lie."

"It's not a lie, it's just not the truth. The whole truth. I really do have an awful headache. Besides, it only counts as a lie if you're the one who makes it up."

Dru crossed her arms, clearly unconvinced.

"Please, I promised one of the patients on the ward that I'd be there to say farewell before her discharge. She's had a terribly hard time these past weeks." Una's mouth was uncharacteristically dry, making it hard to spit out the words. "Kidney stones and gallstones and . . . and . . . prostate stones."

"Prostate stones? I thought you said the patient was a woman."

"Yes, er, she is. A hermaphrodite, actually." She smacked her lips and swallowed. "All the more reason she's had such an awful time. She'd be just heartbroken if I wasn't there to see her off and might even relapse."

Reluctantly, Dru had agreed.

Now, Una strode past the workmen laying stones for the new gatehouse and crossed the lawn. Her tongue remained parched, and she wished she'd grabbed a drink of water or a few sips of coffee before leaving the house. Lying hadn't always come easy to her. The first few times she'd sputtered and stammered like she had a mouthful of flour. But that had been over a decade ago as a child. Now she was a pro and damned well ought to act like it. She'd deceived Dru from the beginning, after all. What was one more lie?

Bald trees and wiry bushes dotted the lawn. Paths crisscrossed the brown grass, connecting the hospital, pavilions, and wharf. A few patients hobbled along on crutches or rested on the wooden benches that lined segments of the path. But the winter cold kept most inside. Una found a bench near the Insane Pavilion. A cluster of overgrown bushes shielded the bench from easy view. If she leaned slightly to the left and cocked her head, though, she had a clear line of sight to the back stoop of the pavilion where the women's ward exited onto the lawn.

Una pulled a book from her pocket and pretended to read. She'd kept close watch of the building these past days in case the coppers returned, peering from the windows of ward twelve between every task. So she knew that the day attendant frequently slipped out onto the stoop to steal a few pulls from the flask hidden in her skirt pocket. All Una had to do was wait. If she could get a close look at the woman in the daylight, Una was certain she'd know for sure whether their paths had crossed before—be it in the slums or the back alley where Traveling Mike had been murdered.

A few minutes later, Una heard the creak of door hinges and looked up from her book. The day attendant had stepped out onto the stoop, just as Una had hoped. She leaned to the side and tilted her head, studying the woman through a small gap in the bushes. The attendant wore a puffy blue cap today instead of her usual greasy headscarf, and her gray-streaked hair was knotted in a messy bun. She glanced around, then sneaked the flask from her pocket and took a long slug. Something in the woman's face—her eyebrows perhaps?—did look familiar. They were pale and bushy, with almost no arc. The right one was broken by a thin scar.

No, maybe it wasn't the eyebrows. But something else about her face perhaps. Una laid aside her book and crept closer until she was squatting at the edge of the bush. Was it her missing tooth? No, half the people in the city had gap-toothed grins. The leafless branches snagged on Una's clothes and scratched her skin, but she continued to press forward. Just a little closer. The attendant took another swig and capped her flask. Her knuckles were knobby and swollen.

"You lose something?" a voice said from behind her.

Una startled, lost her balance, and fell face-first into the bushes. Before she could untangle herself, a thick hand encircled her arm and pulled her free.

"Pardon, Miss Kelly, didn't mean to frighten you," Conor said, setting her on her feet before releasing his grip.

Una brushed the dirt and broken twigs from her skirt and righted her cap. She glanced over her shoulder, but the attendant was gone. Damn it!

"Looks like you cut yourself." Conor pulled a handkerchief from his pocket and dabbed it across her cheek. Her skin stung where he touched her, and the handkerchief came away dotted with blood.

"Just a scratch, I'm sure."

When he moved to wipe her face again, she pulled back, glancing belatedly at the hospital. She'd have a hell of a time explaining such familiarity to Superintendent Perkins. Never mind the way his touch made the skin on the back of her neck pucker with gooseflesh.

She returned to the bench where she'd laid her book. Conor sat beside her. They spoke at the same time.

"I was just—"

"Do ya need—"

Conor smiled and gestured for her to go ahead.

"I was just searching the bushes for . . . er . . . a lost mitten."

"I could help ya look. Where did ya last have it?"

He started to stand, but Una put her hand on his sleeve. "Don't bother. I'm sure I left it at home."

They sat a moment in uncomfortable silence. Una tried not to look perturbed even though he'd interfered with her snooping, and who knew when the attendant would slip out for another nip from her flask.

It was easier to be beside him at mass with the priest's voice filling the chapel or walking back to the nurses' home afterward when the busy streets presented ample diversion. He wasn't a bad man, and she generally didn't mind his company. They could laugh together over things no one at the nurses' home would understand. But strange things raised his dander—street urchins, hucksters, women of the lost sisterhood. He'd rant for a few blocks about how they were poisoning the city, then remember himself and apologize. Una suspected he'd find her equally repugnant if he knew her true calling. Then again, who among her new acquaintances wouldn't?

She liked to think that Dru or Edwin might understand if they knew the particulars of her plight. But understanding and still wanting to keep her company were two very different things.

Finally, Conor cleared his throat and nodded toward the Insane Pavilion. "Heard they had a suicide a few days back."

"I heard that too."

"Shame."

"Mmm . . . Do you suppose—" Una hesitated. He'd think she was crazy enough to be locked up there herself if she told him her suspicions about the attendant. But who else could she tell? "Do you suppose it's possible something else could have caused the woman's death?"

"Like what?"

Una absentmindedly touched her cheek. The scratch had stopped bleeding but still stung. "I don't know. It's just . . . the police were brought in to investigate, and they never did find the rope or belt or whatever it was the woman used to hang herself."

"That why ya loitering about out here?"

She winced and nodded.

"You look like a thief casing a shop, ya do."

"I only thought—"

"What, that that old attendant snuck into the woman's cell and strangled her?"

Una looked down at her lap. It sounded completely ridiculous when he said it.

"And why would she do a thing like that?"

"I don't know. It was a foolish thing to think. I guess the idea of that poor woman killing herself has me a bit unsettled."

He scooted closer to her. "Ya wouldn't be the first. It's bleak work here at the hospital. Sometimes the patients get better. Sometimes they don't. She weren't the first to take her life in there and she won't be the last." He reached out and touched Una's cheek again, tracing the line of her cut with the pad of his thumb. "She ain't worth your pity, a lunatic like that. She let the devil in and now—"

Una heard footsteps approaching and pulled away. Striding toward them down the path was Edwin. "Mr. McCready, I—" His gaze flickered to Una, and he stopped. His jaw slackened and eyes blinked in rapid succession like one who'd just been punched. "I . . . er . . ." He straightened his shoulders and looked back at Conor. "I trust I'm not disturbing you. I'm Dr. Westervelt. I'll be filling in as ambulance surgeon while Dr. Scott is ill and I'd like to see the wagon."

"Of course, sir." Conor stood, glancing back at Una. "Get along now and think on what I said."

Una nodded. What he'd said made sense. Not about letting the devil in or any of that nonsense. Death was a bleak reality here at the hospital. She couldn't run around crying murder anytime it happened. Besides, judging from the flinty look Edwin shot her before striding away, Una had new troubles to worry about.

CHAPTER 30

Una watched them go, hoping Edwin would look back. He did not. A strange, panicky feeling grew inside her. Like she'd swallowed a live eel, and it was still thrashing around in her belly.

Clearly Edwin had mistaken her chance encounter with Conor as an illicit rendezvous. Normally Una didn't care two figs what other people thought of her behavior. But, in spite of herself, she cared deeply what Edwin thought. Yes, she'd rebuffed his courtship. And, yes, she trusted he wouldn't report her to Superintendent Perkins. But even so, she didn't want him to think anything was going on with her and Conor. Didn't want him to think this was one of the secrets she'd alluded to last night.

The wisest course of action was to forget about Edwin and get back to the nurses' home. With any luck, she'd arrive right as the morning's demonstration was ending and could slip in alongside the other trainees on their way to the hospital. No one, save Dru, would know she'd been absent. But instead of heading toward the gate, she wended her way across the lawn toward the ambulance bay.

She flattened herself against the wall alongside the entrance and listened. Conor's voice sounded above the snorts and whinnies echoing from the horse stalls, his brogue all but absent. Edwin replied with uncharacteristic curtness. Their conversation was all business—which supplies were aboard, where they were stored, how the surgeon on-call was notified when a message came over the receiver.

Una waited until their discussion ended and Conor's heavy footfalls drifted toward the stalls before creeping inside. The long line of black ambulances stood at the ready, the first already hitched to a horse. The animal's eyes were half-closed, and one of its hind legs lifted as if dozing. Its tail swished as Una approached, but otherwise it didn't stir.

Edwin stood at the back of the wagon, examining the contents of the medical bag the ambulance surgeons carried. Una watched him a moment from alongside the horse, uncertain what to say. The smart half of her knew she should turn around. She'd already said too much last night.

But the stubborn half of her won out. He had no right to sashay around the hospital grounds, barging in on people's private conversations and perverting their intentions. The horse swished his tail again and lazily raised his eyelid as if to say, *Well, get on with it*. She glared in response—though, of course, the horse was right—and straightened her shoulders. A backward glance at the stables to be sure Conor was still occupied, and she pressed her feet onward.

Edwin looked up as she approached, then back down at the medical bag. "Something I can help you with, Nurse Kelly, or were you looking for Mr. McCasanova?"

"It's Mr. McCready, and no, I was not. I came to see you."

He continued to rifle through the bag, picking out objects and examining them as if he'd never seen gauze or tweezers before. "Well, here I am."

"I just . . . before when . . . it wasn't what it looked like. I'd fallen into a bush, and Mr. McCready was checking to see that I was all right."

"And how does one just fall into a bush?"

Una hesitated. She couldn't very well tell him she'd been snooping around the Insane Pavilion because the attendant not only had a penchant for strong spirits but maybe murder too. Edwin, seemingly reading her silence as guilt, snorted and shook his head.

"Edwin, I—" The gong above the telegraph receiver boomed, drowning out her voice. "I—" She tried to speak above it, but the sound filled the bay. The drowsing horse raised its head, ears perked and eyes fully open as Conor leaped onto the driver's seat.

"Ready, Doc?" he hollered without looking back.

Edwin jammed the medical bag closed and climbed into the ambulance. The final gong sounded. Una tried to speak again, but he cut her off. "I have work to do, Nurse Kelly, and you should be on the ward."

Una's hands tingled as if her heart were pumping fire. She clambered into the wagon just as it started to move. "You don't get to tell me what to do."

"I'm a physician. You're a nurse. Not even a nurse. A trainee. Damned if I don't get to tell you what to do."

The ambulance listed, knocking Edwin to his knees. After years of sneaking onto the streetcar, Una had better sense and had grabbed onto one of the overhead hand straps.

"Hold on!" Conor yelled from the driver's seat. "We're about to really get going once we clear the gate!"

Edwin scrambled onto the bench, looking a bit pale. He paid no mind to his lopsided hat and dusty trousers but clutched the seat like it was a life raft.

Wood paneling enclosed the front half of the ambulance, but the flaps covering the large rear windows were furled, giving Una a plain view of the passing hospital. If she leaped out now, she'd likely manage to land on her feet. But once the wagon picked up speed, exiting would be trickier. Of course, she could always wait for a soft pile of trash or manure, covering her head and rolling as she landed. Una was well practiced at this. When you filched a man's pocketbook, you didn't always have time to wait for the streetcar to stop. But Mrs. Buchanan would throw a conniption fit if Una returned to the home with her nursing uniform covered in horseshit and mud.

And her stubborn half wasn't finished. She freed one hand from the strap and pointed at the hospital. "You can order me about in there. But out here, the only boss of me is me." She glanced down at the hard dirt drive, gauging the wagon's speed. It wouldn't be a graceful landing, but she should manage to stay upright. "Now, if you'll excuse me, I also have work to do."

She turned away from him and was about to jump when the ambulance rocked again, weaving between the stonemasons at work on the gatehouse. As it turned on to Twenty-Sixth Street, Una lost her grip on the hand strap. She stumbled sideways, reaching for hold of something, anything, to keep from tumbling out. The street flashed by in a blur. The top half of her was already out the window when something snagged on her skirt.

A hand. Edwin's. He held her there, half in half out, until he could manage to loop an arm around her waist and pull her inside. They collapsed side by side on the bench.

"My God, Una, are you mad?" His hat sat further askew, and his necktie had come undone.

"I thought I had time to jump."

"Jump! From a moving wagon?"

Una hadn't realized her hands were trembling until Edwin took them in his own. A dirty dress would have been the least of her problems had she fallen face-first at this speed. "I hadn't expected such a sudden turn."

Edwin shook his head, but to her relief, he was smiling. "You are mad."

He started to pull his hands away, but Una held on. Her blood no longer felt as if it were on fire. Instead, a different type of heat stirred inside her. "Nothing is going on between Con—Mr. McCready and me. I promise. I was . . . I was sneaking around the Insane Pavilion. He startled me, and I really did fall into a bush." She turned her head so he could see her opposite cheek. "See, I have a scratch to prove it."

He freed one of his hands from hers and traced the scratch with the pad of his thumb just as Conor had done. Instead of pulling away, Una leaned into his touch.

The ambulance rolled over a pothole, and Edwin pulled away to clutch the seat again.

"You're not afraid of carriage riding, are you?" Una asked.

"'Afraid' is far too strong a word," he said, even as his knuckles blanched from so tight a grip on the bench. "I simply prefer being the one in control of the reins."

"Mr. McCready has assured me he's the best driver in the city."

"I'm sure he has."

"Like it or not, Edwin, Mr. McCready and I are good acquaintances. We attend the same church service, and he's been kind enough to walk me home a time or two. That's all."

"There's something about the man . . . I don't trust him."

She brushed back a strand of hair that had fallen across his forehead and righted his hat. "You don't have to. You only have to trust me."

A pang of guilt followed her words. How could she ask him to trust her when everything she'd told him was a lie? But before she could take the words back, his lips were on hers. This kiss was deeper than their first, insistent and unabashed. Una gave up trying to resist him and matched his intensity. Everything else fell away—the sway of the wagon, the rattle of the medicine bottles in the box beneath their seat, the cool stir of air around them—and with it, her old life, everything she'd been and would one day have to return to. Not even the risk of being seen or the cry for air from her lungs could rend the moment.

When at last they pulled apart, Una's lips were tingling and her heart sputtering.

"Promise me you won't try jumping out of a moving wagon again," he said.

Una smiled and kissed him, so she wouldn't have to lie.

CHAPTER 31

Una had been so caught up, first with anger and then passion, that she'd not considered what to do when the ambulance arrived at its destination. But its slowing wheels jogged her senses. Nurses didn't go out with the ambulance. She doubted Conor would say anything, and the patient certainly wouldn't know better, but how would she explain the situation to Superintendent Perkins if word did reach her?

They stopped on a garbage-strewn street in front of an old wooden tenement. It took her a moment to get her bearings, but when the air changed directions and the scent of blood and entrails struck her nose, she realized they were in Hell's Kitchen.

Edwin grimaced. "What's that smell?"

"The slaughterhouses," Una said without thinking, then hastily added, "We have them in Augusta too."

Hell's Kitchen had never been a regular haunt of Una's. Its saloons and gambling dens and whorehouses drew dupes from all parts of the city. Easy pickings, if it weren't for the gangs of Irish roughs who patrolled the streets, expecting a cut of everything. Between them and Marm Blei, Una would walk away with fewer coins in her pocket than she'd started with, so she generally kept away. Rule number twenty-one: Don't pay twice.

There was a rap on the front panel, and Conor hollered, "We're here, Doc! I'll be with the horse and wagon if you need anything."

Edwin grabbed his medical bag. "Guess we'll just have to get used to the smell." He removed the wagon's tailboard and jumped down, then held out his hand for Una.

She hesitated.

"You're coming, aren't you?"

Una took his hand and climbed from the wagon. She'd be more conspicuous waiting in the ambulance, with every passerby stopping and peering inside in the hopes of spying some battered or bloodied passenger to satisfy their morbid curiosity. Already a small crowd had gathered.

Edwin pushed through the onlookers toward the tenement steps. Una followed close behind. She didn't see the roundsman waiting there for them until it was too late to turn around.

"What's the situation, Officer?" Edwin asked.

"Third floor. Number three-oh-two. A man slipped on the stairs comin' down from the roof. Twisted his leg mighty badly." The roundsman spoke with a thick brogue that, unlike Conor, he made no attempt to conceal. His skin was pasty and his dark mustache overgrown. The brass insignia on his jacket read PRECINCT TWENTY.

The tightness in Una's chest eased enough that she could breathe. She didn't know the copper, and his was one of the few precincts this side of Fifty-Seventh Street she hadn't toured in handcuffs. Even so, she stayed in Edwin's shadow, dropping her chin just enough to obscure her face without seeming shifty.

"Is the leg broken?" Edwin asked.

"Don't know. Didn't take much of a look myself."

"Never mind. Just show us the way."

"You and . . . er . . . the lady?"

"Yes. Nurse Kelly will be assisting me."

The copper shifted his weight from one foot to the other, and the tightness in Una's chest returned. Did he recognize her? Should she run?

Una forced down a steadying breath and lifted her eyes to meet his. To run now would be disastrous. She didn't know this part of the city well and would likely be caught. Even if she weren't, the ruse would be up, and she'd never be able to return to the training school. No, all she could do now was trust her disguise.

His gaze shifted from her to Edwin. "It's just that . . . these slums, Doctor, they're not a pretty sight. They don't live like you and me. It might be too much for the lady."

Una nearly laughed with relief. He hadn't recognized her at all, only thought her too delicate to proceed. "Whatever the conditions, Officer," she said, "you may rest assured I'm well trained and up for the task."

"Suit yourself, miss," he said and led them into the building.

As soon as the door closed, darkness enveloped them. The roundsman unfastened the lantern from his belt and lit it with a match.

"Are there no lamps in these tenements?" Edwin asked.

"Not these older ones, no," the officer said.

"But how do the residents manage? Surely they don't carry a lantern strapped to their belts like you do."

The roundsman chuckled. "No, sir, they don't. Get by with a match or a candle, I expect."

"No wonder the man fell," Edwin muttered, his voice thick with disapproval.

He'd probably never been inside a tenement before, Una realized. A barbed reminder that no matter his affections, they came from entirely different worlds.

The roundsman tossed the smoldering match he'd used to light his lantern onto the floor and started up the stairs. "Mind your step, now."

Una ground the match head to a fine dust with her boot heel before following behind him and Edwin. An old tenement like this likely hadn't any fire escapes either. Una did her best to ignore this fact, despite the uptick of her pulse.

The narrow stairs creaked as they ascended. Vegetable peels, rat droppings, and bits of broken glass littered the ground. The smell of the slaughterhouses mingled with that of rot and urine. Halfway up the second flight, Edwin stopped and lifted his foot. A sticky, goopy mess clung to the bottom of his expensive patent leather shoes. To his credit, Edwin merely scraped it off on the lip of the step and continued.

A muffled wailing greeted them when they reached the third floor. The roundsman rapped once on the door before opening it. They entered a disheveled room perhaps twelve feet square. A rusted kettle rattled atop the stove. Wooden crates and barrels served as the only furniture. Two windows looked onto the rear yard, affording the room at least a semblance of light.

Though Una had lived in worse places, her weeks at the nurses' home with its clean and cozy appointments had weakened her sensibilities. She heard Edwin's sharp intake of breath and struggled to hide her own revulsion. Mrs. Buchanan's enthusiasm for order and tidiness, once so annoying to Una, now seemed positively saintly.

Three children huddled wide-eyed in the far corner of the room. An old, toothless woman rested on an upturned crate nearby. Two more middle-aged women sat near the windows hunched over their needlework, their fingers knobby and thin, baskets of shirts stacked around them. One of them pointed to the adjoining room where the moaning was emanating from.

Stepping around rag piles and ash buckets and rusty pails, they picked their way toward the room. The injured man lay inside on a thin mattress, his wife weeping beside him. A single candle lit the windowless room. But even in the dim light, Una could see the grave state of the man's leg, twisted below the knee and bleeding through his dirty trousers.

The copper hesitated by the doorway, but Edwin grabbed his lantern and hurried in. Una followed. He set down his bag and shrugged out of his jacket, laying it aside without care of dirt and fleas. As he rolled up his shirtsleeves, he said to Una, "Open my bag and find the scissors so I can cut away his trouser leg."

For a single moment, Una stood gaping down at the man, his wife, and Edwin unable to move. It wasn't the man's leg. She'd seen worse at Bellevue and before. But the situation called for a nurse. Not a thief on the lam pretending to be a nurse.

She rattled her head and knelt beside Edwin. Nurse or not, at least she could help. She fumbled with the medicine bag's latch, trying three times before it opened. When she managed to find the scissors, the cold metal felt familiar in her hand. She handed them to Edwin and watched as he cut through the man's trousers. The leg, swollen to twice its natural size, had taken on a waxy, reddish-purple hue. The tibia had fractured and pierced the skin. Blood spread from the wound.

The wife gasped at the sight and continued to sob. The man told her in Gaelic to hush, then turned to Edwin and said in English, "Pull out your saw, Doc, I'm ready."

"I don't think we'll need to amputate. Certainly not here. Once I get the leg stabilized, we'll bring you to Bellevue for further care."

Edwin turned his scissors to the man's boot, but the man sat up and cried, "Not me boot, Doc! It's me only pair."

"Your foot's too swollen to remove the boot otherwise, and we must get it off."

"What about trying a little grease?" Una said. She knew all too well how prized a good pair of boots were.

"I suppose that might work."

Una stood. "I'll fetch it along with some clean water." She turned to the wife. "Perhaps you could help me."

The woman nodded, wobbling as she stood. Una looped an arm around her waist and steered her to the main room. Una's Gaelic was rusty, but she remembered a little of what her mother used to say when tending to the sick and needy. "*Ná caill do chroí.*" *Don't lose heart.* "Dr. Westervelt and I will see that he gets the very best care."

A little grease and the boot came off with a single tug. The man didn't even flinch. Una suspected that had as much to do with the laudanum Edwin gave him as with her gentle ministrations, though. It took only a few minutes in the frigid apartment for the water she'd boiled to cool. Once it reached a tepid temperature, she cleaned the blood from the man's leg. Though only the tibia had broken through the skin, she knew from her nightly study with Dru that the fibula was likely fractured too. She helped Edwin splint the man's leg, ready with oakum packing and cotton bindings before he asked for them.

The roundsman fetched the stretcher from the ambulance, and Una accompanied him to grab a blanket. "You're mighty good with these folks," he said to her as they trudged back up the dark stairs. Una was alert for any hint of sarcasm or suspicion, but his voice was sincere. "I'd heard yous at Bellevue were a new breed of nurses. Now I believe it."

Una found it strangely difficult to speak, as if a lump of coal were blocking her windpipe. At last she managed, "Thank you, Officer."

Back in the small, dark bedroom, they carefully rolled the man onto the long swath of stretcher canvas, then slipped wooden poles through the tubes of fabric along either edge. Una tucked the blankets around him until he was snug as a swaddled babe. He winced when Edwin and the officer lifted the stretcher, but the laudanum kept him otherwise calm.

Una grabbed the medical bag and followed behind the men as they carried the stretcher from the room. She didn't envy them the task of picking their way down the steep steps and held the roundsman's lantern aloft to light the way.

They had packed the man into the back of the ambulance and were about to leave when the wife hurried out from the tenement. She came up to the side of the wagon where Una was seated and held something out to her. "*Go raibh míle maith agat.*"

May you have a thousand good things. Una only vaguely remembered the expression but knew it meant a heartfelt thanks.

She took the object—a small, oval medallion—and turned it over in her palm. One side was flat. The other had a relief of the Virgin Mary.

"I'll see that it stays with him," she said.

The woman shook her head. "No, my friend, it's for you."

The ambulance pulled away before Una could insist on giving it back. It was nickel silver, not the real thing. No fence in town would give her more than a quarter for it. But somehow that didn't matter. She squeezed her fingers around the medallion, then tucked it safely away inside her pocket.

CHAPTER 32

The next few weeks passed without upset. No botched spying attempts from the bushes. No unplanned ambulance rides. No irksome encounters with Nurse Hatfield. The man with the fractured leg was placed in the ward adjoining her own. Una managed to visit him every day despite her growing list of duties. His leg was raised and fixed with traction, but the puncture wound had healed without infection, and the prognosis for his recovery was good. She brought him fresh tea, fluffed his pillow, and read to him when she had the time. He preferred the *Irish American* but would settle for the *World* if that was the only newspaper handy.

Una managed to see Edwin most days too, if only for a fleeting moment when he brought a new ambulance patient to her ward. When Dr. Scott recovered from the flu and returned to his position as ambulance surgeon, she and Edwin contrived to meet in stairwells, storerooms, even the worrisome elevator to share a few words and a hurried kiss. The rare Sunday when neither of them were on duty, they met at Central Park, braving the muddy, less fashionable paths to keep from being seen by anyone from Bellevue.

Una knew their liaisons were reckless. And the more Edwin shared of his life—a favorite hunting dog named Oyster he'd had as a child, a carriage accident when he was nine that fractured his skull and left the driver dead, a half brother he'd met in New Orleans and never spoken to again—the more Una hated herself for deceiving him. But every time she resolved to tell him they were through, her will crumbled.

He was different from past men she'd dallied with. Those men were like her—at once flippant and guarded when it came to matters of the heart. Even Barney, the only other man who'd shown true care for her, expressed his affection in paternalistic terms. Edwin spoke to her like an equal. (When they weren't on the ward, playing, as he'd put it, their prescribed roles.) He flattered her with compliments the same as other men but seemed as interested in knowing her thoughts as he was in kissing her.

Thankfully, no one at the hospital or nurses' home suspected anything between them. Or so Una thought.

One night in early March, as they sat side by side in the library reading, Dru turned to her and asked, "Where do you really go after church on Sundays?"

Una looked up from her textbook, doing her best to appear unperturbed even though her heart had leaped into her throat. For a country bumpkin, Dru's instincts were surprisingly sharp. She cast a nonchalant glance around the room to be sure they weren't in earshot of the other women, then met Dru's gaze and smiled stiffly. "Like I told you, to my cousin's home uptown for supper."

"But you always eat again when you return."

"She's . . . er . . . not a very good cook." That was true enough. Una reached for her cup of milk and took a sip, then turned her eyes back to her book, hoping that would be the end of it.

"Are you having an affair with your cousin's husband?"

Una choked on her half-swallowed milk, coughing and tearing up until her windpipe cleared. If Dru had ever met Randolph, she'd know how ridiculous a notion that was. "My God, what a thing to say! Of course not."

Dru's neck flushed, and she looked down at her lap. "I'm sorry. I didn't mean to cause offense. Mother always told me I'd do well to keep my mouth shut."

Clearly that advice had fallen on deaf ears.

"It's just that . . . well, never mind. I suppose Mother was right." Dru wrung her hands as if she hoped to squeeze out all feeling. "We're still friends, aren't we?"

Una reached over and stilled Dru's hands. "Don't be a ninny, of course we are. I've been called worse than an adulteress before."

"What could be worse than that?"

Trollop. Miscreant. Bandit. Boot-scum. Bogtrotter. Menace. Gutter rat. Una could list dozens of insults slung her way over the years, but she didn't elaborate. She tried to return to her book but couldn't concentrate on the words, rereading the same paragraph about methods for arresting hemorrhages three times before giving up. "What made you think I was carrying on an affair?"

This time it was Dru who scanned the room before leaning in and whispering, "Well, in *The Forgotten Room,* Lady Shuttlecock spends hours primping before sneaking out to meet her lover, Count Wickabee. It's how her deceit is eventually uncovered. Her lady's maid notices and tells the cook who tells the—"

"*The Forgotten Room*? Is that what you're wasting candles on late at night after Mrs. Buchanan turns off the gas? And here I thought you were memorizing the names of the blood vessels."

"You won't tell anyone, will you?" Her eyes fell to her lap. "Miss Hatfield and the others might think it in bad taste."

Una shook her head. For some, reading anything other than the Bible was considered bad taste. Though she wouldn't be surprised if Miss Hatfield had a trove of silly novels hidden away in her room. "So you think I'm like Lady Scuttlebug?"

"Shuttlecock, yes."

"And you are . . . the maid?"

"It's just that I've noticed you take more care with your appearance now than before. Pinning your hair just so. Making sure your buttons are straight and sleeves puffed. Asking to borrow my muff and hat when you go out."

Una frowned. The way Dru talked, she'd been positively slatternly before. She'd just never seen the point of brushing her hair a hundred times or preening in front of the mirror. Una hadn't even owned a mirror. The backside of a spoon worked well enough.

"I didn't really think you were having an affair with your cousin's husband," Dru continued. "But when you insisted that was where you were off to every Sunday when you're not on duty at the hospital, well, I couldn't figure what else it could be. Anyway, Dr. Westervelt will be quite relieved."

"Dr. Westervelt?" Una winced at the shrillness of her voice. She leaned back and said more evenly, "Whatever do you mean?"

"Haven't you noticed? He's smitten with you, Una."

Una tried to laugh, but it came out more like a bark. "Surely you're mistaken."

"Why else would he have snuck us in to see that blood transfusion?"

"He was only being kind."

"Well, he certainly wasn't there to watch the procedure. He hardly looked away from you the entire time."

Una grabbed her cup of milk and drank it empty. But still her mouth felt dry. "You don't think anyone else has noticed?"

Dru thought on this an interminably long time before shaking her head. "Not unless they read a lot of novels. In *The Hidden*—"

"You won't mention this to anyone else, will you?"

"Why? Not even Miss Hatfield could fault you. It's not as if you've encouraged his attentions."

Una had lied straight-faced a million times. To bankers and streetcar conductors and coppers and judges. But now, her goddamn lips betrayed her with a smile. A half smile, really. A twitch.

Dru caught it and squealed. Una hushed her.

"I knew you weren't going to your cousin's for supper."

"It's nothing. We're not . . . we enjoy each other's company. That's all." It was nothing, wasn't it? She'd never actually agreed he could court her, after all. Besides, a man like him, on his way to becoming an esteemed surgeon, and she, a thief in hiding, was the sort of ridiculous pairing that belonged on the pages of one of Dru's novels.

For the first time in all their nights of studying, Dru closed her book without marking her page or glancing at the clock to see if she could squeeze out another few minutes of reading. "Tell me everything."

And for the first time, Una did. The whole truth of it. From the first time she'd seen him on the ward to their latest rendezvous just that morning in the northwest stairwell on her way down to the laundry.

"Is he always as terribly serious as he seems at the hospital?" Dru asked.

Una shook her head. That was one of the things she liked about him—his warm, easy laugh. The way he made her laugh too. She liked that he was thoughtful and curious. He listened without jumping over her words to correct or cajole her. He had his share of pigheaded opinions, to be sure. But, unlike most people, he was not above changing his mind. She liked that he had the courage to stand up to Dr. Pingry. The confidence to inspire ready faith in his patients. And yet, when he and Una were alone, he showed the softer, less certain side of himself, trusting her not to exploit it.

And for once, Una didn't. She didn't keep score. Didn't probe for weakness. Didn't angle for advantage. It was as close as she could come to being vulnerable too.

Una and Dru talked until Mrs. Buchanan shooed them to bed. But Una lay awake long after the house went dark. She waited for the knock of regret, the kind she'd felt after drinking too much whiskey or losing the day's earnings on a game of cards. But it didn't come. Instead she felt lighter. Almost giddy. Further proof that jabbering to Dru about Edwin had been a mistake.

Trouble was, her addled brain didn't much care what proof there was. Nor did the rest of her. Rules be damned, she'd enjoyed sitting with Dru, laughing and whispering, as much as she enjoyed her time with Edwin. As much as she'd enjoyed anything for a long, long time. And didn't everyone, even a lying, thieving slum-dweller, deserve a moment or two of happiness?

Reality would come calling soon enough. It always did.

CHAPTER 33

Like the aftereffects of strong spirits, that pesky feeling of lightness lingered into the next day. Una caught herself smiling while delousing a patient's hair and humming—actually humming!—while scrubbing bedpans. What she needed was a cold pail of water thrown over her head. What came was worse.

Shortly after noon, the head nurse sent Una down to the basement exam room where new arrivals were seen before being transferred to the appropriate ward. An influx of patients was expected after an accident at the nearby tinware factory, and Una was to assist with their intake.

The nurse on duty in the exam room had only a few minutes to show Una where the supplies and medicines were kept before the first ambulance arrived. Three patients stumbled out of the back, bruised and bloody but able to walk. The next ambulance bell sounded only a few minutes later, and two more patients, both stretcher cases, were brought in. Una and the other nurse cleared beds for them, squeezing the first three men onto a single cot. Those patients who arrived on the third ambulance had no place to go but the floor.

Una tended to the less injured men while the other nurse, a second-year, took on the more severe cases. The house physician and his two interns bustled between them, tending those whose wounds were urgent and quickly assigning the rest to one of the upstairs wards.

The small room was as noisy and crowded as a concert saloon. Una had to step over patients lying on the floor and shimmy around others crammed three or four on the beds to reach the supply cabinet. Water from the washbasin spilled on her dress, and her apron was stained with blood. She cleaned and bandaged the men's wounds. Smeared salve over their burns. Assisted the doctors in setting and splinting fractured bones. For each man who was conscious, she filled out an intake card with his name, age, address, and next of kin, pinning it to his shirt before orderlies carried him upstairs. For those patients who were unconscious, Una simply wrote *Unknown*.

She couldn't help but think of her mother as she hustled from one patient to the next. Was this the sort of chaotic scene she'd arrived at after the fire? Had someone asked her name, sighed, and written *unknown* when only a raspy, uneven exhale came in reply? Would it have been better if she'd died at the scene, among the ash and rubble, like many of the others had?

Una pushed the thought aside but took care with each of the men she tended, even those too injured to mutter their name, offering a gentle touch or reassuring smile.

At some point, Edwin arrived, presumably to help identify which patients would need surgery and of what kind. Una registered his presence, and, as always, a pleasant warmth spread inside her. But she hadn't time to seek out his smile or space among her harried thoughts to wonder when they might meet again. Too many patients yet needed her care.

Such was the mayhem that Una didn't notice the arrival of another ambulance until Conor and the surgeon dragged in a new patient. A cot had recently been freed, but Una hadn't yet found a spare moment to change out the soot-darkened and bloody sheets. They dropped the patient onto the cot anyway as there was little better place to put him. As soon as she finished mixing up a new batch of burn ointment, Una would see about fresh sheets and whatever else the patient needed.

Conor passed by Una on his way out.

"Another factory worker?" she asked him.

"Nah, I think that's the lot of 'em. This one's just a drunkard." He glanced at the patient with disgust. No, not disgust. Revulsion. The kind of look usually reserved for an overflowing privy. "Be better off without 'em, this city would."

"I'll get him cleaned up and into one of the alcoholic cells."

"Not a him," Conor said and spat on the floor. "*She's* what passes for a lady in the slums." He shook his head and stomped out. Una watched him go, unnerved by the vitriol in his voice. She'd seen his fits before. Listened to him blather on like a Bible-waving reformer. But this was a hospital, after all. Open to any in need. No one was quite as insufferable as a teetotaling Irishman, her father had always said. And Una had to agree.

She mixed the last of the linseed oil and lime water and brought the ointment to one of the interns. He was tending to a man who lay moaning on the floor. Red, weeping burns covered his face and arms. Una helped the intern bandage the man's wound with ointment-soaked rags, mindful that every inch of burn must be protected from the air. When they'd finished, orderlies carried the patient up to ward nine. She needn't ask whether the man would make it. The doctor's somber, thin-lipped expression bespoke the odds.

But she hadn't time to wallow or return to thoughts of her mother, and for that, Una was grateful. She scrubbed her hands and pulled the last clean sheet from the cupboard. The drunk had not stirred since Conor and the ambulance surgeon had heaved her onto the cot. Una would have worried she were dead, but for her loud, tremulous snoring. A dirty, moth-eaten cloak covered her body, shrouding her face and entangling her limbs, so she looked more like a heap of rags than a woman. Only a few strands of red hair and a shoeless foot peeked out from beneath the fabric.

Una rolled the woman onto her side, bracing her heavy body

with one hand while folding up the dirty sheet with the other. She put the fresh sheet down in its place and then heaved the woman onto her opposite side and repeated the procedure. The woman's snoring faltered a moment only to start up even louder. She might be dead drunk, but at least now she was sleeping on a clean sheet. But when Una returned with an intake card to pin to the patient's cloak, *unknown* already written in place of a name, she found the woman stirring.

"Miss? Miss are you awake?" Una knelt beside the cot and gently shook the woman's shoulder.

The woman startled. She fought at the cloak still twisted around her body, spewing a string of curses. Her voice, though hoarse and muffled, sounded familiar. Before Una could place it, the woman managed to untangle herself and throw off the cloak.

Una gasped when she saw the woman's face. *Deidre?* She caught herself before saying the name aloud. Her thoughts swam like mosquito larvae in a rusty pail. Maybe Deidre wouldn't see past the nurse's cap and uniform. She was drunk, after all. The scent of cheap brandy soured her breath and sweated through her skin.

Una scrambled up from her knees, but before she could fully stand, Deidre grabbed her arm. "Una? Is that you?"

"Miss, you're heavily intoxicated and don't know what you're talking about." She tried to pull free, but Deidre held on to her arm as if it were the keys to a bank vault. An easy fix would be to sock Deidre in the jaw, but that was hardly behavior becoming of a nurse. "Miss, please let go of me before I—"

"I'd sooner be dead than not know you, Una Kelly."

Not wanting to cause a scene and rip her shirtsleeve in the process, Una knelt beside the bed again. "Hush," she hissed through gritted teeth. "Or you'll regret it."

Deidre cackled. "You and your disguises. They don't really think you're a nurse, do they? And here I thought doctors were supposed to be smart."

"I *am* a nurse."

This made Deidre laugh all the harder.

"A trainee anyway. Applied and was accepted same as the other trainees. Not that it's any of your damn business."

Deidre sat up, her hand still locked around Una's arm. "They know you wanted for murder? You put that on your nurse's application?"

Una glanced over her shoulder at the others in the room. Though several of the injured men had been moved up to the wards and one out to the morgue, it was still as harried and noisy as before. The second-year juggled an armful of rags and a basin of water as she tottered to a man with a bleeding head wound in the far corner. The house physician barked orders to his interns. Edwin examined a patient's mangled hand. The orderlies scuttled out with another body bound for the morgue. She turned back to Deidre. "I didn't murder nobody, and you know it."

"Maybe not, but them coppers sure would like to know you're here. They've even got a reward posted. Bet Marm Blei would pay to know too."

Una's heart skipped several beats before jolting back into an uneven rhythm. Panic licked like icy rain over her skin. "You wouldn't . . . Deidre, we're friends."

"Ha! You think I don't know you tried to pin ol' Mike Sheeny's death on me? I knew you would the minute I saw you in that cell." She belched, then smiled smugly. "So I beat you to it."

The cold panic settled in Una's bones, making it impossible to move. Her thoughts continued to swim. Behind her, amid the clamor, she heard Edwin say to his patient that they'd need to operate immediately to save his hand. The sound of his voice—so steady and assured—helped quiet her mind. "Listen, I can . . . I can pay you to keep quiet."

Deidre released her arm. "How much?"

"Five dollars a month."

"Five! I can make twice that in a day dipping pockets."

"Like hell, you can. When was the last time—" Una stopped.

Arguing over Deidre's lousy pickpocketing skills wouldn't help anything. "Seven."

"A month?"

"A month," Una said, even though it would be a struggle to get by on the remaining three dollars of her stipend.

Deidre sucked on her bottom lip the way she always did whenever she was thinking hard. "That's an extra hundred and ten dollars a year."

"Something like that."

"Them coppers only offering fifty."

"Think of all the meat pies and brandy you could buy with the difference." Una glanced over her shoulder. Another patient or two had been taken up to the wards. Most of the others sat bandaged and waiting. The second-year was gathering up the bloodied sponges and discarded bits of gauze from around the room. The doctors were consulting in the corner. Before long, they would want Una's report on the inebriated patient or come to examine Deidre themselves. "Do we have a deal?"

"Throw in a quart of whiskey and a bottle of laudanum, and we do."

"What?"

"You got plenty around here. You telling me you ain't taking a sip or two on the side?"

"No, I ain't. I could get expelled for that."

"Think of what they'd do if they knew you was wanted by the law."

"Fine. I'll slip you laudanum this one time but—"

"Every time. Along with the seven dollars. And the whiskey too."

"I—" Una stopped and hurried to her feet at the sound of approaching footfalls. It was Edwin. He glanced at Deidre with a frown, then said to Una, "What's your report?"

"Vital signs are stable, sir. No injury or ill-health aside from inebriation."

He leaned down and tried to peel back Deidre's eyelid to examine her sclera, but she batted his hand away.

"Don't touch me, you good-for-nothing—"

"I observed no signs of cirrhosis, sir," Una said.

"All right. Have the orderlies take her to a cell to dry out."

"Yes, Doctor."

Edwin flashed her the briefest of smiles and turned to go.

"Oh, Doctor," Deidre said, her voice suddenly sweet. "I wanted to tell you something about this here nurse you got."

Una stared at her with pleading eyes.

"She's . . . she's been right kind to me. Giving me everything I need." Deidre glanced from Edwin to Una. "It sure is good to know that whenever I come back, I'll be cared after just the same, won't I?"

All Una could do was nod.

CHAPTER 34

—»◦«—

Una waited for the first hint of predawn light, then slipped from bed. A chill skittered over her skin as she dressed. It would be several more minutes before Mrs. Buchanan turned on the gas and stoked the basement furnace. Una crept about in the cold darkness, smoothing her hair into a simple bun and pinning on her cap, careful not to awaken Dru.

Her nerves were raw with worry, and she hadn't slept a wink. She counted out seven dollars from the thin stash of bills she kept in her trunk and shoved them into her pocket. Deidre would be expecting whiskey too and a refill of the near-empty laudanum bottle Una had slipped into her palm before the orderlies took her to her cell. One thing at a time, though. Hopefully the money would satisfy Deidre until Una had a chance to sneak into the drugs department and filch the rest.

With dawn about to break, she left the home and hurried across the street to the hospital. Instead of climbing the stairs to ward twelve, she slipped down to the basement. It was warmer here than outside, though she could still see her breath as it drifted upward into the air. The walls had the wet, greenish cast of a sewer grate and cockroaches skittered across the floor.

She passed through a long, open room where the poorest of the city could lodge for the night. Though many had already quit their beds—which were little more than wooden planks—and left to toil away the day begging at street corners or rummaging for rags, the stench of their sweat still hung heavy in the air. Una herself had spent a few nights in public lodging rooms such as these and shuddered to remember the desolation that seemed to bed down alongside her. The only place worse had been the workhouse on Blackwell's Island.

No matter what, Una couldn't go back there. But how long could she go on stealing from the hospital and not get caught? How long until Deidre grew dissatisfied and one bottle of laudanum became two or three or four? It would be easier to mix the laudanum or whiskey with arsenic and be done with it.

Una stopped and shook her head. What kind of vile thought was that? She might be many things, but murderess was not one of them. Somehow she'd have to find a way to meet Deidre's demands. If she siphoned off an ounce or two of whiskey at a time, a drop of laudanum here and there, at month's end she'd have enough, and no one would be the wiser. And there was always Edwin's skeleton key if she came up short, though the idea of pinching it from his pocket made Una sick. She'd leave the stash for Deidre in a secret hidey-hole far away from Bellevue where no one, not even that nosey Nurse Hatfield, would ever see her.

None of that would change the fact that Una didn't trust Deidre any more than a thief in a jewelry shop. Even if Una delivered the goods in full every month, she'd never know peace of mind again. Maybe she ought to cut her losses and run. There wasn't much at the nurses' home she could filch. Adornments of any kind—beads, feathers, ruffles—were forbidden on the wards. So most of the trainees had left their silks and bobbles at home. But Una could get enough to buy a train ticket out of New York. The idea made her stomach turn inside out. Good thing she'd skipped breakfast.

Beyond the lodging room was the alcoholics' ward. It smelled less of sweat here and more of vomit. Cells lined either side of the hallway. Like the Insane Pavilion, each door was solid wood with a small peephole in the center. She peered into each cell as she passed. Most had only one occupant, though Una knew during a busy spell three, four, sometimes five women could be packed inside. Some of the women she saw were curled up on messy straw pallets sleeping. Others paced or sat with their knees drawn up to their chests, riding out the horrors.

Una thought of Conor's harangue yesterday in the exam room. He wasn't the only one who shared that scathing view. Yet it surprised her coming from a man of humble means, who'd doubtless known struggle. In these women, Una saw her father, broken by the war. She saw herself, cold and hungry, craving the fire a good pull of whiskey would light in her belly. She saw the countless women she knew in the slums who drank to numb the pain of their husbands' fists.

She even felt a kernel of compassion for Deidre, who'd certainly known her share of trouble. But damned if Una was going to let her ruin this. She'd worked too hard to get where she was to give it all up now. She raised her chin and squared her shoulders as she approached the last cell. Yesterday, Deidre had the upper hand. Today, it was Una's turn. Rule number eight: Until the brass changes hands, it ain't too late to renegotiate.

But when Una reached the last cell, the door was open. Inside, she found only a helper woman on her hands and knees washing the floor. Otherwise, the small room was empty. Had she passed by Deidre and not realized it? Una checked each of the cells again. Deidre wasn't there.

Had she already been released? That seemed unlikely given the early hour. Then again, if Deidre could sweet-talk her way out of an arrest, she could certainly persuade the dull-witted night attendant that she was sober enough to be let go.

The heavy, icy sensation that had gripped her yesterday returned. She sucked in a deep breath to calm herself. Now was no time to lose her wits. But the dank, sour air did little to calm her.

Would Deidre go to the wards looking for her? To the nurses' home? Would she give up and go to the police? Wherever she was headed, Una had to find her first.

She whirled around and ran straight into Edwin.

"Ed—er . . . Dr. Westervelt," she said, staggering back. "What are you doing here?"

He reached out to steady her. The touch of his hand, usually so welcome, made her all the more frantic, and she shrank away.

"I came to check on the patient we admitted yesterday," he said.

"But it's scarcely dawn."

"I couldn't sleep." He lowered his voice. "Had I known you'd be here, I—"

"She's not here. The patient. Must have sobered up and been released." Una took a step back, glancing over her shoulder at the exit. She had to make sure Deidre wasn't lurking around the grounds where someone might see her. "I . . . er . . . Have a good day, Doctor."

Edwin grabbed her hand before she could turn and flee. "Meet me in the elevator later? Two o'clock."

"I can't. Not today. Maybe, um, next week." She tried to slip her hand free from his, but he held on.

"Next week!" A clatter sounded from a nearby cell, and he lowered his voice again. "Una, what's wrong? You're not yourself this morning."

Una opened up her mouth but didn't know what to say. She hated lying to him. And she didn't have time for long excuses. She had to find Deidre. "I'm fine. Really. Just . . . overly tired."

"It's all this sneaking around, isn't it? I hate it too. Makes me feel no better than my father. I've half a mind to march up to Miss Perkins's office, tell her I love you, and be done with it."

Una's racing thoughts lurched to a halt. "What did you say?"

Edwin looked down, the color deepening in his freshly shaven cheeks. When he met her gaze again, Una searched his eyes for any trace of insincerity. Words were easy, but it took skill to lie with your eyes. "I love you, Una Kelly," he said. His eyes confirmed it.

Una stood dumbfounded a moment before pulling her hand away. Men had told her they loved her before, drunkenly, stupidly. One man had even put it into song. But their glassy, roving eyes hadn't held an ounce of sincerity. This was something different, something terrifying.

The clamor of approaching footfalls saved her from having to speak. Reflexively, both she and Edwin took a step apart. A woman dressed in a plain cotton dress and apron, whom Una guessed to be the ward attendant, scuttled up to them.

"Beggin' your pardon. Didn't hear you two come in." She swiped at the sleep crusted around her eyes and nodded to the last cell where the helper woman had just emerged with her wash bucket. "Sally there's supposed to give a holler when any of youse come down. Guess she didn't hear you neither."

"We took care not to be too . . . er . . . loud," Una said. "Lest we wake any of your patients still at rest."

The attendant snorted. "These women could sleep through a parade. Until they start to dry out, that is. Then even a graveyard be too noisy for 'em."

Una saw the washerwoman cross herself and hurry off down the hall. For a moment, standing alone with Edwin, she'd forgotten how dismal this part of the basement was. Now the cold, rank air was inescapable, pricking her skin and choking her lungs.

"There was a woman brought in by ambulance yesterday and transferred to your ward," Edwin said. His posture had stiffened and eyes hardened. "Red hair. Short in stature. Inebriated, but not to the point of unconsciousness. I came to check on her condition but am told she's gone. Was she released or sent to another ward?"

The attendant's hands fluttered to her apron. "Neither, sir. The house doc didn't tell you?"

"I've not been up to see him yet."

"She died, sir."

The words struck Una like a sudden lash of icy wind off the river.

"Whatever was the cause?" Edwin said. "Aside from having overimbibed, she hadn't any signs of ill-health." He turned to Una. "You made careful observation of her yesterday, Nurse Kelly. Did you note anything?"

But Una couldn't answer. She only rattled her head and whispered, "Died? Are you sure?"

"Yes, miss. It was the laudanum."

"I didn't prescribe any laudanum," Edwin said.

The attendant scurried to a desk at the end of the hall and returned with a small glass bottle. "Found her dead just after midnight. This was in her pocket, drained to the last drop."

Una snatched the bottle from the woman's hand. *Laudanum, alcohol 47%, opium 60 gr. per ounce* was written in red lettering on the label, followed by the words *Bellevue Drug Department*. But the bottle Una had stolen for her had been nearly empty. Deidre couldn't have overdosed on such a small amount.

When she realized both Edwin and the attendant were looking at her, Una said, "She must have snatched this while I was attending another patient. Things were so chaotic in the exam room, I don't even remember when she first arrived."

"It's certainly not *your* fault," Edwin said, then to the attendant, "Don't you search patients and inventory their belongings when they arrive?"

"Aye, we do, sir. But we didn't find anything."

"A bottle this small would be easy to hide," Una said, handing it back to the attendant. "But I don't see . . . How did you know she was dead? Wouldn't she just appear to be sleeping?"

"Was her eyes, miss. Wide open and red as the devil's. Gave me half a fright, it did. I rushed inside and saw she weren't breathin'. That's when I found the laudanum in her pocket."

"But are you sure? Laudanum can slow a patient's respirations. Their heart rate too." Una's voice grew thin and pitchy. "Perhaps she was sleeping and you mistook—"

"The house doc examined her himself and declared her dead."

He could have been mistaken too, dragged from sleep in the middle of the night down to this dark, dingy, rat-hole of a ward. Maybe he'd pressed his fingers against the wrong side of her wrist when feeling for a pulse. Or placed his stethoscope too high or low or wide on her chest. Either way, Una had to see for herself. "Where is she now?"

"The morgue."

CHAPTER 35

The morning mist had begun its slow creep back to the river when Una ascended from the basement. But the morgue, an old, single-story building at the far end of the lawn, was still shrouded in a patchy white haze. She heard Edwin's footsteps on the stairs behind her but didn't slow and was glad when he didn't follow her beyond the gravel drive. She couldn't think of him now, what he'd said, what she hadn't said in return. She could only think of Deidre.

To enter the morgue, Una passed through a small paved courtyard that opened off the lawn. To one side was a long, wooden building that jutted out over the river where she'd heard spare coffins were kept. To the other side was the morgue. A gate leading to Twenty-Sixth Street stood at the far end. More than a dozen coffins were stacked haphazardly in the corner of the courtyard—some large, some so small only an infant would fit inside.

A bearded man with a checkered cap stood in the courtyard, spraying the icy pavers with a hose. He wore no jacket, despite the air's misty chill, only a cotton shirt and baggy wool trousers held up by red suspenders. When he saw Una, he turned off the water and set the hose aside.

"Can I help you, miss?"

"Are you the doctor in charge here?"

He shook his head. "The morgue keeper."

"Yes, perhaps you can help me, then. I came to see a patient—a deceased patient, that is."

He crossed his arms and leaned against the stack of coffins. "You're one of them nurses from the school, ain't ya?"

Una nodded.

"Could tell from your uniform. Rather dour, if you ask me," he said, then added hastily, "But looks mighty pretty on you."

"Pretty is not the point. We nurses dress to work, same as you. Now, about that patient."

"The dead one?"

Una winced. "Yes. Where might I find her . . . er . . . her body?"

"Depends on whether the body's been claimed yet." He rapped on the lid of one of the coffins. "After three days, those that ain't go to potter's field."

"She died only last night."

"Well, then, the body ought to still be inside." He pushed off from the stack of coffins and gestured to the door of the stone building to her right. "Ladies first."

The door opened to a long corridor. Una hesitated, then stepped inside. The morgue keeper followed behind her. A strange smell hung in the damp air: the sharp, eye-watering scent of disinfectant and beneath it, the pungent, almost sweet scent of rot. Una shuddered to imagine how the building must reek in the summer months.

The first room they came to had more coffins, their lids not yet nailed down. The morgue keeper lifted the lids one by one for Una to peer inside. A handsome Negro man whose coily hair had just begun to gray. Another man, German by the looks of him, with a dark, gaping bullet hole to his temple. An aged woman with leathery skin and a toothless mouth. A young girl with the dark features of an Italian whose lips were frozen in a peaceful smile. Almost peaceful. Like the others, cords bound her feet and hands as if to keep her tidily contained within the narrow box.

When the keeper lifted the lid off a coffin little bigger than a shoebox, Una had to look away.

"Found frozen in the streets, this one," the keeper said, seeming to delight in Una's discomfort. "What kind of unnatural mother—"

"The patient I'm looking for is an adult, not an infant. And she was very much alive when she entered the hospital." She glared at the keeper until he slid the lid back in place.

Next, they entered the viewing room. Four stone tables stood evenly spaced in front of a large window that looked out onto the street. Morning sunlight streamed in through the glass around curious onlookers. Atop each table lay a body. Rubber sheets covered their nakedness while their clothes hung limply on the wall behind them. A block of wood was wedged beneath each of their necks, lifting their heads and angling their faces for better viewing. Water rained down on them from dangling pipes capped with spray nozzles. It plinked against the rubber sheets and dripped down onto the flagstone floor.

Deidre's was not among the bodies stretched out here for identification, though Una recognized one of the men killed in yesterday's accident. His soot-darkened shirt and trousers dangled from a peg behind him. Una couldn't help but imagine his wife dunking these very clothes in her washbasin only a few days before and hanging them to dry with care so that they didn't wrinkle. Would she recognize them now, so dirty and tattered?

"What of their clothes if the body goes unclaimed?" Una wondered aloud.

"We keep them for thirty days in case someone recognizes the deceased's picture outside on the wall," the keeper answered. "After they're sent up to the hospital to be washed and handed out to patients in need. Them clothes unfit to wear goes to the Island. Worked up into rag carpet at a factory there, I believe."

Una nodded, remembering the factory, the smoke, and the steam that belched from its pipes. She'd worked many a day of her stretch there, heedless of whence the rags had come. Now, some small part of her ached at the thought. Her mother's clothes had been burned beyond all use, the few surviving threads glued to

her melted flesh. Blue threads, Una recalled, from her soft ging-
ham day dress. The one with a lace-trimmed collar and modest
bustle.

She jogged her head and strode from the room. What would
she have done with the dress had something more than threads
survived? Turned it into a pillow sham? A pin cushion? How
would that have helped Una in the bleak years after? Such foolish
sentimentality wouldn't have mattered then, and it wouldn't help
now, whatever had become of Deidre.

The morgue keeper led her past a storeroom and office to the
very back of the building where autopsies were performed. He
stopped in the doorway, however, blocking her view.

"This really ain't the place for a lady," he said.

"I'm not a lady. I'm a nurse."

He tucked his thumbs beneath the straps of his suspenders and
looked down.

"You've already shown me a dozen other dead bodies. What's
so different about these?"

"It's . . . er . . . not the bodies themselves that might offend
you. It's the state of their undress."

Una tried to step around him, but he blocked her path.

"I assure you, there's nothing in that room I haven't seen before."

He blushed clear to the roots of his beard. Una sighed. Here
was a man crass enough to lounge against a stack of coffins, who'd
delighted in showing her the curled form of a frozen baby, yet who
squirmed at the thought of her seeing a dead man's private parts.

"Nothing I haven't seen in my work as a nurse. Now, step
aside, please."

"Suit yourself."

He moved to one side of the jamb, and Una shimmied around
him. The other bodies from yesterday's accident lay on metal-
topped trestle tables awaiting examination, water showering
down on them. Beside them was another patient, likely from the
maternity ward, her stomach swollen and skin ashen. And then,

at the far end, Deidre. Her red hair spilled off the table, damp and matted. Her arms lay stiff at her side.

Una stood frozen a moment before forcing down a breath and crossing the room. Her boots clattered atop the wet floor, a haunting intrusion on the silence. She stood beside Deidre and waited for some sign of life—a twitch of the hand or flutter of eyelids. When no sign came, Una reached out and laid her hand on Deidre's chest. Her skin was cold, her breast unmoving. Una recoiled.

Had she truly expected Deidre to be alive, sleeping soundly amid a room full of corpses? And yet, Una had to fight back the urge to reach out again and shake her as if that might somehow quicken her back to life.

"I take it she's the one you're looking for?" the keeper said.

"What happens to her now? Will they really"—Una stopped and swallowed—"cut into her and take out all her organs?"

The keeper sauntered over and shrugged. "If the cause of death ain't known."

"A laudanum overdose. That's what the ward attendant said, anyway."

"Probably not, then."

"So she'll go out on display until someone claims her?"

"The hospital will send someone out to notify her kin if any are known."

Una shook her head. "She has no kin."

"Then she ain't likely to be claimed, is she?"

Marm Blei might claim her. Someone from the old crew. Surely they wouldn't let her go missing without checking here. But what about the undertaker's fees and burial expenses? Who would pay those? Considering all the profit Marm Blei had made off Deidre's loot over the years, it seemed only right for her to pay. That didn't mean she would, though.

"If not, she'll be buried at potter's field?"

"Depends." The keeper wandered his gaze over Deidre's body the way a thief eyed a diamond ring. "She looks like choice material for one of the medical colleges."

"What?"

"A certain few of the unclaimed dead are set aside for dissecting. City law and all."

Una remembered what Dru had said during their first anatomy lecture about the Bone Bill, how to stave off the practice of grave robbing the schools were provided with bodies from among the city's vagrant, friendless, unclaimed dead. She reached down and smoothed back the strands of wet hair that had fallen across Deidre's face. It was impossible not to think back on all their escapades together—rowdy nights in the concert saloons, games of euchre by candlelight in their flat. Once, when Marm Blei gained possession of a cache of silk dresses from France, they'd secretly borrowed two of the gowns and passed themselves off as society women at a fancy lunch room on Ladies' Mile. Of course, they'd snuck out before paying the bill. When Marm Blei found out, she'd taken an extra ten percent of their earnings for three whole months. But the caper had been worth it.

"How much do they throw you on the side?"

"I beg your pardon?"

"For choice material. How much do the colleges pay you?"

The keeper tugged on his suspenders again and glanced at the door. "The different colleges allow me something for the loading, carting, and delivering material to them. That's all. Nothing regular. Just what they see fit to give according to the load. I have to pay the cartman, after all."

"How much per body?"

"I ain't never calculated that. They pay me by the load."

"How many bodies per load?"

He shrugged, the soft patter of water filling the silence. "Sometimes one, sometimes two, sometimes as many as eight or ten."

"And how much do they pay you for a load of one?"

"I rarely deliver a single body, unless it's coming along to springtime, the end of the college term, and—"

Una stepped closer to the man and looked him square in the eye. "How much?"

"A dollar or two."

"I'll double that if you promise not to . . . set this one aside."

"What's one dead patient or another to you? You know her or something?"

Una looked down at Deidre again. The attendant had been right; her eyes were horribly bloodshot. "No, I don't know her. But it's my job to care about my patients, and I don't want to see this one cut to pieces on some dissecting table while eager students look on."

"Six."

"Fine." She reached into her pocket and pulled out three dollars. "Half now. The rest in three days if she isn't claimed." She thrust the money into his open palm. "If you renege, I'll report you to the city commissioner."

"Sheesh, you're a tough nut for a nurse." He pocketed the money just as the door to the autopsy room opened. Several men walked in, led by a small man with a crooked nose and thick spectacles, whom Una guessed to be the chief pathologist. The others were interns from the hospital, fresh-faced young men she'd seen on occasion, waddling behind the house physician or a visiting surgeon like day-old ducklings. Thank goodness Edwin wasn't among them.

"What's going on here, Bartlet?" the crooked-nosed man said to the morgue keeper. "Why is there a woman back here?"

"She's a nurse, sir. Came to check on a patient."

The man dropped his chin and eyed Una over the rim of his spectacles. "A patient? There aren't any patients here. Only dead bodies."

"I wanted to be sure, sir," Una said. "Mr. . . . er . . . Bartlet was just about to show me out."

"Sure?" He snickered and walked to the nearest body. He raised one of the arms and let it drop. It struck the metal table with an echoing bang. Una flinched at the noise but otherwise didn't move. "Dead enough for you, miss?"

He reminded Una of the thugs she'd had run-ins with in Hell's

Kitchen or the Bend—he was older and better dressed perhaps, but just as mean. Her rule on the streets, number nine, was to put up her fists as if she wasn't afraid and—when necessary—land the first blow. Though tempting, Una knew that rule wouldn't serve her here. She couldn't afford for word of her visit to get back to Miss Perkins.

"Thank you for your . . . assurances, Doctor," she said. "I'm quite satisfied and shall leave you to your work." She cast a final glance at Deidre. With her hair no longer a lion's mane about her face, Una noticed for the first time a band of discoloration around Deidre's neck. Peering closer, Una realized it was bruising.

"Doctor, there's something strange here with this patient—er . . . body."

The pathologist rolled his eyes. A few of the interns chuckled.

"Nurse, I have five bodies to examine in under an hour. I don't have time for your questions."

"But I think she might have been strangled." The idea hadn't fully formed in Una's mind until she said the words. But, yes, that was precisely what it appeared to be.

The pathologist came over, shaking his head. Una pointed to the swath of reddish-blue skin around Deidre's neck. "See this bruising?"

He spared only a moment's glance at Deidre's body before turning his narrowed eyes on Una. "That is lividity. Not bruising. Had this woman been strangled, one would see a cluster of small petechiae caused by the assailant's fingertips."

"What if he didn't use his hands?"

The pathologist turned toward the group of interns, jabbing a bony finger in Una's direction. "This is precisely why women will never be physicians. A little livor mortis, and they get fantastical ideas in their heads about murderers and ghosts who go flitting around the hospital killing patients at will."

The men laughed.

"I never said anything about ghosts. Only that her neck—"

"The house physician reported to me that this woman died of

a laudanum overdose. I see nothing about the body to contradict that. If you have issue with that, take it up with your superintendent. But rest assured, I shall be having a conversation with her as well."

Una hid her fists in the folds of her skirt. "Forgive my impertinence, Doctor. I have no issue with your studied assessment."

"Good, then see yourself out."

CHAPTER 36

Three days later, Una waited as a small black tugboat pulled up alongside the wharf. *Hope* was painted on the bow. A grimly ironic name. She handed the morgue keeper the remaining three dollars she owed him for sparing Deidre's remains the indignity of dissection along with another dollar for securing her passage on the tug.

"You sure you want to go?" he said, pocketing the money. "Ain't much of a sight."

Una nodded, tightened the knot of her scarf, and stepped aboard. The tug hugged the river's shoreline, backing up to the long wooden building that sat beside the morgue. The boatmen laid a long plank between the building and the deck. Workers from the morgue shoved coffins down the slide, the bodies thudding against the side of their rude receptacles when they struck the deck.

Each evening for the past three days, Una had come to the morgue's viewing window on Twenty-Sixth Street and stood among the passersby. She daren't go inside and risk another run-in with that beak-nosed pathologist. It was easy to identify those who'd flocked to the window out of perverse curiosity from those with earnest intent. The curious pressed their grimy faces against the glass, leaving behind trails of snot and smudge prints.

Or walked by quickly as if they had somewhere else to be and just happened upon this out-of-the-way sight, heads forward but eyes straining at the corners of their sockets.

Those truly searching lingered. They studied the pictures on the wall, the bodies beyond the glass, the clothes hanging on the pegs, at once both hopeful and terrified they might recognize something. Their husband's shirt. Their daughter's face. Their old chum's bright red hair.

Each evening, Una prayed Deidre's body would be gone, claimed by a distant family member or one of Marm Blei's crew. Other bodies came and went. But Deidre's remained.

Una hadn't forgotten Deidre's plan to extort her or how she'd lied to the police. But she couldn't shake this empty, aching feeling, as if her insides had withered away, leaving her hollow. It could just as easily be her lying there on that slab, a constant stream of water dripping onto her breast to keep her flesh from rotting. Just another of the city's riffraff, unclaimed and forgotten.

The morning of the fourth day, before the tug arrived, Una had insisted on seeing Deidre's corpse. She didn't trust the morgue keeper to hold up his end of the bargain any more than she trusted a drunk with a bottle. He'd opened half a dozen coffins in the deadhouse, adding to the already pervasive stench, before finding hers. Deidre's bloodshot eyes were still open, and her skin had taken on a greenish hue. Over the past days, Una had watched the bruising on her neck grow more pronounced, then spread and fade. On final examination, it was hard to distinguish from the general putrefaction that had begun, mocking Una's certainty that Deidre had been strangled.

After the morgue keeper had closed the coffin and nailed it shut again, he'd drawn an *X* on the lid with a brittle piece of chalk. Now, standing on the deck of the *Hope*, Una watched as coffins were shoved down the ramp and stacked in haphazard piles. The trim of the boat seemed the only thought in their placement. Deidre's coffin, with its white *X*, was one of the last brought aboard. She winced as the deckhands heaped it atop the rest as if it were nothing more than a crate of turnips.

With a puff of steam, the tugboat departed from the hospital, chugging upriver amid the chunks of winter ice. It stopped at Blackwell's Island for another load of coffins—typhus victims from the pesthouse and deceased inmates from the prisons—then continued onward.

The sky was clear, and the sun glaringly bright. Seabirds circled overhead, squawking and cawing. Una had never had a tender stomach, but her breakfast roiled with the sway of the boat. Or perhaps it was the smell of its cargo.

Staring out at the river, she remembered a joke from her youth. "If you want to go to Hart Island, break your leg and go to the hospital. The doctors'll get you there quick enough." The humor of it was gone now. But the truth in it remained. Deidre had come to Bellevue whole and healthy, albeit very drunk. Now she was dead. Murdered, if Una's suspicions were correct.

She rattled her head and trained her eyes on the small island in the distance. Even though part of her still hated Deidre, she'd resolved to see her buried. Everyone, even a two-timing swindler, deserved to have someone with them at the end. Hopefully someone would do as much for her. Once this awful day was done, then she'd think about the bruising, what it meant and what she should do.

At Hart Island, the tugboat pulled up alongside a rude wharf, and the coffins were unloaded. Workmen from the Island carted them toward the cemetery with all the care of a busy porter laboring at the train depot. Una followed behind in the company of the captain. In all the bustle, she'd lost track of which cart carried Deidre's coffin but assured herself she'd find it again once they reached the burial grounds.

Una hadn't expected sculptured tombstones or flower-filled urns, but the barrenness of potter's field unnerved her. There were no trees or greenery of any kind. No markers or rough-hewn crosses. Several mangy dogs—mastiffs, judging by the size of them—padded freely about the grounds.

"There's not even a fence," she muttered.

"Aye," the captain said. "But then, what's the point? Those on the outside ain't hankering to get in, and those inside ain't in no position to get out. Besides, the dogs do a good enough job patrolling the place."

They stopped beside two long trenches fifteen feet deep and six feet wide. Una's undigested breakfast inched back into her throat. Surely this wasn't where the bodies were to be laid to rest.

As if in answer, the workers began chucking the coffins into the trench like fuel into a coal pit. Once the first row was laid, a few barrows of dirt were thrown atop the coffins, and a new row was begun. The clatter of wood and plink of soil was deafening. One of the dogs sauntered over, dropping his stick to sniff around at the edge of the trench. Another came up beside him and tried to steal the stick, but he frightened him off with a snarl. He nosed around in the dirt a bit more, then picked up his stick.

No, not a stick, Una realized as he wandered off. A human bone.

She staggered a few feet away from the captain and vomited up a mix of biscuits, coffee, and bile. She wiped her mouth with her hankie and returned to the trench just in time to see Deidre's coffin, its white *X* smudged, heaved inside. Dirt showered down over it, pelting the wood like frozen rain. She cursed herself for not bringing along a flower or ribbon to toss in atop it, but any such sentimental token would simply have been crushed by the weight of another coffin. All she could do was say a short prayer, cross herself, and flee back to the tugboat.

CHAPTER 37

Two nights later, at the end of her shift, when she'd finished explaining to the night nurse what medicines the patients required, whose condition warranted careful attention, and which supplies were in need of replenishing, Una found Dru waiting for her in the main hall. She looped an arm through Una's as they walked back to the nurses' home.

"Hurry to dress and forget about supper," she said.

Una groaned. What was so important to study that they hadn't time for supper? She wouldn't remember a word of it anyway. Una had witnessed her share of horrors in the slums, but that ghastly scene at Hart Island continued to haunt her. Even when she closed her eyes, the sounds came back to her—the thud of coffins, the patter of dirt, the snarl of those flesh-crazed dogs. The training school, Dru's lessons, this elaborate ruse Una had created—what was the point of any of it if she were just going to end up like Deidre, left to rot in some unmarked grave?

"I'm not feeling up to studying tonight."

"Good. We shan't be."

"Then why—"

"No questions. You just have to trust me." They'd reached the steps of the home, and Dru shooed her impatiently inside. "Wear your Sunday dress."

Once they reached their room, Dru was out of her nursing uniform and into a well-cut but unadorned gown more quickly than Una had ever seen her dress. Then she turned on Una, who'd only managed to unfasten a few buttons, batting away her hands and undressing her like a child. Any other night, Una would have protested, maybe even clocked her for being so presumptuous and pushy, but tonight she hadn't the will for any of it. Not even enough to question whether she was fool enough to trust Dru or not.

As soon as they were properly attired, Dru tugged her out of the room and down the stairs. The smell of buttery rolls and roasted mutton wafted from the kitchen. Una's stomach awakened with a growl. She'd skipped breakfast and picked over her lunch. Or was that yesterday's lunch? Perhaps she hadn't eaten today at all. Dru pulled her onward and out of the home where less appealing smells reigned. Her stomach continued to gnaw at itself, however—an old, familiar feeling from her early days on the streets.

They caught the westbound streetcar a block up from the home just before it pulled away. Dru paid the fare and seated them on a bench two dockworkers had kindly vacated. Una had the passing thought that it was dangerous to be out where someone might recognize her, but beyond adjusting her hat so its brim better shadowed her face from the light of passing streetlamps, she couldn't be bothered to care.

Dru talked cheerily above the rattle of the car. A new patient had been admitted to her ward with the most perplexing of ailments, which no amount of cupping or blood-letting seemed to improve. Una welcomed the distraction, listening to the animated cadence of her voice more than the words themselves. Gladness flickered inside her to hear Dru discuss blood and various procedures to evoke it with such aplomb. It sparked again at the mention of Dr. Westervelt, whose clever idea to treat the patient with acetylsalicylic acid had finally yielded improvement. The feeling was soon weighed down by guilt at having left him so abruptly in the alcoholics' ward. But even that emotion could not be sustained, guttering like a weak flame into hopelessness.

They alighted at Madison Square Park, and Dru brought them both a pretzel from a vendor at the corner of the park. Una would have preferred a jug of whiskey, but at least the soft, salty bread quieted her stomach.

"All this way for a pretzel?"

"No silly goose, come on."

They skirted the park, turning down Twenty-Third Street when they reached the Fifth Avenue Hotel. Its gleaming marble facade reflected the soft glow of the streetlamps.

"I've heard it's like a European palace inside," Dru said to her, nodding at the hotel. "Reading rooms and restaurants and drawing rooms all done in the French style. It's even said to have its own barbershop and telegraph office."

While Una had spent countless afternoons in this part of town— the manicured park and fine shops that stretched south down Fifth Avenue were prime hunting grounds for pickpockets—she'd never been inside the hotel. Not even her best disguise could get her past the doormen. But she remembered stopping from time to time in the shade of its awnings and peering through the windows at the splendor within. Someday, she'd thought, I'm going to be as rich and fancy as these bombasts. Now that thought seemed as pointless as it was absurd. All the money in the world couldn't guarantee a death any less ignoble than Deidre's.

They walked on half a block more, then stopped in front of a tall stone building with arched pediments and ornamental trim. EDEN MUSÉE was carved in large block letters above the double-door entry.

"Here we are," Dru said, squeezing Una's hand, her face aglow with childlike delight.

"What is this place?"

Dru didn't answer. She tugged Una up the steps and paid the doorman the entry fee, smiling all the while. They entered a wide, chandelier-lit foyer where an attendant took their coats and ushered them into the adjoining room. Several dozen people milled about inside, stopping in front of crimson-draped alcoves where actors stood in tableau. Good actors. Even at a distance, Una could see that. Not the sort of bawdy ruffians who played in concert saloons in the Tenderloin or the Points. They breathed without the slightest show of it, and their eyes stayed fixed despite the murmurs of the crowd. In stark contrast to the gray, barren trees of Madison Square Park, a profusion of tropical plants bloomed about the room, their shiny green leaves bespeaking of lush, far-away lands.

Una stood in awe of the splendor, her eyes darting from alcove to alcove, plant to plant, uncertain where to focus their attention. For the first time in days, she felt something other than emptiness.

"I knew you'd like it here," Dru said, pulling her toward a large platform at the center of the room where a tableau of actors dressed in royal and religious finery was staged. "A group of second-years were looking at the catalog yesterday and left it behind in the library. The museum opened only last week."

Una fought the urge to elbow and jostle her way closer to the platform, waiting in ladylike fashion beside Dru until a few of the crowd sauntered off to the next display. Up close, Una could see the intricate needlework of the actors' costumes, the glimmering fabrics and shiny adornments. The man in the blue uniform with fancy gold trim was meant to be Emperor William of Germany, Dru explained. Beside him stood Queen Victoria and Pope Leo. But something wasn't quite right about their faces. They wore the same vacant expressions and had the same pale, matte complexions as the corpses Una had seen in the morgue.

She gasped and staggered backward through the crowd, bumping into shoulders and stepping on toes. Her breath came in rapid, shallow pulls. The room seemed to totter, the verdant plants and luxurious draperies blurring in and out of focus. Someone— something—reached out to her. She pulled away.

"They're dead. They're dead," a voice was saying. And Una knew it to be true. Someone had unearthed the bodies from potter's field and dressed them up like actors. She spun around, looking for Deidre, her hands moving reflexively to her throat.

Someone reached for her again. A scream built in her throat. Then, as if through a fog, she recognized Dru's voice. "They're not dead, Una. Listen to me. They're wax."

She let Dru take her hands.

"They're just wax models dressed up to look like real people."

"Wax?"

Dru nodded.

Una glanced back at the tableau, her pulse thudding in her ear. Only wax? She forced down a slow breath. Suddenly she could see it. Of course, they weren't trussed-up corpses. Their features, though deftly crafted, were too smooth, too perfect to be real. Their eyes were painted glass. Their hair, wigs.

Heat flooded Una's cheeks as her breathing slowed. From every corner of the room, people were staring at her. An attendant scurried over. "Perhaps the miss would like some fresh air," he said to Dru. "Or a warm drink in the music hall."

Dru wrapped her arm around Una's waist. "Yes, a warm drink would be lovely."

They passed through a second room of waxwork tableaux into the music hall. Their boot heels clacked softly over the polished tile floor, barely audible above the sweeping sound of the orchestra. The attendant seated them at a table toward the back of the room away from the other guests and then shuffled off to fetch them tea.

"I'm sorry," Una said. "I don't know what came over me." She ran the back of her hand across her forehead, expecting a beading of sweat. But her skin was cool and dry.

"It's my fault. I should have told you in advance that they were wax."

"They don't even look that real. I don't know why . . ." Una trailed off. Of course she knew why. She could hardly close her eyes anymore without seeing a corpse.

"I thought it might cheer you up. That's how much *I* know." Dru looked down and fidgeted with the strings of her purse.

"Cheer me up?"

"You've been positively glum these past few days. I thought it was on account of some disagreement you had with Dr. Westervelt, but you hardly seem to notice when I mention his name. So then I thought it might be some trouble with that smug Miss Hatfield, but she's been gone all week visiting her family in Baltimore. Then I thought—"

"A woman I knew died. Just a few days ago."

"Oh, Una, how dreadful! She must have been terribly dear to you."

Una shook her head. "We were . . . we grew into womanhood together. But we weren't close."

"What was her name?"

Una glanced around the hall, awakening to the danger of being in so public a place. The orchestra captured most guests' attention. Those whom the music had not beguiled chatted quietly with their tablemates or drifted upstairs to the gallery where stereopticon machines cast slowly dissolving images onto the walls. None paid any heed to her and Dru.

"Deidre was her name."

"Perhaps you can make it home in time for the funeral. I'm sure Miss Perkins—"

"It already happened," Una said a bit roughly. "Besides, like I said, we weren't close."

The waiter arrived then with their tea, setting the porcelain and silver service down with a flourish.

"Could we get a glass of brandy as well, please?" Dru asked.

Her words shocked Una as much as they did the waiter, who shifted his weight from foot to foot, gripping his tray like a shield. "I . . . er . . . I'm sorry, miss. We only serve alcohol to ladies when they're in the company of a gentleman."

"I don't want it to get drunk, but for its medicinal properties. We're nurses at Bellevue Hospital where a cup of brandy is prescribed often and to great effect, to soothe a patient's nerves."

"I'm afraid that doesn't matter, miss. This is a first-rate establishment. If you want a cup of brandy, I suggest you find a saloon."

"A saloon!" Dru's eyes widened, and her entire face flushed red. "What sort of ladies do you think we are?"

Una choked back a laugh. She'd never seen Dru angry before.

"Beg your pardon. I wasn't implying . . . I only meant . . . It's management, see—"

"And what would management think if I told them you'd insinuated we were women of ill repute?"

"I didn't say that, miss. I only . . . Please forgive my rudeness."

Dru let the man squirm for several protracted seconds before sighing. "Very well. The tea is fine. Thank you."

The waiter scurried away, and Dru poured the tea as if nothing had happened.

"You're scarier than a runaway horse when you're mad."

"Really, these New Yorkers are so persnickety. I only wanted a little brandy."

Now, Una *did* laugh, loudly enough to draw stares from the neighboring tables. She covered her mouth with her napkin but couldn't stop the rolling waves of laughter. At first, her lungs and stomach muscles were stiff, as if from disuse, but soon they loosened. The rest of her, drawn in on itself like a pill bug, slowly uncoiled as well. She laughed until her sides ached and tears leaked from her eyes. Dru laughed too, snorting between chuckles to catch her breath.

When at last they'd spent themselves, Una reached across the table and squeezed Dru's hand. "Thank you."

"It's hard being here sometimes. The city's so big it could swallow you whole. Thank heavens we have each other."

The lively tune the orchestra was playing ended. Una and Dru joined in the demure applause. A solitary violinist began the next song, drawing his bow slowly across the strings. The sound drew Una back to Hart Island—the gray sky, the freshly dug trench, the plink of dirt atop the coffins. She shivered and took Dru's hand again. "The woman who died, Deidre, she was a patient at Bellevue. I think . . ." Una swallowed. "I think she was murdered."

CHAPTER 38

Dru was quiet the entire way home from the wax museum. What had Una been thinking, revealing her suspicions about Deidre's death? It was the music that had done it—that slow, haunting tune stealing inside her like a phantom. Telling Dru had been the only way to expel it. But so bold a truth was never a good idea.

"Really?" Dru had said.

"Yes, I think so."

"By whom?"

Una looked down at her lap. "I . . . I don't know."

"You must go to the police."

"No," Una said, loudly enough that several people at nearby tables turned to scowl at her. She leaned across the table and whispered, "I can't. If I'm wrong, I'm afraid . . . afraid I'll be expelled from school."

"Have you told Miss Perkins?"

Una shook her head.

Dru leaned back in her chair and pursed her lips. Her eyes drifted toward the orchestra, lingering there until the haunting song was done. Then she'd signaled their waiter and paid the bill, saying nothing more on the subject.

Now, as they mounted the nurses' home's steps, her mind

scrambled for a way to walk back her admission. Dru's unchar-acteristic silence made it all the harder to think. She must believe Una mad. Unhinged. Overworked and hysterical.

Mrs. Buchanan opened the door and waved them inside. "Al-most locked you out, I did." She closed the door behind them and fastened the lock. "Straight up to your room, now."

"Yes, ma'am," Una muttered, shrugging out of her coat.

"I'm just going to grab a book from the library," Dru said.

"It's too late for studying, dear," Mrs. Buchanan said. "I'm about to turn off the gas and head to bed myself."

"I shan't be but a moment."

Una started up the stairs without her. What sort of a textbook did she need at so late an hour? *A Manual of Psychological Medi-cine and Allied Nervous Diseases*? Did she mean to diagnose Una and see her to the Insane Pavilion at first light?

Inside their room, Una changed out of her dress and into her nightshirt. It had been a joke, she'd tell Dru. A fleeting idea of no real substance. Dru arrived a moment later, tossing a book onto her bed before hanging up her coat and beginning to undress.

"About what I said earlier, my nerves were still rather excited and I—"

"Don't worry, I won't tell anyone," Dru said over her shoulder as she unbuttoned her dress. The tautness in Una's hands and neck eased. "Not until we figure it out, anyway."

"Figure it out?"

"Who the killer is," Dru whispered as if afraid the women in the neighboring rooms might hear. Even so, Una detected a hint of excitement in her voice.

"You believe me?"

"Of course I do."

"But I don't know the first thing about solving a murder. Do you?"

Dru stepped out of her dress and horsehair bustle, nodding at the book on her bed. Una crossed the room and picked it up. What she'd thought was some diminutive textbook was actually a collection of stories. The gold lettering on the cover read, *The Works of Edgar A. Poe, Vol 1, Tales.*

Una frowned. She'd never heard of the author, but doubted some silly love story, as Dru was fond of reading, would help them figure out who killed Deidre. "You think the answer is in one of these tales?"

Dru flung on her nightgown and grabbed the book. "Haven't you read 'The Murders in the Rue Morgue'? It's one of my favorites."

Una shook her head.

"I'll read it to you."

Una lit a candle just as the overhead gas lamp flickered out. She squeezed beside Dru on her bed and listened as she began the tale.

"'What song the Syrens sang, or what name Achilles assumed . . .'"

Dru had a pleasing voice when she read, clear and steady, yet animated when the story called for it. Una leaned back against the fluffy pillow and stared at the far wall. In the dancing light and shadow, she could see the tale unfold—the peculiar Mr. Dupin, the winding streets of Paris, the horror-filled apartment in the Rue Morgue. For a moment, her thoughts strayed, and she wondered whether this—lying here beside Dru—was some version of what her life could have been. If she'd had a sister. If her mother hadn't died. If she'd gone to live with Claire instead of staying with her drunken father.

She rested her head on Dru's shoulder. Her nightshirt smelled of lavender and violets. A rise in her voice drew Una back to the story, and she listened intently through to the end. When Dru finished, Una sat up and grabbed the book from her. She flipped through the final pages of the story to be sure she hadn't misheard. "An orangutan? You think an orangutan killed Deidre?"

"No, silly." Dru took back the book and turned to the beginning of the story. "To figure out who, if anyone, murdered her, we have to think like Mr. Dupin." She ran her finger over the lines of words, stopping halfway down the page. "'He makes, in silence, a host of observations and inferences.' That is what we must do. He didn't confine himself to a particular line of reasoning or reject anything out of hand. He visited the scene of the murder. So too shall we."

"The alcoholics' ward? What could we find there? Her body has already been removed and buried."

"See, you're already thinking too narrowly. We won't know what we might find until we go. And you saw the body, did you not?"

"In the morgue, yes."

"If it's not too terribly upsetting, you can relay to me what you saw, and I shall endeavor to imagine it. We can sneak a look at the pathologist's report too. You said he examined the body, yes?"

"But he'd made up his mind about the cause of death before even looking at her."

"We don't have to accept his conclusions. We can make our own deductions from his observations."

"If Miss Perkins or Nurse Hatfield catch us snooping around, there's no telling what kind of trouble we'll get into."

"You and Dr. Westervelt have managed to sneak around without getting caught." She nudged Una playfully in the ribs. "So too can we."

Una winced at the mention of Edwin. She hadn't spoken to him since fleeing so abruptly from the alcoholics' ward. *I love you*, he'd said to her. *I love you.* No man had ever said such things to her and meant it. She rattled her head. That was another mess she'd have to work out. But not tonight.

Dru closed the book and set it on her nightstand. Surely she was tired after so long a day, but her bright-eyed expression was like that of a child in a sweet shop. "Once we solve the mystery—if there is a mystery to be solved—we'll notify Miss Perkins together."

Una climbed from Dru's bed into her own, sinking into the soft mattress. It was a good plan, certainly better than Una could have come up with on her own. Perhaps this Mr. Poe had his merits. But the plan wasn't without risk. And Dru's willingness to help flew in the face of Una's most important rule: Look out for yourself.

She sat up and turned to Dru, who was just about to blow out the candle. "Why are you helping me?"

"We're friends, you goose." She smiled and blew out the candle before Una could correct her.

CHAPTER 39

The following day dawned warm and bright as if spring had finally decided to call. Leaves seemed to have sprouted overnight on Bellevue's trees, and tiny green shoots dotted the lawn. The shadow of Deidre's death remained with Una along with its many questions, but with Dru's help maybe she could solve them. In the meantime, she had to focus on her work. Failing at her studies and getting herself expelled wouldn't help find Deidre's killer—if it had been murder at all. And it certainly wouldn't help her stay out of jail. Una had to keep her wits about her and remain above reproach at the school. No missteps or errors. No skipping out on lectures and no getting caught sneaking around.

The problem remained what to do about Edwin. He was a liability she couldn't afford. At least that's what her head told her. Her heart told her something else.

But Una knew better than to let herself be ruled by such a fickle organ. Besides, Edwin wouldn't want to see her after she'd run from the alcoholics' ward without a word. Or so she tried to convince herself as she climbed the steps of the hospital. The picture of his grandfather hanging in the main hall caught her eye, and her confidence faltered. They had the same sharp nose and tall forehead, but Edwin's eyes were kinder, the curve of his lips more playful. Una's traitorous heart squeezed. He, Edwin, deserved far better than a thief and imposter anyway.

In the past, she'd bluntly rebuffed men's affections. "I'd sooner kiss a sewer rat than you, Patrick O'Hare," or "Save your songs for the whores, Tafferty." Those men who wouldn't be dissuaded, she simply avoided until their blood ran hot for someone else—which never took long. Even Barney, whose devotion seemed more earnest, had likely forgotten her by now.

This latter tactic of avoidance wouldn't work with Edwin, however. The slum might be a wide enough place to disappear in; the hospital was not. And the trainees had been appointed to new wards again, with Una having the unlucky fortune to be assigned to the surgical division on ward fifteen. Not only would she be back under Nurse Hatfield's watchful eye, but also forced to see Edwin, and the odious Dr. Pingry, every morning during rounds.

Una's only recourse, then, was to forget her heart and snub Edwin should he come calling.

Her opportunity came that very morning when Dr. Pingry called her away from the beef tea she was brewing.

He, Dr. Allen, and Edwin hovered around the bedside of a patient who'd been shot twice during a bar fight in the Bowery. One bullet had shattered his wrist, which Dr. Pingry had "most excellently" repaired in the operating theater. The other had entered his back, breaking two ribs before settling somewhere in his abdominal cavity.

"Fetch me the bullet probe, extracting forceps, and one-half grain of morphine," he said to her without looking up from the patient. They'd rolled the man onto his side and removed the dressing from his back. Having been inflicted only yesterday, the wound was still fresh, bleeding but a little, with an aura of blue and red bruising around it. The man groaned as Dr. Pingry placed a finger on either side of the bullet hole and stretched it open to peer inside.

Una hurried to the storeroom and medicine closet. Dr. Pingry could at least have waited until she'd gotten the morphine before examining the wound. She felt a kinship with the man. Even though she didn't know him, she knew what life in the slums of the Bowery was like—hard, violent, and miserable. She placed the probe and medicine bottle on a rattly tray table, along with fresh gauze and a bowl of carbolized water, then wheeled it over.

"I took the liberty of mixing up some disinfectant in case you want to wash your hands or clean the probe before—"

"Had I wanted carbolized water, I would have asked for carbolized water," Dr. Pingry said, shooting her a glare. "Your job, nurse, is not to take liberties but to listen and obey." He grabbed the bullet probe and fingered the porcelain ball at its tip. "Well, did you hear me, girl?"

Edwin winced. Dr. Allen seemed bored.

"Yes, Doctor," Una muttered. "It's just that Lister—"

"Lister! Lister is a charlatan," he said, spittle flying from his mouth and landing on the bullet probe he wagged in Una's direction. "I have been treating patients here at Bellevue for decades with undeniable success. I shall remove this bullet, and afterward you shall see. Rest and quietude are all this man needs."

He bent down over the patient and was about to thrust in the probe when Edwin cleared his throat. "Perhaps the morphine first, Doctor."

"Well, give it, then. What good are you interns if you're going to stand around like pigeons while I do all the work?"

Una watched Edwin draw the medicine into the syringe. He hadn't looked her square in the eye once since Dr. Pingry had called her over. What sort of man tells a woman he loves her, then won't even spare her a glance? Sure, she'd run out on him without so much as acknowledging his affections and taken pains to avoid him these last few days, but he might at least favor her with a glare, a scowl, something!

Instead, he kept his eyes on the patient, injecting the morphine into the subcutaneous tissue of his arm, and watching as Dr. Pingry began the procedure. Una watched too, ready with a small metal basin to receive the bullet once it was retrieved.

Dr. Pingry inserted the probe several inches, rotating his wrist by slight degrees as he followed the path of entry, his face screwed in concentration. He stopped, pulled the probe halfway out, then inserted it again. The patient moaned in his morphine-induced sleep, and his eyelids fluttered.

After what seemed an interminably long time, Dr. Pingry withdrew the probe. Blood coated the shaft to the handle. Instead of using the gauze Una had laid out, Dr. Pingry plucked a handkerchief from his pocket and wiped the tip. Had the porcelain made contact with the bullet, the lead would have left a mark. Dr. Pingry grumbled. Despite no marking, he set aside the probe and picked up the slender forceps. Before inserting them, he stuck his index finger in the wound to scoop out a clot of blood.

After several more minutes of poking around with the forceps, Dr. Pingry withdrew the instrument and threw it onto the tray table, splattering blood and bits of tissue all around. "The bullet is beyond detection." He wiped his hands, then tossed the bloody hankie at Una. "See that this gets laundered and help Dr. Westervelt dress the wound."

Dr. Pingry sauntered out of the ward with Dr. Allen at his heels. Una wadded the hankie in her fist, itching to throw it at the back of his bloated head. The splash of water drew her attention back to the bedside. She watched as Edwin dunked several strips of gauze in the carbolized water, then washed his hands and began to clean the wound.

"How do you stand that man?" Una asked, dropping the crumpled hankie onto the floor before scrubbing her own hands and coming to stand beside him.

"He's a brilliant surgeon."

"Is that you or your grandfather talking?"

Edwin shot her a perturbed glance before turning his attention back to the wound. At least it was something.

"Hand me more gauze," he said.

Una wetted several more strips and handed them to him, the brief contact of their skin sending tiny jolts of energy up her arm like the staccato bleeps traveling along a telegraph wire. She was sure Dru could explain away the sensation using some medical text or other. It wasn't, as Edwin had said, love. But she'd missed the feeling, nonetheless.

"Shall I fetch a needle and sutures?" she asked, trying to refocus her attention.

"No." He squatted down so he was eye-level with the wound. "I'm going to leave it open in case it begins to suppurate. But we'll cover it with an antiseptic dressing."

"Will that kill the . . ." What was the word Edwin had used when telling her about Lister's studies? ". . . the germs Dr. Pingry introduced?"

"No, but it will prevent further contamination."

He worked with careful attention for several minutes, constructing a multilayered dressing of disinfectant-soaked gauze. She couldn't help but admire his quiet patience and steady hand. The longer she watched him, the more her resolve to rebuff him faltered.

"You're not a bad surgeon yourself," she said when he'd finished.

He looked at her with a stranger's coolness, then stood and rinsed his hands. "Cover the dressing with oiled silk. Beef tea and porridge when he wakes. Laudanum as needed for pain."

Una grabbed his arm before he could walk away. "Goddamn it, Edwin, what do you want me to say?" She caught sight of the second-year bustling about at the far end of the ward and let go of his arm, continuing in a whisper, "That I love you too? Fine. I do. I love you."

She hadn't intended to say something so preposterous. She'd never said those words to a man before in her life. Not in jest nor in earnest. But the idea of him walking away from her, from them, made her panic. Now it hung in the air between them. *I love you.* Preposterous. And entirely true. "That doesn't change anything," she added hastily, as much to herself as to him.

Edwin blinked several times, and his face brightened. "It changes everything."

"It doesn't."

A glance at the second-year, and he grabbed Una's hand, tugging her into the nearby storeroom. The tiny room was dark and smelled of disinfectant. Before Una could find matches to light the overhead lamp, Edwin caged her arms and kissed her. Una's resolve failed her, and she kissed him back. She freed her hands and enmeshed them in his hair, mussing the pomade-slickened strands. She wanted to consume him and be consumed in return. They stumbled into a nearby shelf, upsetting the neatly stacked sponges and rattling the newly cleaned chamber pots. They froze, listened a moment to be sure they hadn't raised suspicion, then giggled like children and kissed again.

Eventually, Una's senses unclouded enough to pull away. "I have to get back to work."

"Tell me again that you love me."

She hesitated, feeling the words out on her tongue before speaking. "I love you."

The truth of it frightened her. She felt exposed, vulnerable, like a boxer facing his opponent with one arm lame. "But, Edwin, we can't—"

"Marry me."

"Don't be ridiculous."

"Not now, after you finish your training."

"That's over a year and a half away."

He ran a finger over her cheek and down the side of her neck, sending a pleasant shiver skipping over her skin. "I'm a patient man. I'll wait."

She leaned her head against his chest, and for the span of a few heart beats it all seemed possible—courting him in secret, completing her training and getting her certificate, marrying him and working beside him at the hospital. But then reality bullied in. She was a thief. A thief wanted for murder. Every day would be a lie.

She breathed in his scent—soap and aftershave and a hint of mint—then stepped away from him, straightening her apron and smoothing her hair. "We can't."

"Why not?"

"You're . . . you're not Catholic for one thing."

He chuckled. "So?"

"I *am*." At least when it suited her. "Besides, you're too busy here at the hospital for a wife."

"By the time you graduate, I'll have my own practice, and you can have as much of my time as you require." He looped an arm around her waist and pulled her close again, whispering in her ear. "More if I can help it."

His breath tickled her neck. "Edwin, I have to go," she said but made no move to free herself from his arms. He kissed her again—first her lips, then the tender skin beneath her ear, then the hollow of her throat just above her collar. "Edwin . . ."

"Mmm?"

"We'd better—"

Dr. Pingry's voice sounded from the nearby hallway. "Westervelt!"

Una and Edwin pulled apart.

"Nurse! Where's Dr. Westervelt?"

"I'm afraid I don't know, sir," came the second-year's reply.

Dr. Pingry grumbled, his loud footfalls continuing down the hall.

"I believe you're being summoned," Una said.

Edwin sighed. He straightened his jacket and fumbled for the door. He turned back to her before opening it and kissed her once more. "I'm leaving tomorrow for that symposium on Lister's methods in Philadelphia. Will you think over my proposal while I'm away?"

"Edwin, it's not just that I'm Catholic or that you're too busy with your work, I . . ." But she couldn't bring herself to tell him the truth.

"Whatever it is, I promise you, it won't matter." The scant light that crept beneath the storeroom door illuminated his earnest expression. "Trust me."

Every part of her longed to believe him. She tried again to form the words, but Dr. Pingry's rough voice from down the hall interrupted her.

Edwin cracked open the storeroom door wide enough to slip out. "Just promise me you'll think on it."

"I will," she lied.

CHAPTER 40

⟫•⟪

The warm weather held for several more days, prompting an impromptu visit from Mr. P. T. Barnum and a few of his famed performers.

"Those patients who are well enough may come down to the lawn to enjoy the performance," Nurse Hatfield told Una and the other trainees that morning at breakfast. "Those of improving health who are yet too enfeebled for the stairs may sit out on the balcony. Make sure everyone has a blanket in hand should a breeze stir off the river. Under no circumstances are patients afflicted with pneumonia or hospitalism to attend. When in doubt, defer to the doctor's judgment."

The women hurried through their breakfast, chatting excitedly. The daily routine at Bellevue was rarely broken, especially for so merry an occasion. Many of the women—Una included—had never seen one of Mr. Barnum's shows. The crowds that flocked to his big top events were ripe pickings for pocket divers, but if you were caught, rumor was, Mr. Barnum didn't bother with the police but fed you to the lions instead. Una never put too much stock in rumors but had stayed away just the same.

"This is perfect," Dru whispered to her as they trailed behind the others on their way to the hospital. For once, it had been Dru who'd woken late, rising so sluggishly that morning they'd nearly missed breakfast. And she hadn't uttered a peep about Nurse Hatfield's announcement—or anything else for that matter—until now.

"Perfect for what?" Una asked.

"To sneak down to the alcoholics' ward."

They'd talked over their plan a few times since that night when Dru had read her "The Murders in the Rue Morgue." Each time, Dru had grown more excited to put their observation and deduction skills to the test. Una, on the other hand, had grown warier. If there were a killer lurking behind Bellevue's walls, was it wise to go looking for him? And wasn't Una supposed to be lying low? There was also an unpleasant niggling in her stomach—akin to drinking curdled milk—when she considered how she was embroiling Dru in such a dark and unsavory task. As much as Deidre's murder haunted Una, she'd half hoped that Dru would forget their plans and go back to pestering her about ligaments and bones.

"As soon as we've gotten our patients settled for the show," Dru said, "we can meet in the main hall and head downstairs. Everyone will be so preoccupied by the performers they won't notice we've gone."

"What are we going to tell the ward attendant when we get there? She's bound to get suspicious if she catches us sniffing around."

"I hadn't thought about that."

"And what are you going to tell the second-year on your ward if she asks where you're going? Or Warden O'Rourke when he finds you loitering in the main hall?"

"Well, I'll . . . I'll say that . . ."

Una pulled Dru aside as soon as they passed the laborers at work on the gatehouse. The morning sun glinted sharply off the river. Una tented a hand over her eyes to block out the light. "This isn't some fancy. We can't just traipse around here like storybook characters. Maybe we should call off the plan."

"And never know? What if you're right and the killer strikes again? I couldn't live with myself knowing I might have prevented it. And neither could you, Una Kelly."

Una looked down at the gravel drive beneath their feet. Dru was wrong; Una could live just fine knowing that, thank you very much. But somehow, she didn't want to tarnish Dru's good opinion of her by saying so. Besides, it was clear Dru was not to be dissuaded. "Fine. Once you've got your patients settled on the ward, grab a blanket, and tell the second-year you're going to check on the patients on the lawn. One of them might have forgotten a blanket and be cold. If anyone stops you on your way down, tell them the same thing. And don't wait for me in the main hall. It's too conspicuous. Take the stairs beside the drive down to the cellar and wait for me in the lodging room. It should be empty at that time of day. Got it?"

Dru nodded—too eagerly for Una's liking—and they hurried to their wards.

Midday, with the lawn awash in sunlight, Mr. Barnum's troupe of acrobats and curiosities gathered to begin their show. A long rug had been unraveled over the newly sprouted grass. Beside it stood a table strewn with props. Chairs circled the makeshift stage, and those patients well enough to leave the ward crowded in. Behind them stood the staff. Nearly everyone had turned out to see the exhibition—orderlies, nurses, doctors, washerwomen, kitchen staff. Even Warden O'Rourke and Miss Perkins were in attendance.

The balconies overlooking the lawn were crowded too, with patients leaning over the railing to get a better view.

"Leave the flying to the performers," Una said, coaxing the patients from her ward back from the rail. She made sure each man had a blanket and stool, should he grow weary of standing. The delight on their faces—such a welcome change from that of pain or boredom—made Una linger. She watched the men, even as the show began, smiling not at the daring feats of the performers but the marked improvement in the men's spirits. Surely there was some medicine in this too.

A moment later, Una remembered herself. She grabbed a spare blanket and hurried off, telling the second-year she'd spied a patient down on the lawn shivering with cold. The hallways and stairways were empty, the wards uncannily still. From outside rang cheers and applause, punctuated by long stretches of awe-filled silence.

Una passed through the main hall and out the door just in time to see one performer climb onto the shoulders of another and another until they formed a tower four men high. She clapped with the rest of the audience as she descended the stairs onto the drive that abutted the lawn. With everyone's attention glued to the acrobats, now was the perfect time to slip down to the basement. But when she saw the top performer stretch to his full height then bend his knees and leap off the shoulders of the man beneath him, Una stood transfixed. He somersaulted through the air, making two complete rotations before landing solidly on his feet. A roar of cheers and applause rose from the crowd.

"Quite the show, eh?"

Una tore her gaze from the performers to find Conor standing beside her. "I've never seen anything like it."

"No? Don't they have circuses up north where you're from?"

Her eyes drifted back to the show. The next acrobat in the tower of men leaped from his perch in similar fashion, spinning head over heels twice before landing on his haunches. "Hmm? . . . No . . . er . . . I mean, yes, of course, I've just never had the pleasure of attending."

"This whole island feels like a circus if you ask me. Head down to the waterfront or Mulberry Bend, and you'll see. Freaks and swindlers and other odd folk."

Una's fingers clenched around the blanket. For a former bog-trotter himself, he sure had high-minded ideas. "It's easy to criticize the poor when you've got a full belly and sound roof above your head. It can't have been easy when you first left Ireland."

"T'weren't. Not one day of it. But if you and I can stay away from sin, so can our kith."

Not for the first time, Una imagined how low his opinion of her would sink if he knew who she really was. All the more reason not to argue with him and risk exposing herself. Her fingers loosened around the blanket, and she flashed him her prettiest smile. "Of course, you're right."

Conor returned her smile—men like him were always easy to assure—and they both turned their attention back to the performers.

Not long after, Una spied Dru from the corner of her eye slip through the main doors of the hospital and tiptoe down the stairs. Like Una, she'd grabbed a spare blanket, but instead of holding it nonchalantly, she clutched it to her breast like a shield. Her posture was stiff and eyes darting. When an orderly passed her on the steps, she gave him a too-wide smile. "Don't mind me, I'm just bringing a blanket to one of my patients," she said unsolicited and loudly enough that Una could hear several yards away.

Una winced and shook her head.

"Something paining you, Miss Kelly?" Conor asked.

"Yes, yes . . . Just a little toothache."

"Eating too many sweets, are you?"

Una tried to smile, even as Dru shuffled awkwardly past them.

"Top of the day to you, Nurse Lewis," Conor said to her, tipping his cap.

"Don't mind me, I'm just bringing a blanket to one of my—"

"Look at that!" Una said over her. "A snake charmer."

When Conor turned to look at the performer, Una shot Dru a sharp look and nodded to the basement steps.

"I best be getting back to the ward," Una said to Conor.

"Shame you can't stay. I heard they got a man who can swallow a knife long as my arm."

"Maybe I'll be able to catch it from the balcony."

"See you at mass on Sunday?"

Una nodded and took a few backward steps toward the hospital. The snake charmer held the audience enthralled. The flutelike instrument he played filled the hushed quiet with its melodious tune. Una seized the opportunity to change direction, heading away from the main entrance to the narrow staircase that led to the basement.

Reaching the bottom, she glanced over her shoulder to be sure no one had followed, then opened the door to the lodging room and slipped inside. The snake charmer's song disappeared as the door closed behind her. So too did the light. Una groped along the wall for a gas lamp, stumbling over a small table before finding one. She turned the gas valve and lit a flame with matches from her pocket. With the room now illuminated, she set aside her blanket and looked around. The stench of sweat and urine struck her nose, fainter than the last time she'd been here but still as sharp. Just when she thought the room was empty, Dru popped up from behind a chair in the far corner. Una strangled back a scream.

"What are you doing hiding in the dark?"

"I was afraid someone might see me."

"No one's admitted here till nightfall. You know that." She walked over to Dru and brushed away a cobweb from her shoulder. "Besides, hiding is only a last resort. Better to blend in. Act like you belong."

"Right," Dru said, still clutching the blanket.

"Leave that here, and let's go. We don't have much time."

Una led them through the foul-smelling room and down a dimly lit hall. Dampness clung to the walls, limescale and slime discoloring the stones. Behind her, she heard Dru's breath hitch and falter before evening out.

"It's ghastly down here," Dru said as they passed the staff quarters, which smelled only mildly better than the lodging room. "Miss Nightingale would never approve."

"Beats the workhouse on Blackwell's Island . . . er, or so I've heard."

When at last they reached the alcoholics' ward, Una's muscles stiffened. The dank air, the low cries from the cells, the meager light—it was as if she were stepping back in time, learning of Deidre's murder all over again. A warm hand grabbed her own and squeezed. Dru's.

"Which cell was she in?"

Una nodded to the end of the hall, her throat too tight to speak.

Hand in hand, they progressed onward. Una's feet itched to beat dirt to the cell. The quicker they got there, the quicker they could leave. But Dru walked with interminable slowness, her gaze drifting from floor to ceiling and back, lingering over the cell doors—their locks, hinges, and peepholes.

Near the end of the long hall, they found the cell Deidre had occupied. Another woman was in there now, asleep and snoring on the straw-strewn floor. Dru examined the interior of the cell through the peephole and fingered the rusty padlock on the door.

"Who has the key?" Dru asked.

"The ward attendant, I'd guess."

"Odd that we haven't seen her. I was quite ready to explain our visit so as not to illicit the least bit of suspicion."

Una couldn't help but snicker. "Did the explanation begin, 'don't mind me'?"

"Why, yes. And then I was going to explain in detail how—"

"See, right away that's suspicious."

Dru frowned.

"Maybe just leave the truth stretching to me." Una turned back to the cell. "Now, what are we looking for?"

"Clues."

"What kind of—"

But Dru had already crept farther down the hall before Una could finish. Una sighed and followed. They rounded a corner, and the hall ended in a small room. The ward attendant—the

same woman Una had met when she'd come in search of Deidre—
teetered atop a stack of crates, peering out a sliver of a window
high up in the wall. She was so enthralled, likely by the circus
performers on the lawn, or what little she could see of them, that
she hadn't heard their footfalls. Nearby stood a small desk cluttered with papers, a stack of dirty breakfast plates, a mug of coffee, and a ring of keys. An open door at the far end led to a flight
of stairs.

Not wanting to startle the woman into falling from her precarious perch, Una began to back out of the room. Dru, however,
walked boldly to the desk and snatched the ring of keys, somehow
managing not to make a sound.

"Sneaky as a thief," Una whispered once they'd rounded the
corner and were back in the long hallway of cells. "Where'd you
learn to do that?"

"Miss Nightingale says unnecessary noise is the cruelest ab-
sence of care which can be inflicted on either the sick or the well."
She unlocked the door of Deidre's former cell with equal quietude.
The slumbering woman inside didn't wake.

Una stepped inside and peered around. She wasn't sure what
she'd been expecting to find—a clue of some sort—but the cell
looked the same as it had through the peephole. The smell, that of
sweat and vomit, was sharper inside, as if it had seeped into the
stone walls and could never fully be washed away. The woman's
snores were far louder than they'd sounded from the hall. The air
felt colder too. Damper. A shiver whispered over Una's skin.

Deidre had died here. In this very cell. Alone with her killer.

Yet there was nothing in the cell to suggest who that person
might be. She backed out and waited in the hallway, rubbing her
arms for warmth. It was hopeless to try to figure out what happened to Deidre when so much time had passed since her death.
Half a dozen women must have occupied this cell since then. If
the killer had left any clues behind, they were long gone now.

Dru lingered a minute longer in the cell, then closed and locked
the door. They tiptoed back to the room around the corner at the

end of the hall. The attendant was still at the window, craning her neck to see out the filmy glass. As Dru crept toward the table to replace the keys, she tripped on a loose stone and stumbled into a nearby pail. The pail toppled, clattering against the floor.

The attendant shrieked, twisting around and toppling to the ground. "What in the hell are you two doing here?" she asked, scowling in their direction and rubbing her backside.

"D-don't mind us," Dru stammered, "we've just—"

"We're lost." Una hurried to Dru's side, grabbing the keys from her hand before the attendant could see them. She nodded to the open door at the far end of the room. "Do those stairs lead up to the main floor of the hospital?"

"'Course they do."

Una offered the woman a hand and helped her to her feet, the keys hidden in her other palm. "You see the sword eater yet?"

"Sword eater?"

"I heard it's over two feet long, and he swallows it clear to the hilt."

"Really?" The attendant hurried to restack the crates she'd been standing on. Una seized on her distraction and slipped the keys back onto the table. She grabbed Dru's arm and dragged her to the steps.

"Sorry about the fright," Dru said over her shoulder, but the woman was already back atop the crates, too eager to see the sword eater to pay them any mind.

When they reached the top of the stairs, they found themselves in a short hallway alongside the warden's office near the main hall. Dru closed the door and leaned against the plaster wall. Her eyes fluttered closed a moment. She looked as dog-tired as she had this morning when they'd hurried down to breakfast. "That was close."

Too close, Una thought. And for what? They hadn't learned anything.

Dru opened her eyes and smiled. "But exhilarating too, don't you think?"

"Stupid is what I think. And a complete waste of time."

"But we discovered so much."

"What, that it's cold and dark and stinky? Let's get back to our wards before we find ourselves in real trouble."

Una started off, but Dru grabbed her hand. Her skin was clammy but grip firm. "No, silly goose. We learned two very important things. One, it wasn't all that difficult to sneak past the attendant. The keys were left there on the table for the taking. The cell door opened without a squeak. The walls were thick enough to muffle sounds of a struggle."

"That doesn't tell us anything about the killer."

"No, but it does explain how he could have gotten in and out unnoticed."

"And two?"

Dru lowered her voice to a whisper. "If there is a killer, he likely works here at the hospital. The ward isn't someplace you'd just stumble upon. He'd have to know his way around so as not to be seen."

"You mean like a doctor? Surely, you don't think—"

"Dupin says we mustn't confine our thinking and reject any deduction out of hand. A doctor, an orderly, not even the warden himself can be excluded."

CHAPTER 41

If Una had been distracted before, now she could hardly think straight. Every person she passed in the halls of Bellevue was a potential suspect.

"We don't even know that it was murder," Dru reminded her that evening in the library. While the other trainees sat beside the hearth talking of acrobats and snake charmers and sword swallowers, here they were whispering about a killer whom Una still had no proof existed. "Mr. Dupin says we mustn't—"

"I know, I know," Una leaned back in her chair and freed her hair from its bun. "We mustn't lose sight of the matter as a whole and jump to conclusions." Thanks to Dru, she could practically recite the whole damned story now.

Dru yawned and rested her head on the open textbook that lay between them on the table. Between Una's distraction and Dru's malaise, they managed only a few pages' worth of study. "Tomorrow, we must find a way to get the pathologist's report."

"Leave that to me," Una said. She didn't relish returning to the morgue alone, but the heist would be easier to manage on her own. Swiping a set of keys left out in plain view was one thing. Stealing a report tucked away God-only-knows where in the vilest part of the hospital was something else entirely.

* * *

The next morning, Una left the nurses' home early, slipping out before breakfast and heading straight to the morgue. She snuck past the keeper, who was busy stacking coffins, and into the back room. It was dark and cold inside. Several bodies lay beneath showers of water awaiting autopsy. The *plink, plink, plink* set Una's nerves on edge. She rummaged through drawers and cupboards but found nothing.

With the room slowly filling with daylight and the morning din growing from outside, Una at last stumbled upon a leather-bound sheaf of papers carelessly tucked between specimen jars. They weren't the pathologist's official reports but sketches and scribbled notes on recent cases. Before Una could read through them, approaching footfalls sounded in the hall. She flipped through the pages, glancing only at the date. Luckily, the day of Deidre's murder was seared into her mind. She snatched several pages, all inscribed with the same date, and stuffed them beneath the waistband of her apron.

Una hid behind the door as it swung open. Several men shuffled in. She listened to the clap of their shoes and the echo of their voices—a trick Marm Blei had taught her—to judge when they weren't looking, then slipped around the door and out of the room unseen.

The papers beneath her apron rustled as she walked in a brisk but measured pace from the morgue, arriving on her ward just in time to begin her morning duties. Una was happy to find the patient with the gunshot wound had much improved. He lay nestled amid pillows and sandbags, half-sitting, half-side-lying, so that neither his back nor his bandage-wrapped hand bore any weight. In his good hand, he held a copy of the *Daily Post*. Beside his bed sat a half-eaten bowl of oatmeal. Perhaps Edwin's careful dressing of the wound had helped.

Una cleared away his breakfast dishes, turned the page of the paper for him, and got to work tidying the ward before Nurse Hatfield made her rounds. She managed to secure the stolen notes from the morgue more snuggly beneath her apron so they wouldn't make noise or fall out as she cleaned. Evening seemed an interminably long time away when she and Dru could sit down and study them.

Shortly after noon, however, a new patient arrived from one of the medical wards. Dru accompanied him to relay his condition. She smiled weakly and rubbed her temple before beginning. "Mr. Knauff is a married man, thirty-three years of age, brought here ten days ago after falling from a wagon and fracturing his lower jaw. He is sober of habit with no previous ill-health . . ."

Her report was painfully detailed and precise, and Una only half listened, waiting for the second-year to disappear into the medicine closet so Una could show Dru the papers.

". . . this morning during rounds, Dr. Lawson decided it necessary to encase Mr. Knauff's jaw in a plaster of Paris splint to promote further healing. He conferred with Dr. Pingry, and they agreed to transfer the patient to the care of the surgical department as such a procedure would necessitate the use of ether. Mr. Knauff's bowel evacuations have been regular, and this morning his urine output measured—"

"I have it," Una interrupted once the second-year was finally out of sight.

"Have what?"

"Notes from the morgue." She pulled the papers from beneath her apron. Dru snatched them, her expression brightening.

"What do they say?"

"I haven't had a chance to read them yet. It's not the pathologist's official report but notations he makes during the examination, I think."

Dru moved closer to the window and fanned the pages out between her hands. "He probably uses these afterward when he writes out his official findings."

Una stood beside her and stared down at the sheets of crumpled paper. It unsettled her to think that Deidre and the other patients she'd seen in the morgue that day had been reduced to a few crude sketches and scribbled notes.

"Could this be her?" Dru pointed to an entry that began: *Female, white, mid-twenties*. But a few lines down it read, *fetus in utero estimated eight months' gestation*.

"No, that's not her."

Dru continued to scan the pages, turning them front to back and squinting at the pathologist's sloppy writing. "Here."

Una leaned closer. It was another entry of a woman matching Deidre's description. Further on it read: *Fixed lividity visible on the neck and back. Patchy in appearance. Regular in shape and symmetrical in prominence anteriorly and posteriorly.* "That's her. It has to be. What do you make of it?"

"Hmm . . ." Dru said, rubbing her temple again. She sat down on an unoccupied bed beside the window. "We'll have to consult Dr. Thomas's guide to postmortem examinations and morbid anatomy tonight. Lividity usually becomes fully fixed eight to ten hours after death. But I thought I remember reading it could take longer—up to a full day sometimes—in particularly cold environments."

"Why does that matter?"

"Before it is fixed, when you press on an area of the body colored by lividity it will blanch. A bruise will not. It's possible the pathologist miscalculated the time of death or failed to consider the temperature when making his assessment, thereby confusing bruising around her neck for fixed lividity. Even more interesting—" Dru stopped and winced, gripping the bedsheets.

"Are you all right?" Una asked, sitting beside her.

Dru flashed a thin-lipped smile. "Yes, quite. What was I saying?"

"Even more interesting . . ."

"Yes, even more interesting is the pathologist's description of her fingernails. Several were broken and ragged. He attributes it to her . . ." Dru picked up the paper and read, "'Her likely habitude of slatternliness and intoxication.' But what if—"

"Nurse Lewis, what are you still doing here?"

Una and Dru rose hastily at the sound of the second-year's voice.

"I . . . I . . ."

"She was just finishing telling me about Mr. Knob."

"Knauff," Dru whispered.

"Knauff."

The second-year shook her head. "Well, I'm sure her other patients are long since in want of her attentions."

As Dru hurried off, Una surreptitiously shoved the papers back beneath her apron and returned to her duties. She helped the second-year prepare afternoon medicines between calls for bedpans and extra blankets and cups of water. Several patients had fomentations that needed rewarming and dressings that needed changing. Una stayed so busy she hardly noticed Dr. Allen arrive a few hours later. He lingered over the newly arrived patient's bed before calling to her to fetch supplies for the splinting procedure. His thin, nasally voice barely reached her across the ward, and she realized that in her more than three months at the hospital, she'd hardly ever heard him speak.

Una finished mixing the mustard and linseed poultice she'd been making for another patient, then hurried to the storeroom. She grabbed the necessary supplies along with a basin of water to mix with the plaster and shuffled over to where Dr. Allen was waiting.

He pulled a towel from her arms before she had a chance to lay down the supplies and began shaping it into a cone for the ether.

"Where's Dr. Pingry?" she asked.

"Are you questioning my ability to perform such a simple procedure on my own?"

"No, of course not," Una said, surprised by the edge in his voice. She couldn't tell whether it was nerves or long-suppressed ego.

"Good, now hand me some cotton."

Dr. Allen swiped a few pages of newsprint from a nearby patient's nightstand and rolled it into a cone. He lined the inside with the towel he'd plucked from Una's arms, and stuffed it with cotton.

"Now lie still and breathe deeply," he said to the patient and placed the cone over his nose and mouth. Just as he was about to administer the first drops of ether, Una noticed a smudge of what looked like mutton stew across the patient's shirt. Had Dru mentioned when his last meal was? Una suddenly wished she'd listened better.

"You didn't eat any dinner today, did you, Mr. Knauff?" Una asked.

Mr. Knauff said something that was lost inside the cone.

"The patient hasn't been fasting?" Dr. Allen said.

"I'm not sure. I don't remember what the nurse from the medical ward said. If she said."

"You might have mentioned this earlier."

And you might try being less of an ass, she thought. "I'm sorry, Dr. Allen, I only just realized."

He glowered at her with the same pinched-lip contempt Dr. Pingry often fixed on her and the other trainees. "Carry on mixing the plaster."

"But we can't. The risk of—"

"The risks are minimal."

Was that true? She wished she'd paid better attention during Dr. Clarkson's lecture on the fundamentals of anesthesia or hadn't skipped out on Nurse Smith's demonstration last week about the care of surgical patients. It was a simple procedure, after all.

"Are you sure?"

"Forgive me, nurse, I don't think I heard right. Surely you're not questioning me. Perhaps I should call down Superintendent Perkins, and you can explain your disobedience to her."

Una opened her mouth then closed it again. She suspected Dr. Allen's insistence that they carry on had more to do with his fear of Dr. Pingry than anything else, but to say so would land her in Miss Perkins's office for sure and from there the streets. She grabbed the jar of plaster powder and sifted it into the bowl of water. Dr. Allen smirked and administered the ether.

The procedure lasted only fifteen minutes. Once Mr. Knauff was asleep, Una assisted Dr. Allen in constructing a simple plaster splint that wound around the patient's jaw and up over the crown of his head. They worked in silence. When they were finished, Dr. Allen wiped his hands, listed off his orders—nothing by mouth for four hours, then thin liquids as tolerated, aromatic spirits of ammonia if the patient woke nauseous—and walked away.

Una cleared the supplies and tidied up around the bedside, frequently checking Mr. Knauff's vital signs. As expected, his breathing grew shallower, and he ceased snoring. His pulse slowed, and color returned to his cheeks. Soon he would awaken, talk boisterously until the intoxicating effects of the ether fully wore off, then fall into a natural sleep.

She began a mental list of all the tasks she had yet to complete that afternoon. Leeches had been ordered for two patients, cupping for another, and a purgative enema on yet another. But at least the busyness would keep her mind from wandering to thoughts of Deidre's death and the pathologist's notes still tucked beneath her apron.

Half an hour after the procedure, when Una was just about to leave Mr. Knauff's bedside and fetch the jar of leeches, she noticed a wheezing sound. She leaned closer to him and listened. His breaths, once soft and easy, had grown high-pitched and piercing. She shouted for the second-year, who hurried over, chastising Una for raising her voice until she heard Mr. Knauff's noisy inhales. Her face slackened.

"I'll fetch help."

Soon Dr. Allen, Dr. Pingry, and Nurse Hatfield were crowded around the bed. Mr. Knauff's breathing had grown louder and more ragged. His lips were no longer pink but dusky purple. The plaster cast had already set and had to be cut away with scissors before Dr. Pingry could pry open Mr. Knauff's mouth and look inside. When he could find nothing blocking the throat, he hollered at Una to fetch a scalpel and cut a hole in Mr. Knauff's neck. A tube was inserted into his windpipe. Una and the others waited and listened. Mr. Knauff drew in a tremulous breath. Then another. Then he ceased to breathe at all.

Dr. Pingry ordered artificial respirations, and for the next twenty minutes—though it seemed like far longer—Una, Nurse Hatfield, and Dr. Allen took turns folding Mr. Knauff's forearms over his chest, pressing down, then unfolding his arms and extending them over his head. When at last Dr. Pingry declared their efforts fruitless, Mr. Knauff's face was blue. His eyes had never opened from the ether-induced sleep.

Una sat on the steps outside of Miss Perkins's office, gnawing on the soft skin around her nails. At first, she'd felt a sort of numb disbelief at Mr. Knauff's death as if she and the doctors and poor Mr. Knauff were all part of some waxwork tableau like those at the Eden Musée. But as she'd washed and wrapped the body for transport to the morgue, a quiet grief settled beneath her ribs. She should have listened better to Dru's report. Should have insisted they postpone the procedure.

Nurse Hatfield had come to her shortly after the body was carried away and told her to report to the third floor. "Superintendent Perkins is meeting with Dr. Pingry and Dr. Allen now," she said, not bothering to restrain her smugness. "She'll call you in to plead your case after."

Plead her case? Nurse Hatfield made it sound like Una were on trial.

Now, listening to the soft murmur of the physicians' voices from within Miss Perkins's office, Una felt sick and jittery. She tasted blood and realized she'd chewed her cuticles raw like a trapped rat gnawing off its own tail. When the door opened, and Superintendent Perkins waved her in, Una stood slowly, not trusting her legs.

Dr. Pingry and Dr. Allen passed her on their way out. Dr. Pingry looked annoyed as if meeting with the superintendent had been but one more bother in his already irksome day. Dr. Allen's countenance was more grave, his gray eyes refusing to meet her own.

Miss Perkins did not offer a chair, and Una didn't presume to sit, even though her feet ached and her head was light with hunger. "I'm told a patient on your ward died unexpectedly today."

"Yes, ma'am."

"Dr. Pingry speculates it was due to asphyxia caused by an accumulation of mucus in the trachea during his inhalation of ether."

Una wasn't sure what to say, so she remained silent.

"He further speculates that for such a thing to occur in an otherwise healthy patient, food was likely ingested prior to the administration of the ether."

"I told—"

"Dr. Pingry will deal with Dr. Allen and censure him as he sees fit. For his part, Dr. Allen claims he was unaware of the patient's condition prior to giving the ether, and I am in no position to question his statement. I am, however, in a position to determine what went wrong with his nursing care."

Una's mouth was as dry as tinder, but she resisted the urge to smack her lips or swallow, lest she appear guilty. "I did not feed Mr. Knauff anything."

"So he had not eaten?"

Una's mind scrambled for an answer.

"I trust you understand how serious this is, Miss Kelly. I expect nothing less than complete and honest disclosure."

Una nodded, wishing she'd had a chance to talk to Dru and get their story straight before being summoned here to answer to Miss Perkins. "He may have eaten before he arrived on the ward."

"But surely that information would have been relayed to you when he arrived by the transferring nurse."

"I . . ." Her tongue was so sticky it was hard to form the words. "I don't remember being told whether the patient had eaten or not, but I assumed, as he was being transferred for surgery, that he'd been made to fast that morning."

"You don't remember being told, or you were not told?" When Una didn't answer, Miss Perkins reached for her pen. "I'm afraid I have no choice then, but to—"

"Wasn't told. I wasn't told."

"I see. And from whom did you receive this deficient report?"

Una looked down. She opened her mouth, closed it again, then finally forced herself to spit out, "Nurse Lewis."

CHAPTER 42

⟶∙◦∙⟵

Una fretted away the rest of her shift, of little use to anyone. She knew as soon as she'd left Superintendent Perkins's office Dru had been summoned to give her accounting of the day's events. When she found out Una had implicated her in Mr. Knauff's death, would she point the finger back at Una? It had been Una, after all, who'd cut her off halfway through the report to show her the pathologist's notes.

The notes! Una still had them tucked beneath her apron. If someone found her with them, she'd be expelled for sure. Especially if Dru told Miss Perkins about their scheming to uncover some illusory killer at Bellevue. While the second-year was changing a patient's bandages, Una stuffed the papers into the furnace, watching them catch fire and burn.

She crouched beside the furnace, peering through the grate until her cheeks stung from the heat. Dru would tell Miss Perkins everything. She, like Una, had no choice. Not if she wanted to remain at the school. Which one of them would Miss Perkins believe? Una had the advantage of having told her version of events first. And she knew from experience just how big an advantage that was.

When the night nurse arrived for duty, Una forced her mind to focus long enough to tell her about the more serious cases on the ward who would need special care through the night. In truth, she hadn't expected to make it to the end of her shift without being called again to Miss Perkins's office to face dismissal. She lingered on the ward as the lights were dimmed for the night. Una could hardly breathe for all the guilt inside her. Guilt over Mr. Knauff's death. Guilt for implicating Dru, the one person at the training school who'd been kind to her from the start.

Una walked the short distance from the hospital to the nurses' home alone. Inside, it smelled of ham and boiled cabbage, but she hadn't any appetite. She dreaded seeing Dru. Would she ever be able to forgive Una for this betrayal?

As she stood in the foyer removing her coat, she heard not-so-quiet whispers coming from the library. Una crept closer and listened.

"You're kidding!" one of the women said.

"Nurse Roe confirmed it," another of the trainees said. "She works with Drusilla on ward ten. Drusilla was called to Superintendent Perkins's office late in the afternoon and never returned."

"But how do you know she was expelled?"

Expelled! Una clapped a hand over her mouth to stifle a gasp. She'd thought the worst that might happened to Dru—if Miss Perkins believed Una's version of events—was a demotion to probationer again. Dru had never once been in trouble, after all, or received less than exemplary marks on her examinations.

"She fainted upon hearing the news. An orderly was called to lift her from the floor to the chair and fetch smelling salts. He told Lula in the kitchen who told . . ."

Una pulled her coat back on and hurried to the front door. If Dru had truly fainted, Una must be sure she was all right. She opened the door and nearly collided with Nurse Hatfield.

"And just where are you going at so late an hour, Miss Kelly?"

"Back to the hospital. I heard Dru is unwell." She tried to step around Nurse Hatfield, but the woman blocked her path.

"You cannot see Miss Lewis. At least not tonight."

"She did faint, then?"

Nurse Hatfield nodded. Una stepped back into the foyer, and Nurse Hatfield followed, shutting the door behind them.

"On account of being expelled?" Una asked, her voice warbling.

"That, perhaps, had something to do with it. But a larger part is owed to her fever."

"Fever?"

"Yes. Typhus, we suspect."

Una's limbs went cold. Half of those who contracted the disease died. "But how—"

"There's been an outbreak in the city going on some many weeks. Even a trainee as imperceptive as you must have heard."

"Yes, but typhus patients are sent directly to the Island. How would Dru have—"

"Two weeks ago a patient was misdiagnosed and brought to Bellevue." Nurse Hatfield shrugged out of her coat and peeled off her gloves. Her voice was tired, matter-of-fact, but not unkind. "Miss Lewis cared for him before the true nature of his ailment was discovered. He was immediately transferred to Riverside Hospital, of course. But apparently too late." She turned to Una and smirked. "I'm surprised Miss Lewis didn't tell you about the incident."

Una swallowed her tide of anger. Knocking loose Nurse Hatfield's teeth might feel good, but it wouldn't help anything. And she was right. Why hadn't Dru told her? Fear of having caught the illness must have weighed heavily on her mind. How hadn't Una noticed?

She looked down to hide her reddening cheeks as shame quickly consumed her rage. Had she not been so preoccupied with her own moroseness, with Deidre and the ridiculous idea of murder, she might have noticed. Dru had been unusually tired of late. Pale too and distractible.

"Has she been taken to Riverside too?"

"No, we'll nurse her here in the Sturges Pavilion."

"Can I—"

"No. Only those with the utmost skill and care are permitted to attend her." With that, Nurse Hatfield strode away. She stopped halfway down the hall and said over her shoulder, "Oh, and you might do well to pack up your valise tonight. Superintendent Perkins wants to see you again first thing tomorrow. I don't imagine it's good news."

Una passed a sleepless night and picked over her breakfast the following morning. Not even a steaming cup of Cook Prynne's coffee could thaw her cold and twisted insides. She daren't arrive late to Miss Perkins's office, but each step to the hospital and up its unending stairs tested her will. Dru had been expelled and lay sick—maybe dying. Was Una to be expelled as well?

Miss Perkins admitted Una after her first, timid knock on the door. Like yesterday, she did not offer Una a chair.

"I've considered the events of yesterday's tragedy with great care," she said. Her expression was grave, and her eyes had the watery, red-rimmed look of one who hadn't slept.

Una nodded, unable to speak.

"As you know, this is not the first time your suitability for this profession has been called into question."

"Please, Miss Perkins, I promise to be more—"

The superintendent held up her hand. She stood from her desk and walked to the window. A ring of delicate frost edged the glass, aglint in the morning light. "I've watched you these many weeks, Miss Kelly. This incident notwithstanding, you're unquestionably good with the patients. Never unctuous or aloof. You're calm under pressure and have taken well to your lessons, thanks in no small part to Miss Lewis's tutelage, I presume."

"Yes, ma'am."

"I have no doubt you could become a fine nurse someday. However, I find myself questioning your heart."

Her heart? What did that mean?

Miss Perkins sighed and turned from the window. "We spoke at length yesterday, Miss Lewis and I, before she took ill."

Una winced. Whatever Dru had said, it couldn't be good. Not that Una could blame her after she had fingered Dru in Mr. Knauff's death. Rule number one: Look out for yourself above all others. Una had lived her life by those words. Why, now, did they suddenly sound so hollow?

"Please, Miss Perkins, I can explain. I . . . that is . . . we, Dru and I—Miss Lewis, I mean, we—"

"There's nothing left to explain. Miss Lewis took full responsibility for the unfortunate accident of Mr. Knauff's death."

Una blinked. "She did?"

"She confessed to thinking the procedure would take place the morrow following his transfer, not that afternoon, and fed him his full dinner before bringing him to your ward. She also owned to not relaying that most important bit of information to you when handing over his care on account of being distracted."

"And did she say what . . . er . . . caused her distraction?"

Miss Perkins glanced again out the window. Una followed her gaze. Morning's mist had retreated from the lawn and the Sturges Pavilion—a long, single-story brick building opposite the Insane Pavilion—shown in plain view.

"Of that, she wouldn't speak. I can only speculate it was her illness. The disease can render one quite insensible."

"If that's the case, then must she be expelled?"

Miss Perkins turned back to Una, her weary eyes hardened. "That is not your concern, Miss Kelly. We're here today to discuss your fate, not hers. Lucky for you, not only did Miss Lewis take responsibility for yesterday's tragedy, but she also spoke quite highly of you and your skill."

"She did?"

"'Uncommonly brave and true of heart,' I believe is how she put it. So, despite my misgivings, I'm allowing you to stay."

The coffee Una had drunk at breakfast rose into her throat, tinged with blistering bile. Dru had kept the secret of Deidre and their investigation into her death despite the threat of expulsion. That alone was enough to make Una sick with guilt. But to have spoken kindly of her when Una so little deserved it—she couldn't comprehend it.

"I . . . thank you for another chance."

"Thank Miss Lewis when she recovers. *If* she recovers. Until then, see that you live up to her estimable opinion of you."

That evening, Una resolved to see Dru once her work on the ward was done. She waited until after the other trainees had left the hospital, then crept across the lawn to the Sturges Pavilion. Inside, the lights had been dampened to a soft glow. The night nurse went about her duties, paying Una no mind. Dru's bed was set several feet apart from the others at the far end of the ward. Una pulled up a chair beside her and took her hand. Dru stirred, moaning softly, but didn't wake. Her skin was hot and sticky. An angry rash showed around the sweat-soaked collar of her bed dress.

All day Una's throat had been choked with bile. Now, she felt something different—a trembling and tightness that threatened to give way into a sob. But Una had her rules—number three: Don't cry; number seventeen: Never show weakness—and, with considerable effort, she managed to push down the pesky feeling.

It wasn't her fault Dru was sick. Typhus, cholera, smallpox—even though Bellevue wasn't a pest hospital, there was always a risk to staff. The nurses were no exception. Then why did Una feel so goddamned guilty?

She squeezed Dru's hand, brushed the dampened hair from her face, and promised to return tomorrow.

"I'll fix this," she whispered before standing to leave. "Somehow. Some way."

CHAPTER 43

The next week was a blur of long, harried days and even longer sleepless nights. Una hadn't realized what a bright, anchoring presence Dru had been for her. She missed Dru's cheery smile first thing in the morning. She missed their nightly cups of milk and honey. She even missed their tedious hours of study and Dru's endless chatter.

On the ward, Nurse Hatfield was back to scrutinizing Una's every move. The bedsheets were not smooth enough, the mustard poultices she mixed not thin enough, the beef tea she brewed not strong enough.

With Dru still gravely ill and Edwin off at his symposium, Una felt a strange, new sensation. Loneliness. It settled at the base of her throat like a lump of dry bread. She tried to ignore it. Tried to swallow it down or vomit it up. But the irksome feeling remained. She'd been on her own for years. Why should it bother her now?

To make matters worse, the rough from the Bowery with the bullet wound, who at first seemed to be on the mend, had slowly grown more ill. Pus began to ooze from his wound when she changed his dressing. He no longer could keep down what he ate or drank—not even his laudanum—so nutritive and anodyne enemas were ordered. Dr. Pingry continued to insist the man's condition was stable and his chances of recovery favorable. Instead of cleaning and dressing the wound with disinfectant-soaked gauze, he prescribed the open-air treatment wherein the wound was left uncovered, free to excrete pus and poison until it healed on its own.

The man, who'd been robust as any bruiser when he first came in, now looked gaunt as a skeleton, his limbs spindly as matchsticks and his ribs protruding beneath his skin. Even the obsequious Dr. Allen tried to suggest a more sanitary course of treatment. But Dr. Pingry would not be moved. Any ill effects the patient was suffering, he insisted looking squarely at Una, were due to dangerous odors and pestilent vapors not properly vented from the room.

When Edwin arrived back from Philadelphia and joined the other doctors for morning rounds, his face went blank with shock when he saw the man. "Have we tried to wash out the wound with carbolic acid?"

"Open air is the best option," Dr. Pingry said blithely. "It's draining fine on its own."

The color and animation returned to Edwin's features. "Open air! That's absurd. He'll develop blood poisoning if he hasn't already." He looked to Dr. Allen as if for support but got only a shrug.

"Need I remind you who's in charge here, Dr. Westervelt? You've come back from that symposium altogether too bold. Are you a germ hunter now?" He pointed at a spot on the floor. "Look, there's a bacillus. Catch him!"

Dr. Pingry laughed and walked on to the next patient's bedside. Edwin drew in a deep breath, clenched his jaw, and followed, glancing furtively at Una as he passed her. His eyes softened, but she could see the rage kindling behind them.

That afternoon the patient died.

As she bathed the man for the last time, Una reminded herself she hadn't known him. What was one less Bowery rough? That seemed to be the attitude of Dr. Pingry anyway. Never mind the wife and small daughter that had come to visit the man every evening. Una thought of them arriving tonight, trudging up the stairs to the ward, praying to see some sign of improvement, only to be sent away to the morgue.

Tears mounted in the corners of her eyes. She cursed under her breath and blinked them away. She remembered her own journey to the morgue with her father. He made the identification quickly, but Una had broken free of his handhold and drawn closer to the body to be sure. She circled the grimy table, trying to find some bit of unburned flesh that might be recognizable. A few of her mother's fingers had escaped the flame, the nails neatly trimmed. Bits of her beautiful dark hair. A few threads of her blue dress. Her mouth, so often set in a smile, stretched in a grimace across her once-lovely teeth.

These and more Una recognized, but she hadn't wanted to believe it. For days after the wake and funeral, while her father sat in the kitchen working through a gallon of brandy, Una had curled herself on the sofa and watched out the window, waiting for her mother to come home. Clinging to the hope that the body they'd identified in the morgue had not been hers.

Slowly that hope had hardened into hatred. Her mother had abandoned her. She didn't have to go inside that ramshackle tenement that day. Her father was always saying she ought to steer clear of that low, run-down part of the city. There were plenty of other places in need of her charity.

"That's what you get, *a stór*," he said to Una in a drunken slur as dusk was falling over the city, and her mother still hadn't returned. "What you get when you look out for others above your family. Above your own self." Then he gave her a quarter to fetch more brandy from the grocer down the street. She'd taken a nip of the drink on her way home and abandoned her window-side vigil.

Now, as Una finished washing the Bowery man, her hands shook with such violence she spilled half the basin of sudsy water onto her apron. It bled through her skirt and petticoat. Two orderlies arrived, heaved the body onto a stretcher, and carried it away.

Una asked the second-year to cover for her for a few minutes and climbed out onto the balcony. She'd thought about sneaking a sip of brandy but brought a cup of tea with her instead. It clinked against its saucer in her still shaky hands. Dusk would soon fall, and the yard below was cast in shadow. But the air retained the day's warmth, perfumed with hints of crocus flowers and witch hazel. The waning sunlight glinted off the river as it flowed southward toward the nearly finished Brooklyn Bridge. She sipped her tea and gave up trying to hold back her tears.

It had been years since she'd broken her rules and allowed herself to cry. Tears made you look weak. Weakness got you picked on and exploited. But what a relief it was to let them come, to let them cloud her eyes and dribble down her face. She wasn't sure what or whom she cried for. The man from the Bowery? His wife and daughter? Mr. Knauff and the accident with ether? Diedre? Dru? The tears came harder, mucus clotting her throat. She crouched down, set her teacup aside, and wrapped her arms around her knees. It was her mother she was thinking of. And herself.

She remembered going together to Washington Market to buy oysters and vegetables. On lucky occasions, her mother would add an orange to their basket and peel it for Una on the way home. She remembered sitting on her mother's lap by the fireplace, listening to her read the rare letter her father sent home from the battlefield. Her voice never wavered, not even when news came of the minie ball that had ripped through his leg. That night, though, she let Una crawl into bed with her and held her until dawn.

The years before the war, Una remembered only in flashes and snippets—her mother's laughter, her father's jaunty fiddle playing, the smell of coddle and soda bread wafting from the kitchen. On Sundays they'd walk hand in hand to church, Una in the middle, swinging between their arms.

It was true; her mother had taken to her charity work with particular fervor in the years after her father's return. But by then home had become a solemn place. Her mother seldom laughed. Her father's fiddle went unplayed. They ate supper in silence.

Now Una realized she couldn't blame her mother for needing time away any more than she could blame her father for returning broken from the war. Any more than she could blame her nine-year-old self for mistaking heartbreak for hatred and never truly mourning her mother's death.

Una wept until footfalls rattled the balcony. Glancing up, she saw Edwin approaching. She stood, turning her face away and blotting the mess of tears with her shirtsleeve as he hurried to her side.

"Una, what's wrong?"

She backed away, tripping over her cup and saucer. Tea spilled and splattered, dripping through the lattice of iron onto the balcony below. Thankfully the stoneware hadn't shattered. She and Edwin both bent to pick it up, their fingers brushing as they reached for the saucer.

"I've got it, Doctor, don't trouble yourself."

Edwin frowned and stood, leaning his forearms on the railing. "I hate when you do that, call me 'Doctor' like I'm some stranger. Like I haven't kissed you a hundred times. Like I haven't—"

"Shh, someone might overhear you."

"I don't care if the entire world hears."

She clanked the cup atop the saucer and stood. "Easy for you to say. You don't have anything to lose."

"I'm sorry. I only came out to see that you were all right."

"I'm fine."

He shook his head. "I hate that too. When you lie to me."

She moved to the railing, far enough apart from him not to draw suspicion but close enough to hear the breath whistling in and out of his nose.

"How do you manage when there's so much death here?"

"I try to remember those who live, I suppose. Those whom we help get better." His voice softened. "Is that what's bothering you?"

"No." She looked out over the lawn. A patient with a crutch hobbled along the path amid the newly budding flowers. An attendant sat on a bench alongside the river, smoking a cigarette. A nurse stepped onto the lower balcony catty-corner to where they stood and flapped open a bedsheet, draping it over the rail. Una waited until the nurse returned inside before continuing. "Did you really mean it, before when you said I could tell you anything?"

"Of course I did. I want us always to be open and honest with each other."

"People don't want that—honesty. Not really. They want half-truths and trumped-up stories and sugar-coated lies."

"I do."

She looked at him from the corner of her eyes. Always that damned earnest expression.

"When you got back from New Orleans with your father's body, did you tell your mother how he died? Did you tell her about the bastard brother you'd met there?"

Edwin was quiet a moment. "No."

"That's what I mean."

"I was only sparing her feelings. She'd endured enough indignity at his hands."

"Lies aren't always meant to do harm."

"That's it, then? You would rather spare me whatever it is you think I can't handle and suffer alone?"

Alone. Is that really what she wanted? She ran her hand along the cool iron rail, letting it stop halfway between them. Edwin slid his hand out as well until it rested beside hers, their pinky fingers touching.

"No, that's not what I want anymore." She took a deep breath. "You must promise that no matter what I—"

"Miss Kelly."

The sound of the second-year's voice made Una jump. She pulled her hand away and turned toward the open window.

The second-year poked her head out. "Superintendent Perkins is asking for you."

Una's insides went cold. "I have to go," she said to Edwin when she remembered herself enough to speak. She hurried past him and through the window.

"Her office?" Una asked the second-year.

She nodded, her grave expression compounding Una's unease.

"Did she say what it was about?"

"No, but it's never good."

Una found the door to Miss Perkins's office open when she arrived. The superintendent was behind her wide desk talking with Nurse Hatfield and, strangely, Mrs. Buchanan. When she rapped on the doorjamb, the three women quieted. Miss Perkins waved her in. Una realized upon entering that she was still carrying her empty teacup.

"I didn't have anything to do with that man's death today. I tried to get Dr. Pingry to wash his hands and use clean instruments. I did. Even the interns tried. He refused to change—"

"That's not why I asked to see you, Miss Kelly," Superintendent Perkins said.

Una exhaled with relief.

"I asked to see you because Miss Hatfield has leveled a very serious accusation against you."

She glanced at Nurse Hatfield, then back to Miss Perkins. Had Una neglected something on the ward? Forgotten to close a window or missed a spot while dusting? Surely that wouldn't qualify as *very* serious. Did it have to do with Edwin? Had she seen them together? Whatever it was, Una knew better than to speak beyond a tremulous, "Oh?"

"Theft, Miss Kelly. She says you stole her silk scarf."

"What? That's ridiculous. A bald-faced lie!"

"Then you won't object if we return home and search your room?"

"Of course not," Una said.

She followed the women out of the hospital and across the street to the home. When they reached her room, Una opened the door, and the women filed in. With Dru gone, Una hadn't been as scrupulous about making her bed and winced seeing the rumpled quilt and unfluffed pillow. They weren't here to inspect her bed-making skills, she reminded herself.

Her quilt was one of the first things they removed, anyway. Mrs. Buchanan gave her an apologetic look before pulling it back and inspecting between the sheets. She peeked under her mattress and beneath her bed frame, too, while the other women rummaged through her wardrobe, turning out the pockets of her coat and dresses.

Una watched from the doorway. They would make terrible detectives, these women. She almost laughed in spite of herself. They didn't feel along the tops of the shelves for something tucked out of view. They didn't look for out-of-place seams in the wood where a false wall might have been constructed. They didn't pull up the rug and check for loose floorboards. They didn't knock on the walls and listen for the telltale ring of a hollowed-out cubby.

"See, I didn't take anything," Una said.

Mrs. Buchanan gave a mollifying nod. "I'm sorry, dear. We're almost done." She knelt and opened the lid of Una's chest.

"There's nothing in there but my underthings."

"I'm afraid we must search everything." Mrs. Buchanan unfolded Una's nightdress and turned her spare stockings inside out. Una had stored the worn copy of Barney's magazine at the bottom, along with his bent tie pin and the medallion of the Virgin Mother she'd gotten from the woman in Hell's Kitchen. Mrs. Buchanan looked beneath them, then began repacking Una's trunk.

"Check between the pages of that magazine," Nurse Hatfield said, a hint of desperation in her voice.

Una glared at her, grabbing the magazine from Mrs. Buchanan and thrusting it into her hand. "Here. Check yourself. You won't be satisfied until you've turned every page."

Nurse Hatfield flipped carefully through the magazine, her smug expression falling and cheeks reddening as she neared the end. "I . . . er . . . I don't understand. My scarf has been missing for days. No one but you would have taken it."

Una snatched back the magazine and tossed it into her trunk. It landed against the bottom with a clink. "Well, as you see, I didn't."

"It must be here somewhere. Maybe among Miss Lewis's things." She took a step toward Dru's trunk, but Una blocked her path.

"Don't you dare touch anything of hers." Una had intentionally kept everything—from the half-spent candle at Dru's bedside to the fur muff and cap hanging from her peg—just as Dru had left it.

"None of it belongs here anyway," Nurse Hatfield said. "She's not a trainee anymore."

Miss Perkins, hitherto silent, moved between them. "Enough! Your accusation has proven unfounded, Eugenia. I regret ever indulging you in it. I believe you owe Miss Kelly an apology."

Nurse Hatfield crossed her arms and looked away. She stood silently for several seconds then huffed. "I'm sor—"

Mrs. Buchanan cleared her throat, saving Nurse Hatfield the trouble of finishing. "I'm afraid Miss Eugenia might be right in her suspicions." She held out her hand. In her palm was the silver pocket watch. "I believe this is the watch Dr. Pingry said he lost after his lecture." She turned it over to reveal the letters engraved on the back. "See, here are his initials."

CHAPTER 44

Una stood outside the nurses' home, valise in hand, uncertain where to go. She couldn't return to the Points, and Claire would never take her in. Three months had passed since Traveling Mike's murder, not long enough by a mile for the police to have closed the case and forgotten her. She knew crooks who'd returned to the city after years away only to be nabbed by the coppers. Without her nursing disguise, Una would find herself in the same boat.

Three months—had it only been that long? It felt like a lifetime. She walked down Twenty-Sixth Street with no particular destination in mind. Night had fallen, giving her the cover of gaslight and shadow, but it was not yet late enough that her presence on the street would cause suspicion. The streetcar passed, its wheels grinding over the pavers, and she thought of Dru, still delirious with fever. Now they were both expelled. What a waste her sacrifice had been.

She wandered past Madison Square Park, not stopping until she reached the bright electric lights of Broadway. Hansoms rolled past, ferrying people from their hotels to music halls, theaters, and the opera house. Amusement-seekers crowded the sidewalks too, dressed in their evening finery. With her valise and cotton day dress, Una felt conspicuous here. The busy street and boisterous voices and noisy businesses unnerved her after so many days in the quiet of the hospital. Still, the Tenderloin was as good a place as any to hide out for the night.

A few blocks off Broadway, Una found a two-cent restaurant tucked away in a tenement cellar. It was a small, grimy establishment lit with sputtering oil lamps. Upturned barrels served as tables, and the sawdust on the floor looked like it hadn't been replaced since before Christmas. But for two pennies, she could buy herself a cup of coffee or glass of stale beer and sit all night. Una chose the beer.

Drink in hand, she found an empty barrel in a dimly lit corner, pushing away every wobbly stool but one so as not to invite company. The beer was weak, warm, and sour, and Una gagged on her first sip. Somewhere nearby, a rat scratched at the ground. Cockroaches skittered up the walls.

She longed for the warm, gaslit library at the nurses' home. The smell of books instead of days-old vomit. The taste of honey-sweetened milk instead of rancid beer.

"You've gone soft, Una Kelly," she muttered but couldn't help wincing when a man across the room spit a slimy wad of tobacco onto the floor. The man smiled at her, taking no pains to hide his stained, crooked teeth. She scowled in return.

Edwin's teeth were so white and handsome. His mouth always tasted deliciously of cloves and mint when they kissed. She'd come so close to telling him today of her true past and identity. Thank goodness she hadn't. It was madness to think he'd understand. The smug look on Nurse Hatfield's face when they'd found the watch was enough to remind Una she didn't belong.

Mrs. Buchanan had gaped at her in disbelief, wagging her head like a broken toy. Miss Perkins had been more circumspect. Her expression revealed not surprise or censure but only disappointment. She held her hand up to silence Una's fumbling explanation and insisted she pack her bag and leave the home at once.

It was that disappointment that had wounded Una the most.

She couldn't bear to see it in Edwin's eyes as well, not when he'd gazed more lovingly at her than any man before. Better not to sully her memories of him. They were all she had now, after all.

Una forced the thought of him from her mind. She had to figure out what to do. With only seven dollars in her pocket, her options were few. She couldn't go back to diving pockets when not a single fence in town would buy her loot. Marm Blei would have made certain of that. Anyone stupid or desperate enough to go against her wishes would give Una pennies to the dollar anyway.

There was always factory work, but backbreaking as those jobs were, there were always more hungry bellies than spots on the line to fill. It took grease to get even the meanest positions plucking chickens or bottling pickles. The men at Tammany would help. For the price of a few minutes between her legs.

Una choked down another sip of beer. The idea of sweating over a noisy conveyor belt for ten hours a day, feathers sticking to her skin and the stench of chicken blood filling her nose, made her sick. Not even her worst day at Bellevue would compare. Never mind the foreman with his loose hands and the Tammany men who would come calling.

She dropped her head into her hands. So much for a new profession.

As much as she'd hated life at the hospital in the beginning, over time she'd grown fond of the work. She'd never taken to learning all the stupid Latin names of the bones and muscles like Dru had, but she'd enjoyed her time with the patients—soothing their aches and pains with warm fomentations, buoying their bedraggled spirits with fresh air and sunshine, watching their wounds heal and knowing she had helped.

Her feet had ached at the end of the day. Her head and back sometimes too. But she'd felt . . . useful. Capable. Connected to something larger than herself.

Maybe that had been the trouble. She'd lost sight of her rules. Forgotten that to survive you couldn't get wrapped up in anyone else. And yet, she couldn't bring herself to regret that afternoon on the lake with Edwin or her evenings in the library with Dru. Her only regret was how she'd hurt them.

The man with the stained teeth dragged over one of the stools she'd pushed away and sat beside her. So much for not inviting company.

"What's a perdy gal like you doing alone in a place like this?"

Una rolled her eyes. He couldn't even think of something original to say. "Trying to be alone."

"No one wants to be alone. How 'bout I buy you a drink?"

"I have one."

"Then how 'bout I buy you another? Two drinks are always better than one."

"How about I clock you in the nose?"

He chuckled and scooted closer.

"I'm serious, mister." She raised a fist. "See that scar there? That was an Italian who thought it was sweet to pinch my rear. And this one's from an Irish bloke who tried to kiss me. And this one—"

"Okay, okay, I get the point." He backed away but didn't leave. "Suppose I just sit here a while, and we take things slow."

"I don't wanna take things slow or fast or any which way with you. I want to drink my beer in peace."

The clang of an ambulance bell muffled the man's reply. Her thoughts circled back to Edwin and their ride together to Hell's Kitchen. The blur of the streets. The hunger of his kisses. The shock of arriving at their destination and having to pull away. Another clang, this one closer, and her thoughts were yanked back further still. Back to another dingy saloon. Traveling Mike draining his brandy and flashing her a meaningful glance. The ambulance sounding its bell and stopping nearby just after he'd left.

The man beside Una continued to blabber, but she hushed him with a *shh* and flap of her hand. Something about the memory was different, like a jammed cog suddenly sprung free. She skipped ahead in her mind to the alley. The flicker of Deidre's match. The belt around Traveling Mike's neck. The man in uniform crouched beside him. It wasn't a belt or rope; it was a tourniquet. The dark-colored jacket and short-brimmed cap were those of an ambulance driver.

She closed her eyes and imagined the moment just before the match slipped from Deidre's hand. The chill in the air. The dusting of snow. The stench of urine and rotting food scraps. The murderer looking up at them in surprise.

Una opened her eyes with a start.

Conor.

CHAPTER 45

Una stood in the shadow cast by the broad arch of the gatehouse. The stone structure was nearly complete now. Funny how she hadn't noticed the progress yesterday or the day before or the day before that when she'd walked beneath it to and from the hospital. The workers were packing up their tools for the day while the watchman sat nearby on a pallet of stones, wolfing down his supper.

She'd chosen this hour with care. Like the workmen, the physicians would soon be leaving for home. The nurses and hospital staff would be busy getting supper to the patients. The gathering dusk would afford her the cover of darkness.

Still, Una hesitated. If Nurse Hatfield or Superintendent Perkins caught her here, they'd send for the coppers. New York was gone to her, but if she cut her losses now and ran, she just might make it to Boston or Philadelphia and be able to start anew, grifting. Odious and lonely as that life now seemed to her, it sure beat Blackwell's Island. But she had to tell someone about Conor. If he'd killed Traveling Mike, he might have murdered Deidre and the woman from the Insane Pavilion too. Others at Bellevue might be in danger. Including Dru and Edwin.

Her heart squeezed. What had Miss Perkins said to her? That she ought to try to live up to Dru's estimable opinion of her? Dru always had seen Una in a better light than she deserved. By Una's old way of thinking, that made Dru a consummate dupe. But maybe that was also what it meant to be a friend.

Una took a deep breath and quit her place in the shadows. As always, she bade the workmen a friendly hello as she strode past. Best to seem like nothing was amiss.

"Not workin' today, Nurse Kelly?" one of them asked.

"My day off," she said, smiling and sliding her gaze to the watchman. Miss Perkins might have alerted him of Una's dismissal. Thankfully, he was too occupied with his evening meal of buttered bread and milk to pay her any mind.

She tried to slip into the hospital through the storeroom on the ground level but found it locked. The next door, a side entry into the southwest wing, was locked too. She didn't dare use the main entry. No amount of bravado could see her safely past Warden O'Rourke's office, which sat off the main hall. He most certainly knew about her dismissal and would deliver her to the coppers himself if he saw her.

Left with no other choice, she slipped down the stairs to the basement. The thick wooden door was unlocked, its hinges squealing as she tugged it open. Una didn't know this part of the hospital as well as the others, and navigating through its dimly lit, dank passages made the hair on her arms stand on end. Dru had deduced that the murderer would know these passages well. Well enough to find Deidre's cell, sneak inside, and strangle her with the ambulance tourniquet. The thought sent a shiver down her back. Could Conor be lurking here now, watching her?

She tripped over something cold and hard, shrieking at the ensuing clatter. Panicked, she squeezed herself into a narrow alcove beside a mop and broom and closed her eyes. Echoes of the noise bounced between the walls, then faded. Una took a deep breath and forced her eyes open. The hallway was empty save for an upturned pail. "Looby," she said to herself and continued on.

Eventually, she found a stairwell that led to the main hospital. Her heart continued to skitter as she climbed the steps. She might know her way around up here, but her chances of being caught were far greater too.

She peeked inside the doctors' dining room and the medical board room, careful to stay concealed behind the doorframe. Edwin wasn't in either room. She slipped back into the stairwell and climbed to the second floor. She'd done enough sneaking around with him to know all the lesser-used doors and hallways. To know how each ward was connected and how to slip from one to the other unseen. It was easier, of course, in her uniform to blend in. But there were enough visitors during the supper hour that she hoped to go unnoticed.

When she reached ward nine, she strode boldly in and sat beside one of the sleeping patients, leaning over him and fussing with his blankets as if she were his wife. Nurse Cuddy stood at the main table in the center of the ward, plating supper for the patients. Beside her was Nurse Hatfield.

Una lowered her head. Please don't look this way, she thought. Please don't look this way.

"Mind the temperature, Nurse Cuddy," she heard Nurse Hatfield say. "Nourishment is intended to be hot, not lukewarm lest you offend your patient's stomach and it refuse all food."

"Yes, Nurse Hatfield. I'm going as quickly as I can."

Nurse Hatfield gave a dissatisfied *hmm*—a sound Una knew all too well. She knew the telltale clap of her footfalls, too, and winced as she heard her approaching. Una took the sleeping man's hand and began muttering "Ave Maria," keeping her face downturned. The footfalls stopped at the foot of the bed.

"Is there anything you need, ma'am?"

Una shook her head and continued with the prayer. Her thoughts a nervous jumble, she mixed up a few of the words, but hopefully Nurse Hatfield's Latin wasn't good enough to notice. She got to *amen* and started over. Finally, Nurse Hatfield walked away.

Una waited until her footsteps disappeared into the adjoining ward before looking up. She couldn't be certain Nurse Hatfield hadn't recognized her and wasn't off to alert Miss Perkins, but

Una couldn't turn back now. She caught Miss Cuddy's eye and waved her over.

"Nurse . . . er . . . Miss Kelly, I thought you were expelled."

"Shh." Una glanced over her shoulder to be sure Nurse Hatfield hadn't returned. "I was."

"You really stole Miss High and Mighty's scarf, then?"

"No, but . . . I did take Dr. Pingry's watch."

Miss Cuddy's eyes went wide, then she chuckled. "That old curmudgeon had it coming."

"How's Miss Lewis doing?"

"Taken a bit for the worse today, I'm afraid. But she's a fighter, that one."

Una swallowed and nodded. "I'm looking for Dr. Westervelt. Do you know where he might be?"

"I think he's just finishing up in the operating theater. Late case. Skull fracture."

Una stood.

"I wouldn't go up there if I were you," Miss Cuddy said. "Dr. Pingry and a couple dozen medical students are up there too."

She hadn't thought about that. It wouldn't be easy to get his attention without anyone seeing her. "Can you run up and give him a message?"

"Nurse Hatfield's already on my tail about letting supper get cold. If I'm not finished by the time she comes back, I'll get an earful and then some. Besides, you know how fussy Dr. Pingry is about having too many nurses on stage while he's operating. If it were up to him, not a single one of us would be there."

Una glanced at Miss Cuddy's belly. She'd done a good job fluffing her petticoat and tying her apron a few inches higher to hide the growing baby. Una could still use it as leverage, though. But wasn't it all her angling and bullying and fleecing that landed her here in the first place?

"Listen, I know we're not exactly friends, and I was . . . well, a bit of a bother before. But I've got to see him. Tonight. Patients' lives may be at risk."

Nurse Cuddy frowned and glanced back at the table where supper sat cooling. "Ah, fiddlesticks. What's your message?"

"Tell him to wait for me in the operating theater after the case. I'll meet him there at seven. Tell him it's important."

Una hid in the storeroom until she heard the bells of nearby St. Stephen's chime seven. Then she snuck upstairs. Without the gaggle of medical students peering down from the gallery and bright overhead gas lamps illuminated, the amphitheater had the same eerie stillness as the morgue. The metal table at the center of the stage was empty, and the blood-soaked sawdust had been swept from the floor. Twilight filtered in through the high, arching windows, bathing the room in a pale orange glow.

She lingered in the shadow of the doorway, looking for Edwin. She inched inside to see to the very top of the gallery. The crust of a sandwich and a few stubbed cigarettes littered the stairs, but the gallery, like the rest of the room, was empty. Una bit her lip. Nurse Cuddy had delivered him the message, but Edwin hadn't stayed.

Then the door to the storeroom creaked open. Edwin emerged carrying an unlit candle. The knots that had wound inside her all day loosened. She fought the urge to run to him, taking a measured step into the fading light. "I thought you'd gone."

He looked up but didn't approach her. He knew about the watch, then. She shouldn't have been surprised. Gossip traveled through the hospital as quickly as it did a whorehouse. She tried to read in his eyes whether or not he believed it, but the light was failing, and all she could discern was a hardness that hadn't been there before.

He reached in his pocket for a matchbook and lit the candle.

"Edwin, I—"

"Is it true? Did you steal Dr. Pingry's watch?"

She took a few steps closer, stopping when he made no move to do the same. "I . . . I . . ." She shook the nervous energy from her hands and took a deep breath. "I've stolen many things in my life, including Dr. Pingry's watch."

"Is it some compulsion you suffer from? Kleptomania, I've heard the alienists call it."

"No. I did it to survive, to make a living."

Candlelight flickered across his face. He looked pained. Uncertain. "I don't understand. You come from a good family in Maine. Your father is a—"

"My father is an opium fiend and drunk. I'm not from Maine, I was born here in the city. I . . ." A biting dryness had spread across her tongue. She swallowed and forced herself to continue. "I've been a pickpocket and thief for more than half my life."

"And then what?" His voice was thin, strained. "You just up and decided you wanted to leave behind your life of crime and be a nurse?"

Una looked down and shook her head. "I got caught up in a little trouble with my crew. The training school . . . it seemed like a good place to lie low for a while."

"So you never actually wanted to become a nurse? It all was just"—he swept a hand through the air—"a fabrication. A ruse. And you've been stealing from people the entire time you've been here?"

"No, it was only Dr. Pingry's watch. And only because . . . because he's a pompous old cad who deserved it."

"And Miss Hatfield's scarf?"

"That was a lie."

"A lie!" He laughed, a sharp barking sound that echoed in the high room. The candlelight wavered. "Una, everything you've told me is a lie."

"Not everything. I truly did . . . truly do love you."

"If you loved me, you would have told me the truth."

"Why, so you could laugh at me and call me a criminal?"

"Isn't that what you are?"

Una shook her head. "I thought . . . maybe because of your father you'd understand."

"My father? He doesn't have a damned thing to do with this."

"No, you're right." She took a step forward, the heavy clap of her boots joining the fading echo of his laughter above in the rafters. "He may have been a rake. He embarrassed you and betrayed you, but you've never known what it's like to be hungry. Or so cold your fingers and toes blister when you finally get in front of a fire. You've never known what it's like to sleep on the street with nothing but stray dogs for company. Or to have to fight your way free with your fists and nails and teeth from men who mean to hurt you."

She turned away from his aghast expression. Nothing offended like the truth. The sky outside the window had bruised over into night. The operating theater felt suddenly cold as if its heat had drained along with the light. Una rubbed her arms. "I didn't come here to tell you that. But at least now you know."

"Why *did* you come, then?" Edwin said after a moment.

Una turned back around to face him. "I think there's a murderer at Bellevue."

He seemed to half-laugh, half-choke. "A murderer!"

"Yes, Conor. The ambulance driver. He killed a man. I saw him."

"Here?"

"In an alley near the Points. He strangled him with a tourniquet from the wagon."

Edwin snorted. A vein of wax dribbled down the side of the candle and onto his hand. He dropped the candle, wincing and cursing. The flame flickered out, throwing them into darkness.

Una bent down and groped for the candle. She touched something warm—Edwin's hand—and felt him pull away.

"I can find it on my own," he said and struck a match.

The candle had rolled to the foot of the operating table. He crawled over to it and relit the wick. She watched him clamber to his feet, careful not to burn himself again on the candle's wax. He brushed his hand on his trouser and then reached down to help her up. His hand lingered a moment on her arm after she was on her feet as if he couldn't decide whether to pull her closer or push her away. In the end, he did neither but simply let go.

"I think he killed two patients here at Bellevue too, though. A woman from the Insane Pavilion. And the drunk who arrived the same day as all those men from the factory accident."

"She died from too much laudanum. They found the empty bottle in her pocket, remember?"

"It wasn't but a quarter full. Not nearly enough to kill her."

"How do you know?"

"I gave it to her. In the exam room. Before the orderlies took her down to her cell. She was a woman I knew from the streets. She threatened to expose me if I didn't give it to her. She was there with me that night in the alley." As she said this, Una suddenly wondered if Conor might have recognized her. Deidre had been the one to light the match, after all. He would have gotten a better look at her than at Una.

"This is ridiculous," Edwin said, shaking his head. "You're a thief, who stole laudanum for a friend and is now accusing another man of murdering her."

"Please, Edwin, you have to believe me. I think he might kill again."

"And why would he do that?"

"It's like you said before, a compulsion. Not to steal but to murder. He thinks they're trash, these people. Vermin. A plague on the city. He's said so to me himself."

"He's told you he kills people?"

"No, only how abhorrent he finds them—the poor, the tramps, the streetwalkers."

Edwin raked a hand through his hair. "If he's so dangerous, why don't you go to the police?"

"I . . . er . . . I can't. There's a warrant out for my arrest."

He stared at her as if he couldn't quite comprehend what she'd said.

"The man Conor killed, the police think I did it."

"And did you?"

"No, that's what I'm trying to tell you, Conor killed him and—" She stopped and scrutinized his face. "You think I could kill a man?"

"At this point, nothing you say would surprise me."

Una turned away from him again, watching the candlelight flicker against the wall. A sharp, jabbing pain spread through her chest, like a knife wound cut from the inside out.

"If you won't go to the police, I don't see how I can help you," he said.

The pain didn't subside, but Una breathed through it and turned around. "I want to confront him. I think I can get him to confess. But I need someone else. A witness. You said I could trust you. You said—" Her voice broke. "You said no matter what."

He winced but quickly recovered his hard expression. He thrust the candle into her hand, hot wax spilling on them both. "I'm sorry, Una. I don't . . . I can't . . . Good-bye."

CHAPTER 46

The next morning, Una caught the Sixth Avenue el at Twenty-Third Street heading southward. Walking, though perhaps safer, would take far too long. Especially without her boots. Her feet would be frostbitten by the time she arrived. The unseasonably cold day with its low-hanging clouds and fits of wet snow otherwise worked in Una's favor, though. Fewer coppers would be out patrolling, and she could wrap her scarf up to her ears without looking suspicious.

Even so, it was difficult to keep her hands still and thoughts steady. Her encounter last night with Edwin still pained her. When she'd returned to her cramped, stinky lodging house and unbuttoned her dress to wipe the day's grime from beneath her armpits, she'd half expected to find a gaping wound between her breasts. One of those raw, oozing wounds that never seemed to heal no matter the ministrations.

Worse still, that phantom pain had made her so insensible, she'd taken off her boots to sleep as if she were back in the dignified nurses' home. In the morning, they were gone.

Now, she tucked her sodden, rag-tied feet beneath the seat and tried not to shiver. The city passed outside the window in a gray blur. It hadn't snowed enough to cover the soot-stained roofs or grime-covered streets, only enough to transform the dust, ash, and manure into mud. She reached into her coat pocket where her last few possessions remained—the medallion of Mary, which she rubbed for luck, and Barney's slightly crooked pin. If he refused to help her, as Edwin had, Una had no one else to turn to.

At the Bleecker Street station, a copper shuffled aboard the car. Una wasn't surprised, seeing as they were headed toward the courthouse and City Hall. But that didn't stop her breath from catching in her throat nor her pulse from racing. She kept her head lowered. The benches that lined either side of the car were nearly full, but he squeezed in between two gentlemen directly across from her.

"Some weather, eh?" he said as the train picked up speed again.

Una waited for someone else to reply. When no one did, she raised her head slightly, smiled, and nodded, praying that was the end of his blather. But no sooner had she lowered her gaze, than he spoke again.

"Beats them hot summers, though. Don't ya think?"

She nodded again, tucking her feet back as far beneath the seat as she could. His deep-set eyes and russet-colored hair were vaguely familiar. The timbre of his voice too. Una shifted through her memories, the whoosh of her pulse against her eardrum drowning out the rattle of the car.

Grand Central Depot. The day before her arrest. He was the copper who'd chased her all the way to Thirty-Eighth Street. The only time he'd gotten a close look at her was when she'd turned her coat inside out and pretended to be a ragpicker. Might he remember her face? She cursed herself for toying with him that day and protracting their encounter.

She glanced out the window above his head. There were over a dozen blocks to go before her stop. If she got off at the next station and waited for another train, it would look suspicious. Especially if he saw her rag-covered feet as she exited. No, she'd have to wait it out and pray he didn't recognize her.

"Weather like this puts me in mind of my days as a lad back in County Clare," he said.

How many times would she have to nod demurely before he

stopped yapping? Then again, if he were talking, it meant he wasn't thinking back to that privy yard where they'd met.

"My father was from Clare too."

The copper's expression brightened. "Was he now? What part?"

"Lahinch."

"Really? That weren't but a stone's throw for me own home."

And that was enough to get him rhapsodizing about the old country until his stop at Chambers Street. He tipped his cap to her as he left, saying he hoped they'd meet on another ride soon. Una sighed once the car doors closed behind him, her first full exhale in nearly half an hour. She got off at the next station and made her way through the mud to the Herald Building on Newspaper Row.

The lobby attendant, a spindly man with a bushy mustache far too large for his narrow face, refused to admit her without shoes, forcing Una to wait outside until Barney was fetched down.

"Good God, Una, where are your boots?" he asked when he saw her.

"It's a long story."

With Barney to vouch for her, the attendant made no further fuss about her entry. He did scowl, however, at the wet, muddy footprints she left on the polished stone floor as Barney led her to the stairs.

Unlike the last time she'd been here, reporters and typists crowded the newsroom. Clouds of cigarette smoke curled around the dangling gas lamps.

"Is there someplace else we can go?" she asked above the click of typewriters and clamor of voices. "Someplace private?"

"Mr. Hadley might lend us use of his office a moment. Or maybe—"

"What about the roof?"

He looked down at her feet and frowned. "You'll freeze up—"

"I'll be fine. I'd feel better knowing we can't be overheard."

"Don't tell me you've gotten yourself into even more trouble than before."

Begrudgingly, Barney led her back to the stairs. They climbed several more flights and exited onto the roof through a heavy steel door. The cool, misty air prickled her skin. Melting snow puddled at her feet. The nearby spires of St. Paul's and Trinity churches pierced the low-hanging clouds.

"It's too cold up here," Barney said. "Let's go down. I'm sure we can—"

"There's a killer at Bellevue."

"What?"

"Do you remember several months back hearing about a fence who'd been strangled?"

"Sure, I thought it might be related to those other killings I was investigating in the slums. But the police figured a woman for it. Some pickpocket from the Bend." He stopped and cocked his head, his staid expression morphing into wide-eyed surprise. "Wait a minute. That was you!"

He took a step backward, slipping on a slick of ice. Una grabbed hold of his wheeling arms before he fell.

"Of course it wasn't me. I mean, I was there, but I didn't kill him. I know who did, though." She let go of his arms and tiptoed to a dry patch of roof in the lee of a chimney. Barney followed. There, with the soft murmur of the streets rising from below and the occasional flake of snow still spitting from the sky, Una told him everything.

"Do you believe me?" she asked when she was done.

"I don't know. It's certainly an intriguing conjecture."

"'Intriguing'! Three people are dead. Maybe more."

"Bad choice of words. My apologies." He lit a cigarette and offered one to Una. She reached out to take it, then waved her hand *no*. Barney slipped the cigarette case back into his jacket pocket and continued. "But you're mad if you think we can just walk up and get a confession out of him."

"*We?* Does that mean you'll help me?"

"It would make a great story." He took a long pull on his cigarette and then flicked ash onto the ground. "Only trouble is the how of it."

Una wished Dru were here. She had the mind for such schemes, even if she hadn't the stealthiness to pull it off. Una thought back to "The Murders in the Rue Morgue." How was it that Mr. Dupin got the orangutan's owner to confess?

"I've got it," she said after a moment. "We must lure him out, away from Bellevue, under the false pretense that we have something he wants."

"And what is that?"

Una shook her head. She hadn't gotten that far yet. They couldn't very well put an advertisement in the paper about a missing orangutan the way Mr. Dupin had. She stared out at the city as she considered. From this height, she could see all the way south to Battery Park, its trees faintly green despite the cold. Ships lined the Hudson, masts furled, anchors dropped, while others sailed its choppy waters, navigating around the steamers and tugboats that belched smoke into the air. When she turned her eyes inland, the Five Points intersection was visible, tenements choking it on all sides. She followed Mulberry Street to the Bend, then shifted her gaze northward, hoping to see the sprawling gray fortress of Bellevue. But church spires and smokestacks stymied her view.

What else had Mr. Poe said in that silly story of his? A line near the beginning came back to her: *Deprived of ordinary resources, the analyst throws himself into the spirit of his opponent, identifies himself therewith, and not unfrequently sees thus, at a glance, the sole methods (sometimes indeed absurdly simple ones) by which he may seduce into error or hurry into miscalculation.*

"We must make him think somehow his crimes are about to be discovered," she said. "That will make him rash and more easily fooled."

Barney nodded slowly. "I think I see what you're getting at." He stubbed out his cigarette and turned to her with a mischievous smile. "You said you were friends with him?"

"After a fashion."

"But he likes you. Enough that he would trust you?"

"I don't think he'll hurt me if that's what you're getting at."

"And you say he caught you snooping around after that lunatic woman was killed?"

Una nodded.

"Good, good."

Una couldn't see what on earth was good about that. If anything, it would make Conor more suspicious of her. And she certainly didn't like to think that she'd befriended a killer.

"What if you convince him you've met a woman who shares your same suspicions about the recent deaths at Bellevue and knows who the killer is? This woman—Mrs. Bean, we'll call her—has agreed to tell you the killer's identity, but only if you meet her at Washington Square after dark."

"I don't see how this will lure Mr. McCready out."

"Tell him . . . tell him you're afraid to go alone and ask him to accompany you. By the time you arrive, he'll be so on edge it will be easy to trick him into confessing. Meanwhile, I'll be listening behind a bush. Once he says anything incriminating, I'll jump out and apprehend him."

Una frowned. The plan wasn't as absurdly simple as she'd hoped. "How will I know which bush you're hiding behind?"

"We'll pick a spot."

"What if it's windy and you can't hear our conversation? Or what if there's a copper on patrol who tries to hassle us for loitering after dark? Or worse yet, recognizes me."

"Do you have a better idea?"

Una rubbed her hands together for warmth. "What about one of those panel cribs shakedown thieves use?"

"Panel what?"

"It's a room in a lodging house that's been specially outfitted for robbery. A woman entices a man inside, and her partner—who's hidden away inside a wardrobe with a false back that revolves like a turnstile—sneaks out and steals the man's honey while he and the woman are . . . well, you know . . . distracted."

Barney's ears turned the color of radishes.

"It's the perfect place for you to hide and listen while I trick Conor into confessing."

"I don't know . . ." He fumbled with his tie, leaving it rumpled and askew. "What if something happens to you before I can get out?"

Una fished inside her coat pocket and pulled out his silver pin. She straightened his tie and pinned it to his shirt. "I'll be fine. I told you, I don't think Conor will hurt me."

Barney fingered the pin. "I was wondering where that went."

"I owe my freedom to that thing. Sorry it's a bit bent."

"So how do you plan on getting him to confess?"

"I was hoping you'd have an idea for that."

They sat in silence for a moment, staring out at the city. The snow had stopped and the sky was beginning to clear.

"You said you know what sets him off," Barney said at last. "Use that against him. Get him riled enough, and he's bound to slip up. It's worked for me dozens of times when I'm trying to get a story."

"He'll be suspicious, though, when we arrive, and no one's in the room."

"Tell him . . . tell him the woman must be late. To him, you're just a sweet, innocent nurse, remember? He's got no reason not to trust you."

Una considered this. The entire plan was risky. Only an overeager reporter and a desperate woman would contrive such a cockeyed scheme. But Una was desperate. This was the only chance of clearing her name. Otherwise she'd be on the run, hiding and grifting forever. She tried again to pick out Bellevue among the distant blur of shapes along the East River. More importantly, she couldn't let Conor hurt Dru or anyone else.

"What do you think?" Barney asked. "We can bag the whole idea and go to the police if—"

"No." She stamped her feet to bring feeling back to her toes. "You gotta spring for a new pair of boots, though."

CHAPTER 47

That Sunday at mass, Una was so nervous she stood when she should have knelt and knelt when she should have sat. She mixed up the "Pater Noster" and "Gloria Patri," and tripped on the laces of her new boots on her way to communion. But Conor, seated only one pew away, didn't seem to notice. Seeing him now in the low light that filtered in through the stained-glass windows, she was all the more certain he was the killer. Like always, he waited for her at the base of the church steps when the service was over to walk her home.

"I was worried I wouldn't see you today," he said. "Someone said you'd been expelled."

Even though Una had expected this and practiced her answer, her voice came out thin. "That was Miss Mackinlay. An Ulster Scot by blood, but people were always mistaking her for Irish and mixing the two of us up."

"So you ain't been expelled?"

She shook her head with all too much vigor, then tried to make up for it with an over-wide smile. She needed to calm down. This was no different from any other ruse. Never mind that she had only one shot to lay her trap.

"Well, I sure am glad to hear it."

They walked a short distance in silence, then spoke again at the same time.

"Conor, I—"

"Fine day for—"

Una gave a tittering laugh. "You first."

"I was going to say it's a remarkably fine day after that snap of cold we had. How's about we take the long way by the river?"

"That would be lovely," she forced herself to say, despite the niggling feeling in her gut.

They stopped in the shade of the overhead el tracks and let a carriage pass before heading on toward the river.

"And you?"

"What? . . . Oh, yes . . . I was . . . I wanted to ask a little favor."

He flashed her a rakish smile. "Why, anything for you, Miss Kelly."

"Do you remember when I thought that dowdy old attendant might have killed that woman in the Insane Pavilion?"

His expression cooled. "I thought you'd put that crazy idea out of your head."

"Yes, I had. Completely. But then I met a woman, a patient, who was terrified of falling asleep at night. Wouldn't take chloral or even a nip of brandy after supper. When I asked her what she was afraid of, she said she'd heard of another woman, a friend of hers, who'd come to the hospital after taking too much liquor and been strangled in her sleep. Strangled. Just like the woman from the Insane Pavilion."

"That woman hanged herself."

"Maybe. They never found the rope or sheet she did it with, remember? And this woman—the patient who refused to sleep—says she thinks the man who killed her friend murdered a third person near the Points."

Conor took her arm and pulled her to the edge of the sidewalk beneath a storefront awning. His fingers pressed into her flesh, not so hard as to be painful, but certainly beyond the bounds of what could be considered polite or friendly. He looked behind them at the sparsely populated sidewalk and loosened his hold. "Miss Kelly, you shouldn't pay any mind to such babble. It ain't becoming of a nurse. Or a lady."

"But she knows the man, Conor. Says she could identify him."

He dropped her arm and took a step back. "Did she tell ya who it was?"

Una shook her head.

"Why don't she go to the police?"

"She's too afraid."

"Afraid of what?"

"She has a past. Just what she didn't say. Stealing maybe. Vagrancy. But if she's right, I could go to the police for her."

He shook his head and started off again toward the river. Una took a steadying breath, then hurried after him. "Please, I know that doesn't exactly make her the most trusted of sources, but I have to at least hear her story. What if she's right and this man hurts someone else?" Out of desperation, she looped an arm through his, resting her hand in the crook of his elbow. It was a risky, intimate gesture, but he didn't pull away. "I couldn't live with myself, Conor, knowing I was responsible for someone else's death."

They reached the river, and Conor's pace slowed. The water lapped at the dock, and seagulls called from above.

"I don't see what any of this has to do with me," he said.

"She wouldn't tell me any more at the hospital but said I could come to see her at a lodging house on Baxter Street tonight after she was discharged." Una kept hold of his arm and donned her best doe-eyed expression. "I don't know that part of the city very well. I was hoping you'd come along too, just in case her motives aren't entirely honest."

He looked away from her, first toward the river, then at the hulking gray hospital less than a block ahead. Una followed his gaze. The wine and wafer she'd taken at mass sat heavy in her empty stomach. Bellevue had seemed so dismal when she'd first arrived. A sleeping stone behemoth that might awaken at any moment and swallow her whole. Now it felt like home. The first real home she'd known since her mother's death. Would its high brick walls ever welcome her again?

Conor startled her by placing a hand over hers. "Baxter Street, ya say?"

She nodded. "Near Grand."

"Tonight?"

"Yes, after dark," she said.

"And this woman who thinks she's caught herself a murderer, she'll be alone?"

"I expect so, yes. Will you come?"

"Aye, I'll come." He patted her hand, his faraway gaze sending a prickle over her skin. "You're too trusting, Miss Kelly. Too trusting by a mile."

CHAPTER 48

They'd agreed to meet that night at sunset just beyond Belle-vue's gate. Una waited in the shadows of the narrow alleyway one building up from the nurses' home. As soon as she heard the tread of horse hooves on Bellevue's drive, she hurried out of cover, so when the night watchman opened the gate and Conor drove out, it would seem like she'd been waiting for him outside the home. Light glowed from the ground-level windows, softened by the gossamer curtains. Were the ladies playing whist? she wondered. Studying their notes from the morning's lecture? Her chest squeezed as she thought of Dru. If what she did tonight earned her any goodwill at the hospital, she'd use it to get Dru readmitted to the school.

Conor slowed the ambulance just outside the gate. He'd in-sisted they take the wagon, rather than the streetcar, assuring her the drivers took such liberties all the time when they were off duty. "Gets ya where you're going faster," he'd said with a smile Una didn't fully trust. But she hadn't argued.

She inhaled slowly and crossed the street. Conor jumped down from the driver's bench. He wore a grave expression, glancing around them with unsettled eyes. "You tell Miss Perkins or any of the other trainees about this?"

Una shook her head. "I didn't want to needlessly alarm anyone."

"Good." He glanced about again. Daylight had all but drained from the sky, and the streetlamps had yet to turn on, leaving them to the gathering darkness. Conor's shoulders relaxed, and he helped Una into the back of the wagon. The window coverings on either side had been unfurled and tied to the baseboards, so it was even darker within than without. She tripped over a medical bag before finding the bench and sitting down, trying not to flinch when he closed the back gate.

She flattened her hands on the bench to steady herself as the wagon lurched into motion. There was still time to abandon the plan. She could jump out now and . . . and what? Return to the streets and leave Dru and the rest of Bellevue in danger? The training program had given her a glimmer of life beyond surviving. Of what it was like to care about people beyond herself. True, she'd ended up alone again. But that had been her own doing. Not Nurse Hatfield's. Not Edwin's.

She folded up her regret alongside her unease and stowed them both away. She needed a clear mind tonight. The streets grew more congested the farther they got from the river. Conor steered the ambulance around carriages and streetcars and lumbering mule carts, ringing the gong every so often to clear the way. They turned off Third Avenue onto a quieter street. A polished brougham and a worn-out hansom cab turned as well, but neither kept pace with Conor's speed. Several turns later, Una noticed the cab was still there, now several blocks behind. Were they being followed?

She scooted to the edge of the bench and peered out above the back gate, trying to make out the cab's passenger. The streetlamps had flickered on, casting pools of light over the road. But even with the illumination, the distance was too great to see more than a hazy outline.

The ambulance hit a pothole, bucking Una off the bench and nearly out the back.

"Sorry about that, Miss Kelly," Conor called from the front. "You all right?"

"Fine!" she hollered above the grinding wheels and reseated herself a safe distance from the back. When she looked out again, the hansom cab was gone. Foolish to think that anyone had been following them. Only Barney knew of her whereabouts, and hopefully he'd already arrived at the room and secreted himself inside the wardrobe behind its false back.

A few minutes later, they arrived at the lodging house, an old, four-story building built of wood, sandwiched between two taller brick buildings. A noisy saloon occupied the cellar level.

"Ya sure about this?" Conor asked before opening the wagon's back gate.

"One-forty-four Baxter Street. That's the address she gave me."

He glanced toward the saloon, where an aproned bartender was carelessly emptying a spittoon onto the sidewalk beside the door. "Don't seem like a place fit for a lady."

"You forget I've seen worse at the hospital."

"Maybe I should go up alone. Make sure there's nothing amiss. You can't be too careful when you're dealing with this sort."

"And leave me alone here in the carriage? I'd feel far safer if I were with you." Una conjured a sweet smile and extended her hand for Conor to help her down. "Besides, I don't think the woman will talk unless I'm there."

After helping her to the ground, Conor climbed inside the wagon and checked the lock on the supply box. "Most folks won't steal from an ambulance," he said over his shoulder, "but I wouldn't put it past these gutter rats here." He turned to clamber out and glanced down at the medical bag Una had tripped over. "Dagnammit. I thought I left this back at Bellevue."

"They won't be needing it, will they?"

"Nah, we got plenty of others. But I can't leave it here. Some miscreant will have off with it before we reach the door. Guess we'll have to take it up with us." He grabbed the bag and climbed down.

A shiver worked its way down Una's limbs. She didn't believe for one second that he'd left the bag in the wagon bed by accident.

Not when she knew what was inside, nestled among the other supplies: a tourniquet.

They passed by the door to the saloon, careful to avoid the
sticky spatter of tobacco juice, and climbed a set of wooden steps
to the building's main entry. Inside, a tiny foyer branched off into
a long, shadowy hall and another, unlit staircase. Between the two
was a small desk with a middle-aged woman seated behind it.

"Good evening," Una said to her. "We're meeting someone
here. A young woman by the name of Miss Bean."

The woman looked up from the socks she was darning by the
light of a candle and gave a high-pitched hiccup. "Bean, you say?"
She hiccupped again.

Una nodded. Barney was to have paid the woman well—not
only to secure a panel crib but to direct Una and Conor to it when
they arrived. But her dull, glassy eyes and liquor-infused breath
didn't give Una much confidence. The woman looked from Una to
Conor, who stood a few steps behind her. "I'm gonna tell you what
I told the other feller. You break it or stain it, you pay for it. And
if the coppers make a visit"—she paused for another hiccup—
"everyone's skin's their own."

Heat flooded Una's face. She hoped Conor read it as embarrassment and not panic. "We're here to see a lady, not a gentleman. A *Miss* Bean."

The woman pursed her thin, wrinkled lips. "Same rules apply.
Third floor, second door on the right."

Una hurried up the stairs before the woman could slip up and
say anything more. Conor followed. She stopped on the first landing and fished in her pocket for a matchbook. The staircase was
as dark and cramped as her old tenement. She lit a match and held
it out to Conor.

His eyes narrowed for the flash of a second, and then he took
it. She lit another for herself and continued up to the third floor.
When they reached the room, Una knocked loudly and waited for
several seconds, wanting to give Barney time to situate himself
before they entered. Then she tried the doorknob. Unlocked, as

expected. She opened the door a few inches and called inside, "Hello?"

No answer.

Una opened the door fully and peered in. The room was lit by a single wall lamp, its flue cracked and stained with soot. A wooden framed bed sat to one side. A threadbare rug, ladder-backed chair, and large, unvarnished wardrobe were the only other adornments. The wall facing the door held a small window that overlooked the street.

"Miss Bean must have stepped out for something," she said, stepping aside to show Conor the empty room. "I'm sure she'll be back presently. Shall we wait inside?"

He nodded and followed her into the room, closing the door behind them. He gestured for Una to take the chair, setting the medical bag down on the bed but not sitting himself. To do so would have been baldly suggestive. A gentleman killer, Una thought, though it didn't make her any less nervous.

She watched him study the room. He crossed to the window, peered out, then walked to the wardrobe. Una held her breath as he opened the doors and looked inside. One half of the wardrobe was fitted with shelves and drawers. The other half, a tall cubby for hanging dresses and coats, was empty save for a few rusty hooks. It looked so much like any old wardrobe that Una began to worry the woman downstairs had directed them to the wrong room. Then she heard a soft creak. A louder sound followed—likely Barney's knee or elbow knocking into the false panel. Una winced. It must be cramped as a pickle jar back there, tall as Barney was. And he certainly wasn't the nimblest of men.

"Rats—they're everywhere in the city," Una said with a high, brittle laugh.

Conor shut the wardrobe. "That they are." He thrust his hands into his trouser pockets and leaned against the wall. He didn't look as agitated as he had when they left Bellevue, his fair skin unflushed and posture easy. "Miss Bean, you said this woman's name was?"

"That was the name she told me to use tonight, but I don't trust it's her real name."

He nodded slowly.

"Thank you for coming with me," Una said. "I feel better with you here. You're doubtful, I know. A killer at Bellevue. To say it aloud makes me half doubt it too." She smoothed her skirt, then folded her hands demurely in her lap and stared up at him. Time to lure him into confessing. Mr. Poe's story had made it seem so easy. But that had been fiction. Here, face-to-face with a real killer, it proved far more daunting. She took a deep breath and continued. "If there were such a killer, what do you suppose he would look like?"

Conor shrugged. "I can't say I know."

"I imagine him a little man. Impish, really. Not ugly but plain. Someone you look upon and"—she snapped her fingers—"completely forget."

His eye twitched. It was working.

"I don't imagine him very intelligent either. How could he be if a silly little woman figured him out?"

"Maybe Miss Bean doesn't know as much as she thinks," he said, his neck and ears beginning to color, the brogue slipping back into his voice. "If she knows anything at all. It takes a clever man to hide such a thing for so long."

"Or maybe he just got lucky." Una stood and went to the window. The street outside was dark and empty, save for an idling cab and a few drunks staggering from one saloon to the next. She could hear Conor breathe from clear across the room, each inhale faster and more raucous than the one that proceeded it. Like a boiler ready to explode. Ready to confess. Barney better be listening. "Regardless, he's certainly of a very low class. Dirty, ill-bred, unrefined. A bastard."

Instead of an angry outburst, Una heard a soft click. She turned around and saw Conor had locked the door. "That's not a very polite thing to say, Miss Kelly," he said, his voice low and even. He stole toward her as casually as a man out for a Sunday stroll.

Una's throat squeezed shut, trapping the air in her lungs. She shimmied away from the window and tried to smile. "Miss Bean might be startled to find the door locked," she managed to squeak out. "Perhaps we should—"

"Miss Bean isn't coming." He yanked the window curtains closed.

"Of course she is." Una straightened her shoulders and started toward the door. Conor had hold of her arm before she'd taken two steps. His grip was like a bear trap, his fingers metal teeth biting into her skin. He muscled her back into the chair.

"You should have let things be, Miss Kelly," he said, standing over her. "I told ya as much that day on the lawn, but ya didn't listen."

Fear scrambled Una's thoughts. She'd give her front teeth for a pair of brass knuckles. A billy club. Hell, even Barney's stupid tie pin. Barney. He was still inside the wardrobe. She had to keep Conor talking, get his confession, but how?

"Conor, if you've done something, hurt someone, you've got to come clean. I know you couldn't have meant to do it."

"Me?" He walked to the bed and unfastened the clasp on the medical bag. "Me! What makes you think I've done anything? Did *Miss Bean* tell ya that?" He chuckled, rummaging through the bag. He wouldn't hurt me, Una reminded herself. Would he?

"Maybe it was that red-haired drunkard who told ya." He pulled something from the bag. Not the tourniquet but an ivory-handled trocar. "We'd met before, she and I, in a back alley only half a dozen blocks from here." He strolled the length of the room, dragging the pointed tip of the trocar along the wall. The scraping noise made her skin prickle with gooseflesh.

"You killed her because she was a drunk?"

"Not just a drunk but a thief and whore!" His voice rattled the lampshade, troubling the flame. He stopped, ran the metal shaft of the trocar through his fingers, sighed. "But no, I didn't kill her. Not for that."

He took two quick steps to the wardrobe, then flung open

the doors and kicked the back panel. It swung around on its piv-ots. Before Una could react, he plunged the trocar into the dark cubby beyond the panel. Barney howled and stumbled forward. Conor stabbed him again. And again. Blood spread like an ink stain through Barney's shirt and jacket. He clutched his chest and gasped for breath as if he were drowning.

Una stood, grabbed the chair, and hurled it at Conor. It splin-tered across his back, and he staggered forward, dropping the tro-car. She caught Barney's eye just as he collapsed, a mix of fear and bewilderment in his wide pupils. He toppled out of the wardrobe, landing with a thud on the floor. Una hurried to his side, kicking the trocar across the room before bending down to examine him.

His lips had a dusky hue, and his respirations came fast and ragged. He coughed, spitting up frothy, blood-tinged sputum. He had a wound in his upper arm and two in his chest. One appeared superficial. The other hissed with each breath. Likely as not, the trocar had punctured his lung.

Una clapped a hand over the wound. She needed to dress it with oilcloth and get him to the hospital. But even with the am-bulance waiting outside, the idea seemed impossible. How would she get him downstairs? What about Conor?

Conor.

She glanced up. The impact of the chair had knocked him for-ward into the wall. He stood slumped in the corner now, rubbing his head.

Una grabbed Barney's hand and placed it over the wound where her own hand had been. "Keep pressure there." She scrambled across the room to the medical bag. There was oilcloth inside and maybe something she could use to fend off Conor if he tried to attack again. She rifled frantically through the bag. A brown med-icine bottle caught her eye. Morphine. Buried under other sup-plies, she found a syringe and hastily plunged the needle into the bottle. She'd just finished drawing up the morphine and grabbed hold of the bag's carrying strap when a hand enmeshed in her hair, yanking her backward and throwing her to the floor. The tattered rug did little to cushion her fall. Pinpricks of light flashed across her vision as her head struck the ground. The syringe rolled from her hand.

A heavy weight settled over her midsection. Her eyes focused enough to see Conor straddled atop her, pinning her down. She tried to wriggle free, but Conor's knees tightened around her. He laughed.

"You're quite the woman, Miss Kelly. I liked you. I really did. But you couldn't mind your damned business."

She felt the strap of worn leather in her palm and realized that though she'd lost the syringe, she still had hold of the medical bag in her other hand. Her fingers tightened around the strap.

"I couldn't for the life of me figure out why," he continued. "A nice girl like you. Then it struck me when I saw your face in the match light as we were coming up the stairs." He reached down and clasped his hands around her throat, depressing her windpipe. "Ya always did look familiar."

Una swung her arm with all her strength, smashing the bag against his head. He toppled off her. She rolled onto her hands and knees and upended the bag. Gauze, needles, forceps, medicine bottles, scissors, and other supplies spilled onto the floor. She rummaged through them, finding the scalpel just as she heard Conor groan, and staggered to her feet. When he lunged for her, she slashed him with the blade. It nicked his shoulder and cut a deep gash along his chin. An inch or two lower, and it would have caught his carotid.

As it was, though, he barely flinched. She tried to swipe again, but he caught her hand, bending it back until she dropped the blade. Una kicked and clawed, but after a moment's struggle, Conor was on top of her again. He reached for something amid the mess of medical supplies as she tried in vain to push him off her. When she saw the cloth band with its brass buckle and screw, Una froze.

Conor unfurled the band and loosened the screw. "For years, I ferried boot scum like you to Bellevue. Thieves and whores and drunks. Roughs, gamblers, immigrant filth, opium fiends."

"Please, Conor, murder is a cardinal sin, you imperil your soul by—"

"Greed, lust, wickedness—these are the sins God hates!" His voice was high-pitched and eyes wild.

Una spread her arms, feeling atop the rug for the scalpel . . . oakum . . . strips of flannel . . . suturing thread . . . Then something sharp pricked her finger. She strained her eyes to the far corners of their sockets to see what it was. Not the scalpel blade but the needle and syringe she'd filled with morphine!

She tried to grab it, but it rolled beyond her reach just as Conor looped the tourniquet around her neck. Una stretched out her hand. Her fingers brushed the glass but couldn't grasp it. He threaded the end of the cloth band through the buckle and cinched it so tight that only a narrow stream of air could escape her lungs.

Panic flooded Una's veins and fogged her mind. A few turns of the screw, and she wouldn't be able to breathe at all. She reached out again, stretching her muscles and sinew until they burned. One finger touched the syringe again, reaching up and over its smooth glass body to coax it into her palm.

Conor turned the tourniquet screw a quarter rotation, all but closing off her airway. Una's lungs were burning. Her hands shook and tingled. When at last she had the syringe securely within her grasp, she flattened her thumb against the plunger and raised her arm.

Conor caught sight of her movement. He let go of the screw and tried to pry the syringe from her hand. She slipped free of his fumbling fingers and stabbed the needle into his arm, depressing the plunger, before he could bat her arm away.

She waited, but nothing happened. He pulled the syringe from his arm and threw it across the room. It shattered against the wall. The sound of glass falling to the floor was muffled by the growing thud of her pulse in her ear. Her vision blurred. Each gasping breath brought only a trickle of air. She felt Conor's hands at the tourniquet again, grasping and fumbling, as if he couldn't find the screw. Then, suddenly, he collapsed on top of her, limp and heavy.

Una tried to roll him off of her, but her air-starved limbs were too weak. A pounding sound filled the room, rattling the floor beneath her. Una thought it was the thrum of her pulse about to explode in her brain, then the pounding gave way to a crack. She felt Conor's weight lift off her and the tourniquet loosened about her neck. Air whooshed in and out of her lungs, burning as it rasped through her windpipe. She blinked, trying to make out the shape moving about the room. Barney? Conor? She felt heavy. Tired. She blinked once more, then her eyelids refused to open, and she surrendered to the darkness.

CHAPTER 49

—◆◇◆—

When Una's eyes opened again, someone was shining a bright light directly in her face. She winced and turned her head, only to realize the light was all around her. Sunshine? How long had she been unconscious? Her head throbbed, and her throat burned with each pull of air. But she could breathe! In and out without resistance. She took a deep gulp of air and immediately regretted it as a fit of dry coughs racked her.

"Here, try a sip of water."

Una turned toward the voice. A woman in a puffy white cap and seersucker dress held a cup of water to her lips. A nurse? Miss Cuddy?

Una took a small sip. Her esophagus burned as much as her windpipe and seemed to have forgotten how to swallow. She coughed again, spitting up half the water. But her next drink went down easier.

"Where am I?" she asked in a voice so hoarse she hardly recognized it as her own.

"Bellevue Hospital."

Una looked around the room, its rows of beds and long center table taking shape in the brightness. "How did I get here?"

"The ambulance brought you in last night."

The ambulance? Una bolted upright. Her head throbbed in protest, and the room wobbled a moment before steadying. Last night's events came back to her with pulse-pounding clarity. She grabbed her neck. The tourniquet was gone, though it had left her skin puffy and raw. She kicked at the blankets entrapping her legs and tried to stand. A wave of nausea overtook her before her feet could find the floor.

Miss Cuddy put a hand on her shoulder. Una flinched.

"It's all right, Miss Kelly. Lie back down."

"I have to . . . Conor . . . he's dangerous."

Miss Cuddy pushed her gently back into bed. "The only thing that's dangerous is you trying to stand too quickly. Lie here, and I'll fetch Superintendent Perkins. She wanted to see you as soon as you woke."

"But—"

"Try another sip of water. I'll be right back."

Una let her head fall back against the pillow and closed her eyes to ward off the nausea. The last thing she wanted was another sip of water. The queasiness settled, but her heart refused to slow. Where was Conor? Barney? Who had found her and released the tourniquet?

Footsteps thumped toward her, and she opened her eyes. Miss Perkins approached with two coppers at her side. Una's muscles tightened. She recognized the men at once. Officer Simms and the detective from the Sixth Precinct.

"Glad you're awake, Miss Kelly," the superintendent said. She smiled, but it did little to calm Una's nerves. "These gentlemen have a few questions for you. Are you feeling up to answering them?"

Una hesitated. Could she feign to be too tired and then run as soon as they were gone? Considering she couldn't even stand without becoming nauseous and dizzy, her chances of escape seemed slim. Best to tell them the truth, then, and hope that they believed her.

She nodded, and the men pulled up chairs alongside her bed.

"I'm Detective Collins, and this is Officer Simms. Do you remember us?"

Officer Simms's nose had healed crooked, and he glared at her with the same beady eyes she recalled from the alley when he'd pushed her up against the wall and groped her.

"I remember."

"Then you'll remember the charges of murder booked against you. Add to that assault on an officer of the law"—the detective glanced askew at Officer Simms—"and you're looking at spending the rest of your life on the Island."

"I didn't kill anyone." It came out more a croak than a shout, followed by another bout of coughing. "If you were more than a two-bit detective, you'd know that. Conor McCready killed Traveling Mike. And Deidre and—"

"Five people, all together, we think," the detective said.

Officer Simms balled his fists together, his fat knuckles cracking. "We'll know more once we get him talking."

"What?"

"He's a bit groggy still from all the morphine you gave him," Detective Collins said. "It *was* morphine, wasn't it?"

Una nodded, still confused. "Conor's in jail?"

"He will be as soon as the doctor clears him."

"But how do you know—"

"Your friend, the reporter, told us. He can't speak. Something about a collapsed lung. But he wrote out a statement for us. Dr. Westervelt filled in the rest."

Edwin? Now she was even more confused.

"If you cooperate and give us a statement and promise to show up in court to testify, we'll see that the assault charge against you is dropped."

"You mean that you believe me? I'm not under arrest?"

"Officer Simms here isn't too pleased about it, but no. It was a brave thing you did, Miss Kelly. Rather chancy—"

"Stupid," Officer Simms interrupted.

"But Mr. McCready might have gone uncaught without you."

She tried to speak, but another fit of coughing stopped her.

"I'll come back this evening to get your statement," the detective said, standing.

Officer Simms stood too. "Don't even think about running. If you ain't there singing at the trial, I'll turn out every slum in the city to find you."

You couldn't find me before, Una wanted to say. Instead, she nodded.

Miss Perkins escorted them off the ward, then returned to Una's bedside.

"The officers told me about your . . . er . . . history. It seems you're not the Miss Una Kelly we thought you were."

Una shook her head.

"I suppose I should have guessed as much when you stole Dr. Pingry's watch. Was anything you said in your admission interview true?"

"Parts of it." Una looked down at her hands. Her nails were jagged and broken from last night's struggle. "But not the parts that matter."

"I see."

"The only reason I applied to the school was because I needed a place to hide out from the police."

Miss Perkins's brow furrowed—the only crack in her otherwise inscrutable expression.

"I hated it at first," Una continued, looking around the ward. "All the rules and studying. Kowtowing to whatever the doctors said. But there's something . . . wondrous about seeing a sick patient get well and knowing that I had helped."

"Nursing is not for everyone," Miss Perkins said. "You see every facet of life—birth, death, illness, healing, trauma, madness, despair, joy. To take all that in demands both an iron constitution and a gentle soul. That's the type of woman we're looking for. That's what matters."

Una immediately thought of Dru. She reached and grabbed

Miss Perkins's arm. "Miss Lewis, she hasn't . . . she's not . . . her fever?"

"It broke last night," Miss Perkins said, patting Una's hand. "Word from the doctor this morning is that she's much improved."

Una closed her eyes and exhaled. When she opened them again, tears blurred her vision. Never mind if Miss Perkins thought her weak for crying. Una was too grateful to care. "Everything that happened with Mr. Knauff was my fault. Please let Miss Lewis stay on in the training program. She's exactly the type of woman you're looking for. She deserves a second chance and a far better friend than me."

Miss Perkins handed Una her hankie. "Mr. Knauff's tragic death was no one's fault alone. But it is good to hear you own your share of the blame. The larger share rests with Dr. Allen. As for Miss Lewis, her illness certainly played a role."

"You'll let her stay, then?"

Miss Perkins nodded.

Una smiled, the first real smile she'd worn in days, and blinked back a new wave of tears. "Thank you."

"And what of you, Miss Kelly?"

She shrugged. It was too daunting to think about. She had no money. No place to live. No friends or family to call on. But at least she was no longer wanted by the police. And the people here at Bellevue were safe.

"I cannot let you back into the training program, you understand."

Una nodded. She hadn't expected to be allowed back into the school. It was enough that Dru could stay. But a pang of regret swelled inside her just the same.

"Not officially, anyway," Miss Perkins continued. "But I think after I explain to the board how you put your own life in danger to lure out a killer in our midst, they might agree to keep you on. You could continue learning and honing your skills. You could live again at the nurses' home. You just couldn't be an official graduate at the end of your two years. No diploma. No pin. But I think you'll find plenty of work, honest work, even without such tokens."

"Really? You'd do that for me? Speak to the board?"

"I'm seldom wrong about people, Miss Kelly. In the end, it's a question of heart. I'm no longer in doubt about yours. But you must maintain an exemplary record. No more lies or stealing. Am I understood?"

"Yes, yes. Thank you!"

"Good." She patted Una's hand again. "Now, get some rest."

But Una was too elated to rest. She watched Miss Cuddy and the first-year nurse shuffle about the ward changing dressings, delivering medicines, mixing poultices and lotions and antiseptics. She watched them dust and cut bandages and clean bedpans. She watched them hurry to the side of a patient who was just about to fall. Apply leeches to a feverish patient. Soothe a grimacing, tumor-ridden patient with a warm fomentation. Their work was never ending, and Una wanted to be a part of it. Better to do than sit around idle, her mother had said to her. Better to give than to wait for someone to give to you. And for the first time, Una realized she was right.

CHAPTER 50

That evening, after a bowl of thin gruel and cup of beef tea, Una pleaded with Nurse Cuddy to allow her a short stroll on the lawn, insisting a little fresh air would be good for her lungs. At last, Nurse Cuddy conceded. She wrapped a heavy blanket around Una's shoulders and helped her downstairs. Spring had returned in full force after the week's earlier snow. The lawn was green and fragrant with new blooms.

"I'll be back to fetch you in half an hour," Nurse Cuddy said, after seating Una on a bench. "Mind that you don't overtire yourself."

Una nodded, but as soon as Nurse Cuddy had vanished within the hospital, she quit the bench and snuck into the nearby Sturges Pavilion.

Dru's bed remained apart from the others at the far end of the ward. But instead of lying down, tossing and moaning in a feverish sleep, Dru sat propped against a stack of pillows, sipping a bowl of broth. She looked thin and frail, but her cheeks had regained their rosy glow.

Una hesitated before making her way across the ward. Would Dru forgive her for being such a rotten friend? Maybe she wouldn't remember Mr. Knauff and all that had happened the day she fell ill. Maybe they could go on as if it never happened.

She stopped at the table in the middle of the ward, leaning

against it as she caught her breath. Her throat still burned with each shallow draw of air. She watched Dru take another sip of broth and screwed her resolve. To pretend nothing had happened was tantamount to a lie. And Una was done lying.

Dru spotted Una as she neared the bed. Her eyes widened and lips wobbled before settling into a frown. "Good heavens, Una! What happened to you?"

Una had forgotten how dreadful she looked—throat bruised and eyes bloodshot. She pulled the blanket snuggly around herself and sat down on the edge of Dru's bed. "You should see the other fellow."

Dru didn't laugh but continued to stare at her in confusion. "But you're all right, aren't you?"

"Never mind about me. I'm fine. You're the one who's been sick. Really, I ought to let you rest and come back another time. I'm just glad you're on the mend. I've been so worried. Truly, and I only wanted to say—" Una stopped. She was rambling like a fool.

Dru reached out and grabbed her hand. "Go on."

"It's just . . . I'm terribly sorry, Dru. For everything. Involving you in the search for Deidre's murderer. Ratting you out to Miss Perkins when Mr. Knauff's death wasn't even your fault. Caring only for myself when here you were falling ill to typhus."

Una waited for Dru to let go of her hand and shrink away. To turn up her chin and insist that Una leave. But she didn't.

"There's more. I haven't been straight with you from the start . . ."

Una told her everything. Her voice grew more hoarse and her throat sore. But she continued, staring down at the floor as she spoke, afraid of what she might see in Dru's expression.

Silence greeted her when she finished, and, for once, Una wished Dru would say something. Anything. She dared a glance up. Instead of revulsion, she found kindness in Dru's eyes.

"Oh, Una," she said at last. "No wonder you're so brave."

Brave? That's how Dru saw her? After everything she'd told her? Not selfish or scheming but brave?

Dru squeezed her hand and rested her head back against the pillows. Her eyelids fluttered shut and were slow to open. Una knew she ought to leave Dru to rest. Miss Cuddy would be coming for her soon, anyway. Best she get back to the lawn. She squeezed Dru's hand in return and stood.

"I'm sure Mrs. Buchanan could find you another roommate," she said. "That is, if you want."

"Don't be a goose, Una. But you best be ready. We're weeks behind in our study. We never finished reading about the alimentary system or the respiratory system . . ." She prattled on like her old self for a full minute longer before falling asleep. Una pulled Dru's blanket up to her chin, then hurried best she could—her gait was still a bit unsteady—back to the lawn.

She sat down on the bench and stared out at the river. The waning sunlight played on the water, bathing the sails of the passing schooners in an orange glow.

"Mind if I join you?" a voice said from behind her.

Una turned and saw Edwin. She thought of their last bitter parting, and that stabbing pain in her chest revived. He sat down on the edge of the bench before she could reply. His eyes lingered on her neck.

"Good God, Una, you look worse now than you did last night."

"You were here when they brought me in?"

He cocked his head. "You don't remember? I was the one who found you."

She thought back to the night before, the tourniquet biting into her neck, Conor's weight heavy atop her, the banging noise that reverberated through the floorboards. She shivered. "You were there? At the lodging house?"

"I was about to head home last night when I saw Mr. McCready leave with the ambulance. There hadn't been any gong or call for the surgeon, but I didn't think much of it until I remembered what you'd said. I flagged down a cab and followed him."

Una remembered the hansom cab she'd seen trailing them. "I thought you didn't believe me."

"I didn't. At least I thought I didn't. But I wanted to be sure. When I got to where the ambulance was parked, I didn't notice anything suspicious and assumed Conor had gone into the saloon for a drink. I was about to leave when I saw you in the third-floor window. Then Conor came around a moment later and closed the curtain. I knew something was wrong. I would have gotten to you sooner, but that damned lodge keeper wouldn't tell me what room you were in. I tried every one until I found you." He swiveled around on the bench to face her. "Thank God you'd managed to sedate him. Any tighter and that tourniquet would have killed you." He reached out as if to touch her, then let his hand fall back to his side. "None of this would have happened if I'd believed you from the start."

She'd given him good reason not to with all her lies. But that didn't mean she was ready to forgive him.

They sat a moment in silence, then Una turned her gaze back to the lawn. The shadow cast by the hospital had lengthened, stretching to the dock. A large, dark bird with a spray of white tail feathers swooped down over the water.

"Is that an eagle?" she asked, watching it skim the glassy surface before coming away with a writhing fish.

"Looks like it. It's about time of year they start rebuilding their nests." He sat forward, resting his forearms on his legs, and turned his head sheepishly to look at her. "We could meet at Central Park Sunday and find out."

"Edwin, don't. We can't pretend like the past didn't happen. I'm not the woman you thought you fell in love with."

"Maybe not. But I'd like to get to know the woman you really are."

"That's not how you felt in the operating theater. You could hardly bear to look at me, let alone help me." Her gaze drifted upward from the river to the darkening sky. "I haven't changed."

"But I have. I was angry that you lied to me, yes. Embarrassed that I'd been played the fool."

"I never meant—"

"I know. And once I got over my bruised ego, I realized that

I'd lied to you too. I said you could trust me, implored you to trust me, and then when you finally did, I turned my back on you." He sat up and ran a hand through his hair. "If you give me another chance, let us start anew, I promise not to betray you like that again."

Una glanced at him from the corner of her eye, still uncertain. But he wasn't asking for promises or avowals. Only a second chance. "You haven't forgotten that I'm a thief?"

"Former thief."

"And that I don't come from a hoity-toity family."

"I haven't forgotten, and I don't care."

"Your family will."

"I don't care if they care. An old friend encouraged me to be my own man. I rather think I shall take her advice."

"Miss Perkins said I might be able to rejoin the training school. Socializing with gentlemen, you'll remember, is strictly forbidden."

He flashed her a wicked smile. "I shan't tell a soul. Besides, I happen to know quite a few storerooms and a rather jolting elevator where we can be alone."

Una shook her head and laughed, wincing as she did at the still-raw pain in her throat. "Don't joke. It hurts to laugh."

Edwin reached out again and boldly took her hand. Una's skin sparked at his touch.

"I'm entirely serious." His thumb stroked the top of her hand. "A new beginning, then?"

Una's gaze swept along the northeast wing of the hospital to the river and back. The first of evening's stars twinkled overhead. Not in a hundred years would she have imagined herself working at a place like Bellevue, helping people instead of fleecing them, letting them into her heart instead of going it alone. It bucked every one of her rules. But maybe it was time for a new set of rules.

She nodded at Edwin and laced her fingers through his. "Yes, a new beginning."

AUTHOR'S NOTE

Many times in my career, I felt I didn't quite fit the mold of what a nurse should be. I didn't come from a family of nurses. I didn't grow up wanting to be a nurse. I didn't relate to the meek, saintly images of Florence Nightingale and the nurses of old.

Nursing wasn't who I was. It was what I did.

The Coronavirus pandemic changed that. It gave me clarity of purpose. It affirmed I was making a positive difference, however small that difference might be. It made me proud of my profession and honored to be part of it.

Researching this book had a similar effect. Florence Nightingale wasn't meek. She was a renegade. A trailblazer. And America's first nurses—those who trained at Bellevue and similar schools—came to the profession for a myriad of reasons, not just saintly obligation. Then, as now, nurses weren't born of one mold.

But that doesn't mean Florence Nightingale and America's early nurses weren't influenced and constrained by the prejudices of their day. Doctors jealously guarded against any encroachment by women into their field and insisted upon a culture of obedience that exists to this day. Women of color, non-Christians, and men were belatedly and sometimes begrudgingly accepted into the field. For nearly a century, nurses' behavior—on and off the ward—was held to an exacting and puritanical standard.

The history of nursing, like most history, is messy and, at times, ugly. But nursing's impact on medicine has been monumental.

The Bellevue Training School for Nurses—the first of its kind in America—opened in 1873. Before this, nurses were largely untrained and illiterate. The pay was abysmal and working conditions wretched. In the early part of the nineteenth century, many nurses in New York were conscripted from the local prison and workhouse. In response, a committee of wealthy society women organized by the State Board of Charities opened the nation's first nurse training school at Bellevue. The school's founders solicited advice from Florence Nightingale and modeled the training program after a school she'd established in London a decade earlier. Many physicians opposed the idea, believing women unequal to the serious demands of medical work, and worried nurse training might pave the way for female physicians.

Despite these initial objections, the benefit of professionally trained nurses was immense. The cleanliness of hospital wards improved, infection rates decreased, and patient care flourished.

Initially, the qualifications required of Bellevue Training School applicants were very strict. Only well-educated, non-disabled, Christian, unmarried or widowed women were accepted. The first class had 29 applicants, 19 of whom were admitted, and only 6 of whom ultimately graduated. A year later, over 100 women applied. Twenty years on, the school had nearly 2,000 applicants annually. Within a few years of the school's opening, there were several such training schools across the eastern United States, many of which employed Bellevue graduates as superintendents and head nurses.

Today in the U.S., over 150,000 new nurses graduate each year.

For further reading about early medicine and Gilded Age New York consider: *Bellevue: Three Centuries of Medicine and Mayhem at America's Most Storied Hospital* by David Oshinsky; *New York Nightingales: The Emergence of the Nursing Profession at*

Bellevue and New York Hospital, 1850–1920 by Jane E. Mottus; *The Gilded Age in New York, 1870–1910* by Esther Crain; *Five Points: The Nineteenth-Century New York City Neighborhood That Invented Tap Dance, Stole Elections, and Became the World's Most Notorious Slum* by Tyler Anbinder; and *The Butchering Art: Joseph Lister's Quest to Transform the Grisly World of Victorian Medicine* by Lindsey Fitzharris.

ACKNOWLEDGMENTS

Thank you to the team at Kensington for championing this book and helping it reach readers. Special thanks to my editor, John Scognamiglio, for your trust and patience as I explored this sliver of history and found my story.

Thank you to my agent, Michael Carr, who continues to help me grow as a writer. To my A group, in particular, my early readers Jenny Ballif and Angelina Hill. You helped me not only strengthen the story but believe in myself.

And to my family. Thank you for your boundless love.

THE NURSE'S SECRET

ABOUT THIS GUIDE

The suggested questions are included to enhance your group's
reading of Amanda Skenandore's *The Nurse's Secret*!

DISCUSSION QUESTIONS

1. How was early nursing different from your understanding of the profession today? How is it the same?

2. Did the qualifications required to apply to the Bellevue Training School for Nurses surprise you?

3. What have your experiences with modern-day nurses been like?

4. Great wealth and extreme poverty existed side by side in Gilded Age New York with almost no middle class in between. The rich lived in European-inspired mansions along Millionaire's Row while the poor crowded into tenements—sometimes living a dozen people to a room. How was this reflected in the novel? Does the same degree of class stratification exist today?

5. How did the death of Una's mother shape her outlook?

6. Una has a list of rules to survive life on the streets. How did those rules help her? How did they hurt her? Do you think any of the rules are worth carrying over into her new life?

7. Do you think Edwin and Una are a good fit for each other? Do you think their relationship will endure?

8. Today, nurses are consistently ranked as the number one most trusted profession in America in Gallup's annual poll. Do you feel that distinction is deserved?

9. When Edwin tells Una he doesn't care who knows about their romance, she replies, "Easy for you to say. You don't

have anything to lose." What gender dynamics are at play in the novel? Do those same dynamics exist today?

10. Dr. Joseph Lister came to America in 1876 to share his ideas about germ theory and asepsis, but it was several years before the medical community fully embraced his ideas. Why do you think there was such reluctance? Aside from germ theory, what medical advances in the past 150 years do you think have had the biggest impact?